ea

THE

EATON

"★★★★★ Reading John K. Addis was like reading an eighties horror movie. It's fast paced, macabre and full of gritty atmospheric settings, along with a relentlessly chilling plot from an author who's mastered the genre!" - *Catherine Rose Putsche, Top #40 Regional Goodreads Reviewer, Author of "The Surgeon's Son"*

"★★★★★ The Eaton is the best kind of horror. Some of the images are so vivid that I had to put The Eaton down for a few minutes, let myself relax, take a few breaths, and then I could continue. This book is so well plotted, and the characters feel so real, that you will be as terrorized as they are. You will have to keep reading to see what happens next, even if you are afraid to find out." - *Bill Mackela, Bill's Book Reviews*

"★★★★★ Amazing debut by a really talented author. As the action unfolds, and we start jumping back and forth in time, the narrative becomes irresistible. This is one of those books that will stick with you after you read it—Addis does a great job of putting you in the action." - *Alec Drachman, Goodreads*

"★★★★★ I would recommend The Eaton to anyone who loves a good horror story with rich, well-developed characters who all have their secrets they would like to keep hidden, but are faced with a horror they've never met. If you ever hoped to find tunnels under the floorboards of an old house, or imagined you were on some sort of expedition to discover secrets that have been buried for years, you might want to try The Eaton." - *Melanie Marsh, FangFreakinTasticReviews.com*

THE
EATON

to my
favorite former
neighborhood
troublemaker!

JOHN K. ADDIS

To my Father, for the many late-night
horror movies, and for looking
like Stephen King.

prologue

Jonathan Wesley's head pounded in perfect time to the whiskey-drenched drumbeat of his blood. He tried to force his eyes shut, to drown out the reality around him, but found this sapped the energy away from his fists, as if he could only keep one part of his ravaged body clenched at a time. He chose the fists, looked around again in the dim light, saw the panicked faces of acquaintances and strangers, and the pounding worsened. He had to get out of here, but there was nowhere to go.

Thump. Thump. Thump.

"Help me with this," someone yelled. Two men were moving a piece of furniture. Jonathan remained seated on the ground, his back leaning hard against the cold wall farthest from the door. He registered a new noise, and turned his head to his left—a little too fast, as it made his stomach curdle—and saw Nora shaking and sobbing over the blood-drenched body of a woman he didn't know. The stranger was young, nearly naked, and clearly dead, her insides spilling out onto the carpet, a deep gash from one shoulder having ripped her apart like the flesh of a peach. The rough slice had severed one of her breasts, and only a thin flap of taut skin kept it from sliding off her body and into the gore. Nora wouldn't stop with the damned crying, and the harsh sound of her sobs seemed to be getting louder and louder, taunting him, filling his head. It even threatened to be louder than his heartbeat. Though he had only met Nora two days ago, Jon was overcome with hate for her, and felt a macabre urge to tear off the stranger's dangling dead breast before him and shove it down Nora's fat blubbering throat.

Keep it together, Jon.

He became vaguely aware that there was now a new rhythm in the room, an even deeper pounding than his head, now a full syncopated timpani battle for domination of his senses. It was coming from the other side of the door. His fellow prisoners looked more terrified now, and at least two women had their heads in their hands. One man—Harland, he thought—was praying, on his goddamned knees and everything, begging for forgiveness. Jon wondered what Harland's sins had been. He wondered if he should pray for his own.

Thump. Ba-Thump. Ba-Ba-Thump.

"Can't you *hear* him?" screamed an older woman in white. She was gesturing with intensity toward the door, confronting the men who had succeeded in barricading the entrance with a heavy oak desk. "Can't you hear my son?"

Lady, Jon thought, *even if they could hear him, they're not going to move the desk. Besides, how would it help having another person trapped with us? There was still nowhere to go. And, no more to drink.*

He clenched his fists again. The room appeared to be slowly tumbling, veering off-kilter like a sinking ship. Everything seemed covered in gauze, and his peripheral vision had become black, vignetting the scene like a photograph.

It's shit. All of it.

Jon had always been a mean drunk. Vicious, even. Isn't that what Niamh had said? But perhaps being drunk just revealed the truth. If the past few days had taught him anything, it was that seeing things clearly required a hell of a lot of booze. So it wasn't his fault that, when he saw things clearly, every person on the planet was a worthless, festering pile. Including himself.

All of this, all of life, the shit of bulls.

Jonathan clenched his eyes tight, trying again to block out what remained of the world. But the naked woman was still dead. The old woman was still shouting. A new voice in the corner was beginning to wail.

And the pounding at the door grew louder.

one

"Wake up, Sam."

Sam did not obey. His body lay motionless, on its stomach, a touch of drool dampening a spot of cotton sheet below his mouth. His light brown hair was matted comically to one side, the pillow having frozen yesterday's gelled look into a half-mohawk. Upon a subsequent jostle, a quiet, dull moan escaped Sam's parted lips. It was clear he remained far from consciousness, and as if to punctuate this fact, he followed the quiet moan with a significantly louder snore.

"Samuel, wake up! It's a big day."

This time, Sam's eyes fluttered open, but only briefly. He mumbled something that sounded like "fiber menace," which was more probably "five more minutes," though only in context would Sarah have made that deduction. Even then, with Sam's tendency toward wild, surreal nightmares, a "fiber menace" wasn't outside the realm of possibility, either. Perhaps it was the distant future, and some old woolen blankets had become self-aware, learned to walk, armed themselves with atomic lasers, and were presently terrorizing the streets of Sam's psyche.

Sam's dreams sometimes bled into the real world, too, which is why today was especially significant. After months of fighting with mortgage companies, banks, real estate agents, zoning boards, and even his parents, Sarah's beloved boyfriend was finally going to become the legal owner of the long-abandoned Michigan Central Railroad station in Eaton Rapids, Michigan. And, after an estimated six months of intense repair, restoration, and build-out, this derelict station would be successfully transformed into a chic new martini bar. In Sam's mind, the task was already accomplished—he could picture it so clearly. A signature cocktail would end up on top-ten lists in trendy publications, while respected indie bands would fall over themselves offering to play to the intimate crowd. The establishment's name was to be determined later, as Sam didn't want to jinx the property sale by committing to a specific moniker, but Sarah knew that he was partial to the semi-eponymous "Spice."

Sam let out another deep, tortured snore. Sarah was reminded how their relationship would never had succeeded without her ability to sleep through anything.

"Oh for God's sake," she mumbled, strategizing her next attempt. Sam was still wearing yesterday's undershirt; perhaps she could pull it over his head.

Instead, she leaned in and whispered.

"Samuel T. Spicer, you will wake up this instant, and make wild, ravenous love to your very hot and barely clothed fiancée."

That did it. Sam's eyes opened, and he looked up at Sarah, who was sitting playfully cross-legged beside him. She was wearing a loose-fitting grey tank top, which made both her short, black hair and her porcelain skin pop like an old photograph against the beiges and browns of the blankets and sheets. And, she had been truthful—the tank top was the entirety of her ensemble.

Sam closed his eyes and smiled, stretching out a bit on his side of the bed, the faint odor of sweat and old cologne wafting up around them.

"I love it when you sound all literal," he slurred dreamily.

"You mean literary."

"Yes, literalary."

Sarah rolled her eyes.

"But," he continued, pivoting his body to stretch in another direction, "unless I was talking in my sleep, you are not yet my fiancée."

As his eyes were still closed, he had no warning of the pillow which was slicing through the air toward the side of his head.

Thump.

"Hey!"

Sam opened his eyes and wrestled the fluffy weapon from his giggling attacker. He tossed it off the bed, over his shoulder, and didn't notice that it struck and nearly toppled a lamp on the nearby nightstand.

Sarah was reaching for a second pillow, a back-up armament, but Sam grabbed and pinned her wrists instead. She responded with a smoldering pout, and stared him down as she untangled her crossed legs, letting herself slide along the sheets toward his body. It was amazing to Sarah how much she had grown to trust this man, as it wasn't long ago that she had been frozen with fear at any hint of bondage. With Sam, her lips melted into a smile, as twice she pretended to try to escape the cuffs made by his strong arms.

"Well, you got me," purred Sarah with delicious,

manufactured innocence. "I can't move at all. What are you going to do about that?"

He felt one of her toes snag and tug at the side of his boxer briefs, pulling them down, until he released her wrists and assisted in the maneuver, quickly joining her in lower nudity.

Sarah's arms stayed fixed where they had been, as if pinned against the mattress by invisible hands. Sam took the hint and returned to his previous position of playful dominance, clutching her wrists in his usual mastery of delicate and deliberate. Her green eyes seemed to sparkle at this, and she bit her lower lip, a deliberate act that she knew drove him wild.

"You really are too good to me, Sarah."

"I know. That's why you're going to marry me."

Sam had begun to kiss a trail down her neck and collarbone, pausing at the vaguely Celtic, jet-black tattoo half-hidden by her tank top. He had begun tracing the inked pattern with the very tip of his tongue, but recognized the need for a verbal response to her claim. "Oh yeah?" he offered, distractedly, as he moved south, running his lips over the hard outline of her right nipple, the one pierced with steel and iron, straining through the thin fabric of her shirt.

"Oh yeah," Sarah responded with a confident nod, while wrapping her bare legs against the back of his thighs, pulling him into her. A broad smile crept over her face as his teeth brushed almost imperceptibly against the hard steel piercing her flesh. "And then I'm going to divorce your ass and take your new bar."

Sam's eyes shot up to hers, but his lips and teeth remained in place. He bit down on the piercing, and she cried aloud, some syllable lost between "oh" and "Sam" and "God" and "fuck."

He was going to marry her, alright.

*

Vaughn was waiting for them at the old station, sitting outside on a concrete step in the chilly air. His face exploded into a toothy grin as he saw Sam's Mustang pull into the large gravel space that was once, allegedly, a parking lot.

"I'm going to have to pave this," Sam remarked to Sarah in monotone.

"Maybe if you bought a car with more than two inches of clearance on its ass, you wouldn't have to worry."

Sam thought for a moment.

"The ass of a car isn't the underbelly, it's the trunk."

"What? That's stupid. You sit on your ass. It's closest to the ground."

"No, Sarah, your *feet* are closest to the ground, not your ass. You just think that because you sit around eating bon bons all day."

Sarah laughed aloud, an almost guttural guffaw, and punched his arm. "I'm a grad student. That's what we do. I'm exercising my mind. That involves sitting on your butt."

Sam placed the car in park and removed the keys from the ignition. He turned to smile at her. "I'm still right."

Sarah scrunched her pixie nose in response. "As I may remind you," she countered with playful snippiness, "I am the only one among us with genuine automotive knowledge."

"Helping your dad rebuild cars makes you an expert on simile?"

"No, but being a grad student does. And besides," she added, "what the hell is a 'bon bon'?"

They exited the car as Vaughn jogged up to them.

"Hey man!" called Vaughn with giddy energy. He offered a quick, manly hug to his friend, then turned to nod at Sarah. "Your boy really got something sweet here."

"Why thank you," replied Sarah, all exaggerated sunshine and rainbows. "I think I'm quite a catch myself!"

Vaughn laughed, and caught himself from saying "no, I meant the building," because he knew she knew exactly what he had meant, and was only trying to trap him into an awkward moment. So, instead, he played it smart, and said "you really are somethin', Sarah. *And* this building! Sam's got *two* beauties in his life now!"

Sarah smirked in response, then gazed upward at the dilapidated old train station spread out across the horizon before her. "Yeah, *two* beauties." A moment passed as they all gazed into the future at the work ahead.

"Admittedly," interjected Sam for the save, motioning toward his purchase, "*this* girl's more of a fixer-upper."

The long side of the structure had seven boarded-up windows and a large, imposing door. Each short side of the station had just two windows, as it was a rather narrow rectangle of a box, and Sam's agent had warned him of this potential shortcoming early on in the process. "I'm not sure it's large enough for the kind of club you're imagining," she had explained. "There's a lot of character, sure, but practically, wouldn't you like a property a bit more…square?" But something about this building had just seemed *right* to Sam. With its tall, coved ceilings, beautiful dark wood molding (which was still in decent condition), all-original paneling, and float glass, this was the type of construction that just wasn't made anymore. It had class, a sort of regal dignity, that demanded respect, even after— and in spite of—so many years of neglect.

The three walked closer to the entrance, but Sam stopped short. Vaughn faltered a pace later, and turned back to his friend.

"We're not going in?"

"I don't have the key yet. Janet's coming any minute now."

"You were at closing for, like, three hours, and they forgot the key?"

Sam laughed. "Actually, I think Janet just wanted to be here when we made it official. She put a lot of work into this sale, too. Besides, I'm pretty sure she's bringing champagne."

She was. Janet Blair pulled up seconds later in an ugly but allegedly expensive blue Volvo sedan, leaping out of her vehicle with cheerful impatience, clutching a bottle of Moët & Chandon.

"Sammy! Sarah! You guys excited?" She beamed at them through her bulky sunglasses and bleached-white teeth, her hair over-permed and, with her short stature, altogether resembling something of an over-caffeinated Muppet in a burgundy blazer. Her stubby legs, already having to take two steps for every one of a tall person's stride, were restrained further by a tight matching skirt, which required her to take more than fifty steps to travel from the Volvo to the door of the station less than twenty yards away. She handed the champagne bottle to Sam, almost peremptorily, brushing past them on her way to the front door.

"Vaughn," said Sam, by way of introduction as Janet fumbled with the keys, "this is my Realtor, Janet Blair."

"Nice to meet you, ma'am." Vaughn, a former Michigan State basketball forward, towered over the small middle-aged redhead like a great oak over a dandelion. She glanced up at him with annoyance.

"You're blocking my light, there, Shaq."

Vaughn blinked twice and looked pleadingly to Sam, who shook his head and offered a quick shrug, as if to say "don't worry, she's not racist, she's just weird."

Janet had been a friend to the Spicer family for as long as Sam could remember, and had always been a bit of a character. He remembered her popping by the house unannounced with plates of cookies, even though she lived an hour away. He remembered her talking about guys she was enamored with, only later to describe them as "worthless ass-nuggets"—a colorful phrase which got Sam's mouth washed out with soap when he repeated it the next day. He remembered her wedding, at which Sam met a girl he would disastrously date for months, and he remembered her bitter divorce, after which Janet stayed in the Spicer family's guest room for weeks as she bawled over every shared detail of marital hell. And he remembered how, with each passing year, she seemed to get shorter, spunkier, and frizzier.

"Success!" screeched the Muppet. Sam smiled and grasped his girl's hand. Sarah gazed with pride at her trembling pre-fiancé. Vaughn let his bright, signature grin melt across his face once more.

The ancient door creaked, lightly trembled as it cleared the molding, and opened.

two

The building took an audible breath of fresh, crisp Michigan air. Freed dust particles danced happily in the welcome rays of sunlight. A musty smell engulfed Janet, Vaughn, Sarah, and Sam as they stepped through the threshold.

"Wow," breathed Vaughn and Sam in unison, before looking at each other and cracking up.

Sarah was thinking "wow" as well, calculating all the work and time and money that would be needed to reinvent this place as something approaching "hip." She opened her mouth to speak, but one look at Sam's drunkenly happy visage convinced her to keep such boring, practical thoughts to herself. This station was his baby, and you don't remind a proud new daddy that he's going to be changing a thousand diapers.

"Finally sinkin' in, huh?" Janet had removed her sunglasses and was gazing over the wreck, hands on her hips, like the queen of a conquered land.

Sam smiled. He had been waiting for this day for seven months, from the first time he found the building up for sale, to the time he found century-old pictures of the station on Google's image search, to the time he hired Janet as a reluctant buyer's agent, to the time he convinced her to break into the property the day the combination on the key box inexplicably failed, to the time the bank finally approved his loan after months of battles, to...well, there were about a hundred specific, detailed memories of this journey, each frustrating milestone pushing him a small step forward to the ultimate goal of ownership. Having only lived in apartments and rented rooms since leaving home, it was intoxicating to be standing inside the first property that was finally, uniquely, irreversibly, his.

"So," declared an energetic Vaughn, determined to break the reverent silence, "you're putting the bar against this wall, right?" He leapt over some fallen boards and pranced to the southeast corner. "I'm thinking…something really smokin', here. Like, glass, with underlights, or some really cool curved limestone, or maybe just a giant sheet of black onyx."

"I'm actually thinking concrete." Sam walked over to Vaughn's location, and spread his arms to illustrate the size of his imagined creation. "I've been reading up on concrete countertops online, and you have infinite flexibility. You can build them yourself, get the shape you want, the color you want, and it's just labor—the actual, physical costs are next to nothing."

"Ha!" interjected a new voice from the doorway. "*Just labor?* Because, shit, what's *labor?* Labor's nothing. Sure, go ahead, give it a shot." Then, dialing the sarcasm knob further into dripping territory, "I'm *sure* it will look super-duper pro."

Sam choked back a retort, and forced a laugh. "Guys," he explained, motioning to the backlit figure, "this is Albert. He's the restoration expert I found who's going to be helping us out."

"Al," revised Al, offering his hand to Janet. "And this boy's gonna need it."

Without another word, and without introducing himself to Vaughn or Sarah, Al proceeded to kneel and study a nearby baseboard, as if he was alone in the room. A dusty, world-weary man of fifty, but looking sixty, Al was right at home among the disrepair and the rubble. He moved swiftly, efficiently, yet respectfully along the walls of the station, stopping every few moments to touch a particularly interesting gouge, scrape or natural imperfection in the rich wood paneling.

"Where'd you find this guy," whispered Vaughn.

"He's the best," came Sam's swift, defensive reply. "I met him a few months ago when he was repairing Beaumont Tower's carillon—for free, just cause he loved the shit."

"Is he working for free for you too?"

Sam smiled. "Let's just say he has a lifetime gratis bar tab when we're up and running."

Al was on his knees, knocking meaningfully at a floorboard, grimacing for no apparent reason that Sam could detect, then moving a few inches further, peering closer, and knocking again.

Janet broke the awkward silence with a clap.

"Oh! I almost forgot." Janet tittered over to Sam with his new key, complete with a large, impractical four-inch plastic keychain emblazoned with the realty company's hideous logo. "She's all yours." Then, adding, "as long as you keep up with the payments."

Sam chuckled. He was well aware what he was getting himself into. Even if all repairs and design went as scheduled, he still had at least half a year's worth of monthly payments on a property that couldn't make a dime until they opened for business. And even then, it would take time to turn any sort of profit, if ever. Eaton Rapids was a city of just 6,000 people, and even with the new condos and developments going on at the old mill, and a surge of young people emigrating from nearby Lansing, this was an unlikely location for an upscale club. The banks thought so, too, and Sam had been rejected for more than a dozen small business loans. If this was going to work, he had to do the heavy lifting himself. Hence, a homemade concrete bar, not onyx.

"We'll make it happen," Sam declared in preemptive triumph.

"Uh huh," muttered Al, who began knocking on walls this time, listening closely, the chiseled lines across his face wrinkling deeper, as he jotted notes onto a tattered paper pad he had retrieved from his back pocket.

Although the building had been neglected for many years, the structure was sound. The mullioned windows, which were high and arched at the top, were still intact, and the rich wood molding around them had suffered little damage over the decades. The paneling, which ran up from the floor to about waist-level, was in a more battered condition, as if many years of clumsy movers had knocked furniture against every possible board at every possible height. Above the paneling, sickly beige paint was peeling off the walls in great scabs, all the way up to the high ornamented ceilings, which was to be expected from a building suffering without climate control through a dozen baking summers and freezing Michigan winters.

Sam's mind flashed back to his childhood, the day his family moved into their first real home, after years living in a trailer park of, he would learn later, some ill repute. Their new home had a modest square footage for its neighborhood, but compared with the trailer, it was a castle. It had three full bedrooms (though Sam would remain an only child), an office, a real dining room, an attic with dormer windows, and a basement half-finished and half-creepy—the creepy half leading Sam on an endless futile search for hidden passages and buried treasure. Though only six years old, the memories of exploring this new castle for the first time remained among the strongest of his childhood.

"So Vaughn, is there really enough room for a dance floor here?" Sarah was trying to imagine the setup, and having trouble visualizing a workable layout. Vaughn had been spinning as "DJ Knight" at a much larger club in Lansing for the past year, and Sarah found it hard to believe such an intimate setting would service his boisterous style.

"Absolutely. Remember, I do weddings, too, and those fold-out dance floors are no bigger than this. There's an upside to tight—people have to be closer together, and nothing's hotter than bodies grinding in a confined space."

"Literally," interjected Al from the far side of the room, "since there's no air conditioning."

"We'll fix that," promised Sam.

Vaughn shrugged. "Ya sure? Cold temps might cut into drink sales."

"I'll keep that in mind."

Janet was kicking some fallen boards from her path. "I wish the seller had at least cleaned up the place. You need a good junk guy?"

"I kinda want to go through everything piece by piece first," replied Sam, gazing around at the smattering of old boards, upholstery, and papers. "You never know what you're going to find, especially in a place with this much history." He was thinking of the old military discharge papers he had once found lodged under boards in the closet of his childhood bedroom. Although left behind by the previous owner, Sam had imagined they were hidden on purpose by a time-traveling super-soldier, to be retrieved only when the robot apocalypse had begun.

Al had left the main area, and was poking around in the other section of the property, a back room which would have been "employees only." Curious, Janet made her way to join him.

"Have you decided what you're using that area for?" Vaughn began walking to the employees area as well.

"Well, there has to be some storage, and expanded bathrooms," offered Sam. "I'm really not sure. We still might have to add on to the back so there's enough space, as long as the city lets us, and that would be a good place to remove a wall."

Vaughn nodded, then disappeared into the small room. Sam was about to follow, but felt a hand on his arm. Sarah tugged his shoulder downward, so she could whisper in his ear.

"We need to kick your friends out and christen this place properly," she cooed.

"You don't want to share the champagne?"

"You know that's not what I mean."

"Oh, I know."

Sam smiled and brushed his fingers across her right cheek. She closed her eyes and returned the smile, resisting the impulse to turn and bite his hand, as was her usual response to such mushy gestures.

"We should probably wait until I get the power and heat turned on," explained Sam. "It'll be a few days."

Sarah pouted, but did not otherwise object to this cruel but practical observation. It was indeed quite cold. In fact, Sarah was convinced that it was colder inside than it had been in the parking lot, even if logic demanded the opposite. The October day had been sunny, but crisp and windy— "good football weather" as her father used to say. At least inside they were sheltered from the moving air. But the chill persisted, as if her legs, and the back of her neck, were exposed to some unseen draft, that followed her body no matter how she happened to turn, or where she happened to move.

"Yeah, yeah," she agreed. "Besides, Kedzie will be coming by after she gets off work, and probably wouldn't appreciate the show."

"Really? From what I know of Kedzie, I bet she would."

Careful, Sam thought.

Sam led Sarah into the back area, where Janet and Vaughn were watching Al rip blue, stained low-pile carpet from one corner. The main room had wood plank flooring, as expected, and Sam had assumed this smaller room would have a similar composition, once this unattractive covering had been removed.

Al looked up. "I'm assuming you don't want to keep this," he said to Sam, gesturing to the carpet.

"Oh, God, no," Sam replied.

Without responding, Al continued with his work.

"Need a hand with that, man?" Vaughn knelt down and started tugging as well. The fabric began to crack and crumble beneath his strong hands, and he wondered if he should be wearing a respirator. "Damn, how old *is* this shit?"

Sam and Sarah bent down to help as well. Only Janet demurred, preferring to act in the role of supervisor. "That corner's sticking," she chirped unhelpfully, and "roll it up tighter to save space," and "pull a little harder," and "it's sticking on that nail, see it?"

The flooring underneath was indeed the same hardwood as the main room, but in far better condition, having been protected and preserved under carpet for many, many decades. Curiously, there was even an inlaid parquet pattern in the center of the room, which was unmatched by anything in the rest of the station. Small pieces of dark wood created a looping design resembling a lowercase "e" repeated as a border.

"Now why would they bother with something so fancy in what was clearly an employee's area," Janet inquired to the room, though looking squarely at Al, the only one who might have the qualifications to venture an accurate guess.

Vaughn answered instead. "Maybe this was for the boss's desk. Can't blame the big dog for wanting a little class under his feet."

"Eaton Rapids, you may recall, was a pretty big deal when this station was built," offered Al. "It was the so-called 'Saratoga of the West.' Back when Michigan was still 'the West.'"

Sarah scoffed at this. "Here?"

"That's right," explained Al, still scraping and rolling carpet away from the center of the room. "Lots of wealth came through here. Luxury hotels, mineral baths…Eaton Rapids was the place to see, and be seen."

"Not just blankets and ice cream, eh?" Sam was referring to Eaton Rapids' most popular turn-of-the-century industries, notably the woolen mills and Miller Dairy Farms. Janet got the reference, but Sarah and Vaughn, not originally from the area, exchanged a lost look.

"That still doesn't explain why builders would lay down a nice inlay in the private part of the station," complained Janet. "The main area's floor is pretty boring. No offense, Sam."

The carpet was rolled in a tight tube against the far wall now. Al stood up, brushed his hands on his jeans, and admired the pattern before them. It was indeed a complete square, about five feet along the edges. After a short examination, he cocked his head, and smiled. "Now *this* could be interesting," he mused.

Sam couldn't see what Al was referring to. "The pattern? Looks like a lot of letter 'e's. For Eaton Rapids, I suppose?"

Al shook his head. "No. Well, maybe. But I don't mean the pattern. Here, listen." He crouched down, and began tapping his knuckles against the floorboards, first inside the pattern, then just outside of it. He glanced up, looking for a sense of understanding on Sam's face. Finding none, Al tried again, knocking slower this time, in series of three, first outside the square, then inside.

Vaughn noticed the distinction. "Yeah…I hear it. Inside

the square, it's more of a hollow sound, right?"

Al stood up. "Right."

Sam turned to Janet. "Does that mean there might be a crawl space after all?"

"No," the Realtor replied in the tone of an expert. "This is just a slab foundation. Having a basement of any kind would have been extremely rare for this type of structure, especially of this period."

Sarah was crouching down now, examining a conspicuous seam between the parquet pattern and the surrounding planks. "This here…there's a bit of a gap, isn't there? That's what you saw, right?"

Al peered down again, as did Sam. "Fascinating," Al concluded after a long period of study. "Here, stand back."

The group took a step away from the square as Al proceeded to jump up and down on each corner of the pattern, then again on each full edge. The solemn look of concentration on Al's face as he did this made the act look particularly absurd. Vaughn shot Sam a look that seemed to ask "no, seriously, who *is* this guy?" Sam opened his mouth as if to offer a defense, but responded with a shrug.

Al stopped, though it was not immediately apparent from his face whether he had successfully observed what he was expecting, or had given up. He instead left the room without a word, and exited the station itself. The remaining group exchanged confused glances, and Sam was about to apologize for Al's behavior, when they heard a trunk slam, and Al returned to them. In his hands was a large crowbar, and he wasted no time in crouching down once more, jamming the sharp edge in between the gap Sarah had observed moments ago. The nearby wood splintered, making a dull, crunching sound like boots marching on dry Autumn leaves.

"Hey, wait," Sam protested. "Don't fuck up the floor—it's vintage, and can be restored, and…"

And…it moved. At first, just a fraction of an inch, barely perceptible from the overhead view of a standing man. But then it was clear what Al was attempting. By driving the crowbar further between the gap, he was able to pull the entire square upwards, as if prying off a large floor tile. Yet rather than pop out of its slot, the massive wooden square began to pivot, opening smoothly, like the lid of a gigantic jewelry box. Two massive iron rocking hinges, embedded beneath the floor, assisted Al's motion, and soon he wasn't exerting much effort at all, the five-foot square opening itself a full 90 degrees, standing upright like a monolith in the center of the dusty room. With a soft thud, it found its resting place, and Al shot a broad smile at the building's new owner, whose own jaw had dropped as low as the section of floor had once been.

Sam blinked, then stammered. "What the hell?"

The massive trap door hadn't just revealed a crawl space. The five peered down into a darkness that must have been at least ten feet deep, for the meager light in the room couldn't reveal the eventual bottom of this very black pit.

But they could see the stairs.

three

Every summer, little Sammy Spicer would spend several weekends at his aunt's house in Mio, Michigan, a small unincorporated village a few hours north of his family home in Eaton Rapids. He liked Aunt Eleanor very much, for she was always sweet to him, and always had sweets *for* him—homemade pies, cookies, cakes, and a particularly memorable homemade chocolate fudge, which seemed to take a great deal of time and concentration stirring a large wooden spoon into a heavy saucepan over an open flame. Even after Aunt Eleanor had given Sam's mom the recipe, giving into Sam's persistent pleadings, it was never the same at home. At first bite, his mom's attempt tasted just like he remembered, but it didn't, as they say of wines, "finish well." It was somehow less rich, and a little gritty, just an understudy to the real deal. Perhaps it was the extra care his aunt was able to devote to the task, or maybe, looking back, his mom's electric cooktop just couldn't compare to that ancient green gas stove that Aunt Eleanor had mastered. Or maybe, in a playful act of sibling rivalry, Eleanor had omitted just one, simple, secret ingredient that assured her own creation was free from competition.

Visiting Aunt Eleanor's would have been perfect, if not for two unfortunate caveats named cousin Matt and cousin Pete. Both older than Sam, Matt by three years and Pete by four, they had grown up not with a father, but rather an endless string of unworthy boyfriends of their mom's. As the real "men of the house," they therefore tried to act older than they were, and so frequently tried to parent—and punish—young Sam. Not in a big brotherly way, but in the manner of a drunken stepfather. They would spend time with their young cousin, invite him into their world of "adult" interests such as violent sports or dangerous risks, and Sam would do his best to keep up and have fun and try and be accepted. But at some point in each activity, Sam would be too scared to go the one step further, or to climb the one branch higher, or commit to the one final act which would make him one of the big kids. When this happened, Matt and Pete wouldn't call him a "baby" or a "pussy" or a "fag" or any of the normal playground insults. No, they'd use far more sophisticated, and therefore more hurtful words, such as "immature" and "disappointment" and, worst of all, "embarrassment."

One of these weekends, Matt, Pete, and Sam had been playing the rule-free game of "dare." Sam was eight years old, and was finally able to keep up with at least some of the tasks at hand. He was able to drink a sip of water from the brown creek. He was able to throw a rock at a passing car. He was able to make a blowtorch from a lighter and his aunt's aerosol hair spray. He was even, once, able to swallow a live bug. On this occasion, he was winning "dare" for the first time, as both Matt and Pete had each failed a request, but Sam had not.

"Ya know," said Pete, eyeing Sam thoughtfully, "there's one thing that both Matt and I have done before, that you haven't."

"What?"

Pete glanced behind his shoulder, motioning with his chin to the low wooden door in the ground behind the house. "The root cellar."

Sam stiffened. "What about it?"

"You ever been in there?"

Sam shook his head.

A slow smile crept across Matt's face. "It's dark," he explained. "And deep. And there are spiders the size of your head."

"So?"

"So, I *dare* you to go inside, shut the door, and stay in for two minutes."

"*Five* minutes," Pete modified. "Five."

Sam said nothing. Didn't offer a word of affirmation, or of protest, or of bargaining. He just thought. Could he do it? Would this win his cousins' respect? And what would be worse—to chicken out now, to say "no," and have them laugh, or to say "yes," but *then* fail, to burst out of the doors sobbing in seconds, to even greater laughter and insult?

Then again, he might succeed.

"Alright, guys," came the eventual, soft reply.

Matt and Pete grinned. They weren't expecting this. In that moment, they may have even given Sam a little credit, for they each had been terrified of the decrepit cellar at Sam's age and even older.

The three boys walked to the old French-style doors, installed in the ground at a far steeper angle than seemed practical or necessary, and smiled at each other conspiratorially. Matt and Pete each took the handle of a door and opened them in tandem—two lips of a great sideways mouth preparing to gobble its next young victim.

There were stairs going down into the cellar, but they faded into blackness. The little remaining light of dusk revealed only five or six steps, though Sam was sure there must be more. The darkness was so great, Sam was convinced the pit must go on forever.

Matt smiled at his little cousin. "Your move, kid."

Sam took a step back.

"Aw, he's not gonna do it," taunted Pete. "You chickening out, Sammy? It's okay. We won't tease. No one expects that much of *you*."

Sam closed his eyes, silently counted to three, then without thinking, as if commanding his muscles to move before his mind had committed, Sam walked into the cellar, taking each downward step to the beat of a metronome, until he was at the bottom and his feet hit clay.

He had counted just seven steps. The clay ground just hadn't been able to reflect light. It wasn't so deep after all.

The young boy turned around and looked up the stairs with defiance.

"Alright, kid," said Matt, glancing at his green plastic digital watch. "Five minutes starting…now."

The two brothers smiled again at each other, and closed the doors. The light, little that there had been, was now gone.

Sam had a panicked thought. What if his cousins had locked the doors as a prank? *Was* there even a lock? He couldn't remember. He tried to picture the two doors, before they had been opened, but all his memory would reveal was an image of the entry already uncovered, the all-consuming blackness staring him down. He closed his eyes to think harder, but realized this was pointless, as his brain could detect no difference in light between eyes open or shut.

Another thought occurred to Sam. What guarantee did he have that Matt and Pete would count the five minutes honestly? They could make it ten. Or twenty. Or go in the house and have fudge and say they "totally forgot" about Sam, and were "so sorry" he had been stuck in that horrible place for a half hour or more.

No, they didn't hate him. They just wanted him to grow up. This was part of growing up. *I'm growing up*, Sam thought. *I'm growing up.*

He could feel his heart beating through his shirt, and imagined he could *see* it beating, pounding against the fabric, if there was only a little light. He thought vaguely that his eyes should have adjusted by now, but there was nothing to adjust to. There was no nightlight. No filtered blue light from streetlamps seeping in through closed blinds. This was true darkness. Six feet underground.

Sam wondered what was down here with him. Was it jars of fruit preserves? Was it tree roots? Were there…bodies? Was Aunt Eleanor secretly a serial killer, and used this place to store the skeletons of her victims?

No. It was just, a cellar. That's all. To Sam's knowledge, they never even used it, unless they caught wind of an approaching tornado.

The room was quiet for a long time. And then, Sam heard the faintest, barely perceptible scratching noise. The kind of sound you couldn't notice under normal conditions, but stood out when deprived of all other senses. It wasn't a scary sound by itself—rather like fingernails brushing against an empty drinking glass—but in this place, it popped like a snare drum. Sam caught his breath, waiting to hear if the sound returned...and it did, louder this time, he believed, and maybe closer.

Sam stood his ground. He wasn't going to run up those invisible stairs, pound at those invisible doors, be let out and be laughed at. He was going to stay put, and wait, and wait, and wait, even if he pissed himself, a fate which seemed more and more likely with each slow-moving second.

It had to have been five minutes, hadn't it? It seemed longer.

He took a deep breath. He had a moment of complete, sophisticated calm.

Then, something scampered across his left shoe.

The shoe was thick, and he barely felt it, but he *knew* he felt it. In his mind, he thought he even *saw* it. Something had run across his foot. What was it? One of the head-sized spiders from Matt's warning? Or something which actual teeth, like...a rat?

Sam held back a tear, but again he stood firm. If he couldn't see the rat, the rat couldn't see him, right? The would-be critter wouldn't even know he existed. He was just running that way anyway. Maybe had to get to the other side of the cellar in a hurry, for food.

Then again, perhaps the rat was being chased. Is that why he was running so fast? Was a bigger predator coming after him? Would Sam soon feel the weight of another creature on his shoe?

For a few desperate seconds, nothing happened. But then, Sam felt tiny *hands* on his right ankle. The rat was trying to crawl up his leg!

Sam couldn't help himself. He screamed, and began shaking and stomping his right foot. He stomped and he stomped and he stomped onto the hard clay earth, trying to hit the creature who had touched him, or at least trying to scare the thing far away, to leave him alone, perchance to die, die, *die* before it could reach him again.

All was still for a moment. Sam was trying not to cry. He pleaded with himself not to let tears come. He begged to God, *please* don't let me cry. But when he saw those big wooden doors up the staircase open again, he couldn't help it. He sobbed and sprinted upward, stumbling on the last stair, until he was out in the "light" of the past-sunset sky.

Matt and Pete were stifling laughter, but there was something different in their eyes. Something approaching respect. Sam knew, without being told, just from their faces, that even though he had gotten scared, even though he had screamed, *he had made it the full five minutes.* He was sure of it. And they knew it, too. He composed himself, wiping his cheeks, and offered a weak smile.

"Congrats, Sam," said Matt. "Even Pete would have shit himself at your age."

"Fuck you, you fuckin' liar!" Pete punched his brother in the arm, and laughed.

Sam managed another smile. He was a big kid now. He had made it. And he'd been braver than Pete—*Pete*, who wasn't even scared of playing chicken on train tracks.

The laughter subsided. Matt looked down at his cousin. "So Sammy, what made you scream?"

Sam looked embarrassed. "I…thought I felt something trying to crawl up my leg."

Matt chuckled derisively, but then his eyes drifted down Sam's body, down his legs, and to his feet. And his playful expression vanished. He took a step forward, toward Sam, staring at his right shoe, trying to get a clearer picture in the dim light of the sky.

"Shit, dude," he said. "Holy shit, dude."

Sam, nervously, let his eyes fall to his feet as well. At first he saw nothing. Just his tennis shoes, and the dirt and patchy grass beneath them. But soon, he saw the eyes. He blinked, convinced it was just an illusion, a trick, something in the ground. It wasn't. There were two small, black eyes, popped violently from their sockets, hanging on by gooey threads from the flattened face stuck with blood on Sam's right foot. And Sam realized at once what must have happened. He had stomped on and squashed a small, grey field mouse, whose bleeding corpse had caught in the treads of his shoe, and whose crushed skull was now staring up in anguish at the little boy who had slaughtered him.

Sam's mouth opened wide to scream, but no sound came. His body convulsed in disgust and terror. He tried to scrape the animal off, on the ground, on the dirt, but those bulging, dangling black eyes wouldn't leave, they wouldn't stop following him, staring accusingly, hatefully up at their killer. Sam twisted, tripped, and fell, and finally kicked off the shoe altogether, hurling it into the night, then ran crying with a limp into the safety of Aunt Eleanor's warm cabin.

But worse than anything, worse than the fright, worse than knowing he had killed a living creature, worse than the shock of finding the carcass embedded in his shoe, worse than the panic he felt when it couldn't be scraped off, far worse than these things, was hearing Matt and Pete roar with laughter behind him. Sam could hear them howling, screaming, guffawing at his expense, every second that he was running, all the way to the safety of the house, and could still hear them laughing, muffled, after he shut the big door behind him.

He was not brave. He was not one of the big kids.

He was an embarrassment.

*

In the station, Sam stared down at the steps below him. They were wooden, and seemed a little steep, but not in disrepair. Although he couldn't see more than five or six steps before they gave way to the blackness, he could see they flared out a bit as they progressed, and there were handrails starting at about the third step down. As his eyes adjusted, he could even see the floor. It was not bottomless. It was just a cellar. That was all.

Sam took a deep breath, trying to drown the voice of the knot in his stomach urging him to flee, to get outside this creepy place, back into the sun. The cellar at Aunt Eleanor's consumed his thoughts, but he was determined not to show fear in front of Sarah. He straightened his back, and stared down the challenge.

"Vaughn," he said abruptly, taking charge. "You have

your van here, right?"

"Uh, yeah man."

"Your equipment?"

Vaughn didn't see what he was getting at. "You wanna hear some tunes?"

"No, your lights. You still have those battery-powered LED things?"

Vaughn got it. "Oh, yeah dude, sure. They should be all charged up and everything."

"Get them."

Vaughn took a long, slow look at the pit, then left to get the equipment. He returned with two battery-operated American DJ spotlights on small metal tripods, and flipped them both on.

"I have a flashlight here, too," offered Janet, retrieving a small but bright keychain-light from her purse. It, too, boasted the hideous realty logo.

"Alright," said Sam, taking one of the spotlights from Vaughn. "Are we all going down?"

Sarah stepped closer, and rested her hand on his shoulder in affirmation. Al said "well shit, I'm not going to miss this." Janet nodded, somberly, but fascinated.

"Then let's go."

Sam led the way, wielding the closed metal tripod light like a club in one hand, and holding Sarah's hand with the other, as they stepped down together into the basement room. Vaughn followed close behind, then Janet and Al, until all five had traversed sixteen full steps, landing on a wood floor of similar style to the room before.

"This doesn't make any sense," Janet complained.

"These ceilings must be twelve feet high. For a *basement*?"

Sam and Vaughn panned their spotlights around the room. It wasn't a large space, but it was oddly empty—no shelves, no furniture, no boxes. It was completely bare. The walls had the same wood paneling of the upstairs rooms, with one noticeable exception: an arched, boarded-up doorway directly in front of their path. As it seemed clear to Sam, and everyone else, that the designed purpose of the staircase must be to direct people through that doorway, the boards would have to be removed.

"Al," began Sam, "do you still have…"

"Way ahead of you, Sammy." Al had the crowbar out and began to remove the first long plank blocking the entrance to…well, whatever the entrance was to. But after a few boards, it became apparent that there wasn't a hidden door or hallway behind the barricade, but a large, iron cage. The bars of the cage were vertical and tightly packed, and at first seemed to be uniform, but as Al continued to work, ornamentation was revealed near the top of the bars, of the same "e" pattern of the parquet in the previous room.

"Uh, Sam," Vaughn said, uneasy. "We just pried open a hidden section of the floor, revealed this creepy-ass room, and Al here is pulling off boards covering up a big fucking cage. I know this is your digs and all, but don't you think it's possible that maybe the previous owners knew something you don't? And, maybe, we should keep those boards right where they are?"

Sam didn't reply, but saw Janet stepping closer, her eyes wide.

"Guys, it's not a cage," said Janet in disbelief, as Al

finished one of the last large barrier boards. "Look inside. Look at the buttons."

They all peered in.

Sarah gasped. "It's an elevator!"

The group was silent for a long moment. Even Al had taken a break from removing the final large board at the bottom of their new discovery. They stared at the row of circular brass buttons on the far wall of the cage, which was indeed, quite clearly now, a rather ornate turn-of-the-century elevator car. The numbers were elegantly carved into the brass, and legible even from their current distance. But what really struck Sam, and the others, into a prolonged state of silence, more than even the sheer impossibility of finding an elevator in the basement of a basement-less building, was the fact that there were not merely one, nor two numbered buttons, but twelve.

four

No one said anything, but Sam reached for and found Sarah's hand, clutching it for support. While he had dreamed as a child of finding hidden passageways, as all children do, Sam found he wasn't quite prepared for actually discovering one. His heart beat faster, but he couldn't determine whether it was from excitement or fear.

"You know, it's not like this could be functional," Vaughn argued, breaking the silence and gesturing to the elevator car. "I mean, what's more likely—that someone installed an old replica down here for safe keeping, or that it actually goes twelve stories down."

"Oh, *down*!" exclaimed Janet. "I was trying to figure out how we missed an adjacent eleven-story building."

Vaughn blinked. "You're kidding."

"Yes," Janet admitted. And after a pause, defensively: "I'm really quite funny."

Al stepped forward and tried opening the gate. He figured out the mechanism, and it became clear there were *two* gates, perfectly aligned, one connected to the walls of the room, and the other to the car itself. He slid both gates to one side, allowing entry, and entered.

"Wait! Dude." Sam placed an arm on Al's shoulder across the divide. "That can't be attached to anything anymore. It could fall straight down. And besides, I told you, power doesn't even get turned on for a few days."

Al said nothing, but gestured upward. Sam poked his head into the elevator car, and saw a dim amber light glowing above the number "12."

"That's...not possible," was Sam's eventual, paradoxical response.

Sarah peeked in to see the light as well. "Well, this doesn't make sense anyway. Shouldn't the floors be 'B1,' 'B2,' and all that? Wouldn't the numbers increase as you get deeper?"

"She's right, Al," Sam agreed. "Why would they call the floor we're on '12,' if we're at ground level? *Below* ground level, even."

"Guys," said Al, offering a helpless, open wave with his arms. "I don't have any answers here at all. This is your baby, Sam. But we're definitely on the twelfth floor according to these numbers, which means there's eleven floors beneath us. I say we grab those party lights and check them out."

Sarah shot Sam a panicked look, unmistakable even when obscured by the spotlighted shadows of the room. *There's no hurry*, she seemed to be pleading. *Let's go upstairs and talk about this.* But her boyfriend's unease had melted away, and he now seemed drunk with curiosity. Sam's eyes had opened wide at the revelation of the lighted number, and had stayed wide, joined now by a goofy grin. While Sarah may have been thinking *this is dangerous*, Sam was thinking *this is the coolest thing that has ever happened to me.* Which, admittedly, made Sarah a little jealous by comparison.

Sam had made a decision, and turned to Vaughn. "You

in?"

Vaughn glanced back and forth between his friend's hopeful face and the creepy magic elevator. "Well, you know I'm with you…but shouldn't someone stay back in order to call 911 if something goes wrong?"

"This guy's right," added Janet, forgetting Vaughn's name. "There's no way I'm gonna get phone service down there. And we haven't even tested the thing."

A reasonable thought.

Sam turned back to the elevator car. "Al, how do we test it?"

"It doesn't *need* to be tested," came an irritated reply. "These things were built to last hundreds of years." Sensing a losing battle, he added "this is *Victorian craftsmanship*" with a dramatic flair. "It's not some modern piece of junk. No built-in obsolescence here. If it's powered, it'll work, end of story."

Sarah was looking just outside the elevator car. She asked Sam to shine the light her way, to which he obliged.

"Here," she gestured. "It's a call button. We can send the car down, then call it back up. That's our test."

"The elevator's not going to move with the door open," Al scoffed, still standing alone in the car. "Look, if you're scared, I could just go down myself, count to ten, and come back up and get you kids."

"No, no," Sam insisted. "If anyone's going to go down alone, it should be me. My property, my risk."

Sarah rolled her eyes. "Okay, I love a good dick contest as much as the next girl, but you're both being stupid. The buttons are on the opposite side of the car, right? We can push one of them with the butt of a light stand after we've closed the gate from the outside."

"But what if the elevator doesn't come back up?" Sam protested.

"That's the whole point of the test, you idiot." Her smile softened the insult.

Al was annoyed. "I really don't mind going down alone."

"No, it's okay. Come on out. Sarah's right. We have the ability to do a safe test, and should take it."

Grudgingly, Al stepped out of the car and closed both gates behind him. They locked with a satisfying click, and Al took the opportunity to point out this solid craftsmanship to Sam with a brief nod and a hand motion, as if to say, "see?"

Sam assured the tripod legs of the light he carried were securely closed, then threaded them through a set of bars nearest to the circle marked "1." With a deep breath, he gently pushed the light stand forward, and activated the button.

The elevator whirred to life and began to descend. He quickly pulled the tripod back through the iron bars and into the waiting room, almost clipping its metal feet against the ceiling of the moving car. Without a modern, solid external door, the shaft and operating mechanism were visible through the outside gate during the car's descent. As they shone light upon the chains and motors, it also became clear that Al was correct. Everything was in eerily impeccable shape, and in perfect operating order.

"This is un-fucking-real," Vaughn interjected. The rest assented this notion with silence.

The elevator was slow by modern standards, and it took a several minutes before a dim, mechanical "thud" signaled the elevator car's arrival at its destination. Sam turned to Sarah and nodded. She returned the nod and pressed the solitary, unlabeled button to the right of the opening. Again, not more than an instant after the button was pushed, the machine whirred to life once more, and after another two minutes, the car was safely back in place, just as they had found it.

Al stood straight, puffing his chest in triumph. "*Now* can we go?"

Sam turned to Sarah with puppy dog eyes, asking not only for permission, but for her enthusiastic accompaniment. She gave both, and grasped his right hand, before taking out her cell phone. "Let me text Kedzie real fast," she explained. "So someone knows where we are."

Vaughn and Al didn't need encouragement. Soon, the committed four stepped into the car together, and turned back around to Janet, who seemed to be on the fence.

"Come on, Janet," teased Sam. "You only live once."

"I know," she responded. "That's precisely why I don't take risks."

"You can stay and keep watch if you like."

She considered this option, but was bored by the thought of sitting in a dark room while four lucky others made what could be the find of the century.

"Ah hell," Janet decided, stepping forward at last, joining the group inside the gate. "I'd rather kick myself for missing my next appointment than kick myself for missing this."

It took a few moments to decide whether to press "11,"

thereby exploring the closest level first, planning to move deeper as they went, or to press "1," going deepest first, planning to work their way up. Sam made an executive decision to start on "1," deducing that an etched double ring around the "1" made the floor special, and whatever was stored there would make the most interesting find. After a collective, fingers-crossed intake of musky air, the group agreed, and Sam had again pushed the brass circle "1," this time inside the car, with an index finger.

As the car descended, Al observed that the functionality was surprisingly modern for an elevator this old, and expressed relief that the elevator didn't require a trained operator. Still, as they had observed, it was slower than a modern descent would be, which was particularly noticeable as the car passed ten other floors, each slightly visible through the gate. Vaughn and Sam tried to shine the spotlights through the gate and see what each floor had to offer, for none of the floors were lit, but the glare against the vertical bars and the varying depth of the levels made it impossible to adjust one's eyes to the view beyond. Most floors revealed, if anything, simple hallways, but little else of note. The tenth and fifth floors had been different, with clear brickwork, and higher, arched ceilings, but even with the deliberate pacing, it was too difficult to discern specifics in the dark.

Finally, they felt their transportation slow further and stop at the bottom of its track. For a moment, nobody moved, paralyzed either by caution, fear, or just the understandable twinge of second thoughts. It was Al who first stepped toward the opening, unlatched both gates, and entered the large room.

It had taken longer to travel between the second floor and the first, even when accounting for a reduction in speed, and now it was apparent why. The ceiling on this level, like the original room they had found, was at least twelve feet high. Sam was initially convinced they had arrived at a great cavern, for his spotlight seemed to be drowned out by darkness too far away from his location. But as he moved his light around, and looked closer at each illuminated spot, he *could* see the ceiling above them, the tiled floor beneath them, and eventually, the large, imposing desk which faced them, beckoning, fifty feet away.

"Hey Janet," Sam mused. "How many square feet is my property again?"

"Don't get too excited, kid. There's no way all of this is still directly under your little train station."

"I don't know," Al interjected a few paces away. "We still might be below the parking lot. Anyone remember which direction is north?"

"I think you give my parking lot too much credit, Al. This place is huge."

Sarah was again clutching Sam's free hand, and with a quick jolt, she felt an unwelcome shiver down the base of her spine as they continued into the room.

"Are you cold?" asked Sam.

Sarah paused. "Actually, no. Shouldn't I be? Shouldn't it be freezing down here?"

"Or hotter," Vaughn said with a dry chuckle. "This much closer to hell, and all."

Sam was still curious. "What do you think, Al? Climate

control?"

"Possibly," came Al's reply, without any trace of sarcasm, unaware that Sam had been joking.

Vaughn's spotlights were a poor match for this wide open space and its uncompromising darkness. They were battery-powered LEDs, meant for accent lighting, not room illumination. Janet's pocket flashlight was similarly underpowered for the task. Only small pieces of the puzzle could therefore be seen at any one time—two large French doors to the left and right; a handful of Victorian armchairs in red fabric; the deep mahogany and long curve of the center desk, which was now close; black, wrought iron light fixtures eight feet up on the walls.

Janet had noticed the fixtures as well, and deduced they must be electric. "Anyone see a light switch?"

Al seemed to have the same thought. He had already reached the long desk, had quickly maneuvered behind it, and was feeling along the wall with both hands. "Hey," he called, "could you shine one of the lights my way?"

Sam and Vaughn both complied, and Al was able to discern a small rectangle carved dead-center into the back wall behind the desk. He identified the rectangle as an inset door, and after a little trial and error, opened in outward. Inside, there were five dial-based switches, each angled upward and to the left. In quick succession, Al switched all five of these to the right, and waited.

At first, there was just a dull whir, like the sound of distant machinery. But then, the two lights above the desk faded up to full brightness. Additional light fixtures became activated at other points of the great room, most of which had been undetected in the spotlight sweeps. Soon, the area was awash in so much amber light that Sam had to squint to allow his eyes to recover.

He had begun to make the assumption, as they all had upon seeing certain elements in the spotlights, that this must be some sort of lobby. But Sam had not been prepared for a *lobby*. Indeed, everyone had gasped—loudly, and in unison—when the lights came up and the truth was revealed. Janet had even dropped her flashlight, which made a small echoing "thump" by her feet and switched itself off. No one even flinched, or noticed.

Sam gave voice to the thought lingering thick like fog in the room.

"Holy shit."

The lobby, and it was most certainly that, was breathtaking in its design and elegance. The walls were painted in regal reds and browns, which explained why the spotlights had been so ineffective against them. Deep, rich elaborate molding adorned every angle between floor, walls, ceiling, and doorways. Tasteful gold accents were embedded in the desk, the visitors chairs, and even the floor tile.

But what held Sam's attention, more than any other feature of this impossible place, were the large, gold, gothic letters dead center on the wall before them, proudly declaring the name of where they had ended up:

THE EATON

Sarah, realizing the only plausible explanation, asked softly, to no one in particular: "…a *hotel?*"

Al stared at the letters in utter astonishment, as if he had solved some ancient riddle. He thought of his childhood, his Grandpa, and of all the buildings he had explored and restored over the years. Then, he laughed aloud. As he was still standing behind the large concierge desk, Al turned to his companions, feigned an air of sophistication and belonging, and placed his hands down on the shiny, lacquered wood.

"Why yes, ma'am, and welcome," he said in a mocking tone of professional courtesy. "Would you ladies and gentlemen happen to have a reservation?"

five

The first floor of The Eaton was massive by comparison to the defunct train station above it, but quite intimate when compared with a modern hotel. The main floor was divided roughly into thirds, with the lobby, desk, and a small posterior employees area making up the center column, a ballroom and bar through double doors to the left of the lobby, and a dining room and kitchen through double doors to the right. Al estimated the entire size of the level at about 5,000 sq ft., perhaps 70 feet square. The ballroom had a small brass sign listing its capacity as 80 persons, and the dining area, with a portion cut out for the kitchen, had a listed capacity of 65. The luxury apparent in every detail seemed designed to impress an elite group of guests.

Sarah had been drawn to the dining room. There were fifteen tables, three rows of five, with padded wooden armchairs arranged around each. Each table was dressed with a crisp, white thick linen tablecloth, and a small brass candle holder at each table's center. A few extra chairs ran along the far wall, near a small serving area which connected with a back kitchen. The lack of cobwebs and significant dust struck Sarah as quite odd, for if they had truly stumbled upon a long-closed hotel, she assumed there would be more evidence of neglect.

Al startled Sarah as she was running her finger along the server's countertop, checking her dust hypothesis. "We're underground," he said.

"I'm sorry?"

"It's a sealed space. Dust has to come from somewhere. In fact, most dust, in a house or office, is nothing but dead skin cells. I'm guessing there hasn't been any skin down here in over a hundred years."

"That's…disgusting."

Al shrugged, unaffected. "It's true. I used to sell Kirby vacuums when I was right outta high school. One of the sales pitches we were trained to use was sucking dust out of a person's mattress, then peeling the sticky, dusty film out of the canister, explaining to the client how we were holding a sheet of their rotting skin in front of them. The first woman I tried this on just ran to the bathroom to vomit, which convinced me I had lost the sale for sure. But then she came back with her checkbook and bought the premium model."

"As gross as that story is," Sarah continued with a disgusted shudder, "surely you must find the condition of this place a little too good to be true."

"Oh, no doubt," Al eagerly admitted. "This is fucking golden."

"But it doesn't make any sense."

"Well, that depends. If I'm right about the climate control, I believe that a consistent temperature, in a protected underground environment, might very well hold up a hundred years or more. But I'm not saying it ain't weird. How often do you get the chance to walk back in time?"

Sarah and Al heard Sam calling to them from the lobby.

They left the dining area and found him, standing near the entrance of the ballroom, beckoning them to follow.

Vaughn and Janet were already inside, Janet sitting at a barstool, with Vaughn behind the bar. He had retrieved an old bottle of scotch, and presented it with with pride to the entering patrons.

"Guys, check this out. It's a 12-year-old scotch. From 110 years ago, according to the label. Which means…it's a *122-year-old scotch!* We have to try this."

Al rolled his eyes. "Scotch doesn't age in the bottle. It ages in the barrel. A 12-year-old bottled scotch 50 years later or even 100 years later is still a 12-year-old scotch."

Vaughn looked disappointed, then recovered. "But dude, seriously. You're not going to try some?"

Al cracked a smile. "Well, I didn't say that."

"That bottle might be worth a lot of money," Janet protested. "You sure you want to waste it?"

Sam stepped in. "I believe Vaughn's response would be that drinking quality alcohol would never be considered 'wasteful.'"

Vaughn smiled in concurrence. "And besides," he added, "I bet there are a hundred unopened bottles in these cabinets. I think we can spare one for celebration."

Al sat down next to Janet, and Sam and Sarah embraced momentarily, holding hands again. Sam looked into his girlfriend's eyes with such vivacious intensity that she almost burst out laughing in response. She hadn't seen that look since the first time they had made love two years ago.

"I'm a little jealous, sweetie," she admitted. "You're looking at The Eaton with more love than you look at me."

"Oh, Sarah," Sam protested in response, "I *am* looking at you. I wouldn't be this excited without you here. I'm excited for the future this could mean for both of us. What good is finding treasure without someone to share it with?"

Sarah beamed at this. But she saw a hint in his eyes that wasn't just excitement, or love for this discovery, or love for her. It was something different, something new, as if their natural blue color had gained an attractive new sparkle. And as she leaned back to observe him more carefully, she realized it wasn't just his eyes. Sam's posture had changed as well, and he stood a little straighter, as if in uniform. Since they had been together, Sarah couldn't remember a single time he had appeared to her in this condition, and it soon dawned on her what it was: *pride.* He was exuding a sense of accomplishment that, even on his best days, had always eluded him. He had found this old train station. He had gone through hell to buy it. And now, mere hours after signing the documents and getting the keys, he didn't even have to wait a year to see if his proposed nightclub would be become profitable. Rather, with this discovery, he had become a success *today.* And he knew it.

Sam couldn't resist snapping a few quick photos with his cell phone, including a selfie with Sarah, though naturally they were too far underground to have cell service, and The Eaton was a hundred years too old for hotel wi-fi. Still, it would make one hell of a post later.

Vaughn had poured five drinks, and managed a gentle, impatient cough to persuade Sam and Sarah to sit down. They obliged, and each lifted a heavy, leaded glass into the air. Vaughn opened his mouth to speak, then silenced himself, deferring to Sam with a nod. His friend took the cue.

"To The Eaton," Sam declared in triumph.

"To The Eaton," his friends repeated.

Each took their scotch in a single gulp. All but Al gasped and choked before the empty glasses clinked back down to the bar.

"Christ," coughed Sam. "Is it supposed to taste like that?"

Al closed his eyes and smiled. "Only when you're lucky, kid."

Sam regained his composure, turned back to Sarah, and kissed her on the cheek, a gesture of thanks for partaking in the fire water. She squeezed his hand in reply, and again had a smile for him.

"Okay," Vaughn said, looking around the room. "Now what?"

Sam spoke up. "I say we finish exploring this level and work our way up. I just peeked in that back room, but I'm guessing if we dig around further, we could probably find room keys, assuming there are rooms, right?"

"Yeah, that makes sense," Al agreed.

"Then let's go."

Vaughn was about to cork the scotch, but Al stopped him, taking out a hip flask from his pocket. "No reason not to take some for the road," he explained with a wry smile.

"Only if you share, old man," said Vaughn.

The group proceeded back to the lobby. Sam and Sarah opened the door to the back office and began to look around. The rest followed, though the space was tight for five people, leading each person to examine just the area within their immediate reach.

A small desk in the corner contained a series of large black ledgers, and Sarah opened one.

"Hey, look at this. It's a reservation book." She leafed through the pages. "But...it's empty." She tried another book, and this one had writing, but only in the first few pages. "Here we are. We have reservations starting Friday, September 15, 1905. That must have been the first day they were open."

Sarah turned the ledger around so the others could see. Names were printed in perfect penmanship, and beside them, room numbers. Dr. Henrietta Carr, room 702. Dr. Alexander Winchell and Wife, room 801. Waldorf Astor, Master. The names continued on through the first weekend, with more being added Saturday, but no check-out times were recorded at all, despite a column dedicated to such entries.

"And that's where it ends." Sarah frowned. The rest of the book was blank. "They were only open for a single weekend?"

"I'm more concerned with the fact that they didn't check out," replied Vaughn. "Sam, I love ya man, but if we find skeletons in those rooms..."

"I'm sure it's just an oversight," Sam responded with confidence. "The hotel must have run out of money, or something. Maybe financiers didn't come through after all. Who knows. But if people had died down here, that means they would have gone missing, and we'd have grown up telling ghost stories about it."

"Technically," Janet interjected, "the fact that none of us knew anything about this place, not even as legend, is what worries me. How could such a thing be kept a secret?"

"It must not have been secret at the time," said Sarah, pointing to the names. "These people knew about it. And I'm guessing these are people with money."

"Maybe the hotel was only open in secret to an elite few," Sam reasoned. "Perhaps the grand opening would have come later, but some special individuals, powerful men and women with connections, got a sneak preview."

Sarah was still puzzled, a crease deepening between her eyebrows. "But this place must have cost a fortune to put together. A luxury hotel completely below ground? You'd think it would have been open for decades, especially if you're right that Eaton Rapids once had money."

As Al had referenced earlier, the city had once thrived as a tourist destination, attracting the wealthy from across the country and beyond. The land had indeed been blessed with a vast reservoir of magnetic mineral springs, which were quite popular—and profitable—to those who believed in the water's curative powers. In the late 19th and early 20th centuries, Eaton Rapids boasted a number of luxury establishments, each boldly advertising spas and mineral baths and miracle cures from any imaginable ailment.

Sam realized something, and turned to Al to confirm it. "This place…we're going to find mineral baths here, too, aren't we?"

Al nodded. "Yes, I suspect as much. This would have been near the end of the magnetic mineral bath boom, although we only recognize the downturn through the benefit of history. At the time, I'm sure the builders of this hotel assumed the bath's popularity and subsequent riches would go on forever."

Janet felt understanding creep across her face in the form of a smile. "Oh, of course," she began. "The wells that found the springs had to be a hundred feet deep, right? About as deep as this hotel. So imagine the marketing of it—only 'The Eaton' has mineral baths that come *right from the source*."

"I see what you mean," agreed Sam with enthusiasm. "Why settle for hotels that bring the healing water to you, when we can bring you to the water!"

"I'm also guessing," added Al, "that we're also going to find an underground water wheel wrapped around one of the springs, which is powering all this. In fact, Sam, when you're ready, I'm sure there's enough left over to power your club up there, too."

"Really?"

"Of course. Even the old mill on the corner once had all its electricity powered by a water wheel. And if it's enough to power a huge industrial complex, I'm pretty sure it'll be enough to cover some cheesy disco lighting."

Vaughn stiffened a bit at "cheesy disco lighting," but said nothing.

Sarah was beginning to feel relieved. This had all been so bizarre, she hadn't known what to think. But hearing the seemingly inconceivable attributes of the hotel described in practical detail, she began to realize that what they had discovered wasn't impossible after all. It was turn-of-the-century science, not magic. The miracle was in finding the place intact, not the place itself. Maybe now she could greater share in her boyfriend's giddy excitement, without the "this isn't right" pit in her stomach.

Janet found the key box. It was hidden behind an old framed photograph on the back wall, embedded into the plaster like a gun safe. Opening revealed fifty sets of keys, each one with a label describing the room or location number. About forty of these keys were rooms, and the rest were staff locations—housekeeping, linen closets, and maintenance, though most were abbreviations that weren't obvious out of context. She strung the keys onto a large brass keyring which sat at the bottom of the box.

As Janet had the only purse, she was nominated for the task of carrying them all. After feeling the extra weight on her shoulder, she made an annoyed grunt, asking "didn't these people ever hear of a skeleton key?"

Vaughn found something interesting, and useful, as well—several copies of a mimeographed sketch of a cross section of the entire hotel. The first floor, as expected, was labeled "Lobby | Ballroom | Dining." The second floor said "Laundry | Maintenance." Floors three and four were each labeled "Single Rooms." The fifth floor just said "Baths," confirming Sam's hypothesis. Six and Seven were "Double Rooms," Eight was "Suites," Nine was "Gameroom | Apothecary," Ten was "Transit—Coming Summer 1906," and Eleven was "Mastersuite." An icon showed the twelfth floor as the exit, the room they had discovered the elevator, and there was a drawing of the train station at the top, which would have theoretically been level thirteen, but was unlabeled, as the elevator didn't travel that high.

"Funny how the 'Mastersuite' is still the top floor, even though it's underground," remarked Janet. "Can't imagine it has much of a view."

"Kinda slick that it's a single word, though," said Vaughn. "*Mastersuite*. Sounds sophisticated."

Sam was struck instead by the description of the tenth floor. "Transit? Transit to where? Eaton Rapids doesn't have a subway system."

"Maybe they would have," Sarah replied, "in 1906."

"Hmm."

Al interrupted. "Hey, Sam." Al had found something as well—a gun. It was sitting at the bottom of a cabinet along with boxes of ammunition.

"Whoa, wasn't expecting that," Sam responded.

"Oh sure," teased Vaughn. "Cause all this other shit, you were *totally* expecting."

Al gingerly picked up the weapon, being sure to aim at the ground, just in case. "Looks like a Colt double action revolver, from…" Al was squinting at numbers etched into the grip. "From 1895 or 1896, I'd say. UMC ammo here, 38 caliber. Damn good gun."

"How do you know so much about handguns," Vaughn asked.

"Lived in Detroit for thirty years. You pick some things up."

Vaughn laughed. "Come on."

"Nah, my dad had a lot of old guns. He may have even had one like this, or even an older model. It should still fire just fine, and the ammo looks new."

Sarah was uncomfortable. She had never liked guns, and

lacked Al's confidence that a 100-year-old pistol was "just fine." She imagined it going off on its own, taking off one of their feet, or worse, in the process. "Can we just, put that back, please?"

"Are you sure?" asked Al. "It's a hell of a find."

"No, she's right," Sam concurred. "I want to leave everything just where we found it, at least for now. I gotta come down here with a good camera, and maybe Professor Ransom from MSU. This needs to be well documented. And besides, Sarah's right, I'd feel safer with it back in the drawer, to be honest."

Al shrugged. "Hey, your hotel," he said as he replaced the revolver.

Sam couldn't help smiling at this. *My hotel.*

"So are we ready to go?" Janet was by the door.

"Absolutely," said Sam. "Vaughn, let's bring your spotlights, just in case we need them. Otherwise, let's look around here a little more, and then move on to..." He paused, glancing at the mimeograph in his hand. "Laundry and Maintenance," he finished.

They all left the small office, but Sam stopped and turned back around as he reached the exit. "Hey, I'll catch up," he called to the others. "I want to bring the ledger."

Sam reasoned that it might be fun, if not altogether useful, to bring the record of which rooms had been rented, and by whom, as they explored the higher floors. And, he thought, if they found anything left behind, they'd be able to place it to a specific person. "We found the lost watch of Mr. Richard Porter," he could proclaim at the inevitable press conference that awaited him. "And we know that the founder of Miller's Ice Cream once occupied the penthouse suite, as evidenced by the following…"

His thoughts stopped cold. Something had caught his subliminal attention, near the far floor. He had felt a breeze brush past him, and there had been a quick movement of something, *by* something, visible only from the very corner of Sam's eye.

Sam's breath quickened, along with the pace of his heart. Was it just his imagination? Surely there couldn't be anything *alive* down here. Surely it couldn't have been…

But it was. *A mouse.*

It ran out from behind a bookcase, fearless, directly at Sam, running straight up his left leg. Sam's blood-curdling scream echoed like a foghorn through the lobby, and Vaughn and Sarah raced back to the room to see what had happened. They found Sam stumbling, ghost-white, panicked beyond all reason, flailing his hands wildly, kicking with his feet, shouting "get it off get it off get it off!"

Vaughn caught his friends body almost in mid-air, and Sarah helped brace him on the other side.

"What, Sam, what is it?" demanded Sarah.

"A mouse!" he shrieked, momentarily ashamed at the unmanly sound.

"Sam, where?"

But it was nowhere. Sam couldn't see it. It wasn't crawling on his body anymore, and didn't seem to be anywhere on the floor. He instinctively, and with dread, checked the bottom of each shoe, just in case. No mouse. In a moment, he calmed down, embarrassed, but was still trembling as they joined the others in the lobby.

"There *was* a mouse," Sam explained, sheepishly.

Janet chuckled. "You had the balls to take an elevator to nowhere and you're scared of a little mouse?"

"He's *terrified* of mice," Sarah explained, in Sam's defense. "Since he was a kid."

"There wasn't any mouse," said Al.

"Yes there was. I'm telling you, it crawled up my leg."

"It couldn't have been a mouse," explained Al. "They wouldn't go this far underground unless there was food, and there's no food here. Some old canned shit in the kitchen, but that's it. Nothing a mouse could eat, not in a century."

Vaughn spoke up. "If Sam said there was a mouse, then there was a mouse, and that's that."

Al began to protest, thought better of it, and held his hands up in surrender.

"It's alright," said Sam, without enthusiasm, but regaining a measure of excitement. "Let's go check out the next level."

They turned and walked in the general direction of the elevator, but as they got closer, it was obvious that something was wrong. It took a moment for someone to realize what it was.

"The elevator!" Sarah gasped. "It's not here!"

The elevator car was indeed absent. Just one gate, the gate to the empty shaft, remained.

"Now, don't panic," said Sam, reassuringly. "It's probably programmed to return to the top floor after a while, just like the elevators of above-ground hotels are programmed to return to ground level."

"Not sure how you think a Victorian elevator could be

'programmed,' Sam," Vaughn remarked dryly.

"*Late* Victorian," Al corrected. "Queen Anne."

"But look," Sam persisted, pointing above the elevator entrance. There was a curved brass line with numbers 1 through 12 etched above it, and a black arrow that now rested on the "12."

"See? It's fine. We just have to press the call button to bring it back."

Before anyone could press the button, however, they heard the dull whir of the motor, and the floor indicator began to move, to "11," then "10," then "9." Sam shot a quick glance to Al.

"Don't look at me," Al protested. "I didn't touch a thing."

The elevator car continued downward, to "5," then "4," then "3," then "2," until they could see the bottom of the approaching car through the exterior gate.

Instinctively, uneasily, Sam took a step back.

six

Sam had once teased Sarah that her friends from high school had been largely like herself, in that they were all trying desperately to be unique. He pointed out that they each had at least one tattoo with some supposedly spiritual meaning, they each had at least one piercing which their parents did not know about and would not approve, they each smoked clove cigarettes they did not inhale, they each had nearly identical music collections of unintelligible metal and underground folk, and they each wrote endless streams of dark, non-rhyming poetry with at least one gratuitous use, per poem, of the word "fuck"—or, when they were older and even more angsty and anarchistic, "cunt." When a parent or teacher would stumble upon one of these scribbled pseudo-gothic ramblings, each young middle class rebel would scream the same tired argument of "you just don't get me," slamming their bedroom door behind them in a dramatic act of sedition. Then, ultimately, each would sob to their friends via telephone or, when it became popular Sarah's senior year of high school, the online blog community of Livejournal.

"That's a pretty damned sexist generalization of my friends," Sarah had countered, and further retaliated by pointing out the "layered levels of loserdom" that comprised Sam's own chosen companions. But she grudgingly agreed with Sam's observation that every one of Sarah's "type" seemed to have one friend on the side who didn't fit this mold, who wore floral skirts instead of studded black jeans, who dated the handsome jocks instead of the brooding bass players, and who enjoyed playing the game of pretty, preppy, and popular. Sure, these "outcast" friends would never have hung out with Sarah's *group,* but one-on-one, the friendships were real. There seemed to be, Sam argued, a genuine need of every rebel girl to connect with at least one person who wasn't. For Sarah, that friend was Kedzie Duffield.

Going by "Duffy" in high school and "Kedz" in college, Kedzie was well-liked, fun, confident, and, yes, popular. She had a smile that came almost too easily, in any situation, as if her gums were lubricated and any twitch could cause an involuntary full-faced grin. In high school, of course, she had been Homecoming Queen, and then Prom Queen. Every boy she dated looked like he belonged in a pinup calendar of shirtless firemen. And all the while, Sarah both despised and loved her.

Kedzie and Sarah could each have excelled in academics, but both chose, for their own reasons, to be *good* at high school without being great. They ended up being accepted to, and attending, the same college—and as luck would have it, each ended up in the same dorm, one floor apart, their freshman year. While their friendship was a relative secret in the cliquey world of the ninth through twelfth grades, in college, having a variety of different, interesting friends was encouraged. There were no weird looks when they sat together at lunch, so they ate more lunches together. Though they each retained separate interests, they even

JOHN K. ADDIS

developed, for the very first time, a few mutual friends.

Sarah soaked up the additional intellectual challenges of college, and had continued onto a Master's program, while Kedzie had entered the "real world" first, working as a receptionist at a local law firm. Sarah had been pushing Kedzie to become a paralegal, and maybe even attend law school, but she had shown no real interest. Kedzie wanted to find a cute boy, settle down, and be a mom. Sarah would rant and rave at this, quoting everyone from Gloria Steinem to Ani DiFranco in her defense, but Kedzie would remind her friend that *even these* feminist icons were, in fact, married, and that it was her choice to prioritize work and family as she saw fit. To Sarah, this suggested weakness, but to Kedzie, it felt like something she could control.

It didn't help matters that every boy Sarah dated would become a drooling mess at the sight of her friend. Even Sam had conspicuously asked, on more than one occasion, that Sarah should "see if Kedz wants to come out, too." But through it all, her friend had been there for her every time it had mattered, through bad breakups, through a DUI which involved vomiting on an officer's boots, through the emotional breakdown that led Sarah to call a professor a "fascist" in front of a packed classroom, through "the Tony thing," and a hundred other minor and major life crises that only Kedzie, and maybe Livejournal, knew anything about. And Sarah had been there for Kedzie as well, through similarly bad breakups, failing classes, the death of Kedzie's mom, and most recently, the unplanned pregnancy, which she was choosing to carry to term, despite the father dumping Kedzie the second he found out.

Sometimes, two people just have to be in each other's lives, for better or for worse, to depend on each other through both love and, occasionally, hate. Even when Kedzie had slept with Sarah's college sweetheart years ago, Sarah knew she couldn't stay mad forever, and was still quite glad to see her at the end of their subsequent month of silence, just as she was glad to see her now.

"Jesus Christ, Kedz! You scared us half to death." Sarah ran up to the elevator gate, unlatched it, grabbed the hand of her friend, and pulled her into the lobby. "Guys, this is my friend Kedzie."

Al and Janet smiled and said hello. Sam and Vaughn already knew Kedzie quite well, and offered a more colloquial "hey."

Kedzie smiled back, but her eyes were already darting around the incredible room. "My, my, Sam," she said. "You didn't tell me about all *this.*"

"I didn't know," Sam replied. "None of us did. Al here was just peeling back carpet and we found this trap door, and this elevator and, well, we're still a little in shock ourselves."

Kedzie walked a few steps more into the great room. She burst into one of her trademark smiles.

"Well, I think this is going to make one hell of a club after all," she giggled. Then, to Sarah, "I'm sorry I called your boyfriend a loser for buying this dump."

"You know," said Sam, "I can still hear you."

Kedzie flashed him a playful grin. "So show me around, stud."

Sam and Sarah walked Kedzie through the rooms they

had visited, told her about the history of the place they'd uncovered so far, ending at the grand ballroom, with its ancient stash of high-end alcohol. At this, Vaughn ran in to greet them, followed by Janet and Al, and offered Kedzie a shot of scotch, too, to join in the celebration. Kedzie laughed and shook her head politely.

"Now Vaughn, you know I can't," she said, patting her belly. "Not with little Sammy Jr. in here."

"Yeah, I'm going to go with 'not funny' on that one," Sarah responded, with an exaggerated narrowing of her eyes.

"Oh come on," chirped Kedzie. "It's a *little* funny. Besides, I can't name him after his real dad. You try explaining to a kindergarten teacher why your kid is called 'Fucking Deadbeat Loser.'"

"*Jr.,*" added Sam.

They laughed.

"So what are you even doing here," asked Sarah. "Shouldn't you still be at work for another five hours?"

Kedzie shrugged. "The guys were going to be in court the whole afternoon, so they let me go early. I went back to the apartment and hung out a bit, but then I remembered you were getting the keys to this place today, and thought I'd swing by. It took me a while to figure out where you had gone, since your cars were here but no one was answering my hellos, but I found the elevator and, well…ta-da!" Kedzie made a theatrical gesture with her arms, as if announcing herself to the stage.

"You got my text, right?" added Sarah.

Kedzie paused for a moment, then grinned. "Of course!"

Sarah frowned. She thought her text had strongly

implied not to join them, since then there would be no one left in the outside world who knew where they were. She would have to check how she worded that later. Then again, Kedzie wasn't one to do as Sarah asked.

"Hang on," said Janet. "You came by, couldn't find us, discovered the elevator, and just thought you'd call it up and try pressing '1'? That's pretty reckless, kid."

Kedzie shrugged. "You only live once."

"That's what Janet said," teased Sam.

"We were just about to explore the second floor, before you arrived," Al interjected with a touch of impatience.

"Oh! Mind if I tag along?"

"Of course not," said Sam. He turned to where Vaughn was opening low cabinet doors behind the bar. "Coming, Vaughn?"

Vaughn closed one of the cabinet doors and said he'd be just a second. He had decided to take the extra time afforded by Kedzie's arrival to do a more thorough inventory of the bar's stash of liquor, but was surprised to find most of the cabinets empty. In fact, he soon realized that there were only a dozen or so bottles of alcohol in the entire area. Even with the small capacity of the hotel, there should have been hundreds of bottles for guests to choose from. Perhaps the owners had moved inventory out of the hotel when they had to unexpectedly shut down. Vaughn was about to bring up the lack of spirits to Sam, but decided against it, as he had been the one to convince them that opening a bottle would be no big deal.

The expanded group made their way back to the lobby, and approached the elevator.

"Congratulations, by the way," Janet said, glancing down at Kedzie's belly as they walked, though Kedzie was not yet showing. "I'm sure he or she will be a beautiful baby, even with the father thing."

"Er, thanks!" Kedzie responded after a pause, perhaps feeling this to be a little too personal a statement from a stranger, but accepting the compliment. "What about you? Any kids?"

Janet paused for a moment, then smiled sadly. "No," she said. "No kids. Some great nephews, though."

The elevator car stood empty before them, as imposing, yet as inviting, as ever.

"Sure we can all fit?" asked Kedzie, as Sam unlatched the gate.

"I hope so," said Sam. "There aren't any stairs."

"What are you talking about," sneered Al. "You can't have an elevator without stairs. They're over there."

Sam looked to where Al was pointing. There was a simple door on the right side of the room, which Sam had assumed was a second door into the dining area. But the dining area must have been cut a little short, for upon examination, there was indeed an etching of a staircase pattern near the door's trim. Sam walked over to the door, opened it, and looked up. Sure enough, it was a narrow staircase, at least ten stories high.

"But…there weren't stairs in the elevator room," Sam protested. "There weren't even any doors. There was just the elevator."

"We must have overlooked them," reasoned Al.

"No, no." Sam shook his head. "We would have seen

them up there. A door, at least. The walls were paneled, remember? Besides, if there had been stairs, we wouldn't have risked the elevator."

Kedzie looked concerned. "Wait, what do you mean, 'risked'? What's wrong with the elevator?"

"Nothing's wrong with the elevator," insisted Al. "Sam's just a big ol' pussy."

Sam sighed, and closed the door to the stairs.

"Alright," Sam agreed. "We'll deal with that later. For now, we travel in style."

The six visitors boarded the elevator. Sam closed both gates, turned behind him, and pressed the number "2." He smiled at Sarah, to his side, and then stared ahead through the gate as the lobby vanished beneath them.

It was a tight fit in the old fashioned elevator car, and so Sarah didn't notice when Kedzie coyly, fleetingly, and purposely brushed her hand against Sam's ass.

seven

The second floor (or "eleventh sub-basement" as Janet called it) lacked much of the ornate detail and design of the lobby. The floor, ceiling and door moldings were still cut and carved from quality wood, but the walls were drab in color, and the layout pedestrian. It also seemed, at least from the length of the hallway, that this floor had a smaller overall footprint than the lobby, and Sam began to wonder if each floor would get progressively smaller as they traveled upward, like an underground pyramid. This might be normal for an above ground structure, as lower floors would need to be as wide, or wider, than floors above, but in a basement model, such construction made less sense.

"So Al," Sam began as they exited the car. "As far as we can tell, this hotel was built years after the depot was up and running. Isn't it difficult to dig a basement—particularly one this deep and wide—with a building already on top?"

"Well," Al explained, "it wasn't quite as uncommon as you might suppose. Even today, many Victorian homes have basements that were carved out after the fact. The annoying part is having to remove all that dirt and clay."

"Yes, but those are just eight-foot basements, if that. This would be twelve stories worth of dirt and clay. It would have taken forever."

"Well, who's to say it didn't? For all we know, they started planning this hotel from the moment the depot opened, and took as many years as they needed to."

The hallway was lit, but dimly. There were additional light fixtures on the wall that were not illuminated, but when they first had passed by the floor on the elevator ride down to the lobby, this floor (and all the others) had been *completely* dark. Sam reasoned that one of the master switches Al had activated behind the lobby desk must also have activated a basic lighting system for the whole hotel. Sure enough, when he turned back toward the elevator, he saw two wooden push buttons on that wall, positioned so that someone could turn and reach them, even in the dark, after a single step out of the elevator car. Sam walked back, pushed both buttons, and the hallway was fully illuminated.

Al had arrived at a door marked "Maintenance," stopping to listen to a muffled mechanical whir on the other side. Al smiled to Sam, then to Janet, nodding for her to retrieve the appropriate key. She fumbled in her purse for a bit, and found the appropriate key on the ring, handed it to Al, and waited as he unlocked and opened the door.

The six visitors entered the room, each surprised at the volume—and quantity—of the machines. Al had been right about the water wheel, but even he was surprised at the sheer size of the contraption. At the far wall, there was a large cutout directly into the clay, with a six-foot-wide water wheel spinning along by the power of a visible stream of flowing underground water. Attached to this wheel, and all through the room, was a series of tubes, some copper and some glass, to other components along the other three walls. Most of these large components were unlabeled, though one was marked "heat," and it too had a visible flow of water coming down from the ceiling, passing through it, and exiting out the side to join the other pipes. Al inspected this box for a few moments, then smiled and turned to Sam.

"Steam heat," he shouted over the machinery. "This must have been pretty cutting-edge at the time. I'm guessing we're going to find both radiators *and* forced-air duct work on the higher levels."

Vaughn was fascinated by three large metal discs, about five feet each in diameter, each embedded vertically about six inches deep into the nearby wall. They seemed to be made out of a variety of flattened, smaller discs in a concentric circle pattern down to a black hole in each center. Vaughn laughed as he realized why they reminded him of.

"Hey, Sam, check it out. LPs!"

Sam laughed as well. They did indeed look like large steel-plated vinyl records.

"What do they do?" asked Kedzie.

"Nothing, I guess," shrugged Vaughn. "They just look cool."

"Oh," said Kedzie with a smirk. "Kinda like you."

Al had walked over to examine the discs as well. Eventually, he nodded, shot a knowing smile to the rest of the group, and activated a large mechanical lever near the farthest metal plate. At first, nothing happened, except a dull rumble hardly audible over the other noise in the room. But then Sam began to feel the hairs on the back of his neck stand up, and the room acquired a subtle, subsonic vibration. A few seconds later, and with a speed that startled everyone, including Al, all three discs were quickly covered, then uncovered, by thin metal sheets from the top, acting as three hidden guillotines. Sam thought the effect was like staring into the circle of a very large cigar cutter, with a very large blade, and a very fast operator aiming for the cleanest possible cut. Seven seconds later, it happened again, and kept happening in regular intervals, each time just as unsettling as the time before.

"What the hell are those things," demanded Sarah. "Giant cheese slicers?"

Vaughn was getting out his cell phone, preparing to snap a picture. "They're sweet as hell, is what they are," he decided.

Al spoke up, and called to Vaughn over the noise. "Hey, unless that thing's all plastic or aluminum, you might want to be caref—"

But it was too late. Though standing more than ten feet away from the nearest silver "album," Vaughn felt the phone slip out from his fingers, as if being yanked by an invisible hand. The phone flew across the room like a dart, striking the metal disc and breaking in two, both pieces sticking hard to the metal surface like glue.

"My phone!"

Within two seconds, right on schedule, the sharp guillotines snapped down and shattered the phone into a thousand pieces—some of which, the little plastic parts, flew off in all directions into the room, while others, metallic parts, re-adhered themselves to the circle.

"Dude, what the hell?" shouted Vaughn to Al.

"It's some sort of magnetic generator," Al shouted back. "Look at the water pipes around it. I'm guessing it's helping to boost the power of the magnetic mineral springs, or maybe getting power *from* them."

Another seven-second slice, on schedule.

Vaughn was still pissed. "Then what's with the fucking blades?'

"Maybe it's transmitting the charge back to the other side," Al answered. "Or re-calibrating."

Sam was growing irritated. "Could you just turn the damn thing off, Al?"

Al complied, pulling the large lever down, disengaging the circuit. The deep, bass hum and whir began to power down, and the three large circles were just decorative wall art once again. In a few moments, some of the little remaining pieces of Vaughn's destroyed cell phone began to slide down the surface of the LP's as well, as the magnets began to lose their power.

"I really liked that phone," Vaughn pouted.

Janet, who had observed the whole scene in silent wonder, gasped aloud when she turned to Kedzie.

"Oh! Dear, you're bleeding!"

Kedzie followed Janet's gaze down to her shirt, near her navel. There was a small but growing blood stain on her white blouse. She lifted up the shirt to get a better look, and saw that a sliver of gray plastic must have shot out like shrapnel during the destruction of Vaughn's cell, pieced her shirt, and had embedded its sharp point into her abdomen. She pulled the piece out with her fingernails and tossed it on the floor.

"Yuck," she said, frowning.

"Are you okay?" Janet seemed disproportionately concerned, considering the superficial nature of the wound.

"I'm fine," laughed Kedzie. "Really. I didn't even feel it." She was pushing her hand against the small wound to stop the bleeding, but the existing blood on her shirt popped against the white fabric like a crime scene.

"What about the baby? Is the baby okay?"

Kedzie shot an annoyed look at this persistent old woman.

"The baby is fine," Kedzie snapped.

Sam and Sarah exchanged a puzzled glance. Janet's panic seemed unwarranted. Sarah thought of a way of diffusing the tension.

"Hey Janet," Sarah said. "You have the keys. Let's go across the hall to housekeeping and see if we can't find a couple of clean towels for Kedzie here, okay?"

Janet agreed, and the two left. After an awkward silence, Vaughn spoke up.

"Well, it's silly to just wait here. We all should go. We haven't seen that room, either." Vaughn turned again toward the evil metal circles on the wall. "Besides," he frowned, "this place is giving me the creeps."

They all nodded, and Vaughn and Al, being closest to the door, left first. But Sam pulled Kedzie back for a moment, before joining the others in the hallway.

"Kedz," he said with delicacy. "You're okay, right?"

Kedzie smiled. "I'm fine, Sam."

Sam paused. "And…you're *sure* it's not…"

Again, Kedzie smiled, this time less brightly. "I'm sure. I was already two weeks along then—I just didn't know it yet. I think that's why my hormones were so out of control." She rested her right hand on his hip, and looked up at him.

"Believe me, I wish it was yours."

Sam stiffened. "You don't mean that. Sarah's your best friend."

"And your fiancée," she replied, with just a hint of disdain, or maybe jealousy. "But I'd be a lot prouder to carry your child than the real asshole's. It just didn't work out that way."

It wasn't the first time she had made this comment, but Sam was touched by it, though no less uneasy at the thought. With different timing, their one moment of weakness could have ended with him losing Sarah forever, destroying a 15-year friendship between two best friends, and requiring him, for life, to help support a child he would always know came from an unfaithful, drunken one night stand. Was it selfish to think "thank *God* the baby isn't mine?"

"Hey, she's not my fiancée," he said, with a pang of guilt, for he understood his motivation behind the comment. Even now, Sam couldn't tell if he genuinely felt ashamed, or if he just felt he *should* feel ashamed. Somehow, after the fact, he had deluded himself into the idea that he, as a man, was entitled to one last "lap around the bar" before his circumscription was made official through jewelry. He even found a way to justify the betrayal as an act of nobility, to get things out of his system before it was too late, to assure that he wouldn't cheat on Sarah "for real" when they were married. The rationalization was so complete that he almost felt pride.

A month later, he had purchased the ring. He had it with him today, planning a beautiful proposal in the center of the hollowed out train station once everyone else had left. When he shared the idea of this plan, his mom had been worried it would seem narcissistic, and suggested that his proposal should be all about *her*, not all about *him*. But in his mind, he felt this would be a romantic act, showing Sarah he was combining his loves and interests and futures together. He supposed, however, that's just what a narcissist would think.

Sam knew he loved Sarah. He knew they were right together. But it was impossible to look down into Kedzie's beautiful blue eyes, smell the sweet fruit from her perfume, feel her hand softly resting against his body, and not remember every detail of that one amazing mistake, and want her all over again. Only this time, he imagined a scenario in which she would come on to him again, flirting wildly, biting his earlobe like she had a few months ago, but *this* time he would say "no, no….I'm taken…it isn't right…but you're *great*, though. You're really *great*." And he'd leave her apartment with nothing more than a peck on the cheek, the faithful, valiant, virtuous hero. He'd imagine her either sobbing with what might have been, or better yet, fantasizing about him long after he left. Oh, that would feel good.

"Alright Kedz, you said the exact same thing to me last time we talked about it. I believe you." He gave Kedzie's left hip a mildly inappropriate squeeze, before he added "come on" and led her across the hall.

"There you are," said Sarah as they arrived, holding two hand towels, one of which she had dampened with warm water from a nearby faucet. Observing a mild look of surprise on Sam's face, Sarah explained: "yeah, running water—neat, huh?"

"Well hang on," Kedzie protested. "There's no way I trust that water." She motioned to Al. "Can't you use some of that guy's booze instead? It'd be more sterile."

Sarah looked at Al. He shrugged and offered his flask.

Kedzie hopped up onto a nearby countertop and lifted her bloody shirt. Sarah dabbed some of the alcohol onto a new towel and began to clean the small wound. It had already stopped bleeding, but had made a bit of a mess on her bare stomach.

Vaughn and Al were busy looking at a row of large tubes on the far wall. "Pneumatics," Sam heard Al explaining. "See, they could fill one of these canisters here with a couple towels, bed linens, you name it, and then they put the container in here, and the air pressure moves the canisters up to the different floors."

"Oh, like those weird tubes at the drive-up banks," Vaughn responded, understanding. "Only bigger."

"Exactly."

Sam was going to ask a question about this, but his gaze wandered over to Janet, who was staring at Kedzie, and looking increasingly uncomfortable. The corners of her mouth arched downward, and her color was off.

"Hey Janet," said Sam. "You feelin' okay?"

Sarah was drying Kedzie's abdomen with the second towel, and was pulling her shirt back down to make sure the stain had dried. "Well," Sarah said, "if you soak the blouse later, I think you'll be good. It's not much blood."

"Yeah," responded Kedzie, looking down at her shirt. Then, snapping her eyes up to meet Janet's gaze, she said, quite decisively, "it'll be fine. *I'm sure it will come out in the wash.*"

The energy in the room shifted, and Janet turned white. She took a step back, bumping into a wheeled cart and knocking over a tin of powdered detergent.

Sam inched toward her. "Janet? What's wrong?"

Janet looked around in a panic. Her mind became cloudy and her vision blurred. "I'm going to be sick," she said, covering her mouth with one hand. She noticed a large "Soiled Linens" container to her right, ran over, and lifted the lid, opening her mouth wide to vomit into it.

But her mouth just locked open instead. She stared into the can for several long seconds, then screamed.

She fell backward, and Vaughn stepped over to catch her, helping her fall to the ground with as much grace as possible. Sam ran to the canister instead, and looked in to see for himself what was wrong.

Inside, there was a crumpled, two-foot pile of white bedsheets, each stained with deep, red-brown splotches. In particular, the sheet on top looked like it had been soaked with the stuff.

Al peered in as well, then met Sam's gaze.

"Oil?" Sam offered.

Al considered this for a moment, then slowly shook his head "no."

Vaughn was comforting Janet on the floor. She was sitting upright, but trembling. Sam knelt down to her, placing a hand on her arm.

"Janet, it's alright. Al thinks it's just oil, not blood or anything." Sam shot a look to Al, making sure he stayed silent. "It's not scary, it's fine."

Janet looked up at Sam with intense, quizzical desperation. Her eyes darted back and forth between his own, searching for answers, or at least something that would make sense of what he had just said.

"Really," Sam insisted. "It's just dirty sheets."

Janet blinked, bewildered. "Who gives a damn about the sheets," she responded through tears. "*What about the dead fucking baby?*"

eight

Sam and Sarah couldn't convince Janet to look inside the bin a second time, so they tipped the container over and spread the dirty linens on the floor before her. At first, Janet still thought she saw an outline of an arm, or a head, and came close to screaming again. After staring at the sheets for several long seconds, however, she began to calm down, acknowledging that what she had seen must have been an illusion.

"It's okay," consoled Al. "Hell, Sam here thought he saw a mouse, and his scream was girlier than yours."

Sam narrowed his eyes in Al's direction, as if to telepathically convey the message *I did see a mouse, you bastard,* but Al shrugged in response, either not receiving the transmission, or choosing to ignore it.

"I could have sworn there was a tiny body in there," Janet said, still in a bit of a trance, as if recalling a dream. "I'm not good with blood. Not at all. And I just knew I had to throw up, watching...you know, and..." Janet stammered a bit, having trouble meeting Kedzie's eyes across the room. Kedzie had one hand held protectively over her abdomen, and Janet realized she must have scared the poor girl. "I'm sorry, Kedzie," she said at last. "I truly don't know what came over me."

Something about the way she said this last part stuck Sam as odd, and he had a thought that Janet perhaps *did* know, at least partially, what had come over her. There was a strange tension between Janet and Kedzie, considering they had only recently met, and Sam was certain it had something to do with Kedzie's pregnancy.

Sam thought back to something Janet had said during their first meeting about the property, many months ago. She had asked if he wanted a family—specifically, if he wanted children. He had told her things with Sarah had been getting serious, but he wasn't sure about her views on kids. When he asked, as tactfully as he could, if Janet herself had ever wanted children, she had paused, offered a sad smile, and said "only for a moment." At the time, this had awakened a childhood memory of eavesdropping on his mom consoling Janet many years ago. He didn't understand the conversation as a kid, but he knew Janet had been pregnant, and then she wasn't. He remembered his confusion at the idea of "losing" a baby, and believed Janet must have been quite careless. In fact, Sam was even going to offer to look for the child, but changed his mind, as he shouldn't have been spying in the first place. As Sam thought back to the memory now, he realized for the first time that the miscarriage must have been a factor in her subsequent divorce. It involved something her husband had done, or maybe said…but he couldn't remember.

Sam noticed Sarah had sat down beside Janet, placing a reassuring hand on her shoulder. "It's okay," she said. "This place is a little spooky."

As were, Sam thought, the stained sheets. Baby or no baby, the sheets didn't seem to tell a happy tale. Vaughn gave voice to the lingering thought in the air.

"So, The Eaton closed its doors weeks after opening. And it never reopened, and no one talked about it afterwards, at least not enough for it to even become a local legend." Vaughn glanced down at the sheets, then at Janet to make sure she was comfortable with his discussing the matter, and continued. "In fact, it seems the last guests left in such a hurry they didn't even bother checking out. So what in the hell happened?"

Al, who had been leaning against a wall of pneumatic tubes, cleared his throat.

"This doesn't change the plan," Al said. "We still need to go floor by floor and see what we can find. Maybe we'll uncover more evidence, and maybe we won't. But there's still a lot to explore."

Sam turned to Janet. "It's okay if you want to take off," he suggested. "I'm sure you can come back another time."

Janet shook her head, and seemed to regain a level of composure. "No, no. I've already let my little panic attack waste enough time, and I'm not letting you go through this place without me." She got to her feet and brushed dust off the back of her skirt, glancing around at the room as if satisfied it served no future purpose. "Let's go."

"Are you sure?" asked Sam.

"Of course," Janet replied as brightly as possible. "Besides," she added, holding up her purse, "I have the keys."

*

As it had on the maintenance level, a few dim lights

illuminated the third floor hallway, and a light switch panel found near the elevator turned on the rest. More than anything the group had seen to date, this floor was more reminiscent of a standard hotel, with neutral tones for the carpet and paint, and a symmetrical layout of four rooms to the left, and four to the right, each with a large brass room number plaque affixed on the corresponding mahogany doors. A narrow door at the end of the hallway led presumably to the staircase they had observed on the other levels. After some hesitation, they picked the closest numbered door on the right, and opened it.

The room was empty, and immaculate. It was also small by today's hotel standards, and Sam was disappointed that the rooms in his new luxury hotel might not be as luxurious as he had hoped. There were classy, tasteful furnishings, and some nice Victorian flourishes on the door molding, but otherwise it paled in comparison to the grandeur of the foyer and ballroom.

Al could sense Sam's mild disappointment. "You know, this actually would have been considered a pretty high-end room when this was built," he assured him. Al motioned to the open door on the far wall. "I mean, look—that's a private bathroom."

Sam walked over and peered inside. It contained a toilet and sink, and a shelf for linens, but that was it.

"Not sure I could rent this room without a shower," Sam said.

Al laughed. "Sam, you forget why people would want to come here. The baths are two levels up."

Sarah opened the top drawer of a dresser across from the

bed. It was empty. "What, no Gideon Bible?"

"A little early for that," Al answered. "Try the others."

Sarah tried each of the remaining three drawers, but all were empty.

Vaughn sat on the edge of the well-made bed, and bounced a little to test for springiness. It sagged in a lopsided fashion, but he imagined this may have represented the best in mattress design at the time. He glanced up at Sam. "Maybe this room hadn't been rented yet."

"Maybe," shrugged Sam. "Want to check the rest of the floor?"

"Hell yes," said Al.

They exited the first room. It would have been easy enough to split up to search the other seven, covering more rooms at a faster pace, but an unspoken acknowledgement of the growing creepiness of the situation kept them in a group. One by one, they searched the remaining rooms, which were more or less identical to each other. None contained anything of interest, except the last room, which contained the only bed they had found unmade. It gave everyone a bit of a start, as if they had intruded on a living resident, and even Sam stepped back into the hallway for a moment upon viewing the oddity. But even this room, like the rest, had empty dresser drawers, and was clean in every other regard, save the turned back comforter and sheet.

"Anyone see the maid service door hanger?" joked Sarah.

"If they all had been like this," Sam mused, "it wouldn't be so weird. But why one? Why *this* one?"

"How's your place at the moment," asked Janet.

"What do you mean?"

"Are all the rooms clean?"

Sam thought about it. "Yes, I think so."

"Is the bed made?"

Sarah laughed, adding that "Sam *never* makes the bed."

Janet crinkled her nose. "Bleh. I can't stand coming home to an unmade bed. I'd rather be late for a house showing then leave before making the bed."

"How delightfully OCD of you," remarked Sam.

"So after an apocalypse," Janet continued, "if visitors from the future were to view the contents of your apartment, do you think they'd ask the same question? Why the rest of the home was clean, but only the bedroom was left unkempt?"

Vaughn stiffened a bit. "Do you think an apocalypse happened here?"

"No, I'm not saying that. I'm just pointing out it's impossible to form opinions or judgments on this sort of observation. If I were to die today, for example, and the police or my family or whoever was going through my place, do you know what they'd find? Branches. In the kitchen."

Sam cocked his head. "Branches?"

"Yep. About a dozen skinny branches taken from the old tree in the back. Right there on my kitchen table. And do you know *why* I have a dozen branches on my kitchen table?"

Nobody hazarded a guess.

"Exactly. You have no idea. You can't even speculate. And I'll tell ya, years after my death, when my family would gather around and talk about me—which *would* happen, by the way, I'm very memorable—someone would bring up 'the branches,' and they'd all offer opinions, and they'd debate opposing theories, and they'd never guess the real reason. Because it doesn't even matter."

Vaughn nodded. "I have a dress shoe sitting in my bathroom sink right now."

Sarah chuckled. "Just one?"

"Just one," Vaughn confirmed.

"Where's the other one?"

"I donno. Probably on the floor in my bedroom."

Sam had a guess. "Did you step in dog shit or something?"

Vaughn laughed aloud. "That's really close, Sam! It was someone's vomit in the hallway of my apartment building."

Kedzie made a face. "You need new neighbors."

"Yeah, well. College town."

Sarah shook her head. "Wait a minute, that one's not too hard to figure out. But kitchen branches?"

Janet grinned. "I'll give you a hint: I have a gas stove."

Al was growing impatient by this pointless conversation. "Come on guys, we have eight more floors to cover."

Sam was a tad amused by Al's frustration. "Nothing weird at your place, eh, Al?"

"No. Can we go?"

"Sure, sure, we can go."

They began to file out of the room, with Al taking the lead.

Sam was the last to leave. For some reason, he had an impulse to face the interior of the room as he was closing the door, rather than shutting it absentmindedly behind his back. This may have been a mistake, as Sam could have sworn he saw a shadow move across the bed, just for a moment, as he eyed the shrinking sliver of view before the door closed.

nine

The second floor of single rooms was so identical to the first that if their elevator had possessed a solid door, instead of a see-through cage, Sam would not have believed the elevator had transported them at all. Kedzie had suggested they try the stairs, but Vaughn objected, as he was still lugging around the two battery-operated lights, and insisted they were "heavier than they looked." No one wanted to separate from the group.

The first room had been occupied. There were men's and women's clothing in the armoire, and luggage by the foot of the bed. Three hard-bound books were on the nightstand, along with a pair of earrings. Sarah picked one of the earrings up and examined it in the light.

"Real diamond, I think. These are nice."

"Well I should hope so," observed Kedzie. "I don't think they had cubic zirconia back then." After a second, with a sly smile, she turned to Sam. "Maybe you should compare it side by side with the zirconia engagement ring Sam has in his pocket."

Sam felt himself turn white, but tried to cover it up. "Very funny, Kedz," he said with a laugh that sounded forced to his ears. He glanced at Sarah with what he hoped was nonchalance, but he could not read the coy expression she shot back at him.

"Do you think I should take them?" Sarah glanced

around the group to see if there were any moral objections. The group responded with a communal shrug. Sarah smiled broadly and put the earrings in her pocket. "Thanks, Sam!"

"Anytime," Sam offered. "I had them placed there, you know. It's one of the reasons I bought the place."

"How thoughtful and romantic you are," Sarah purred. "I'm a lucky girl."

Kedzie made a face. "And I'm going to barf. Where's my jewelry, Sam?"

"I'm sure we'll find more treasures along the way," Sam reassured her. Then he thought for a moment. There might indeed be all sorts of valuables in the hotel rooms, but some may have historical significance. Things would need to be cataloged. There may even be a need to place certain items on display in a museum. It was possible that there were people of note who stayed here during the hotel's brief run, and surviving descendants as well. What would be the legal issues surrounding property thought lost a century earlier? Did the great-grandchildren of The Eaton's occupants have a legal claim of inheritance? Sam had no idea.

As if reading his thoughts, Janet suggested a compromise. "I'm not exactly sure that everything we find here becomes Sam's just because he owns the building. In cases where a seller forgets items in the home, they don't automatically become the buyer's property. But it's something we can look into. I'd say there's no harm for now in taking souvenirs, but don't sell anything on eBay just yet."

"Well," asked Vaughn, "are we even sure all of this is Sam's building? I can't imagine the property deed mentions a twelve-floor underground hotel."

"No, I'd have noticed that," chuckled Janet. "But in general, when you buy a parcel of land, you own everything from the property line down through the earth. It's the same principle that gives you rights to any oil or precious metals found anywhere on your property, regardless of depth."

"Well perfect," cooed Sarah, lightly tapping her pocket. "*These* precious metals were definitely found below Sam's place. So there."

Al, who had been silent thus far, seemed anxious. He glanced at his watch and shuffled his feet. Finally, since Sam didn't seem to be taking the nonverbal bait, he cleared his throat and motioned to the door. "The other rooms, guys?"

"Sorry," said Sam, with a little impatience of his own. "Is exploring a hidden underground hotel a little too dull for you? Do you have more interesting plans later?"

"Must be a hell of a hot date," chuckled Kedzie.

Al narrowed his eyes. "I do not find jewelry and old clothes particularly fascinating. What I'm interested in is the higher levels. I can only imagine the suites are more architecturally interesting, and I can't wait to see if the baths are still operational."

"Fair enough," Sam acknowledged. "But I still like the idea of going in order. Besides, what's wrong with building a little suspense?"

Al chuckled with a touch of derision, but then shrugged his shoulders in acquiescence, as if to say "you're the boss."

Sam smiled. "Alright then, next room."

As they began to file out into the hallway, Sarah noticed a reflective glass object in the far corner. She approached and knelt down to pick it up.

"What's that," asked Vaughn. Sarah handed it to him. It was a glass bottle, resembling an fifth of alcohol, but without a label or identifying marks. It did not have a stopper, and was bone dry.

"They must have had a bit of a party," observed Sam as he took the bottle from his friend. "I wonder if this was from the bar."

"Well you did want your club to have bottle service," Vaughn remarked. "Maybe it already had."

"Indeed."

Sam set the bottle back down on the ground, and they joined the others in the hallway. Janet had already opened the next door and had stepped inside.

This new room, like so many on the first level, looked untouched. The bedspread was neat, the armoire was empty, and the nightstand was free from both objects and dust. Sam glanced at Al, who had waited in the hallway this time, trying not to look bored.

Sarah noticed it first. It crept into her mind like a shadow, hinting at itself while revealing nothing concrete. "Hey, be quiet a sec," she requested, and everyone complied. Sam and Sarah exchanged glances. At first it sounded like a dull hum, perhaps from the machinery that powered the lights and heat. But then a faint rhythm became clear, and it wasn't a mechanical rhythm at all. It was music.

Sarah walked over to the far wall and placed her ear against various points along the surface. "It's coming from the next room," she declared.

"Maybe someone left a TV on," Janet remarked dryly.

They joined Al in the hallway and opened the door to the adjacent room. Although inaudible from the hallway, the quiet sound of music was more obvious once inside. Yet it was not clear where the music could have been coming from. This room, like the one preceding, appeared unruffled, with a nicely made bed and no sign of past occupation.

"The armoire," directed Al.

Sam was closest, and so opened the heavy doors of the armoire. Inside the armoire sat a beautiful Berliner gramophone, with music emanating from a brass horn facing the room. The album was nearing completion, and as the final chord faded into silence, Sam watched in awe as the careful mechanics of the antique machine began to slow and click to a stop.

"That was Liszt," Sarah announced. "One of the short piano pieces."

Vaughn lifted the needle and examined the record. Rather than having a modern label, the small seven-inch disc had the title engraved in the shellac. It was indeed Liszt, Short Piano Piece #1 in E Major, performed by Arthur Friedham with a recording date of 1898.

Al was impressed. "And just how in the hell does a young punk girl such as yourself recognize a piece like that?"

"My dad played piano for us growing up," Sarah explained. "He was in a band on the side. Nothing major…local bars, Amvet halls, that kind of thing."

Al raised an eyebrow. "And this band played Liszt?"

"No, no, nothing like that. They played classic rock."

"Or as I knew it, 'rock,'" Al mused.

"Yes. But he was classically trained. When he played for us, it was as likely to be Beethoven as it was the Beatles. We had this old upright in the dining room—really bright sound, practically a tack piano—and we'd sing songs together after dinner, or on holidays, you know. But the classical stuff he'd play at night for us to sleep to. My sister and I had bunk beds in a room which shared a wall with the dining room, so we could hear it really well, though it was muffled of course. Sometimes at night he'd play Mozart, or Bach, or even a little Rachmaninov before his tendonitis got too bad." Sarah smiled at the memory, and gazed at the gramophone as if it were a treasured photograph. "Liszt was one of his favorite composers, and these little piano solos were special treats. Especially as they were short enough to keep a child's attention span."

Vaughn operated the hand crank and started the record from the beginning. Even with the limited acoustic range of the monaural equipment, the melody was clear, and rather haunting. For Sam, the inescapable dreamlike coloring to the entire day was further heightened by this impossible musical discovery. That the recording was one of his fiancée's most beloved songs from childhood added an otherworldly depth. It felt magical yet creepy, comfortable yet ominous.

"Not to interrupt your music appreciation seminar," Vaughn said, "but are we seriously not going to talk about how fucked up this is? There's no power option for this device. It's hand-crank only. How did the thing just start playing?"

"Perhaps it was queued up all this time," offered Al, "and

our footsteps and door closings nearby just bumped a hair-trigger mechanism."

"You think the tension in the crank held for over a hundred years?" Vaughn remarked with skepticism. "That seems unlikely."

Al shot Vaughn a sly smile. "The alternative, my boy, would be a ghost."

Janet had taken time to inspect the rest of the room. Curiously, she found no additional sign of occupancy. The nightstand was empty, there were no clothes, and the bathroom was untouched. There were not even any additional gramophone records. She frowned.

"So, what is this here for? Do you think whoever rented this room forgot their record player behind?"

"Maybe it belonged to the hotel," ventured Vaughn. "It's pretty bulky to be a travel unit."

Sam chuckled. "Did they even have travel units back then?"

"Look, man, my first record player was a dual-turntable Numark mixer kit. That's as far back as my knowledge goes. I don't know anything about creepy Victorian shit playing by itself in haunted hotels."

Sam stiffened a bit at this. "It's not haunted. No one thinks it's haunted." But that wasn't true. Vaughn may have been the first to vocalize the idea, but every single one of them had thought it over the last two hours, except for Kedzie.

"Oh my God, you all are looking like you've seen a ghost," Kedzie chirped. "But there's no such thing as ghosts. It's always just a guy in a mask."

"Well, jenkies," replied Sarah. "In that case, there must be nothing to worry about, huh."

Sam laughed. "Come on, gang. Let's try another room." He leaned over to turn off the gramophone, but Sarah halted his hand with hers. She looked at him with something approaching panic, but her face soon returned to normal.

"Sarah? What is it?"

"I...don't know." But she did know. When she saw Sam's hand approaching the off switch, Sarah had been consumed with an irrational sense of dread. It spread through her body in a violent jolt, and she became momentarily convinced that, if the music were stopped, her father would be killed. This feeling was all the more irrational due to the fact her father had passed away several years ago.

Sarah's father had actually owned an old gramophone like this, but it had never worked, at least not in any of Sarah's recollections. Like most of his musical possessions, they had been taken by her older sister Amy, who was the musically gifted one. Sarah had instead received her father's old books, art supplies, and architectural tools. Even though Sarah's inheritance was more valuable and useful to her own interests, Sarah was always jealous of Amy's share. After all, her greatest memories of her daddy were his playing music, not reading books or using a protractor. She thought about Amy, and wondered if she still had the old record player tucked away in an attic somewhere. Maybe she'd ask if she could have it.

"Sorry," said Sarah, coming out of her trance. "It's fine, shut it off."

By then, however, the final chord had played once more, and static had again filled the small space. Sam docked the needle. Sarah's dread did not return.

They left the room, and explored the other rooms one by one. Other than a few pieces of old clothing in one armoire, and another empty bottle of some sort of spirit, the remaining rooms were essentially empty.

When it was time to leave for the next level, and they had loaded the elevator car, Sarah looked wistfully through the cage at the closed door which had held the Liszt, and the memories of her father the discovery had awakened. She began to remember other things, too—the time her dad had taken her to the circus and she had dropped the cotton candy, and the time she had ridden on his shoulders to see the Christmas parade, and the time they had built a puppet theatre out of scrap wood and deck screws, and the time he had cried when he had lost her at the department store, when she had decided to play hide and seek in the middle of a clothes rack. She wondered what her father would think of her life today, if he would be proud of her academic accomplishments, her increasingly feisty spirit, or her charity work. She wondered if he would approve of her politics, her tattoos, and even if he'd approve of Sam.

"On to the baths," announced Al in the manner of a tour guide, pressing the brass "5" before him. Sam found Sarah's hand and gave it a good squeeze. She smiled up at him with gratitude. He smiled back, and turned to watch the floors change.

Sarah ultimately decided she was happy they had found the gramophone. She reasoned that although the discovery may have been unusual, like so much of this mysterious place, it was not creepy or haunted. And besides, if it *had* been a ghost, why couldn't it have been a friendly one? Surely an evil ghost would have found something more ominous to frighten them with than two minutes of piano music. Perhaps it was even her father, smiling down on her, sharing one last musical memory with his little girl, to comfort her as she explored this bizarre, abandoned underground world.

The elevator arrived at its destination. For a long moment, no one said a word, except for Al.

"Well, wouldya look at that."

ten

For the first time of their entire adventure, Al seemed truly awestruck. His jaw was slack and his eyes were like saucers. He opened the elevator gate, but no one moved for several moments. Then they all stepped into the luxury together.

The elevator emptied into a small waiting area with a pair of enormous doors straight ahead, which were open wide and beckoning. The rest of the floor appeared to be a single, cavernous room, and was already lit with more than a dozen warm electric lights. It was closer in size and style to the impressive lobby, with its high ceilings and ornate designs, but was altogether more opulent in both scope and fine detail. There was an active but quiet fountain in the center of the room, inlaid with green tile which seemed to emit a certain phosphorescence at certain angles. Stone statues were carved into the center of the fountain, and reflected a Greek style without referencing specific gods or historical figures. Unlike the rich wood walls of the lobby, the walls were also stone, though carved with the similar looping "e" pattern which had been etched into the lobby trim. Along the left and right walls were eight large baths clad in gorgeous cerulean blue tile, with each tub thrusting halfway into the room and remaining halfway embedded into the walls, as if carved directly out of a rock face. The far wall was comprised of six showers with half-height dividers, as well as deep open shelves containing large folded towels.

Presumably, the shower stalls were used for changing as well, as it was the only place for possible privacy. There was also a door on the far wall, which presumably accessed the stairs.

The baths themselves were filled with gently bubbling water. They did not possess the powerful jets of modern hot tubs, but Sam was surprised to see any bubbles at all, always having assumed that mineral baths of the past had been still. He dipped his fingers into the water, and found it rather warm, like a toddler's bath. He turned to Sarah, who had followed him to the closest tub, and motioned for her to try the water as well. She did, and grinned with mischief.

"Let's kick everyone out and stay here for a while," she cooed.

Vaughn overheard her remark from the other side of the room. "Hey you're not trying these out without us!"

Sarah laughed and looked up at her boyfriend. "Whaddya think, stud?"

A broad smile spread across Sam's face. He began to unbutton his shirt. "Why the hell not?"

Sam, Sarah and Vaughn all began stripping down. Al and Janet exchanged awkward glances, but Janet eventually laughed and started removing her blouse as well. "Don't get any ideas, though," she warned Al with a chuckle.

"I didn't bring a bathing suit," Al said. "And I don't have a change of underwear."

Sam overheard this remark, and took the lead by removing his own boxers first and stepping naked into the bath, followed by Vaughn, and then Sarah, though she was a little more coy, making sure to cover her exposed breasts with gently crossed arms. Janet was next to disrobe, though made the decision not to hide a thing, and joined the three younger occupants without any lingering embarrassment.

Each tub was designed to fit ten full sized adults, but Al decided on taking his own tub adjacent to the rest of them. "Nothing personal, guys…just a little old fashioned." Only Kedzie remained clothed, and stayed standing by the fountain.

"Can't join us at all, Kedzie?" Vaughn seemed disappointed.

"Aw, Vaughn, you know you don't get to see me naked that easily."

"Dip your feet in," urged Sarah. "I'm sure the baby will be fine!"

"Sounds like famous last words to me," Kedzie responded with a shake of the head. "I'm fine just admiring the fountain, and I'll be your little towel girl when y'all are finished swimming in each other's juices."

"Just my own juices here," corrected Al.

"Okay, enough with the 'juices' talk," laughed Sarah. "I'm already suspending disbelief and pretending there's chlorine in here."

"So what *is* in here, Al," asked Janet.

"Oh, probably lime deposits, iron, silica, that sort of thing. Some salts and sulfurs. But remember, what really made these waters special was the magnetism."

"That's actually a thing? Magnetic water?" Janet was skeptical.

"That's right," Al replied. "A neutral iron or steel rod could be placed in this water and, after a short time, become a magnet with measurable polarity."

Vaughn laughed. "Dude, how do you *know* all this shit?"

"Hey, I grew up with this 'shit.' My parents and grandparents believed these waters could cure anything. Rheumatism, dyspepsia, sciatica…"

"Well now you're just making up words," Vaughn scoffed.

"Ha, ha. But don't forget, magnetic therapy is used all over the world. Magnetic energy affects all living things, and keeping your own electromagnetism in balance is thought, by some, to be the key to good health and long life."

Janet spoke up. "By 'some,' of course, you're referring to the hippie chicks at music festivals selling magnetite rings to make your internal energy totally more groovy?"

Al smirked. "Something like that."

"Well then," she said. "I'm taking some with me." She leaned over the tub to grab her purse, retrieving a half-filled plastic Aquafina bottle. She dumped its original contents onto the floor, then plunged the container into the bath. She capped it and held it above her head in triumph. "To an extra year of life!"

"Oh yeah?" Sam laughed. "Then I'm going to live forever!" He descended into the bubbles, immersing his head under water. He popped back out after a moment, spit a stream of water in the manner of a fountain sculpture, and shook his hair like a wet puppy.

"Hey," chided Sarah with a smile, as she brushed away droplets from her forehead.

Sam tickled her right thigh under the water, and nibbled her bare shoulder as he cuddled closer. She squealed with delight and pulled his face up to kiss him on the lips. The kiss was short but deep, and left a distinct, lingering metallic flavor on her tongue.

"Um, excuse me, middle-aged Realtor present," said Janet, leaning over to place the bottle back in her purse. Vaughn smiled and slid a bit closer to her as she returned.

"Feeling left out?" he asked, with a suggestive smile.

"In your dreams, mister."

Vaughn laughed, then shrugged his shoulders, defeated. He turned to the only remaining female. "Come on, Kedz," urged a jovial Vaughn. "Just dip a nipple in."

Kedzie snorted at this crassness, but then smiled with mock seduction, and slowly lifted up her shirt as if starting a strip tease. But when she revealed her abdomen, Vaughn stopped smiling. "What," she asked, looking down. She was surprised to see that the skin around her navel was soaked red with blood.

Sarah noticed too, and got out of the water, first instructing Vaughn to "turn around." She first jogged to the far wall for a towel, motioning for Kedzie to join her. Sarah wrapped a towel around her wet body, then eased Kedzie into the light.

"Does it hurt?" asked Sarah.

"No, not really," Kedzie answered.

Sam had gotten out too and was walking toward them, cupping himself in his hands in an act of modesty. He also grabbed a towel and wrapped it around his waist.

"Everything okay over there?" Vaughn called from the tub.

Sarah gasped when Kedzie lifted her shirt. The small cut had stretched from a quarter-sized slit to several full inches in length. The wound was still shallow, but blood was seeping from it like an overflowing tub. Sam and Sarah both froze for a moment, then Sarah grabbed a clean towel from the shelving and pushed it against the wound. Sam grabbed a few more towels and lay them on the ground so Kedzie could lie down comfortably.

Upon hearing Sarah's gasp, Vaughn had jumped from the tub and ran over to them. He saw the cut and the blood, and knew what to do.

"Ninth floor, Apothecary," he said.

Sam nodded. "Go."

Vaughn raced, naked, to the elevator, closed the gate, and pressed "9." Janet and Al looked at each other from their respective tubs.

"Well, there's something you don't see every day," Janet remarked.

"Maybe we should get out," Al replied. "Can someone grab us some towels?"

Sam nodded and grabbed two more towels from the shelves, jogging them over to Al and Janet, then returning to Kedzie and Sarah.

"It's not deep…I'll be fine," Kedzie insisted.

Sarah was still frowning. "But the cut was so small. I don't understand why it's bigger now."

"Maybe that's just something that happens to pregnant bellies," Kedzie offered.

"But you're not even showing."

Kedzie shrugged.

Although Sarah was pressing on the wound with the towel, she noticed a few drops of blood had dripped onto the tile beneath them. She removed the towel again to examine the wound, but this time, she thought she noticed something else as well, perhaps something to do with Kedzie's navel. Sarah puzzled over it for a moment, then a thought began to form, just a tickle in the back of her mind. She was experiencing a moment of déjà vu from the time she had first cleaned the smaller wound. Something was clearly bugging her on a subliminal level. But what was it?

She looked up at Kedzie for answers, and their eyes locked for a brief moment. But these eyes were unreadable to Sarah, as if they reflected a mix of contradictory and jumbled emotions. She thought she saw panic, anger, hunger, and hate, all at once, and all in a split second. It so startled Sarah that she forgot about the puzzle her subconscious was working on, and she was immediately concerned for Kedzie's well-being. Was she going into shock? Was she about to pass out?

Sarah opened her mouth to speak, but didn't get the chance, as right then, without warning or so much as a flicker, the lights went out.

Someone cried aloud. Sarah was pretty sure it was Janet. She heard Sam say "hang on, don't panic." Sarah reached for Sam's hand and he took it, squeezing it once, but then letting go, leaving her alone in the pure, impenetrable blackness. She instinctively stood up and looked around, but it was as if her eyes were shut, and she became disoriented. She knelt back down and reached for Kedzie, but she couldn't feel her, either.

"Kedzie? Sam?" Sarah's voice cracked in panic. She felt as if she were under a blanket.

"Hang on!" Sam shouted from another direction. "I'm finding them!"

"Finding what?" asked Sarah, bewildered.

Sam didn't answer. He was feeling along the baths and the walls, following the layout of the room as close as he remembered, in order to locate the elevator door. But it wasn't the elevator itself which interested him. Rather, Sam remembered that Vaughn was still lugging the battery powered lights from floor to floor. He only hoped that his friend had taken them out of the elevator car, as he had on the previous floors, and set them beside the elevator call buttons. If instead, in the shared awe of observing the bath level for the first time, he had left them in the elevator, then the lights were with Vaughn on the ninth floor, and would be no help to them.

"Just give me a minute," Sam called back.

The intensity of the darkness was unrelenting, and Sarah was becoming more anxious. Above ground, true darkness was rare. It may feel as if the universe was black the second any lights went out, she realized, but once your eyes adjusted, you could regain your bearings. Perhaps the faded LED light from an alarm clock, or a streetlight filtering in through closed blinds, would light a path if you waited just a few moments. But down here, there was nothing. Sarah tried again to reach down to find Kedzie, to comfort her, but felt only the cold tile. "Kedz?" she called once more. Still no response.

Before she could try again, Sarah felt something brush against her back, like someone running behind her, but without sound. She spun in place, though she still could not see and could not even know if she had even turned around.

"What the hell was that?" Sarah cried in a panic. "Who was that?"

"Sarah?" called Sam, concerned. "What's wrong?"

"I don't know! I can't find Kedzie and someone just brushed against me!"

"Wasn't me," called Al's voice from behind her.

"Me neither," said Janet. "I'm staying put."

There was no answer from Kedzie.

Sam debated abandoning the quest for the lights, and running back to where he heard Sarah's last call. But he knew he was close to the lights, if they were here, as he had just reached the wall he was aiming for, and was certain the units would be just a few more steps from his position. He didn't want Sarah to be alone and scared, but he couldn't give up now.

"Hang on," Sam said. "I'll just be another minute! I'm trying to find Vaughn's lights!"

"Okay," said Sarah shakily. "Kedz, if this is your idea of a joke, if you're trying to scare us, it's not very fucking funny!"

White light pierced the room. Sam panned the DJ light across the floor and across the baths, finding Al, Janet, and Sarah. No Vaughn, of course, since he was still in the Apothecary, but also no Kedzie.

"What the hell?" Sam was more confused than alarmed. "Kedzie, where are you?"

No response. Sarah ran to each tub and looked inside, certain that Kedzie would be found face-down and lifeless in one of them, but each were empty. The water was calm, as whatever electricity source had powered the lights had also powered the gentle bubbles.

"Well she couldn't have taken the elevator," Sam observed, "and she couldn't have just vanished, so she must have taken the stairs." He gestured to the single door on the far wall. Sarah walked over to it and reached for the handle, but it turned on its own. Sarah gasped and jumped back as the door opened inward into the room, then calmed as she realized it must be Kedzie. But it wasn't. It was Vaughn, holding an ancient first aid kit in front of his genitals.

"Jesus, Vaughn, you scared me." Sarah admitted. "Did you see Kedz?"

Vaughn gave her a confused look. "What do you mean?"

"She's gone," Sam explained, walking over to them with lights in each hand. "We figure she must have taken the stairs, since you had the elevator and she's not here." Sam motioned with the DJ light to reveal the empty room.

"I didn't see her," Vaughn said, finding his clothes.

"Why'd you take the stairs," Sarah inquired. "Does that mean the elevator's down?"

There was a pause as Vaughn considered this. "Yes," he concluded, "whatever took out the lights must have also stopped the elevator. That's why I couldn't use it to come back."

Sam nodded. "Okay, well, maybe this makes sense. Kedzie couldn't have gone upstairs because you would have seen or heard her on your way down, so she must have gone downstairs to where we've already been."

"She probably panicked and ran back to the maintenance room," said Al behind them. "That's what I might have done, to try to get the lights back on."

"But its pitch black down here," Sarah protested.

"I'm sure she has a cell phone light or something. A 'flashlight app,' as you kids call it."

Sam was nodding. This made sense.

"Okay, so we all get dressed and go down there and find her, agreed?" Sam saw nods. "We have to try to get the power back anyway."

"Well hang on," Janet interjected, her right hand raised like a schoolgirl asking a question. "Even if Vaughn didn't run into her, she may just have easily gone upstairs to try to get out. If I was scared and trapped underground, my instinct would be to go *up* as fast as I could, not *down*."

"So we should go up?"

"We should do both," said Janet. "We have two lights, after all. Two groups, and we each take a light."

Sarah stiffened. "Split up? Are you kidding? Sam, she's kidding, right?"

Sam was horrified by the idea as well, but the logic was sound. Kedzie was frightened and was now lost, and could only have run in two possible directions—up the staircase, or down the staircase. Ordinarily, they could stand to wait where they were for a while, in the hopes that Kedzie would return, but Kedzie was hurt, and bleeding. What if she were to pass out? If she wouldn't answer their calls, she could not assist in her own rescue. She would have to be found, and if she was injured, it would have to be fast.

"Alright," said Sam decisively, after everyone's clothes had been thrown back on. "Kedzie's hurt. So first, we check and see if there's a blood trail in either direction. If there is, we follow it together. If not, Janet's right, and we have to split up, and check up and down simultaneously. But we don't have to be dumb about it like cheesy movie victims. Each team will have a light, and each team should keep someone in the staircase at all times so we can shout to each other, while someone else explores the floor. The team going down should try and get the lights on, too, agreed?"

The gang agreed. But upon inspecting the stairway, no droplets of blood could be seen in either direction. Sarah held onto Sam's arm, and tried to communicate a telepathic message: "please, please, please be on my team." Sam nodded to her, understanding.

"Okay," he said. "How about Janet and Al go up, Vaughn, Sarah and I go down. But I'll run back and forth to help communication too."

"Old versus young, eh?" cracked Janet.

"I like it," said Al in response. "She's more likely to be downstairs anyway, which means you and I get to explore the uncharted waters while the kiddies are stuck in a rerun." Al turned to Vaughn. "You remember how to get the lights back on, though, right?"

Vaughn nodded. "Piece of cake."

"I bet she's fine," assured Sam. "Just scared." Sam took the first aid kit from Vaughn and removed some bandages to give to Al. "Take these, just in case. Just holler if you find her. One of us will be in the stairwell at all times."

Al took the bandages, nodded to Janet, and they began their ascent with one of Vaughn's lights. Sam, Sarah and Vaughn headed down the stairs with the other.

Please let her be alright, Sam prayed. He squeezed Sarah's hand. She squeezed back, and the three friends returned to the deep.

eleven

Although he was tempted to skip the two floors of single rooms and head straight for Maintenance, where power might be restored, Sam also understood that if Kedzie was lost on one of those floors, and they missed it, Kedzie might try to move to an upper area they'd already cleared, such as the baths. Sarah protested this decision at first, but Sam insisted "it will only take a few minutes per floor, and then we'll know for sure." Vaughn agreed to be in charge of holding and aiming the lights, and Sam volunteered to stay in the stairwell, in the dark, in case Kedzie tried to pass by, or in case Al and Janet had to shout something down to them.

"Oh shit," said Sam. "I just realized we don't have the keys. Janet does."

"I don't think we need them," Sarah suggested.

"You don't think we locked up any of the rooms we unlocked?"

"I don't think so. But even if we had, Kedzie couldn't have gotten into a locked room, so it doesn't matter."

"What if she locked herself in a room?"

"Why would she do that?"

"Just in case, though, maybe we should get the keys from Janet."

"Sam, by that logic, Kedzie would be just as likely to have locked herself in a room *they're* exploring. But I don't think she would do that."

Sam nodded. "Alright. I just hope we didn't lock the maintenance room."

"I don't think so, man," ventured Vaughn. "Who would we have been trying to keep out?"

The three had arrived at the fourth floor, which was the second floor of single rooms they had originally explored. Sam motioned to Sarah and Vaughn to go on.

"You sure you'll be okay in here in the dark, babe?" Sarah was concerned.

"I'm fine," said Sam, although there was a crack in his voice. He was thinking of mice and cellars. Then he remembered his cell phone. "I can get a little light with this," he said, and turned it on. Its light was feeble compared with Vaughn's DJ equipment, but it would do to prevent fear in the stairwell.

"Alright," agreed Sarah. "Here we go."

Sam watched as Sarah and Vaughn entered the floor. Sam kept the door propped open with his foot, so he could observe his friends' progress while staying in the hallway, watch for Kedzie, and hear any shouts from Al and Janet above.

Sarah and Vaughn moved quickly, efficiently, and a little nervously. They re-entered the room with the gramophone, thankful that it was not again playing. They entered the rooms which had been empty, and all remained so. Finally, they got to the far end of the hall with the elevator. Sarah tried the elevator buttons, and as expected, nothing happened. Then, she was struck by an unpleasant thought.

"Vaughn," she said, "should we check the elevator shaft?"

"Hmm." Vaughn looked puzzled. The gate was in place, and would have to be opened manually to peer down into the darkness. But he cocked his head in a thoughtful gesture, told Sarah to stand back, and unlatched the gate.

Sam was observing their actions at the end of the dim hallway, but was uncertain as to what they were doing. "Guys?" he asked.

"Checking something," replied Sarah. "Just a moment."

Vaughn shone his light down the elevator shaft. Sarah peered in as well. At first, it appeared the LEDs weren't powerful enough to illuminate the ground floor. But as their eyes adjusted, they could make out the shaft mechanics, and see the empty square floor where the elevator would rest in the lobby. Thankfully, there was no body. Sarah exhaled, and Vaughn restored and latched the gate. The two began walking back to Sam.

"This floor's clear," Vaughn reported brightly. Sarah added a hopeful smile.

"Okay," said Sam. "On to three."

The team traversed another flight, and followed the same procedure. Sam stayed in the stairwell with his feeble cell phone light to keep him from panic, and Sarah and Vaughn began re-entering the first series of empty rooms. One by one, the rooms were thoroughly checked, and each remained as barren as ever.

"I'm not sure if this is making me feel better or worse," Sarah admitted as the last room was cleared. "How far could she have gotten? I'm not even sure she had her cell phone. She could be in complete darkness."

"No," said Vaughn. "She must have had something. A

lighter, maybe? Something. She couldn't have gone ten feet in this blackness without some sort of light."

Sarah felt a slow chill slithering up her spine. Everything about this was wrong. She couldn't conceive of a reason that her friend would vanish under such circumstances. When the lights go out, you stay put. You don't go exploring, or even attempt to escape, without telling anybody. And still, Sarah tried to commit herself into accepting that Kedzie had taken off, because she was trying very hard to suppress the alternate theory that couldn't stop picking at her—that Kedzie did not "run away," but was taken.

Back in college, Sarah and Kedz had a period during which they attended frat parties. In Sarah's case, she was going "ironically," determined to judge the other attendees, careful not to have too much genuine fun. Kedzie, of course, threw herself into any situation, and was the life of the party. And the boys loved her for it. Sarah was hit on at these parties as well, as she was quite attractive even with the "otherness" vibe. But the boys always seemed drawn to Kedzie on a different level, something more primal. When boys were talking to Sarah, she sensed their interest, and sometimes their desire for her, but never their need. With Kedzie, the boys *needed* her, and gazed upon her not as one would look upon a potential girlfriend, or date, or even as a sex object, but as food. Sarah couldn't believe how brazen the frat boys would be, looking Kedzie up and down without any discretion, mouths open and panting, even licking their lips. They wanted not to talk to her, but to consume her, and became mind-numbed drooling animals in the process. For her part, Kedzie would encourage, laugh, flirt, and ask boys to get her another drink, but she didn't take it seriously. "You know I'm going home with *you*, Sarah," she would say. "Don't be jealous." Sarah wasn't jealous. She was worried her friend had no idea what these hungry men were capable of, outside of the safety in numbers of well-illuminated frat house ballrooms. So for the most part, Sarah watched out for Kedzie, never taking her out of her sight, no matter who Sarah was talking to herself.

One time, though, she did lose her. They had been at a party for more than two hours, and Sarah had been signaling her desire to leave, but Kedzie wouldn't hear of it. "Oh come on," she pouted. "I'm having fun. And besides, look at that cute boy that just walked in."

Sarah looked, and flushed. The boy was not only cute, he was staring right at her. Not at Kedzie, or even at Kedzie and Sarah together, but just at Sarah. It was unmistakable. His dark eyes seemed to see right through her, and with the slightest of nods, he conveyed a simple message: "I am talking to you first." He poured himself a beer from the keg, gestured to a few guys he recognized from across the room, and walked with confidence over to where Sarah and Kedzie were trying to pretend not to notice him.

"Hello," the stranger had said. He looked at Kedzie, then Sarah, but his eyes stayed on Sarah.

"Hi," said Kedzie with her usual, bubbly charm. The stranger smiled politely at this, but took no special notice. He turned back to Sarah, awaiting her greeting, which was his purpose.

"Hello," said Sarah. "What's your name?"

"I'm Tony," he answered. "And you?"

"Sarah."

"And I'm Kedzie!" Kedzie flashed the brightest, flirtiest smile she had in her.

Tony smiled again at Kedzie, but in a perfunctory way, as if she had handed him a business card. "Nice to meet you," he said to her, before turning back to Sarah. "And you," he said, with more weight.

Kedzie read the situation, and gave Sarah a knowing smile. "Well, I was just about to run back to continue my fascinating conversation with Peter and…Mike…*Matt*… over there, so I'll leave you be. It was nice to meet you, Tony!"

"Likewise," Tony replied.

Sarah watched her friend leave, but Tony was determined to hold Sarah's attention.

"Please tell me," he began smoothly, "what you study."

"I study journalism," Sarah lied. It was her standard answer. She couldn't for the life of her remember when or why she had started answering this way, but figured she had observed just the right balance of interest and disinterest with this response in the past, and so it came to her now on auto-pilot. The truthful answer would have been "sociology," but for some reason this admission had, in the past, either sparked unwanted debate, or stopped a conversation cold. "Journalism" was interesting but not *too* interesting, and could be as mundane or controversial as she wished to portray it, based on whether she wanted a short conversation or a long one.

"And what," Tony asked, eyes locked to hers, "do you journalate?"

Sarah blinked, then giggled, which was unlike her. "I journalate whatever I care to, Tony. But please tell me you know that's not a real word."

"I think anything can be a real word in a living language," he countered. "Words are made to be created, revised, tested, and perfected. You understood the question I was asking. There was no confusion. A real word is that which conveys meaning. It does not have to be in the dictionary. At least, not at first. Why, I bet people used the word 'sexy' for years before someone decided it was a 'real' word, and I bet no one had any trouble understanding what 'sexy' meant when they heard it aloud before they read it in a book. 'Sexy' is a word that just makes sense in context. And I bet, Sarah, that you're very sexy when you journalate."

Sarah couldn't decide whether she adored or despised this talkative, showy, forward young man. But she was suitably intrigued, which is a higher compliment than she had ever bestowed on a boy at a frat party in the past. She was compelled to determine whether Tony was genuinely interesting or just a player with some unique pick-up lines, and that could only come through additional conversation. Maybe she had a streak of journalism in her after all. So they talked, and laughed, and drank beer out of red plastic cups together, and Sarah forgot about Kedzie for a solid thirty minutes.

"Hey, one sec," Sarah said. She looked around. Kedz was nowhere.

"Looking for someone?" asked Tony.

"Yeah, the girl I was with. We're watching out for each other."

Tony nodded knowingly. "Sure, I understand. Want to walk around a bit, look for her?"

"Can we? I know that sounds paranoid."

"Not at all," reassured Tony. "I'll come with."

As they walked from the party room to the dining room to the large open kitchen, Sarah felt a pit in her stomach. Where *was* she? Had she been talked into going upstairs into one of the bedrooms? *Dammit, girl.*

"Kedzie?" Sarah called, trying not to sound concerned or motherly. "Hey Kedz, ya still around?" But she wasn't.

"She probably found a cute boy and is making out somewhere," teased Tony. "Come on, don't worry about it. She your little sister or something?"

Sarah ignored him, and kept scanning the crowds. No sign.

What's wrong with me, thought Sarah. *I'm not her guardian angel. She's probably having fun. Lighten the fuck up.*

Sarah was by the staircase now, debating whether to continue the search upstairs.

Then she heard the scream.

There's no question it was Kedzie's. Sarah knew it, viscerally, in her gut. She raced up the first flight of stairs, not waiting to see if Tony was still behind her. She arrived at the hallway, and looked around, frantic. There were so many doors. Where was she?

Then she heard her. "Nooo!" Kedzie was screaming. It was coming from the left, maybe two doors down. Sarah raced to the door, and without knocking or even thinking, she turned the doorknob and bolted in.

"Kedzie?" she cried.

Kedzie was there, alright. With a boy. But she wasn't in danger. She had her shirt off, though not her bra, and the boy had his shirt off too, but he wasn't hurting her. He was drawing on her taut stomach with ice cubes.

Sarah replayed the screams in the recorder of her mind. What had sounded like terror must have been the playful shouts of someone being teased by ice, enjoying the cold but being shocked by it. She hadn't saved her friend by barging in. She had embarrassed Kedzie. And herself.

"Oh, God," Sarah stammered. "I'm so sorry. I heard screaming, and run up…"

Kedzie shot her a furious look. But the boy was laughing. "Holy shit, girl, I told ya you were being loud! Especially if they could hear you downstairs." The boy looked past Sarah to the guy standing behind her. "Is this the guy you brought with you to stop the evil rapist?"

Sarah turned and saw Tony. He was smiling, too.

Relieved, Sarah allowed herself an embarrassed chuckle. "Well, shit, Kedz."

Kedzie was still pissed. She grabbed her shirt, then barked "close the door—we're leaving in five minutes." Sarah and Tony backed out and did as ordered.

"I guess she wants to leave," Sarah said, sheepishly. "I'm going to get yelled at."

"Don't worry," Tony smiled. "I'm sure in time she'll be flattered that you care enough to try and protect her."

"Right?" agreed Sarah. Then she sighed. "I guess it would be pretty insulting, though, if someone felt they had to look after me all the time."

Tony nodded. Then, he looked around, and snatched a

dry erase marker from a nearby bedroom door. He fished a receipt from his pocket and wrote a phone number on the paper, testing the dryness afterwards with a finger. The number held together.

"This is my cell," he said, handing it to her. "Give me a call if things calm down tonight, or whenever. If you like."

Sarah took the paper. "Sure thing, Tony. Good to meet you."

They shook hands in a playfully formal manner, just as a newly clothed Kedzie opened the door of the ice man's room. She glanced dismissively at Tony, then took Sarah's hand and led her down the stairs and toward the exit. Sarah was going to get an earful, alright.

"You think I can't tell the difference between a nice guy and a rapist?" Kedzie demanded after they had exited the fraternity. The air had become chilly, and Kedzie shuddered, though it could have been the lingering effects from the ice.

"I don't think *anyone* can tell the difference. Otherwise the assholes couldn't get away with it."

"That's bullshit. I can smell a rapist coming a mile away."

Sarah scoffed at this, and rolled her eyes, though a week later, Sarah would find herself wishing Kedzie's claim had been true.

"Look," Kedzie said, after a pause. "I do know that you care about me. But I'm not a kid. I'm not a ditz either, by the way. I can make my own choices, and my own mistakes. Okay?"

Sarah sighed. "Yeah, I know."

"Do you?"

"Yeah."

"Well okay then," Kedzie smiled brightly. "Let's order pizza."

They walked in silence for a bit, Sarah trying to determine whether Kedzie's restored joviality was genuine or a cover. She supposed she did tend to think of Kedzie as younger, though she wasn't, and ditzier, though she wasn't that either, at least not really. Why was Sarah so protective? Kedzie just seemed more carefree than Sarah had ever been, and the brightness in her spirit was so clear. Perhaps, although Sarah hated to admit it, at times she was a little jealous too.

"We could get you a Kubotan," offered Sarah.

"What's a Kubotan?"

"It's a self-defense thing. Goes on a keychain."

"Pepper spray?"

"No, it's more like a piece of hard plastic or metal. I've been thinking of getting one. It can cause pain if applied to certain sensitive parts of the body."

"Like the dick?"

Sarah laughed. "I suppose that would be painful."

"Nah, that's what knees are for."

"True enough."

"I *am* tough, ya know."

"I know, Kedz."

"Someday I'm going to get a tattoo that says 'one tough bitch,' just so people don't fuck with me." Kedzie giggled and beamed. "Ya think?"

"Could work," Sarah acknowledged.

"Of course, that means I'd have to deal with the pain of

the tattoo needle, and I hate needles."

"Who's the tough bitch now," Sarah teased.

Kedzie sighed. "Maybe I'll just get the Kubotan."

"We'll order them together."

"Engraved," added Kedzie.

"*Tough bitches forever.*"

The next morning, they had purchased Kubotans together at a head shop near campus. They were made of solid iron, and were identical in size and color, so Sarah thought fondly of her friend whenever she noticed or felt the small weapon on her keychain in the days that followed.

Their friendship had faded somewhat in the past two years, as Sarah had become serious with Sam. She supposed that was normal, for when you live with a significant other, they're bound to become your best friend, and when you're planning a future with someone, priorities change. She had hoped Kedzie would meet someone just as special, because then they could have couples nights and do couples things, and they'd all be friends together. Unless she chose a real douchebag, that is. But now, Kedzie's "plus one" would be a newborn baby, and their life paths would diverge even further.

As Sarah and Vaughn made their way back toward the staircase of The Eaton, thoughts of Kedzie's friendship years ago were replaced with thoughts of Kedzie's unusual behavior in the past few hours. Sarah knew there was something "off," but couldn't place it. Then again, even Vaughn seemed a little "off" at the moment. Maybe she was "off" too, merely being "Sarah-ish" instead of Sarah, not quite feeling herself, as they all navigated this new and bizarre reality a hundred feet below the earth.

Reuniting with Sam in the stairwell, the three walked down to the maintenance level, opened the door, and peered down the empty hallway. Once again, cries of "hello?" and "Kedz?" darkly lingered in the hollow air, unheard and unanswered. Sam nodded to Sarah and Vaughn, indicating they would repeat the procedure of previous floors, Sam standing guard by the stairs while the others explored the floor.

Sarah thought this hallway felt just as quiet, but somehow not as empty. There was a faint, dank smell which could have been semen. Sarah tried to track the odor to a specific place but could not; it seemed to enter and exit her perception without pattern. She followed and watched as Vaughn lit the laundry room, but it was as empty as everywhere else. They shrugged to each other and returned to the hallway.

"Well, at least let's get the lights on," sighed Sarah, gesturing to the maintenance room.

Vaughn smiled and led the way.

twelve

The hallway of the first floor of double rooms looked more or less like the hallways of single rooms, but with fewer doors; instead of four rooms on each side of the hallway, there were three rooms on each side. *Not quite "double" rooms,* Al thought.

Al held the light as Janet checked each of the doorknobs to assure they wouldn't turn.

"Shouldn't we open them?" Al asked.

"The doors?" Janet shrugged. "What for? If they're locked, she couldn't have gotten in."

"What if she found one that was unlocked, went in, and locked it from the inside?"

"Why would she do that?"

"Why would she run off in the first place?"

Janet smiled. "I think you just want to keep exploring. But this is Sam's place and we should wait for him."

"I suppose so."

"Besides, if we search all the rooms it would take forever."

"Well, at least knock on each door, just to make sure she's not inside."

This compromise seemed wise. Janet knocked on a door and called Kedzie's name, listened intently for a few seconds, and moved on to the next. Soon the first floor of double rooms was clear.

At the end of the hallway, Janet tried the elevator button just in case, but without power, everything remained silent.

"Onward and upward," advised Al, gesturing back toward the stairs.

As they walked together down the dark hallway, Janet asked Al how he had gotten into the restoration business. Al described his early days in Detroit, fixing up old buildings before it was "cool," and how he eventually and almost accidentally became an expert in "adaptive re-use."

"Adaptive re-use?"

"It's when you take an old structure and use it for something new, like converting a warehouse into loft apartments," Al explained. Then he gave her a teasing smirk. "I thought you were in real estate."

Janet stiffened a bit. "I do mostly homes," she explained. "But I'm quite familiar with adaptive re-use; I just never called it that."

"What do you call it?"

"I dunno," she replied. "Renovation? Restoration?"

"It's partly that, but I think if you just restore something, you're intending to return it to its original purpose. With adaptive re-use, you're turning it into something new that people need in the modern world. Especially old factories and warehouses in downtown districts, which are now prime real estate. Developers just want to tear down these century-old buildings and put in cheap-ass drywall boxes." Al shuddered. "So many beautiful buildings that could have stood for a thousand years have been destroyed and replaced with crap that won't last fifty."

"Why'd you leave Detroit? Seems no shortage of old

buildings to restore down there."

Al laughed. "Yeah, but no money to do it. The big guys are doing fine, but smaller developers are spooked. They see the city getting smaller every year. There are maybe six or seven blocks in the whole city that were worth restoring, and they're already restored. I know, because I worked on half of them."

The pair had taken the stairs to the next level, which looked so much like the previous floor Janet was half-convinced they hadn't moved at all.

"Is this your first time on an Eaton Rapids project?" asked Janet, as she tried the first room door.

"No, I've poked around here for years. I had some experience working with Albert Kahn buildings in the D, so one day a guy calls to see if I'd help make a restoration plan for the old Horner Mill."

"Kahn did the Fisher Building, right?"

Al nodded. "That and about half the city. The architect of Detroit, they called him."

"But the mill's older than that, right?" Janet asked, after testing and knocking on another door.

"Some of it, sure. But when the mill needed to expand back in the day, they got Kahn to design the expansions and the new buildings. It doesn't look as distinctive as some of his high-profile work, because he wanted to blend his style with the existing structures so it all felt right. But the guys who own the Horner Mill now wanted my expertise in preserving Kahn's badassery while making cool lofts with modern amenities."

"Is that when you moved from Detroit?"

"Yep. To Lansing, though. Lots to do there, too."

"You must be pretty respected."

"I'm the man," claimed Al. In truth, though his knowledge and experience were genuine, his reputation had suffered significant damage in recent years. Untreated alcoholism resulted in a number of burned bridges, and he was fired from more than one well-paying gig due to tardiness and a negative attitude. When the owners of the Horner Mill contacted him for a quote, he cut his rates in half to assure the gig, using it as a way to escape Detroit and start a new life, making new connections. So far, it had worked well, and he had talked his way into a project manager position on a number of small but decent gigs. His apartment was affordable, and without family his expenses were low, so he was able to offer low rates in return, making him affordable even to kids like Sam Spicer. Although, even before the discovery of this underground hotel, he would have taken Sam's job for free, just in case.

There was one door left for Janet to check, room 706. She was so surprised when the knob turned that she jumped.

"Live one, eh?" said Al, turning the light so they could get a better look.

Janet called out Kedzie's name, then opened the door. They peered inside together, and cautiously entered.

The double rooms were indeed larger than the singles, and seemed better appointed, with nicer headboards, armoires, and wood detailing, assuming this room was representative of its neighbors. The private bathroom was more spacious as well, with a clawfoot tub and a floor-length mirror. But Kedzie was nowhere to be found.

There was evidence of past occupancy, however. Three glass wine bottles, all empty, lay beside one end table. The armoire contained several hanging men's dress shirts and a pair of folded pants. Two large hardcover books sat on the edge of the bed, which seemed to have been made in haste.

Al picked up one of the books with his free hand and read the spine. *Love and Mr. Lewisham* by H.G. Wells. He returned it to the bed and examined the second, which was *Jude the Obscure* by Thomas Hardy. Neither Al nor Janet had heard of either title. "Obscure is right," noted Janet. But Al noticed that this second book seemed to weigh less than it should. He set down the DJ light and opened the novel with both hands, wherein he found a large L-shaped hole cut into the pages, hollowing out the insides. But the hidden compartment was empty.

"Huh," said Al.

"Looks like the shape of a gun," Janet remarked.

This was plausible, observed Al. A revolver would fit quite well in this cut-out space, and would be just the sort of thing you might want to hide while traveling.

Al frowned. "So this guy took his gun when he left, but not his books? Or his shirts and pants?"

Janet said nothing. She was anxious and uneasy, and shuffled her feet a bit on the floor. "We should keep looking for Kedzie," she suggested, and Al agreed. He picked up the light and the two made their way to the stairway once more.

The two traveled up an additional flight to the suites level, one floor below the Apothecary where Vaughn had gone for a first aid kit before the lights went out. This time, the hallway contained just four doors, two on each side. The doors were wider and more ornate than the standard room doors they had seen so far, and the molding around each door boasted a more intricate design in a Victorian style. The hotel room numbers were large and brass, and to the left of each entrance, like a home address, rather than affixed to the doors themselves.

"Oh, come on," pleaded Al. "We have to go into one of these."

"Perhaps," was Janet's noncommittal reply.

The first door Janet tried was locked. But the second door, room 802, was open. Janet called out "hello," and as usual, no one responded. As Al did a sweep of his light across the room, however, the pair let out a gasp. This room looked like it had been trashed by rock stars. Most of the furniture was overturned, and clothes were strewn across the floor, as if someone had tossed them out of a suitcase in a frenzy. Al shined the light up near the ceiling, revealing a large gap in the crown molding over the bed, with clear evidence of damage to the surrounding wall, suggesting the missing piece had been ripped down with intent.

"Jesus," Al remarked.

Al could tell the suite had been luxurious, and must have cost a fortune compared to the rooms they had seen so far. There were additional electric lights, and even a ceiling fan, though nothing had power at the moment. The room even had a window, framed by expensive fabric, looking out into an oil painting of a spring garden embedded a few inches into the brick. But it was hard to appreciate the beauty of the surroundings when they were covered in such destruction. Someone had either lost something vitally important and had to find it in a hurry, or this was the aftermath of a very, very bad domestic dispute.

As Janet and Al explored the suite further, they found more than a dozen empty liquor bottles in the bathroom, a few of them broken, as well as a cracked mirror dangling above some unsettling dark red spots on the tile below. At the sight of the dried blood, Janet let out a choked sob, and pulled Al's shirt, pleading with him to return to the hallway with her. Al complied, and Janet closed the suite door with a forceful flourish, determined to never set foot in there again.

Instinctively, Janet started toward the stairs, but stopped when she realized Al wasn't following.

"Where are you going?" asked Al.

Janet stopped. "I don't know," she admitted.

"There are still two more rooms to check."

"Al, she's not here," Janet announced with authority. "Let's try another floor."

"We should at least knock on the other two doors," Al persisted.

Janet said nothing, and the two stared at each other for a long moment. It was hard to gauge Al's expression, for the light he was carrying, aimed outward, cast himself in dark shadows. But his resolve seemed to be holding, and Janet couldn't very well go exploring on her own without their primary light source. She considered her pocketed cell phone, which had a flashlight application, but reasoned it would be no match for the uncompromising tomb-like blackness.

She threw up her hands.

"Fine, have it your way." She stomped over to the nearest door on the other side of the hallway and tried to turn the knob. Locked. She pounded on the door and called to Kedzie to come out if she was in there. No answer. Janet shot a look back to Al, who remained silent. She traversed the hallway to the last suite, 804, and her light man followed. This doorknob did turn, which gave Janet pause, and she considered for a moment pretending that it was locked. Had Al seen the knob turn? Could she get away with faking it? She decided that would be silly. After all, Kedzie was indeed missing somewhere, and an unlocked room would be as good a place to hide as any.

Fuck it, she told herself. *I'll open the damned thing.*

"Kedzie?"

Janet pushed open the door. Al swept the light into the room.

A body hung motionless from the ceiling.

thirteen

"Right here." Vaughn tapped a specific fuse in an ancient fuse box. Sarah removed the fuse, which was the size and shape of a laboratory test tube, and held it up to Vaughn's light. A metal filament inside was burned through.

Sarah stepped back and looked around for a box of replacement fuses, which she reasoned should be close by. After some digging in a nearby cabinet, she found a dozen new fuses stacked in neat rows at the bottom of a shallow drawer. She picked one at random, examined it under the light to ensure it was intact, and walked back to the fuse box. Before she could put it in, Sam was shouting something down the hallway.

"What's that, Sam?" asked Sarah.

Sam stepped into the hallway. "I think I heard a scream up the stairwell. It might have been Kedzie, or maybe Janet, but I'm going to check it out."

"Want us to come?"

"No, stay here and get the lights on. I'll be back!"

Without waiting for an answer, he began racing up the stairs. Sam used the dim light of his cell to see where he was going, but it was difficult. He lost track of the number of flights he had climbed, but was sure he must be close. "Kedz?" he called out. Then, "Al? Janet? Where are you?" There was no response. He strained to listen for sounds, but if there was anything to hear, it was no match for his labored breaths and pounding heartbeat. He raced up another flight. "Anyone? Hello?"

He was about to try another, when the dim light of his cell caught motion on the next step. Was Sam seeing things? He took another tentative step, and again saw movement. A mouse. No, two mice. No, *five*. Sam angled the light upward. He couldn't hear them, but he knew they were there. One of the stairs looked like it was jiggling, like jelly. But as his eyes adjusted, it was clear that *this* time, the supposed creatures had just been a trick of the light, affected by the shake in his hands from his jackhammering heart.

"In here, Sam!" It was Al's voice, from below, muffled through the stairway door nearby. Sam snapped out of his panic, raced down the stairs and burst through the door to find Al holding the portable light in one arm and a sobbing Janet in the other.

"I heard a scream," Sam gasped.

Al chuckled. "Told you he'd hear you all the way down there," he said, giving Janet an affectionate pat. She did not seem amused.

"What happened?"

Al turned the light toward the open suite door, nodding to Sam to see for himself. Sam looked into the dark room and cried out. A dark body hung by its neck, suspended from a ceiling fan. It seemed to be shivering, swaying a bit, though it might have been an optical illusion caused by the shadows of the hand-held light-source. Sam realized who it must be.

"Kedz!" he choked, leaping forward toward the hanging form.

"No, wait! It's—" But Al was too late. Sam had reached the body and swung it toward him, just as Al moved the light further into the room, allowing Sam to face the frail skeleton now sagging in his arms. The bones crackled and snapped under the force of his embrace, and Sam leapt backward, stumbled and fell to the ground, eyes still transfixed on the crumbling creature before him. The skeleton had been held together by its last remnants of mummified flesh, and by the fabric of a dress, but now had lost any ability to retain a human form. Within seconds, the skeleton was nothing but bones and dust lying in a heap under a swinging rope.

"Jesus Christ. Jesus fucking Christ!" Sam tried to scoot backwards but hit the wall behind him, causing a painting to tumble off its nail and land with a crunchy thud to his left. "Fuck!" he screamed again, squeezing his eyes tight and trying to calm his nerves.

"Sorry about that," said Al. "I just thought..."

"You could have fucking warned me, Al!"

Janet stepped into the room to comfort Sam, though she avoided looking in the direction of the pile of bones. "Come on," she said reassuringly. "Let's get you out of here."

She helped him to his feet, and they stepped around the bones with caution as they exited the suite together, rejoining Al in the hallway.

"Fuck," said Sam again. "I thought it was Kedzie."

"I know," said Janet. "It's this awful light. Everything's hiding in the shadows. You can't get a grasp on anything."

"No luck with the power?" asked Al.

"They're working on it," Sam barked. Then, to no one

in particular, "What the hell is wrong with this place?"

*

Six floors below, Sarah had snapped the fuse into its socket, but nothing had changed. She removed the fuse, again examined it under the light to confirm it was intact, and put it back. Still nothing.

"There must be some sort of reset button," Sarah observed, running her hands along all four sides of the fuse box, then stepping back to examine the wall for a switch.

"What about that big lever?"

"What lever?"

"The one Al used."

Sarah remembered. The one that activated the metal magnetic discs and choppers which destroyed Vaughn's phone. Vaughn angled the light toward that side of the room and Sarah approached the lever, stepping on a few pieces of pulverized metal and plastic from the last encounter. "Here goes nothing," she said.

The machine was silent at first, and Sarah stepped toward the discs to examine them closer. Eventually, a deep subsonic hum filled the space, and the discs on the wall began to spin. Soon the lights faded in, at first imperceptibly, as slow as a sunrise, and just as welcome. Sarah flashed a relief-filled smile to Vaughn, who smiled back. The large discs were spinning faster now, much faster, and the first metal screech of the chomping guillotine made Sarah flinched. Being in close proximity to the magnets was making her whole body tingle, as if her blood was tickling her skin from the inside out. The sensation was not altogether unpleasant, and at first she was reminded of the soft vibrations felt in the afterglow of an orgasm. But when the second guillotine slashed down, just inches away, the tingles devolved into a shivering dread. Something was wrong.

Sarah felt a new tingling sensation, this time concentrated on her right nipple. For a moment it felt quite good, and then rough, as if someone was trying to yank her nipple off with pliers. It took just a moment for her to logically put this sensation together with her surroundings, but by then it was too late. Against her will, she felt her breast being pulled the inches between her body and the nearest spinning circle. It felt like it took a long time, as if she could make choices and push and pull with free will, but by the force with which her body was slammed into the magnet, she knew it could only have been a fraction of a second. It felt not only as if she were being pulled toward the device, but pushed from behind as well. The steel and iron nipple piercing was now glued to the magnet, an attraction too powerful to resist the thin fabrics of her bra and tight t-shirt, and she couldn't break away.

"Vaughn!" she screamed. "Vaughn, help!" She tried to turn toward Vaughn, against the hard angle, but couldn't see him clearly, except to know he hadn't moved. She turned the other way, to try and reach the lever which would shut the thing off, but it was out of reach.

How many seconds had it been since the last slice? Three? Four? In a panic, she tried to pull at her trapped breast with both hands, crying out in pain as she tried turning, twisting, and yanking the nipple free. It felt as if the steel bar was going to slice right through the front of the nipple flesh, and soon Sarah was hoping—praying—that that's what *would* happen, because the alternative...

"Vaughn!" Sarah screamed again. Why wasn't he helping? He just needed to grab her and pull her back. Or reach the lever and shut it off. Or pull the fuse out of the box behind him. Anything other than just standing there. Was he even still in the room? Once again, it felt like something was pushing against her back, and Sarah became certain that a magnet by itself couldn't be strong enough to pin her in place, but when she strained to look behind her, she saw the space was empty.

Sarah felt isolated, helpless and bewildered. How many seconds had it been? She tried again to reach for the lever, stretching her body like silly putty, until the tips of the fingers of the right hand just grazed the top of the damned thing, still needing another inch. She cried out, giving it everything she had, knowing she was almost there, when she heard the guillotine come down, felt the tug against her skin, sending her flying, falling beside the lever, knocking her head on a nearby shelving unit and calling out again.

Her first thought was that she had done it, she had hit the lever, euphoric in the blissful fractions of seconds before pain kicks in, and then she felt it, in a wave, like being stabbed in the breast with a knife, and she dared looking down. There was a hole in her shirt, and where her right nipple had been, there was barely more than a stump, squirting blood in time with her pounding heartbeat, into the room and onto her body. She looked up at the big spinning discs, her nipple bar and a large chunk of her nipple spinning along with the magnet, and she screamed and screamed and couldn't stop for several seconds. Soon the logical need for medical attention brought her back to reality, and she stood up, still bleeding everywhere, and looked around the room. Where the hell was Vaughn?

She knew she had to press a hand against her breast to stop the bleeding and did so, applying as much pressure as she could stand while still being able to walk. Staggering out into the hallway, she first headed for the stairwell, but then remembered the power was on and tried the elevator buttons instead. She left a bloody fingerprint on the call button, but nothing happened. The elevator was still not functioning. Maybe it had to warm up? Either way, that was time Sarah didn't have. She needed medical attention.

She turned and ran down the hallway toward the stairwell side, almost slipping on a trail of blood by the maintenance door. As she opened the door, she cried out for help, screaming Sam's name up the stairway as loud as she could. She started to climb the stairs but was too nauseous to get more than halfway up a single flight. Her insides flipped, and she nearly vomited. She collapsed on the stairs then, certain she was going to pass out, when she heard Sam's voice calling down to her.

*

When the lights had come back on, Sam and Al had decided to re-enter the room with the skeletal remains. Janet stayed in the hallway, under the excuse that she needed to listen for signs of Kedzie.

It was the first time Al had seen one of the suites in its fully lit glory, not swept by a DJ's LED spotlight. The architecture, the furniture, the upholstery…everything was impeccable. In fact, if not for the pile of bones by the bed and the crude homemade noose hanging from the ceiling fan, it would make a hell of a resort photograph.

Sam noticed a notebook sitting on the far end table. He approached it and picked it up. It appeared to be some sort of journal. He thumbed through the pages and found dates and details spanning several weeks, apparently a sort of travelogue. About halfway through the diary, the writer begins to describe the start of their stay at The Eaton. Sam turned back toward the suite room door, and was about to describe to Al what he had found, when Janet appeared in the doorway.

"Hey, I think I hear something in the hallway," she said. "I think it's Sarah! Someone's shouting 'Sam.'"

Sam dropped the diary on the bed as he raced out the room and into the stairwell. It was indeed Sarah, and she was calling for him, in a panicked voice he had never heard from her, not in his life. He began to race down the stairs, first stair-by-stair and then using the railings to leap whole half-flights at a time. When he found her, he cried out in shock, for her shirt was drenched in blood, and her eyes her closed. But when she heard his cry, she opened her eyes, looked up at him, and was so relieved she laughed aloud.

"Sarah! What the hell?"

"My nipple bar," she explained with a dark chuckle. "The magnets."

Sam had no idea what she was talking about until Sarah mentioned Vaughn's cell phone. Even though that had happened just hours earlier, the memory felt months old. "Oh, shit, Sarah," Sam said in sympathy. "Oh my God. What do you need?"

"I need to get the fuck out of here."

"Okay. Okay, anything."

"The elevators are still out," Sarah said. "We'll have to take the stairs."

Sam nodded, but he also remembered that they hadn't seen any stairs in the outside world, just the elevator. He doubted the stairs went to the surface.

As if reading his mind, Sarah said "they have to get to the depot somehow. It'd be a fucking fire hazard."

Sam nodded again. "Alright. I'll carry you."

"Up twelve flights of stairs? Good luck."

Sam knew she was right. He wasn't strong enough for that. But Vaughn...

"Hey, where's Vaughn?"

"Hell if I know. He took off."

"He what?"

"I don't know, dammit. He just stood there as my nipple got sliced off and now he's nowhere. Probably found Kedzie and they're off in some room fucking each other's brains out somewhere. I don't know, I don't care, just get me out of here." Sarah was losing her patience and was feeling sick to her stomach again. She knew she reeked of blood and sweat and she just needed to return to the real world. Her left hand was still pressed over her right breast trying to stop the bleeding, but wasn't sure she was succeeding. Sam helped her to her feet, and she leaned on him for support as they walked up several flights.

Janet was standing on the landing of the suites floor when they came into view.

"Oh my God! What happened?" she exclaimed.

"There was an accident," Sam explained. "We have to get her to a hospital and the elevators still aren't working. We're going to see if these stairs make it out."

"Al, get over here!" Janet yelled. Al came hurrying into the stairwell, the diary from the skeleton room tucked under his arm. Sam explained the situation and Al offered his sympathies immediately.

Janet fumbled through her purse until she located a small bottle of ibuprofen. Sarah took the container, opened it, found six remaining tablets, and swallowed them all with a swig of the water bottle from Janet's purse. It tasted warm and vaguely metallic, and Sarah remembered that the bottle had been filled with the water they had been bathing in.

"I can stay and wait for Vaughn and Kedzie," Al offered.

"Not me," said Janet. "I want out too."

Without another word, Janet turned and began to climb the stairs, followed by Sam and Sarah. As they ascended, Sam kept glancing up the center of the stairwell, and could indeed see that the stairs would not go enough flights to reach the surface, but it wasn't the end of the stairs that stopped their progress. When they turned the third corner of stairs, their path was blocked, not by a wall or a ceiling, but by another body. And this one was fresh.

fourteen

He hadn't meant to cheat on Sarah, not really. Sam just wanted the satisfaction of knowing that he *could* sleep with such an attractive woman if he wished. He had been playfully hitting on Kedzie the whole night, but even though she had encouraged him, Sam was careful to only say and do things right up to the line, so he'd have a plausible "out" if she got offended. He kept waiting for Kedzie to rebuff a wayward caress, or express shock at a sexual comment, so he could claim he was "just kidding," but she never did. As the night progressed, Sam felt she was almost daring him to see how far he would take the game. It made him feel alive, and desirable, and powerful. When it became clear that Kedzie's drunken flirtations would lead somewhere if he decided to pursue them, it was adrenaline more than desire that pushed him over the edge.

Sarah had been out of town for a few days visiting family, and Sam had found himself chatting with friends online, including Kedzie. She had messaged him first, asking for advice, as she was trying to decide whether to break up with a guy she found "great but dickish." Sam suggested they talk over drinks at a new martini bar in Lansing. "It'll be good for you to get out," he had typed, "and we can try out potential drink options which could make it on my bar's permanent menu." At that point, the dream of owning the old depot had just begun to take shape, and he was still working with Janet to make an offer on the place. But Kedzie had admired his ambition in the attempt, and said she would be honored to help in any way she could.

They agreed on a time to meet, and Sam made a joke that she "better look hot." She responded with the promise that she would, followed by an emoticon wink, before logging off. Something about this innocuous wink made Sam excited. Of course, nothing was going to happen. They were just friends, and more importantly, Sam was in love with and living with Kedzie's *best* friend. There was no possibility anything at all would progress between them. And yet Sam felt an overwhelming desire to look hot, too. He took a shower, put on cologne, and even did a little manscaping, which he felt ridiculous doing, as no one was going to see him down there until Sarah returned from her trip. He went back and forth between two different shirts, and even changed from one to the other when he felt his shoulders didn't look broad enough in his first choice. He realized he was behaving like a teenager preparing for a first date, and he was both amused at and ashamed of himself. He tried to come back to reality, and even debated not brushing his teeth, to prove it was just an evening of hanging out, but he couldn't help himself. Sam was going to be having drinks with one of the most physically attractive women he had ever met, and he was determined to bring his A-game, even if it was just for solitaire.

He arrived first at the bar, picked a table for two with high stools, and positioned his body so Kedzie would see his best side when she entered. He casually ordered a Bombay Sapphire and tonic, his favorite, then wished he could take it back and order something more manly, like a Canadian bottled beer. As he waited, he began to feel silly, then nervous. Was he trying too hard? Would Kedzie notice at once that he had done his hair for her? That he had actually ironed the shirt he was wearing? That he smelled a little too perfect? And what would she say to Sarah? "Uh, your boyfriend said he just wanted to hang out, but then looked like he was expecting something more..." Yikes. Maybe he could come up with some excuse for looking so awesome, like having dinner with his mom earlier or something. Ugh, no that's awful. A meeting with potential investors? Better.

And then she walked in, and Sam heard the entire bar's sharp intake of breath.

He had seen Kedzie look amazing before, particularly on nights she went clubbing with Sarah and their mutual girlfriends. But this was different. Tonight she was looking amazing *for him*. And she was showing off. Clingy, low-cut little black dress revealing all the right places, hair teased in a professional-yet-slutty way that suggested a recent romp on a conference table, and lips so full, shiny and sparkling he was somehow certain they would taste like strawberries. As she flashed an excited smile and slinked over to his table, Sam knew every man in the place was thinking "that guy is one lucky motherfucker." And they were right.

Over the next three hours of drinks and flirty conversation, Sam felt like he was in another universe, a place where everything he said was witty, where he could do no wrong, and where all his stated dreams and aspirations were already assured. This beautiful creature before him knew it, too. He deserved a great life. He deserved *her*. Even if they were just roleplaying, even if this fantasy talk would end the moment he walked her through the parking lot to her car, Sam was determined to enjoy every second of it.

Only he didn't walk her to her car. He walked her to his.

There was no discussion. Neither of them even acknowledged that Kedzie's own vehicle was being ignored. Sam simply walked with her to the passenger side of the Mustang, pressed his body into hers as he opened the door for her, helped her inside, and knew the rest of the night was set in stone the instant the car door closed. She was in his possession now, and there was no going back. Only forward. Very forward.

The deep bucket seat had hiked Kedzie's dress halfway up her thighs, but she made no effort to reclaim modesty. Sam didn't say a word as his free hand caressed her beautiful bare legs as they drove, and Kedzie offered no resistance as he tested how far his fingers could explore. By the time they arrived at his apartment, she was trembling, breathing heavily, and as full of raw desire as Sam had ever seen in a woman. They barely made it through his front door before they were clawing at each other, tearing clothing apart, fucking against the wall, on the counter, over the back of a couch, anywhere and everywhere. Not sex born from love, or even desire, but need.

The next morning, there were no awkward moments. No talk of regret. No assurances that it was just a "one time thing" or to keep it secret. All that was understood. Sam drove Kedzie back to the martini bar parking lot, walked her to her car in the crisp morning air, kissed her cheek with genuine tenderness, and returned home to clean up. He straightened the furniture. He returned knocked-over items to their proper positions. He changed the sheets, though the bed was the one place the two hadn't had sex. Methodically, he restored his surroundings to normal.

When he was done, Sam sat down and thought about what last night had meant, and how it might affect his relationship with Sarah. He knew he had to decide whether he could live with himself given what he had done, and after replaying some of the most incredible moments of the previous evening in his mind, Sam decided that he could. He reasoned that last night had been a lose-lose situation, for although it was possible he'd regret it the rest of his life, if he hadn't slept with Kedzie the one time he had the chance, he might have regretted *that* for the rest of his life instead. And, don't they always say a man on his deathbed will regret the things he didn't do more than the things he did? Sam was pretty sure that's what they said.

That night was the first time Sam had seen Kedzie naked. This was the second.

Her body lay broken before them, sprawled across a staircase as if caught in free fall, skirt hiked up to her waist and her shirt missing, mouth agape, eyes wide and staring blankly up at absolutely nothing. Sarah screamed, and Janet once again buried her head in Al's arms, but Sam couldn't look away. The shock was too much. There was nothing that could explain this. Nothing could rationalize this. There was no way this was happening. And yet, there she was.

"We have to get out of here," Sam choked. No one moved. Kedzie's body was blocking the steps. But, Sam knew the steps wouldn't go high enough anyway.

Beside him, Sarah passed out. Janet half-caught her on the way down, preventing her head from hitting the landing.

"We need to get her to a hospital," said Janet.

"The elevators are still down, I think," replied Sam. "And the stairs don't make it all the way."

"Let's get her some water," offered Al. "Quick, let's get her down to the baths."

"Are you crazy?" cried Janet. "We have to get her up, not down!"

"Vaughn left a first aid kit down there," Al said. "Let's get her gauzed and alcoholed and woken up, and we can try to fix the elevator."

"What about her?" asked Janet, motioning to Kedzie's body without looking at her.

"One thing at a time," insisted Al.

Sam snapped out of his trance and nodded his head. "Al's right. Hurry."

Al helped Sam lift Sarah over his shoulder, only to find he wasn't strong enough to carry her himself. The two quickly shared the duties, Al holding Sarah's legs and Sam the arms as they progressed back to the fifth floor. Sarah let out a moan while they were carrying her, which was encouraging, and in no time they were removing her blood-soaked shirt and cleaning Sarah's wound. Al produced a flask from a pants pocket, took a huge swig, and offered the rest to Janet, who initially declined, until she realized he was offering it as antiseptic, not a beverage. She took the alcohol, went through the first aid kit and did what she could with the mangled breast, an injury which was beginning to clot, before applying several layers of gauze to the area and wrapping tape around her chest and back. Sam removed his button-down shirt, and threaded Sarah's arms through the fabric and buttoned her up. He now felt a touch cold in only a white cotton undershirt, but he realized the shivering could have been caused by the panic of it all.

Sarah began to come to, and Janet gripped her hand to offer support. When her eyes opened and she realized where she was, she sat up in an instant.

"We're still...why didn't you get me out of here," she demanded.

"We're trying," assured Sam. Indeed, Al had pressed the elevator button several times on this level without success. "The stairs don't make it far enough."

"Are you sure?" she demanded.

"I am," came a voice entering from the stairwell door. It was Vaughn.

Sam was glad to see his friend, but Sarah's reaction was blistering. "Where the fuck have you been?"

Vaughn stammered. "I was...I was just..." He started walking towards his friends, but Sarah shouted at him to stay put.

"Sarah, what the hell?" insisted Sam.

"He let this happen to me," Sarah spat. "He stood right by and let that magnet thing slice me open. He didn't lift a fucking finger as I screamed for help."

Sam looked back to Vaughn, his fierce eyes demanding answers.

"That's not true," protested Vaughn. "I don't know what

she's talking about. The second the power was back on, I raced to the stairwell to find you, Sam, but you had run up instead, so I ran up too. But I couldn't find what floor you were on so I kept running. Which is…where I found Kedzie." He took a breath. "Sam, Kedzie's dead."

"I know that," Sam snapped. "We just came from there, so where the fuck were you?"

"I kept going," said Vaughn. "To get out, to get help. But the stairs just stop. There's no way out there. I tried. So I came back down and found you." He walked a few steps toward Sarah. "I'm so sorry. I had no idea…"

Sarah wasn't convinced. "Vaughn, stay the fuck back. You hear me? Back."

Vaughn froze.

Sam turned to his girlfriend, eyes pleading. "Sarah…it's Vaughn."

"Yeah, and he's the only one who wasn't with us when Kedzie was killed so I don't want any fucking excuses. Tell him to stay away!"

Vaughn looked confused and hurt. He sulked back to a corner of the room and slunk to the floor beside one of the baths.

"Sarah," whispered Sam. "You can't be accusing Vaughn of…"

"Of what?" she interrupted. "We're the only ones down here. What do you think happened? Kedzie decided to take her clothes off and tripped?"

"Damnit, Sarah, Vaughn is my best friend…"

"Yeah?" said Sarah. "Well Kedzie's mine. *Was* mine. So fuck you!"

Sam looked so instantly, deeply wounded, that Sarah wished she could have taken it back. He stood up and walked to another empty corner of the room, standing still for a long moment. He couldn't believe that Sarah had accused Vaughn of such violence. But he also couldn't believe Kedzie was dead, and no explanation, not even Sarah's insinuation, made any sense.

The silence was broken by Al.

"Guys, it looks like the elevator is stuck on one of the upper floors." He had pushed the protective cage open and was using Janet's Realtor penlight to peer up the dark shaft. "If we go up, and fix it, we can get out."

Janet, who was still kneeling beside Sarah, took Sarah's hand in her own.

"Dear, can you walk?"

Sarah stiffened but made it to her feet.

"Yeah," she said, as soon as she knew for sure. She was still weak, but determined to leave this place at any cost. "Let's go."

"Well, hang on," said Al. "If Vaughn didn't kill Kedzie, who did?"

"Al," said Sam impatiently, "we just have to get out of this place."

"But that's what I mean," Al explained. "Kedzie tried, right? And didn't make it. So if it wasn't Vaughn, and it wasn't some freak accident, then there's someone else in the hotel."

They all had been thinking it, each on some level, but everyone froze when it was said aloud. Sam, Sarah, Janet, and Vaughn all looked around at one another, for confirmation that their own fears weren't unique.

"So?" said Sam to break the silence.

"So," explained Al, "we should go back down to the lobby and get the gun."

Sam turned to look at Sarah. He was expecting her to say something like "no fucking way" or "that would only make things worse." But she surprised him by nodding emphatically, saying "let's go," and charging down the stairs ahead of them. Sam never gave her enough credit for complexity, he realized for the hundredth time. He also recognized that he had been hoping she *hadn't* been receptive to the gun idea, as he really was terrified of such weapons, and would rather have opposed the move using the excuse of a peace-loving girlfriend, rather than reveal his own insecurities. Sam also hated admitting to himself how much he admired Sarah at times like this, where she was the strong one, more likely to protect him than the other way around.

The group walked down the stairs more or less together, with Sarah in the lead and Vaughn at the rear. The further they descended, the heavier the atmosphere felt, until it was almost suffocating, and Sam realized he was walking slower. Janet, too, seemed to be slowing down, and it wasn't until she turned to face Sam did he notice she was crying.

"Janet?"

"I have to get out of here, Sam," she responded in a whisper.

"I know," he replied. "We all do. And we will."

"I mean it. I can't do this. That girl's dead. Why are we going down. We need to be going up. We can't..." Janet's voice trailed off. They had arrived at the final landing, and Sarah was opening the door to the lobby.

"It will be okay."

"Why can't Al and I work on fixing the elevator," pleaded Janet. "You can meet us back with the gun."

Sam shook his head. "We're not splitting up again. Are you kidding?"

The lobby seemed to have lost some of its former luster. It was still beautiful, but somehow darker, less impressive, and much less inviting. Sarah walked straight to the back office, where Sam had seen the mouse, and returned holding the revolver and a box of cartridges.

"Load it," she ordered Al.

Al took the weapon from her and did as she was told. He placed a bullet in each chamber, six in all, and offered the loaded gun back to Sarah.

"Test it," she commanded.

Al stiffened. "I don't…"

"Fire the fucking thing."

No one said a word. Al shot Sarah a puzzled, pleading expression, but it was returned with a cool stare. He felt the weight of the weapon in his hand, shifted his body from side to side, and resigned himself to the logic of her request. With care, Al raised and aimed the pistol at the ground a dozen feet in front of the group, took a deep breath, and fired.

In the silent space, the report was louder than anyone had anticipated. Al was so shocked he dropped the gun, which fell and clanged on the tile. Janet screamed. Even Sarah seemed jolted from her determined demeanor and clutched Sam's right arm for support. It was several seconds before Al could steel his nerves enough to bend down and retrieve the gun, which now seemed heavier than moments earlier. He turned to Sarah and raised an eyebrow.

"Replace the empty shell," she said, admitting a slight crack in her voice, unable to maintain the same degree of unquestioned authority she had held before. Still, Al did as he was told, surprised by the heat of the gun chamber this time, restoring the gun to its full complement of six rounds.

No one said anything for several seconds. The only sounds in the room were from Janet, who seemed to be trying to stifle a whimper.

"Okay," said Al at last. "Now what?"

Sam opened his mouth to speak, but realized Al had directed his question to Sarah, not to him. Despite the hotel being Sam's, Sarah seemed to have taken charge, and all eyes were upon her.

Sam was reminded of their third date, when he had planned what he thought to be a fun evening of live music at a coffee shop followed by a bit of bar-hopping, ending up at a club where he could impress her by knowing the DJ, expecting Sarah to be dazzled by his preparation and connection to someone as cool as Vaughn. Truthfully, "planned" was a pretty strong word for his idea, but he felt he could pull off the cocky confidence necessary to make it seem like it took a degree of effort and coordination, something he presumed most men to lack. Besides, he reasoned, it was the mythical "third date," where the chance of a first-time sexual encounter was heightened. But when he had picked Sarah up from her apartment and explained his plan, she had dismissed the whole thing as something they could do anytime, and instead suggested (or, rather, informed him of) the different direction the evening would take. At first, Sam had been a bit taken aback at what he perceived as rudeness, and told her so, albeit in a way that hinted he was kidding should she have taken offense. But Sarah argued, quite effectively he had to admit, that the rudeness was with Sam for assuming that he would always get to decide what they did on any particular evening, considering he had controlled the first two dates. Sam relented, offered a mea culpa for his caveman ways, and admitted he was intrigued by the idea of not being in charge for a change. She flashed him a triumphant smile that was just about the sexiest thing Sam had ever seen, grabbed his hand, and said "let's go."

He began to regret his decision to let her run things when she informed him of two other guys they were picking up. Sensing his annoyance, Sarah assured him that it was still a date, and they were only giving them a ride there, not back. Sam still hadn't been told where "there" was, but he agreed, and followed Sarah's directions to a duplex on the other side of town. The two guys hopped in the back, and barely introduced themselves before breaking out a small sheet of what Sam thought were stickers. Before Sam could comment, they each placed a small strip of paper in their mouths, leading Sam to belatedly realize that it must have been LSD. Sam had never seen acid in person and had no experience with it at all, and was somewhat relieved when Sarah declined to partake. He wondered at the time if she had sensed his uneasiness and was staying clean for his sake, but later discovered that she, like him, had no interest in it. As they drove on, seemingly to the middle of nowhere, following Sarah's directions from a handwritten sheet of paper, Sam decided it was okay to lose control a bit. If Sarah wanted to run this night, he'd just have to sit back and let her. After all, he didn't think he was being used, or taken advantage of, or lied to. Rather, he just felt led.

Sarah directed him off the main roads, through small side streets, and onto a dirt road Sam wasn't sure was a road at all. The night had smothered the last of the ambient blue, and they seemed to be driving deeper and deeper into a forest. Sam's mind began to offer protest. Where were they headed? A cabin? A tent? A place of demonic sacrifice? But he tried to play it cool, like it was the most normal thing in the world for a third date to involve acid-tripping strangers and a car trip to nowhere. He didn't believe Sarah was setting him up. He just couldn't wrap his head around how different the night was progressing from his original plan. And if there was a bit of fear and anxiety mixed in with his curiosity, it only made the night feel more exhilarating. He loved not knowing what was going to happen next.

They arrived at a clearing, where more than a dozen other vehicles, all unoccupied, were parked. Sarah reached over to squeeze Sam's right thigh, assuring him "you are going to love this." They exited the vehicle and Sarah pointed to a barely visible walking trail entering another section of woods. Prepared for the darkness, Sarah retrieved a small flashlight from her purse and led the way. The four walked together through the dark trail for what seemed like ten minutes before Sam heard the faint sound of distant drums. *Holy shit,* he thought. *It* is *a demonic sacrifice!* But Sarah grabbed his hand, reassuring but playful, and increased their pace. A minute later, Sam could smell smoke, and the drums got louder, and it at last dawned on Sam what Sarah had gotten them into.

"A *drum circle?*" Sam asked, incredulous.

Sarah beamed. "I told you you would love it."

Sam was transported back to their very first conversation, at the party where they had met. He had been trying to impress her by name-dropping the neo-paganist quasi-religion of Wicca as they talked, even though he knew nothing about Wiccans and was gambling that this darkly hot girl, with her goth hair and body piercings, would at least feel that Sam must not be as square as he looked. When she had asked if he was a Wiccan himself, Sam laughed and replied "no, I couldn't be satisfied with a life of playing bongos around a bonfire all night—I want to make something of myself!" When she had dryly responded by detailing her Master's studies, and describing a more impressive future life plan than Sam had ever considered for himself, he was sure he had blown it. But they continued to talk all night, found they had quite a bit in common after all, and he had gotten her number. And now, Sarah was getting her revenge, commandeering their third date to play bongos and sit around a bonfire.

The crowd was about forty in all, ranging from pentagram-wearing pagan girls celebrating something called the "Sabbat" to grey-haired hippies with their own didgeridoos. A few, like the guys Sam and Sarah had picked up, seemed only interested in getting high and watching the fire, while others took the opportunity to dance for hours without a break. It was not, to say the least, Sam's "scene," but it wasn't Sarah's, either. She was able to introduce him to a few friends, and they even took a turn at some primitive instruments together, but as relative outsiders, they shared a winking bond. They sat by the fire, leaning into one another, Sam's arm around her, both feeling profoundly comfortable and at home.

At around four in the morning, as the fire had gone down and some in the crowd had begun to pack up their things, Sarah had kissed Sam's neck and asked him to take her home. They had gone back to her place, where they had helped each other undress, and taken a shower together to wash away the smells of sweat and smoke. It was the first time they had seen each other naked, and the fact that it wasn't in an act of sex, but of cleanliness, made it all the more intimate. With the tenderness of long-time lovers, they touched each other under the water, washed each other, and dried each other, before heading naked, holding hands all the way, to Sarah's bed. They curled into each other, kissed twice, and closed their eyes, and as the sun began to rise, both drifted off together in the blissful weight of extreme exhaustion. And only the following afternoon when they awoke, entangled in each other's bodies, did they have sex for the first time, followed by the second, and third, and fourth times, never leaving each other for a moment for the entire weekend, dressing only for the pizza delivery man.

Sam nodded at Sarah across the lobby of The Eaton. If she was willing to lead, he would follow.

Al was still waiting. Sarah winced in pain, her breast

throbbing, then smiled grimly.

"Now," she answered, "we get the hell out of here."

fifteen

There was momentary disagreement as to the exit strategy. Sam preferred checking floor by floor to see where the elevator had gotten stuck, since he believed the stairs could only take them so far. Sarah reasoned that they should take the stairs as far as possible, reasoning that they must exit somewhere, and she no longer trusted the power to remain reliable. When Sam reminded Sarah that such a strategy meant having to encounter Kedzie again, Sarah responded that she had no intention of leaving her body in here a moment longer than necessary, and they would have to carry her out. This made Janet anxious, and she tried to argue that they shouldn't touch the body until the police arrive, but Sarah was adamant. "But, *you're* not touching her," she snapped at Vaughn. "Just in case."

As they approached the stairwell, Sam caught Al sneaking a shot from his flask. Based on the angle of the swallow, Sam guessed it was the last sip. It made him nervous that the one responsible for the gun had not chosen to stay sober, but decided not to bring it up. After all, Al was the only one among them with any experience handling a weapon, and a buzzed shot from an expert trumped a sober shot from a scared amateur. But Al was acting a bit funny as well. He said nothing as they trudged up each set of stairs, and seemed almost as uneasy as Janet, who was now consistently trembling, expecting evil around every corner.

They were almost to the turn that would reveal Kedzie's body, and Sam squeezed Sarah's hand, helping to brace them both for the impact. But when the corner came, the shock of the empty stairs trumped any horror they had expected.

"What the hell?" Sarah stepped back, checked the floor number on the wall, then sprinted up several stairs to turn another corner, again seeing nothing.

"She was right here!" insisted Sam, to no one in particular. They all knew her body had been there, and now it was gone.

"Maybe she wasn't dead," offered a hopeful Al.

"There's no way that's true," said Sam, shaking his head. "She was dead. We all saw that. Someone moved her."

"Who the hell could have moved her?" demanded Janet, who was getting close to unhinged. "There's no one fucking here."

"Logic would argue otherwise," Al deadpanned.

Sarah was still standing a few stairs above the rest of the group. "Come on," she urged. "We have to get out."

There was no argument. The group sped up the stairs, only to confirm Sam's theory that the stairs did not go all the way to the surface. They stopped at 11.

"The Mastersuite," Al remembered.

Sam tried the door, which was of a higher quality wood than the doors to previous hallways, but it wouldn't open. "It's locked from the inside," he explained, motioning to Janet. She understood and fumbled through her purse to retrieve the key ring. Sam took it from her and found the proper key, which turned freely in the lock mechanism, but the door could not be budged.

"Is it stuck?" asked Sarah. Sam shook his head. The door wasn't stuck, for it seemed to give a fraction of an inch or so as he pushed his body against the wood. It seemed instead as if the door was blocked by something on the other side, perhaps a large piece of furniture.

"I think," Al opined, "that this door doesn't open into a hallway like the others, but directly into the Mastersuite itself. Like a top floor penthouse, the entire level might be one beautiful rentable space, no hallway required."

"So what," remarked Sarah. "We should still be able to get into the back door."

"Not if some idiot decorator put a 400 lb. armoire in front of it," scoffed Al.

"Well we have to try," Sam argued, and there were nods of approval as he used all his weight against the stubborn door. Still nothing. Vaughn and Al then tried together, but even the two of them ramming their bodies against the wood only moved the door an imperceptible distance.

The aggressive physicality of the act did succeed in jarring Al into feeling some effects of the recent alcohol. A seasoned drinker, the amount in the now-empty flask hadn't been enough to cause any real impairment, but his vision had been affected, for when he had been inches away from Vaughn as they rammed the door together, Vaughn's skin had appeared to flutter and grow darker, almost rippling like a puddle of ink in front of his face. Al had stepped back from Vaughn and blinked a few times to reset his eyes, and saw nothing unusual, except a tall black man shooting him a quizzical expression.

"Y'alright there?" Vaughn asked.

"Yeah, sorry," Al stammered, shaking his head. "Just got a little spacey there for a second."

"Scared to be that close to a black guy, eh?" Vaughn laughed and patted Al's shoulder. "Come on, man. This is Eaton Rapids, not Detroit."

Al laughed awkwardly, as did Sam, who remembered Vaughn using that exact same line once before at a Fourth of July event at Island Park.

"We need to try the floor below," said Sarah.

Janet stiffened at this. "We need to go *up*. We need to get *out*."

Sarah threw up her hands, then wished she hadn't, for it stretched the bloody skin on her breast and sent a searing pain through the left half of her body. "What do you want us to do, Janet? We're as high as the stairs go, and this door's blocked. I say we try the next door that might actually lead somewhere, if that's okay with you."

Janet let out a choked sob, then turned toward a corner and said nothing.

"There has to be a way to the surface," Sam assured her. "Either we find the elevator and take it up, or we find some other stairs. There have to be stairs leading out of this place, not only for if there was a power or safety issue, but because the elevator itself had to be built by someone, right? How would the builders have gotten up and down without stairs? They're here and we'll find them. Or the elevator. Either way, we're getting out and we're getting help. I promise."

Janet shut her eyes tight for a moment, then nodded. "Alright."

"The next floor down," observed Al, "is Transit. Seems as good a place as any for an exit." He did not remind her that the lobby sign had said Transit was "coming soon."

Janet nodded again, and the group walked down a level, grateful for gravity's aid in their descent, after a rough eleven flights up.

Sarah arrived at the door first, opened it without hesitation, and walked onto what must have been an ancient subway platform.

"Holy crap," she said.

Like the first floor lobby and the fifth floor baths, the tenth floor transit level had higher ceilings and boasted a more ornate design aesthetic, with richer woods, tiles, and extra touches throughout. Arched brickwork over the doorways conveyed the grandeur of a big city train depot. Easy chairs and Victorian benches lined a cobblestone strip which resembled an old European city street. The electric lamps were encased in glorious iron chandeliers, hung high against a dark blue ceiling which suggested a night sky, masking any immediate confirmation of being underground. It was like stepping back in time, but to a time that only existed in the fantasies of steampunk graphic novelists and fanciful film directors.

For all its majesty, however, it was unfinished. Large portions of the back wall were incomplete, with piles of bricks and bags of concrete waiting in a corner. There was a steel train car, with small, narrow windows, but no markings. Before it lay a tunnel, which seemed to penetrate further horizontally than any floor they had seen so far, filled with scaffolding, tarps, and even a few abandoned workmen helmets. A booth labeled "Tickets" was completely empty, lacking even a single chair, counter, or cabinet.

Beside the unfinished subway tunnel, in its expected position, was the elevator shaft, though a quick look through the cage showed no elevator car. Sam tried the call button just in case, but nothing stirred. He turned his attention to the tunnel instead, hopping down to the track to inspect the tight space, then looked back to Al. "Could this train even fit through that tunnel?"

"It had to be tight," answered Al. "I think it's pneumatic."

"Like the bank teller tubes we saw down in Maintenance?"

"Yeah, I think so. Look at the train car. There's no engine. It's passive. It would need to be sucked through the tunnel or pushed out."

Sam peered into the tunnel. It went at least another fifty feet, but got darker as the lighting receded, which made an accurate estimate impossible.

"Hey Vaughn," he called back from the entrance of the tunnel. "You still have the DJ lights?"

Vaughn gave Sam a look that said *do you see them in my hands?* Sam did not. He realized they must be several floors below.

"They had to have some work lights," called Al, helpfully.

Sam looked around, and spotted two trapezoidal contraptions plugged into long cords traveling many yards behind him. He found the on switches, and soon the tunnel was flooded with light. It went on for the length of a football field, much farther than the footprint of the train station or its parking lot, but did seem to stop at some point, although it was hard to see clearly from this distance. Sam began to walk further into the tunnel, but heard protests from Sarah back on the platform.

"We have to go forward," argued Sam.

"No, we have to get out of here," Sarah countered.

"That's what I'm trying to do. The stairs stop and the elevator's inoperative. This tunnel has to go somewhere. There might be ladders up to old manhole covers, or maybe even into another building's basement."

Sarah hesitated, but agreed with his logic and stepped down to join him. Respecting her leadership, Al and Janet followed, but Vaughn stayed put on the platform, close to the door. "Someone should stay here, just in case," he said. He didn't say in case of what.

"Alright," Sam agreed. "We'll shout back to you if we find an exit."

"Just don't take off again," demanded Sarah.

The four slowly made their way into the tunnel. When they were twenty yards in, Sam observed two more flood lamps, which he turned on to illuminate the deeper passage. The soft electrical hum of the lamps made Sam uneasy, and he looked back behind him to see the train lobby and train car. Given the necessity of a tight space to make the pneumatic system function, there was no margin for error that could fit, say, a person stuck on the track. If the pneumatic system was activated, and the train car decided to move forward, there was nowhere to escape. Janet must have been thinking the same thing, for her pace slowed, as if considering making a run for it in reverse. But soon they had reached an unfinished portion of the tunnel, without the tight arched brickwork encasing them, exposing rough wood beams and the clay of the earth. A few yards further, the cave widened a bit, and the tension eased.

There hadn't yet been any evidence of an exit, but there was something peculiar. Before them, the cave narrowed considerably, revealing an entrance to a smaller, natural tunnel lined in hard stone and clay. Another flood lamp was pointed toward this tunnel, and so Sam flipped it on to see what the builders of The Eaton had been looking at. At first, Sam saw nothing unusual, but as his eyes adjusted, there was indeed something special about this underground passage. The natural stone walls had dozens of detailed carvings which looked to Sam like the primitive drawings on Egyptian tombs. On the ground beneath the pictures were pieces of paper and a few primitive-looking pencils, as if a school group had been making impressions of the carvings and taking notes on them.

Sarah and Sam exchanged a confused look.

"Hieroglyphics?" Sam pondered aloud.

"Close," answered Al. "They're petroglyphs. Native American. They're a lot more common in the Southwest, where it's drier so the preservation is better. But they're not unheard of in the Midwest. Sanilac Park's just up in the thumb, and their carvings were famous even when I was a kid."

"We took a school trip there once," Sarah recalled. "There were birds and swirls and doodles, right? I remember thinking I was a better artist than they were."

"To be fair," said Al with a smirk, "those artists had to etch their doodles into sandstone, using sharp tools and incredible patience. They didn't have a 64-pack of brightly colored crayons."

Sam peered over the carved symbols. "Will we be able to translate it?"

"It's not like that," replied Al. "It isn't like hieroglyphics. Petroglyphs are just pictures, not language. Whatever they depict, that's all there is."

What the carvings were trying to convey wasn't clear, but the story did not seem a happy one. Nearest the entrance to the discovered tunnel were crude stick figure drawings of people lying on the ground, and deeper into the cave revealed figures running with their hands up in the air. It seemed to Sam that these images were meant to denote the passage of time as you traveled out from the cave, not inward, and so the people had been running in panic, then ended up dead. As one ventured further into the narrow passageway, the images became less coherent, and several depicted beings in transition from one animal shape to another, such as a snake into a bird.

Near the end of the tunnel, the cave walls opened up somewhat, revealing a larger room containing a boulder nearly seven feet high and five feet across. The boulder itself had carvings on its surface that seemed to lack defined shapes at all, each one resembling a crude ink blot, with no two shapes alike. On the walls to the left and right of the boulder there were more carvings of animal transitions, only this time, the shape nearest the boulder was always an amorphous blob, while the shapes beside it seemed to evolve the blobs into figures of animals and people.

"Sam, look there, on the ground." Al pointed to white scrapes in the stone floor to the left of the boulder, which seemed to have been caused by the boulder being pushed or dragged several feet from its current position. As the floodlight angle and distance was no longer ideal this far in, it took a moment for Sam to realize that the boulder had once been sitting in front of yet another tunnel offshoot.

Sam removed his phone from his pocket, activated the flashlight app, and peered into the new passage. What the boulder had been blocking wasn't another hallway, but a small room, closed on all sides, maybe thirty square feet in all. A musky mushroom smell emanated from the space, and Sam thought the far side of the dank cell was wet. He peered closer, allowing his eyes to adjust, and realized there was a small, waist-high flow of water running along the rock wall, a sort of underground spring. It was scarcely more than a trickle, but it was there, and from the look of the erosion on the wall around it, it had been trickling that way for centuries. Other than that, the room was empty—not even a single wall carving. What, then, had the boulder been covering up?

Sam turned off the phone light and turned to face his friends in the room. "Nothing in there," he explained with a shrug. "It's not another tunnel, it's just a small room."

Sarah wasn't paying attention. Her fingers were caressing one of the carvings of a person who seemed to have emerged from another of the blob shapes. She wasn't sure what connection her mind was trying to make, and then, in an instant, she was. Sarah gasped, snatching her hand away from the carving as if it were hot to the touch, and shot a look of sheer terror in Sam's direction.

"Oh shit," she said. "Oh shit." She closed her eyes and began shaking her head emphatically, as if trying to scare off a swarm of insects.

Sam sprinted toward her and grasped her shoulders, then when she wouldn't respond he used a hand to lift her chin up to his, forcing her to look at him. "Sarah, what is it?" Her face was awkwardly illuminated by the floodlight from around the corner. It made her eyes appear sunken, and her features half-finished, as if he was looking merely at a mask of a person rather than the woman he loved.

Sarah tried to answer him, but no words came. Her mind was consumed by images of Kedzie's exposed midriff in The Eaton's laundry room, then again of her crumpled, naked body on the staircase, both pictures seared into her mind—then earlier, months earlier, in Kedzie's apartment, the night she revealed in private that she was pregnant, and how she had lifted up her shirt to show the Celtic tattoo she had just had inked around her navel days before, still healing, and her jokes about what a waste of money it had been since it would now get stretched out and destroyed as the baby grew inside her—and now, Sarah's absolute certainty that the tattoo had not been present, not a trace of it, at any point today.

She felt Sam's hands shaking her. He was concerned. He was expecting an answer. He kept saying her name. She had to respond.

"Sam…" she began.

Behind them, the floodlight switched off.

*

Ba-Ba-Thump. Ba-Ba-Ba-Thump.

Jon opened his eyes again, expecting something to have changed, anything, but nothing had. The damned woman was still screaming about her son.

"I hear him too!" someone shouted, insistent. It was Clem, who Jonathan had known for ten years. In fact, Jon had invited him along in the first place. Why was he getting involved in this dispute? What did he think he heard? God, that man was an asshole. They're all assholes. Maybe everyone was an asshole, himself included. But Clem, hell, he's their king.

"Let him in!" The old bat was panicked now. She tried to move the desk herself but it was far too heavy. Her whole body was shaking with the exertion, and the jewels on her multiple necklaces scraped against each other in a soft metallic sound Jon was shocked he could hear over the chaos.

"No, dammit, sit down," ordered one of the furniture movers. "You're sober and you know it!"

Jonathan couldn't help himself, and laughed aloud at this. In what other universe would such a statement make any sense at all? He wished he had his journal to record that one. Alas, it was still in his own room, on the end table with the ink pens, drowning in the dark shadow of the swaying, hanging body of his wife.

How many others were trapped here, Jon wondered. He glanced around, remembering to move his head slower than the last time. Between the living and the dead, he counted fourteen. Were they the last? He remembered thinking how large and luxurious this room had seemed to him at first. Now it was small and dark like a tomb, overwhelmed with the musty stink of sweat and death, bodies huddled and trembling in its corners. The single electric light above seemed to glow weaker by the minute. Perhaps the generators were failing. Or, perhaps he was passing out.

"But I hear him also! It's his voice, I know it!" Jon didn't know this new speaker, but saw him stand up to side with Clem and the old woman. "Just listen, damn you!"

The men listened. Jon listened, too. He heard the deep knocking, but nothing else. He thought maybe he should say something, adding his own drunken insight, but decided against it. After all, what was the point? They would be fooled again soon enough.

"Well I don't hear it," snapped one of the movers. Jon recognized him as Alroy A. Wilbur, a noted furniture salesman and undertaker up in Lansing. He had given a rather pompous toast in the dining room their first night, and Jon hadn't had the desire or occasion to talk to him since. He had been Lansing's mayor years ago, and now it seemed he wanted to be in charge again. So be it. "Step back," Alroy barked.

Something seemed to snap in the old woman's mind. Her face distorted into a parody of rage, like a child's drawing of a monster from a bad dream. She flung herself violently into the desk, pushing it away from the door with a force that at first startled Alroy into complete inaction. After a quick beat, he recovered, and with another man's help, he stopped the desk from advancing further, while shouting at the woman and the man who had taken up her cause.

The knocking grew louder, more insistent, more dire. It rattled the desk, even with multiple hands upon it. Alroy reached into his coat and withdrew a Browning pistol, leveling it at the woman with a trembling hand. "I told you to *step back*," he affirmed, a break in his voice sapping some of what would have been a commanding presence. But Alroy could tell it was falling apart. All of it. Even if the woman was stopped, the desk would not hold.

With a banshee wail of desperation, the woman lunged at Alroy, gnashing her teeth as if to bite him on the face. Her supporter grabbed at her body to pull her back, but was too late. Alroy's pistol went off, exploding the woman's skull just a foot in front of his hand. The sound in the enclosed space was as deafening as a cannon, and both the pounding in Jonathan's head and at the door were replaced by a pure, high-pitched ring of bliss. Jon smiled at the mercy of it, even as he saw what must have been the woman's brains splattered against the artwork hanging on the far wall, and as he saw Clem and another man attack Alroy, wrestling him for the gun, seeing (but not hearing) it go off again, and then a third time, the new bullet hitting the chandelier in the center of the room, plunging them all into complete and utter darkness.

As his ears attempted to make up for the uselessness of his eyes, Jonathan became aware of people screaming all around, crawling over his legs, running futilely back and forth, the chaos of the situation unbearable to everyone but him. He knew there was an epic battle underway for the door, perhaps over whether to let someone out or let someone in. He knew it didn't matter. With several recursive layers of hangover and crippling intoxication, Jon would have thought he could have accepted reality and resigned himself to his fate, but instead his tension increased. It wasn't logic, but the survival instincts and adrenaline of an animal that compelled him to go on. He tried to summon the strength to stand, but a spasm of pain shot up his leg, and Jon realized he been injured by some debris from the gunshot—glass from the chandelier, perhaps, or a piece of shaved iron. So he slumped back, and heard the pounding once more, both in his head and from the other side of the door, now more in unison than before, and faster, too, working up to a frenzied climax. He wondered which would give out first, the door or his heart.

It was the door. As his ears registered more and more screaming, as he could taste the tang of gunpowder on his lips, as the rancid smell of vomit began to mix with the metallic scent of blood, and as he could feel his own blood pooling in his lap and onto his fists, Jonathan Wesley saw a crack form in the unprotected half of the door. In the absolute blackness, the jagged sliver of hallway light appeared to be drawn into thin air, like a bolt of lightning crackling in the sky but refusing to fade away. Another loud thump, and the crack got bigger, and the slivers multiplied, and the wood seemed to melt away. And Jon laughed, drunk and delirious in the panic of it all, terrified at his upcoming fate but finding comfort in its inevitability, choosing to see the cracks of light as angels, even after he saw the light extinguished by pure, oozing blackness, and Jon's hands finally relaxed, as he at last heard the screaming and the pounding stop forever.

sixteen

It was just two weeks earlier when Jon had received the mysterious letter. On exquisite paper and scripted in an elegant hand, it had been addressed to "Jonathan Wesley, esq." Along the reverse seal of the envelope had been printed the word "CONFIDENTIAL" in large block letters, so even his wife Niamh hadn't opened it. When he read the letter the first time, his impression had been that it was an elaborate prank. The idea that someone was a month away from opening a twelve story underground hotel somewhere in Eaton Rapids was preposterous, for surely no construction of that magnitude could have been kept secret long enough to have built it. But the builders of the hotel seemed to have made an interesting discovery, a series of ancient stone carvings, and Jon was the only person in the area qualified to assess them. The letter even contained a paper rubbing of one of the carvings in question, to make it clear that the builders were sincere, and their trust in him unquestioned. It had been signed "The Eaton."

In just ten days, The Eaton was to have a soft launch for twenty or so invited guests of substantial repute, to join the builders and owners in an introductory celebration of their success. Even some of the laborers had been granted free rooms for the weekend in exchange for their continued discretion. It appeared that Jonathan was perhaps the only outsider, other than the high-class first guests, who knew anything about the hotel at all. The letter stressed the absolute need for secrecy, but made an interesting proposition to Jon and his wife. If they were free during the weekend in question, The Eaton would spring for a beautiful suite with all expenses paid, in exchange for his examination and opinions of their underground discovery. If he liked, he could even bring an assistant, who would also be given free lodging, though with regret they had reserved the last full suite for Jon, and an assistant would stay in a basic room. Given the time frame, they requested a written acceptance or rejection of the offer within the next one or two days, to allow them to make alternate arrangements to attract an archeologist "of similar skill."

Once Jon had decided it was, in fact, a genuine request, he told his wife, and she agreed with his decision to say "yes." The acceptance letter was placed in the post the next morning, and Jon was confident The Eaton would receive it promptly, given Eaton Rapids' close proximity to their Lansing address.

That afternoon, Jon made his way to their local library, near the State Capitol building, to start comparing the rubbing with known American Indian pictographs and petroglyphs. The rubbing had been a tease, for the letter had boasted that these three shapes represented but the smallest taste of the full carvings. By the time the library closed for the day, Jon felt confident they were authentic, at least 500 years old, and might represent the most significant find of its type over a region of several states.

The next day, he purchased a new blank journal, as was his pattern before any such adventure. He dated and began the first entry with a description of the mysterious letter, a brief summary of his research findings so far, and a note expressing his wife's excitement for the weekend away.

"We needed this, Jonathan. It's a sign from God." Niamh held one of his hands in hers, and closed her eyes in silent prayer. It was true, they did need it. When Niamh had been unable to conceive after many years of trying, she had fallen into a depression which itself had done more damage to their marriage than absent children. Jon's work took him away for weeks or months at a time, and it wasn't often that she was permitted to join him. Even during his time at home, he was distant, preoccupied, and seemingly uninterested in her. This made her even more depressed, which made her more silent, which made her even less interesting to her husband.

"It will be grand," Jon agreed, reaching up to caress her fair skin with the fingers of his right hand. A soft red curl fell across a freckled cheek, and he tenderly brushed it back into place. She blushed. Jon couldn't remember the last time his touch had affected her so. An adventure might be just the thing to remind them both of why they fell in love in the first place.

The following day, Jonathan had lunch with his occasional assistant Clem Bevans, telling him of the invitation and asking him to come along. He was glad to discover Clem also had no prior knowledge of the secret hotel, which reassured Jon that he wasn't out of the gossip loop. A young man, unmarried and without substantial hobbies or outside interests, Clem said he'd be delighted to come, as he quite literally had nothing else to do. Jon smiled at this, as it was precisely Clem's lack of any social obligations that made him such a dependable assistant, though in truth Jon would have respected the man more if he had shown an interest in building a life for himself. Jon had always supposed that some men become great, some try and fail, and others have no particular interest in greatness at all; Clem was clearly of this final type. Jon couldn't honestly say that he cared for Clem, but one didn't have to be friends with one's colleagues, and in fact, it was often preferable not to be.

On the Tuesday preceding the weekend, Jon and Niamh received printed train tickets in the post, including a third ticket for Clem, whose address Jon had not provided and the hotel staff did not know. Curiously, there was no accompanying itinerary or directions from the train station to the hotel. Just tickets. Under normal circumstances, Jon may have assumed there had been an oversight, and perhaps been concerned that they wouldn't know where to go. But as everything else about this event had been planned with such care, Jon figured that there must be a reason to maintain the secrecy of the hotel's exact location, and reasoned that transportation from the station to the hotel must have been arranged as well. "I'm sure they'll be sending a carriage," Niamh had said, and Jon agreed.

Clem met them at the Lansing depot Friday morning. He was dressed more casually than the occasion warranted, but didn't seem to notice when Niamh cast him a disapproving glance. The train was on time, and they were pleased at their good fortune of sitting next to a wealthy couple who was also attending The Eaton's opening night.

"Oh my," the wife had declared after revealing their shared destination. "I suppose I was supposed to keep that secret, wasn't I?"

"It's alright, madam," replied Jon. "I suspect that they won't be able to keep it a secret after this weekend. And why would they want to? The best publicity is free publicity. When we return home and describe our experiences, everyone will want to see what the fuss is about."

"Presuming it's as impressive as they've hinted," the woman teased. "Maybe it's secret because there won't be much to tell."

"I'm anticipating," Niamh interjected, "that they will have the finest mineral baths in the city."

Jon turned to his wife with curiosity. "Whyever do you say that? The invitation mentioned no such thing."

"Come now, Jonathan," she teased. "Why else would they bother to build the place underground?"

Jon thought about it, and realized she had a point. He had been so preoccupied with wondering why the Indian carvings had been underground that he hadn't taken the time to seriously consider why the hotel had desired to be underground as well. Access to Eaton Rapids' famed mineral springs was indeed a compelling reason.

"Niamh, my dear, I truthfully hadn't thought of that, and I believe you may be right."

She beamed. A compliment from Jon was rare enough, but one coupled with an admission of his own shortcomings was rather exceptional.

"*Neeve?*" inquired the woman across from them. "How do you spell that my dear?"

"My wife is Irish," Jon answered for her. "It's the traditional spelling of N-I-A-M-H. But you're correct that it's pronounced 'neeve.'"

The posh woman chuckled. "My, my. You'd think an immigrant to our nation would modernize the spelling so good English-speaking Christians would have a fair chance. Or are you Catholic, my dear?"

Niamh bristled. "I *am* Catholic, which also makes me a Christian."

"Of *course* it does," the woman replied, turning her attention to the window to end the conversation.

They exited the train at the small depot and, seeing no arranged transportation, entered the station and had a seat. Both the man and woman they had sat with were also looking around expectantly, finding nothing. After several moments, a young gentleman in a dark tail coat approached them.

"You're waiting for The Eaton," the man inquired by way of a statement.

"Yes, that's right," said Jon.

"We're just waiting for some of the other travelers to leave the station," he explained. "Then we'll close up and take you down." He smiled, gave a slight bow, and walked across the room to deliver the same message to several others.

Clem looked puzzled. "Take us down? Is The Eaton here?" He instinctively looked at the floorboards by his feet, as if he had the ability to see through solid wood.

"That can't be right," Jon replied. "This station's been here for decades. How could they have excavated twelve stories of dirt from a standing structure?"

"What if they came in from the side," offered Clem, miming the procedure with his hands. "Reinforced the foundation, then tunneled in from one side and kept digging down?" Jon was irritated that Clem had thought of this before he had.

"But why would they do that," Jon protested.

"To keep it secret," Niamh reminded them. "Besides, if I'm right about the springs, then they had to dig where the springs were. It couldn't have been just anywhere. And they couldn't very well tear down the village's only train depot in the process, now could they?"

Again, his smart, Irish Catholic wife had a point. Jon hoped the bigoted woman from earlier was listening.

As the station began to clear out, Jon counted those remaining. It seemed about thirty relatively well-dressed individuals were sitting with their luggage, looking around as he was, waiting for the next move by The Eaton's staff. At last, the final uninvited train passenger departed the station, and two staff members closed and locked the station doors. One of the men, whom Jon had spoken to earlier, cleared his throat and commanded the crowd's attention.

"Thank you all for your patience and patronage," he said. "My name is Oliver Stanton. I'm the hotel manager here, and am excited to formally welcome you to our inaugural weekend. As some of you have undoubtedly surmised, The Eaton is indeed an underground hotel, underneath this very station. It took four years of careful planning and secret construction to bring us to this point, and you will be the first to experience these new facilities. Indeed, you in this room are the only ones outside the builders and staff who even know of its existence. After a memorable stay with us, our hope is that you will share your excitement with your friends and families, and let them know of our grand opening in just four weeks' time."

"But who financed this project," a man interjected from a few seats over from Jon. "Who were the investors?"

Oliver smiled. "I am also *the* Oliver Stanton."

There were some excited utterances from the crowd, and a few murmurs of disbelief. Oliver Stanton was the name of a well-known but reclusive financier who had helped with several high-profile products in Eaton and Ingham counties, but who preferred to do business almost exclusively by mail. Few, if any, had ever met the man, and most would have assumed him to be a rich old millionaire, not a kid in his mid-thirties.

"Yet you said you're the hotel manager," someone protested.

"This is true," Oliver replied. "I am the owner and manager. This has been my dream since the single-room schoolhouse of my youth. Now, I see a few of you are looking concerned, such as you, Mr. Barclay." Oliver stepped closer to his acquaintance. "But I assure you that I am still committed to funding your mill, sir." He turned to his left, addressing an elderly woman traveling alone. "And you, Mrs. Miller. Your husband's restaurant will open on time and on budget." This seemed to ease some of the tension in the room, as the crowd began to accept that the man was indeed who he claimed to be.

Jonathan was about to speak up, to ask about the cave

carvings, but thought better of it. It was possible that Oliver and his staff had hoped he'd keep the matter secret, even from the other guests, as not to detract from the glory of the hotel itself. Still, he smiled at Oliver when he found his eyes upon him, and Oliver smiled and nodded back, acknowledging he knew who Jonathan was.

"Now," Oliver said with pride, "please gather your things and follow me."

The invited guests followed Oliver and another employee to a back office which had no apparent exits, staircase, or elevator of any kind. Oliver only allowed a few inside, as not to crowd the space, as he and the other gentleman walked toward opposite sides of a pattern in the floor. It was a large square surrounded by wooden inlays resembling lower case letter e's. Oliver directed a few of the guests to stand further back against the wall, "outside the square," and once they had complied, he directed his associate to kneel down beside him along one edge. They each removed a small metal cube from their pockets, pressed them together against one of the inlay panels, and the large square section of the floor shook and moved upward at an angle, along some sort of hinge. Several in the crowd gasped as the staircase became apparent, and Oliver and the other gentleman walked around to the front to be the first to descend. Cautiously, a few of the braver guests followed them, and soon more than half of the crowd was staring at the lit elevator in front of them.

"The elevator can take eight people at a time, plus luggage and the attendant," Oliver explained, motioning toward his silent assistant. "Matthew will take you down in groups to the main lobby, whereupon you will check in, receive your room keys, and have the opportunity to relax and freshen up. It's just after one o'clock at present, so feel free to explore the baths, the Gameroom, and the bar, all of which are open for your enjoyment this afternoon. At six o'clock sharp, we invite you all to join us in the ballroom for champagne and a four-course meal prepared by our executive chef. It is there we will be giving a brief presentation of how the hotel was constructed, more of what makes it unique, and where we expect to be in the future. If you have any questions, please seek me out, and feel free to address me as Oliver. Now, may I have the first volunteers to venture into The Eaton?"

There was a moment of brief, anxious mumbling, followed by a few affirmations and excited acceptances of Oliver's offer. Four couples joined Matthew in the electric elevator (which itself was exciting,) the gate was closed, and they shared nervous smiles with those on the other side as they began their descent. Jonathan, Niamh and Clem watched the first guests enter, but positioned themselves closer to the gate so that they could be in the next group. Oliver stepped forward to formally introduce himself to Jonathan, kissed Niamh's right hand in a chivalrous greeting, and gave a smart but courteous nod to Clem upon Jon's introduction of him.

"If you wouldn't mind, sir," began Oliver in a somewhat conspiratorial tone, "I wonder if you and your assistant could join me on the tenth floor after checking yourself in. I assure you that you'll have plenty of time to explore the hotel's amenities this weekend, but I would love to get your eyes on the artwork as soon as possible."

"That would be fine," replied Jonathan. "You do believe it is artwork, then? Not a message?"

Oliver was hesitant. "I actually am not certain of anything, which is why you are here. I can only hope it is artwork, I guess I'll say."

Before Jonathan could ask a follow-up question, the elevator returned, empty except for a smiling Matthew.

"You seem quite pleased with yourself," Oliver remarked with his own smile.

"The guests are impressed so far," replied Matthew. He did not add that one of the guests had given him a ten dollar tip, a value which exceeded the wages he was due to receive for the entire weekend's labor.

"Well, then." Oliver turned to the crowd. "Who's next?"

Jonathan and his wife held hands with excitement as the elevator gate closed and the descent began. Niamh smiled bravely at Jon, though she was masking a touch of nervousness as well. She could count the number of times she'd ridden an elevator on a single hand, and all had been up to a higher level, not down into the earth.

"I once stayed at a hotel with electric lights in every room," said a man in the back of the elevator car. "The Prospect House, up in the Adirondacks. Jay Gould was there on the same night I was. Though I suspect he had a larger suite."

"A better view, too," remarked another passenger. There were a few chuckles at this.

"We do have electric lights in every room as well," observed Matthew. "Modeled after the Grand Hotel in

Florence. Somewhat of a practical necessity in a basement establishment, I suppose. They have to run at all times, or there's no light at all."

"Do you get your electricity from the city?" asked Jonathan.

"Actually, no," Matthew replied proudly. "We generate our own through water wheels and steam power. A benefit of being this close to the mineral springs."

The elevator car arrived at the lobby, and Matthew opened the gate. As they stepped into the beautiful space, Jonathan could not believe they were still underground. The ceilings were high, the lighting was bright and plentiful, and the air was clean and fresh. Jon observed the tile and woodwork to be exquisite, and the furnishings ornate but tasteful. It may not have been the finest hotel lobby he had ever seen, as its compact size prohibited any sense of true grandeur, but it held its own against the most impressive hotels in the state, and that was truly something for a small town like Eaton Rapids.

Niamh clutched his arm as they walked toward the front desk. "Oh Jon, this is so lovely!"

Jon turned to his wife and smiled. He was proud to have been invited to such an elite affair, even if it was for his knowledge, not his social stature. "We seem to be part of a rather historic event," he mused.

"Yes, historic," Niamh agreed. "And you get to be a part of it this time. Isn't it nice to be a part of something new, rather than always researching the past? *Living* the history, not just observing after the fact?"

Jon understood she was teasing. It was not the first time

she had accused him of being an observer of life, rather than living in the moment. But this time, it was in good humor.

"I suppose," he said. "If this type of underground hotel takes off, we can say we were guests of the first one, on the first night."

Niamh smiled. "But will anyone believe us?"

"Maybe we can pilfer an embroidered bath towel," he chuckled.

They approached the front desk, checked in, and were invited to have a glass of wine at the bar, on the house. Jon declined, as he had to get to work, and Niamh rarely imbibed, but Clem was excited at the prospect, and asked permission from Jon to have a glass before they had to meet Oliver. Jon agreed, as it would give himself and his wife time to see their own room, and so they walked back to the elevator with the room key in hand. The last of the upstairs guests had just arrived, so the elevator was free. They joined two other couples on the way to their own rooms, and marveled together at the amazing space.

When Jon and Niamh arrived at their suite, the pair was giddy with excitement, as if they were a young couple again. They explored the beautiful space together, unpacked some clothes, and Jon changed into a work shirt so as to not spoil his good jacket, which he planned on wearing that evening. He kissed his wife before he left, which made her blush, and told her to feel free to explore without him. She agreed that she would, Jon grabbed his journal from the end table by the door, and she closed the door behind him.

Clem was already at the 10th floor station when Jon arrived. Oliver was talking to a construction worker, but acknowledged them both with a nod and a raised hand indicating he'd be with them in a moment. Jon took the opportunity to study the beautiful tile of the subway station, marveling at the attention to detail in every inch.

Jon turned to Clem, and asked, "where exactly is this station supposed to connect to? Above ground? Does it connect to a train line?"

Clem shook his head. "No, at least not yet. It's pneumatic, Jon. Something new. They're building the tunnel to Charlotte now, which will be ready in just under a year. That's why this floor is so grand. To many visitors of The Eaton, they'll arrive by pneumatic rail, and this will be the first of the hotel they'll experience." Clem leaned closer, and Jon could smell red wine on his breath. "The thing is, Jon, no one's ever tried a pneumatic transit system of this size. A lot of the tunnel was already in existence, part of the cave network and underground stream system, and the team that hollowed out the tunnel and has begun laying the track doesn't even know about the hotel or the pneumatic mechanism. They're just told to…well, dig, I suppose."

"But why Charlotte?" Jon didn't find Charlotte particularly interesting, and couldn't imagine the considerable expense it would take to build an underground train system to a modestly populated village.

"Well, remember, they're the county seat, and expanding. A lot of money going in. You know J. L. Dolson?"

"Sure, he started the Dolson automobile company last year, right?"

"That's right," Clem explained. "He's ramping up his

Charlotte production lines in the next year or so, to compete with Olds Motor Works in Lansing. But he's got more money and better ideas. He's developing a 'mile-a-minute' touring car that's better than anything on the market. Oliver's seen the prototype. And did you hear about the estates people are building out there? Some of the grandest homes in Michigan. Charlotte will be as big as Detroit by mid-century."

Jon nodded. "So Oliver's no fool. He can build a direct line to the center of Michigan industry, if he's right."

"That's the idea."

"And what if it doesn't happen? What if Lansing keeps growing and Charlotte stays small?"

Oliver approached them, smiling. "Then I guess I'll have built a tunnel to nowhere."

The men shook hands.

"I must ask," Jon inquired cautiously, "how you've managed to keep this so secret. My assistant explained about the tunnelers working in the dark, so to speak, but what about the hotel? Surely you haven't built this all yourself."

"Well almost everything was designed to be modular, built in pieces above ground, by companies that had no idea what it was all for. So the construction team who worked down here was a skeleton crew whose job was to follow plans and assemble everything to my specifications. But yes, certainly my workers would have loved to share information with their friends and family, which could have been a problem." Oliver motioned for the two to join him down the platform. "So I offered them all a rather substantial bonus if the secret remained until today. Double their wages if nothing gets out. They protect the secret, and watch over each other too, to make sure no one's caught writing anything they shouldn't, or taking plans with them to the surface. Even their families aren't being told, under our contract. But I'm paying them well enough that the wives don't ask."

Oliver led Jon and Clem to a short staircase where they could descend safely onto the track itself.

"The thing is," Oliver continued, "there's a huge financial incentive for me as well, keeping this a secret I mean. It's not just about the marketing prospects. The way the county's outdated building codes are set up, I can avoid all taxes, regulations, and bribes if the city doesn't know about a project until it's complete. It's like building a barn on your own property. If they catch you building it, you have to follow the laws and pay fines and inspectors and Lord knows what else. But once it's complete, they can't do anything. It's part of your property now."

"But Michigan Central Railroad owns the depot above us," Clem protested. "You must have gotten permission from them, and the village."

They were walking together down a dimly-lit, half-finished tunnel, but Jonathan could see Oliver grinning like a Cheshire cat. "My dear boy, did you not know that the M.C. Rail is now owned by New York Central?"

Clem did not.

"And did you know, as part of the acquisition deal, ownership rights of individual stations were won by high bidders, in exchange for offering guaranteed 99-year lease agreements to New York Central, so that New York doesn't own a single depot in the state of Michigan, despite now running all Michigan Central lines?"

Jonathan got it. "So no Michigan taxes for New York Rail."

Oliver nodded in triumph. "Exactly. They own all of M.C. Rail, but not a single piece of property in Michigan. New York Central leases the depot above us, from me. Or, I should say, a small corporation I control. But they only lease the depot itself. The building. Not the land. And clearly not any of this."

"Was this your plan, then?" inquired Jon. "From the beginning, when you purchased the depot?"

Oliver smiled. "Sometimes you don't know what you have until you start digging."

He stopped walking, and gestured to a small, natural tunnel which shot off the main path. An electric work light was pointed toward the cave, but Oliver leaned down to light two oil lanterns for Jon and Clem as well.

"There, you see?"

They did see. The carvings were deep, detailed, and numerous, and seemed to continue deep into the tunnel.

Jon and Clem said nothing as they examined, touched, and admired the carvings before them. Jonathan took out his journal and began sketching some of the shapes. Clem observed and offered commentary as his mentor sketched, occasionally pointing out when his sketches deviated from the image, allowing Jon considerable accuracy.

"These are like Greenleaf," Clem commented.

"That's Sanilac, right?" Oliver knew enough about the petroglyphs to know to call on Jonathan, which means he knew about the Sanilac carvings uncovered a generation prior. It could be assumed that he also knew that Jonathan had been the one to research and publish the anthropological papers on those carvings.

Jonathan nodded. "Yeah, this is a lot like Greenleaf. But a later period, I think. The detail is better. Though the shapes, the language of the art, is similar. Especially here." Jonathan pointed with the tip of his fountain pen to several swirl shapes carved in succession. "This is practically a quotation from the Greenleaf sandstone."

Clem and Jon exchanged a knowing smile. This was the part of the job they loved.

"There are more of those shapes deeper into the tunnel," Oliver advised, leading them further into the tight cavern.

As Jonathan examined the artwork, a slow feeling of dread crept across his back, arms, and neck, causing an involuntary shudder which Oliver must have noticed.

"Jonathan?"

Jon nodded but said nothing, and continued his examination of the pictures. *What were these images trying to convey?* Some sort of shape-shifter, Jon supposed, but did American Indians in Michigan even have a shape-shifter legend? The *East* Indians did, with the Rakshasas, the carnivorous demon man-eaters of the Hindu epics. Many other civilizations had similar lore, from Ancient Greece to Norse mythology to the Far East. But he had never heard of such legends coming out of this region. The closest would be the skinwalker myths of the Navajo out West, but skinwalkers were human beings who could assume the form of an animal, not a creature which could assume the form of a human, as these drawings described.

More worrisome than the depiction of a shape-shifting creature was the fact that the artists seemed to make very, very clear that one should not move the boulder before them. And it had indeed been moved, revealing another cave behind it. Jonathan peered into this new darkness with his lantern, and could only see a small, empty rock room with a slow stream of water running in a natural trench, maybe two inches wide. As far as he could tell, there were no petroglyphs inside the space.

Jonathan stepped back into the preceding cavern. He turned to Clem, who shrugged, and then to Oliver.

"Was something in here?" Jon asked.

"No," said Oliver. "Nothing. It was empty."

"But it wasn't open when you found it."

"No."

"So your men moved the boulder, despite the warnings?"

Oliver stiffened. "Well, I'm not sure we interpreted them as warnings, really. My thought was that a lot of effort seemed to have gone into detailing something important behind the boulder. When we forced it open—which took a great deal of manpower, by the way—we were pretty disappointed. One guy thought maybe it was the small stream of water that was being protected, some sort of fountain of youth perhaps, but we tested it and it's the same mineral composition as any Eaton Rapids spring."

"So then you wrote me," Jon continued, "to see if I could help you figure out why the cave was empty?"

"Not quite," Oliver admitted. "We wrote you to see if you could tell us what we had found *before* we attempted to gain entry, to see if it was worth the effort. But we couldn't wait. I couldn't wait, anyway. In fact, we just moved the rock two days ago."

seventeen

"Come on," urged Sam. "We're almost there."

Though the work lights had shut themselves off, plunging the four into complete darkness, they had managed to make their way back to the tunnel proper, where they could see the faint light of the station off in the distance. Guided by this dim illumination, they sprinted toward it, being careful not to stumble on the track beneath their feet.

As their eyes adjusted to the station light, Sam called out for Vaughn, who he did not see. There was no response.

"What the hell," cried Sarah. She, too, shouted his name, to no avail.

Sam looked around on the floor a bit, peeking again in the unfinished train car and the empty ticket booth. Nothing.

Janet was shaking. "Something took him," she muttered to herself. "Something's going to take us."

"Now, hang on," cautioned Al. "We don't know that." He padded the journal he had retrieved from the suite. "We need to read this."

"We don't have time to read a damned book," Janet snapped.

"This journal," Al explained, "was written by the only other people who stayed at this place. Aren't you a little curious? Maybe we'll discover how to get out."

"If the author of that journal knew how to get out, they would have done so, and taken their book," Sarah remarked dryly. "They wouldn't have hung themselves from the ceiling."

"We don't know for sure that the writer is the one who killed herself," Sam offered.

"Sam's right," said Al, who had turned to the first page. "The writer was male." Then, after a moment of skimming the content of the first entry, added: "He was with his wife. That must be who we saw."

Janet seemed comforted at this thought. Perhaps the writer of the journal *did* make it out, and left his journal behind due to the stress of finding his wife's suicide. She turned to Al.

"Alright, read the thing."

"Well hang on," protested Sam. "We have to find Vaughn."

"Says who," Sarah deadpanned.

Sam ignored the sarcasm, but turned to her. "Sarah, what was it back there? What did you see?"

Sarah hesitated. If what she suspected was true, she couldn't trust that Al or Janet were who they said they were. She would have to talk to Sam alone.

"This is interesting," said Al, who was now several pages into the manuscript. "This guy, Jonathan, was hired by the hotel management to examine the carvings we just saw."

Sarah bristled. "What does he say about them?"

Al didn't respond at first. His brow furrowed as he read with increased concentration.

Sam studied Sarah's concerned expression, then turned

back to Al.

"Al?"

"I'm not sure, Sam," he responded. "He wasn't sure what they meant either. Native American, yes. But, there's something else." Al's eyes traveled up from the page, finding Sarah, and repeated Sam's question. "What *did* you see back there, Sarah? You figured something out, didn't you."

Sarah nodded, but cast uneasy glances at Janet and Sam, uncertain whether to share her suspicions in public. Finally, she said, "it's Kedzie. It...wasn't Kedzie."

"What do you mean?" Sam didn't understand.

Sarah shifted on her feet, more nervous than she had ever remembered being in her life. In a small voice, she continued. "Kedzie had a tattoo, around her navel. It was new. But it was pretty big. You couldn't forget it."

"No she didn't," Sam protested. "We just saw her."

"Actually," Sarah said, "I don't think we did."

At last, it dawned on Sam what she was getting at. His mouth dropped open, but no words escaped.

"So," hoped Janet, "it wasn't her body on the stairs? It was an illusion? Some sort of trick, like the dead baby, and she's still down here somewhere?"

Sam turned to Sarah, and they shared a knowing look. "She's saying," Sam said, "that Kedzie was never here. The girl in the laundry room didn't have a tattoo, either."

Janet scoffed at this. Despite being able to accept an illusion of a dead girl, the thought of a living, talking, touchable ghost was too much. "That's ridiculous." She turned to Al for support, but Al, who was once again buried in the journal, said nothing.

Sam thought for a moment, replaying his conversations with Kedzie in the past few hours. It was inconceivable that the person he had been talking to, even touching, hadn't been the real Kedzie. He had known her for years. She even *smelled* like Kedzie. Uncertain, he turned back to Sarah, and said what he knew was required. "I believe you."

The group continued to be silent as the implications sank in, but Janet was shaking her head in defiance. "No, no, no that's bullshit. That's bullshit!" She began gesturing with her hands in a manic, unfocused fashion, mentally at her breaking point. "We just have to get out of here," she shouted. "Now!"

Janet made a break for the door to the stairwell, moving as fast as her short legs and tight skirt would allow. But when she arrived at the entry, Vaughn blocked her path.

"And where the hell have you been," Janet spat.

"Hey, sorry, I was trying to find…" Vaughn trailed off as he read the situation. Something had happened. Everyone was panicked.

"What, are you a ghost, too?" Janet barked. Vaughn's eyes widened.

"What are you talking about?" he stammered in response.

Janet turned and gestured savagely to the rest of the group. "They say Kedzie wasn't real. They say we're seeing imaginary people. So for all I know, you're not real either, Blacula."

Something had caught Janet's eye. She pivoted toward Sam, Al, and Sarah, and realized that behind them, the elevator had returned.

"Free at last!" Janet shouted, and pushed past Al on her way across the platform. Al lost his balance in response, and dropped the journal as he used a hand to steady himself against the wall. As he turned toward the elevator, he saw a strange shimmer across his vision, as if the elevator car was in place, and then wasn't, and then it was back again.

"Thank God," Sam had exclaimed, and was also making his way toward the elevator, watching Janet as she yanked the protective gate open allowing access.

Al knew something was wrong. "Wait," he said sharply.

But it was too late. Janet had stepped over the threshold, tripped, and fell down the shaft where the elevator had never been. There was a thud, and Sarah screamed.

They had all seen the elevator through the gate. And then it had vanished before their eyes.

Yet the thud had come quickly. She couldn't have fallen far. Sam continued racing to the elevator.

"Be careful," Sarah cried after him.

Sam heard a moan, and it sounded close. He peered down the shaft and saw Janet's body, lit from one side, on the roof of the elevator car.

"She's alive," he called back to the others. "The car must be right below us!" Janet had fallen about six feet, and now lay on her back, dazed but conscious. "Are you okay?" Sam asked.

"I don't know," she croaked. "I think...I may have broken something. And my head..."

Sam instinctively grabbed his cell phone to dial 911, but there was still no service. He turned back to the others. "Al, Vaughn, can you help? We need to get her out."

Vaughn hurried over, but Al was hesitant, eyeing Vaughn with suspicion, then Sarah, then the elevator. He seemed to have lost his trust for everything and everyone. Rather than help, he picked up the journal where he had dropped it, and backed toward the door to the stairs.

Sarah's attention had been toward the shaft, but now she watched Al with amazement. "Hey, what are you doing?"

He turned to her, offered an apologetic smile, and then sprinted for the stairway door.

"Al, get back here!" Sarah raced after him, but by the time she passed through the door herself, Al was several flights below and continuing to descend. She heard Sam calling her name from the transit platform and so returned, raising both arms in exasperation. "He just took off!"

"Where did he go?" Sam asked.

Sarah shrugged. "Down. Where else could he go?"

"Maybe he went to see if he could fix the elevator on level nine," Sam guessed.

Sarah shook her head. "No, he went further than that. I could still hear his steps when you called me back."

"Hey, you're supposed to be getting me out of here," Janet protested, sounding a little stronger than she had before.

Sam decided to jump down to Janet, where he planned on helping lift her up to Vaughn's stronger arms above. When he was standing beside her on the roof of the car, it was clear that they were trapped between levels, as there was about a four-foot opening into the hallway of the ninth floor. Sam realized it'd be safer to help her out horizontally, into the hallway, rather than try and lift her vertically back to the transit level.

"Vaughn," Sam called up, "I need you to go down a floor and help me get her out that way."

Vaughn didn't move at first. "Are you sure? I think I can lift her."

"No, this way is better," Sam insisted. "The elevator car seems to be stuck between the ninth and the top of the eighth floor. I can get her into the hallway this way and she can go down rather than up." He turned to Janet. "It will be better for you if your leg is hurt." She nodded in agreement.

"Alright," said Vaughn, masking his reluctance. He ran to the stairwell. A few seconds later, Sam saw him racing toward him in the hallway.

Sam helped Janet position her body to be carried from the top of the car to Vaughn's waiting arms below. She cried out in pain a few times, but insisted they continue, and once Vaughn had her in safety, Sam leapt down to the hallway as well. Sarah had joined them all on the ninth floor, and helped Vaughn lower Janet to the hall carpet.

"Are you okay?" Sarah asked her.

Janet managed to laugh. "No, I can't say that I am. But I'll live." She looked around. "Did Al leave?"

Sarah nodded.

Janet's face fell, and a blend of pain and fury swept over her. "Is it really so hard for us all to stay together? We wasted time searching for Kedzie, and Vaughn, and now Al? That's time we should have spent getting the fuck out of here!" Janet seemed once again on the edge of panic, her muscles tight and trembling, and her eyes snapping back and forth across the hall.

Something clicked with Sarah, and her eyes went wide. "It was S'mores, wasn't it," she asked.

Janet looked confused, and then her attitude softened as a chuckle escaped her lips. "Yes, honey."

Sam cocked his head to one side. "Sarah?"

"The stick," Sarah smiled. "That she had in the kitchen. The branches, and the gas stove. She was roasting marshmallows over the flame."

Sam had almost forgotten Janet's anecdote from earlier. "How the hell did you figure that out?"

"I don't know," Sarah admitted. "It just came to me." She did not add that she had been desperate to come up with something to say that would break the tension and pull Janet back from the cliff.

"I suspect the fear of seeing me killed before giving you the answer must have forced it into your mind," Janet suggested.

Sam smiled. Sarah always had a knack for saying just the right thing to diffuse a situation. He turned back to the elevator.

"So what's making this car stuck?" Sam started to walk toward it, but Vaughn stopped him with his arm, preventing his approach.

"Hey, don't get too close," he said. "It doesn't seem stable."

As if on cue, the elevator car shifted, falling an inch or two and shimmying, accompanied by a disconcerting screech of metal.

"Besides," Vaughn added, "we need to help Janet, and find Al."

"And we need to get out of here," Sarah added.

"All in time," Vaughn said.

Sam nodded. "Right, okay." He turned to Janet. "What do you think? Is your leg broken?"

Janet shook her head. "No, but I don't think I can walk on this ankle. Can you check in there?" She gestured a hand across the hallway to the Apothecary. "There might be a splint, and," she winced, "painkillers."

"Century-old morphine should do the trick, eh Janet?" Sam teased.

Janet moaned, but recovered with a chuckle. "Sounds perfect."

"Alright then." Sam looked to Sarah. "Want to check in here with me?"

Sarah was unsure. She was still distrustful of Vaughn, so she didn't want to leave him alone with Janet. But she didn't want Sam to go alone, either. "Will you be okay here?" she asked Janet.

"Of course."

"I'm sorry I took your last Advil," Sarah said.

Janet smiled. "Oh, I think a sliced nipple beats a sprained ankle any day, dear."

"Alright." Sarah walked with Sam across the hall to the Apothecary, where they began to search through the shelves.

"I bet the good stuff is behind the counter," Sam reasoned, and hopped over the locked half-gate separating the back from the general store.

Sam was surprised at the relative emptiness of the store shelves. Some areas appeared rummaged through, and there were a few empty containers whose contents appeared to have been drained on the spot. Still, he and Sarah were able to find bandages, a splint, and an amber glass bottle of liquid pain medication, and brought the items out into the hall. Sarah braced herself for the possibility that Vaughn and Janet would be missing, but they hadn't moved.

"Excellent," Janet exclaimed as she eyed the bandages. Vaughn helped hold her still as Sam and Sarah braced and wrapped her injured right ankle. The pain medication contained a glass eyedropper but no instructions for use, so Sarah reasoned one dropper full would be the adult dose. Janet winced at the bitter taste, but was grateful, and sighed peacefully, leaning her head against the hallway wall, closing her eyes a moment to allow the medicine to kick in.

Sarah took a dose of the medicine as well, her mutilated breast never being far from her thoughts, then knelt beside Janet and held her hand. "We all saw the elevator," she said.

"There's a big difference between an imaginary elevator and an imaginary person," Janet responded warily, perhaps reconsidering her earlier defiance.

"Yes there is," Sarah agreed. "We have to be on guard." She turned her head to glare at Vaughn.

"What did I do?" Vaughn shrugged.

Sam shot an irritated glance at his girlfriend. "We're all real here."

"What about Al," Janet asked.

Sam furrowed his brow. "Al, I think, freaked out. But remember, all of us, except for Kedzie, were here from the beginning, *before* we entered The Eaton."

This made sense to Janet, who became thoughtful. Then her face took on a look of concern. "Sam, what if Al found a way out, from the journal, and escaped without us? What if it's something we couldn't find for ourselves?"

"Al wouldn't do that," Sam assured her.

"Really? How well do you know him?"

Sarah turned to Sam as well, also curious about this man she had never met before today.

"Well enough," was Sam's weak reply.

"Well enough," Janet responded with derision. "Well enough to entrust your life to him?"

"Not when you put it like that," Sam admitted. "But well enough to believe he wouldn't put our lives at risk by abandoning us."

"No one's lives are at risk," protested Sarah. "The only person we saw get killed wasn't a real person to begin with."

Janet stiffened. "Excuse me honey, but what if the elevator had been five floors down instead of five feet? I could have been killed."

"Either way, we need a plan," said Sam. "Vaughn, you and I should see if we can get this elevator unstuck. It's blocked by something."

"I don't think I want to try that elevator again, Sam," Vaughn argued.

"Well we can't get out any other way," Sam said.

Sarah stood up, offering her hand to Janet. "We need to find Al first," she said. "He has the journal. And the gun."

"Down is the wrong direction," Janet moped, though she grudgingly agreed with the logic of finding the only person who may have answers. "And I'm not sure I can stand yet."

"Let's try," Sarah insisted, her hand still extended.

With Sarah and Sam's help, Janet managed to get to her

feet. "Were there any canes in the pharmacy there?"

"I don't think so," said Sam. He went in again to look, but came out empty-handed.

"There might be a pool cue in the Gameroom," Sarah reasoned.

Janet leaned on Sam and they limped together to the Gameroom, followed by Sarah and Vaughn. The walls were rich and wooden, and attractive amber chandeliers hung from the ceiling. A dozen or so leather-backed chairs were paired up with end tables and ashtrays. And, there were indeed two billiard tables and a cabinet of pool cues. The cues all seemed the same size and level of sturdiness, so Janet selected one that complemented the color of her burgundy blazer. She experimented with which side of the cue should serve as the bottom of the impromptu cane, and practiced walking with it.

Sarah noticed a small latched door, about the size of a pizza box, on the far wall near an attendant's podium. To the side of the door was a call button, and three other buttons labeled "Bar," "Laundry," and "Mastersuite." She slid open the door revealing an empty serving tray.

"Dumbwaiter," explained Sam as he approached her. "Maybe so people in the Gameroom could order cocktails from the lounge bar, or towels perhaps for the Mastersuite."

"I'll take a beer," called Vaughn.

"I don't think anyone's down there to take our order, Vaughn."

"Al might be," Janet said. "Maybe that's where he went, to get a drink. I know I could use one."

Sam thought about this. Al certainly loved alcohol, but

Sam couldn't believe he'd race down ten flights of stairs to get a drink without explanation. Was there another reason he might have returned to the lounge? What had he read in the journal that affected him so? He looked at Janet.

"How do you think stairs will be for you?"

"I may need a little help," Janet admitted. "Just, go slowly."

"Okay."

The four left the Gameroom and entered the stairwell from the hall. Janet limped along with surprising efficiency, using the handrails and her makeshift cane. They descended three levels before they began to hear the sound of sloshing liquid. By the time they had reached level five, they could go no further, as the stairwell was flooded, filled with brown, stinking water.

eighteen

"I'm telling you, it was Danny!" Niamh was in tears, but her voice and her grasp on Jon's arm were firm and unyielding.

"Niamh," Jon said softly, "your brother died when you were kids. He isn't in this hotel with us. Do you understand?"

"You didn't see him, Jon," she cried. "He looked exactly the same as I remember. He was even wearing the same shirt I last saw him in."

"Yes, Niamh. But that was twenty years ago. He wouldn't be the same age, would he."

Niamh's expression turned cold, her Irish temper simmering below the surface. "I'm not saying he survived. I'm saying his ghost is in this hotel."

"But that makes even less sense than him surviving," Jon explained.

"Does it? Does it Jon? Do you know everything? With all your world travels and exploring, can you tell me there's not one damned thing you've ever seen that you can't understand?"

Jonathan said nothing. He had not told Niamh about the content of the petroglyphs on the cave walls yesterday, nor the whispered comments he overheard at breakfast this morning about the strange claims of a construction worker named Tim, who swore he saw the pneumatic train car immersed in a sea of flames, which turned out to be false.

Jon did not want to worry his wife, who suffered from anxiety and depression, and he certainly didn't believe she saw a ghost. He began to wonder, however, if there was some sort of hallucinatory effect from the deep magnetic mineral water which surrounded them. It might even explain the wall carvings and the empty cave room covered by a boulder. If the natives had been exploring the caves and succumbed to a similar psychosis, perhaps one had seen a monster, and others had seen unexplained people and animals, and they convinced themselves that a shapeshifter lived among them, to be captured and detained.

"I'm not saying I don't believe you," Jon said, taking one of her hands in his. "I just want you to think logically. Your brother is dead, and there's no such thing as ghosts." As she seemed unmoved, he continued. "I suppose it's possible that there's an unanticipated effect of being this far below ground. We're a full 24 hours without sunlight now, and," he smiled, "we barely slept last night."

Niamh smiled back at him, the first smile since she had seen her brother. The night before, there had been a party in the lounge hall, and they had eaten imported cheeses and mingled with a few of the county's most elite residents. Wine had flowed for hours, and they both had indulged themselves. They had danced together for the first time since their wedding, falling into a comfortable groove as if they attended such lavish affairs with regularity. By the time they had returned to their room, his hands were all over her, caressing her neck and arms and breasts, helping her to remove her gown, furtively kissing her collarbone and shoulders, until they made love with an intensity that rivaled anything in their first year together. As they held each other afterwards, Jon could smell the sweet wine on his wife's breath, and her perfume-bathed sweat, and felt lucky for the first time in ages. This morning, he had helped her dress, which somehow seemed more intimate than removing her clothes had been the night before. He kissed her with sweetness before he left to meet again with Oliver, but she had been a different person when he had returned. At least now her tears had begun to dry, and there was still a trace of a smile from the memory of making love.

"Oh Jon," she said. "He was so real. He even spoke. He knew my name. The name only he called me—Neevie."

"What did he say?"

Niamh paused. "He said he was thirsty. He said he was dying of thirst, and wouldn't I help him get something to drink." She burst into tears again, burying her head in Jon's chest.

"What is it, my sweet?"

Niamh looked up into her husband's confused eyes, but shook her head. "I can't," she whispered.

"You don't have to," Jon assured her. "But you can tell me anything."

Niamh remembered back to the afternoon Danny died, drowned in the freshwater lake half a mile behind their house. It had been a beautiful but uncharacteristically hot Autumn day, and Danny had indeed been thirsty. He had asked his older sister to get him something to drink from the house, or from the well beside it, for he had twisted his ankle falling out of a tree the day before, and knew she could run the distance easier than he could. But Niamh was consumed with picking wildflowers, and instead suggested that Danny drink from the lake. He agreed, and that was the last she saw him alive.

Jon knew that Niamh hated flowers. He found that out early, when he arrived with flowers for their second date and her older sister, who had answered the door, shook her head in a panic and instructed Jon to hide or destroy the bouquet before Niamh could come down the stairs. Months later, when he had asked her about this unusual aversion, she had admitted to him that she had been picking flowers when her brother had died, and so forever after they had an unpleasant association. But she had not described the manner of Danny's death, nor her years of guilt for having suggested her injured brother drink from a lake rather than running to the house for him.

Now, in Jon's arms, she was about to reveal the whole story, when they heard a woman scream.

Jonathan ran to the door and into the hallway, though he motioned for his wife to stay inside their room. At first he saw only a man and woman staring ahead at the black door to the stairwell, but as he looked closer he could see the flies. There were thousands upon thousands of them, covering every square inch of the door, and bleeding into the surrounding woodwork.

Before he could act, Jon heard the elevator open behind him at the other end of the hall. It was his assistant Clem.

"I heard a scream while coming up," Clem said, exiting the elevator. "Is everyone okay?"

"The flies!" Jon shouted, gesturing toward the far door. The number appeared to have grown, and the insects were starting to buzz, or maybe it was just the flapping of so many small wings in such a tight space.

"What flies?" asked Clem, continuing forward down the hallway. He was so close that Jon could smell the whiskey on his breath.

"Right there," shrieked the only woman in the hallway, whom Jon assumed had been the source of the scream. But as she pointed, and they all looked, the flies seemed to melt away, some seeming to fly into unseen crevices, others dissolving into the air without a trace. All that was left was a wooden door, which had never been black at all.

No one said a word, until Jon confronted Clem. "You didn't see that? You didn't see them disappear?"

"Jon, there was nothing there," Clem said. "Honestly nothing." In truth, Clem thought that he *had* seen something, a strange black mass pushing against the door, but he didn't want to admit it, attributing it to the fog of alcohol.

"But we all saw it," Jon retorted. "All the rest of us, right?" He turned to the other three guests, who each voiced their agreement. "Thousands of them!"

"We need to leave this place," a soft voice intoned behind them. It was Niamh, standing at the doorway to the suite.

"Now hang on," Clem said, with a touch of belligerence. "I don't know what you thought you saw, but it appears to have been an illusion."

Jon scoffed at this. "An identical illusion shared by three different people?"

"But nothing was there," Clem protested. He took a step back and bumped against the wall.

"Well," Jon deduced, "maybe you had so much to drink it affected your eyesight."

"My eyes are fine," Clem snapped. "And we're not leaving. Tonight's the big dinner." Jon observed that Clem slurred the word "dinner."

The door to the stairwell opened.

"Hey," said Oliver, entering the hall. "Someone said they heard a scream a floor below. Is everything okay?"

Over the next few minutes, Oliver heard a competing narrative from the three who saw the flies and Clem who did not. Niamh also spoke up, describing but somewhat downplaying the vision of her brother she "thought" she saw. She seemed embarrassed and uncertain to share her story, and was torn between wanting to support her husband and wanting her usual privacy. Worse, she wasn't sure if the look Jon was giving her was one of thanks or one of consternation.

"Alright," Oliver said at last, throwing his hands up and appealing for a truce. "The truth is, I saw something too. But it wasn't an illusion. I saw the banquet our chef is preparing tonight, and it's amazing. Is it possible that the proximity to the magnetic fields and mineral springs can cause harmless, mild hallucinations? Seems doubtful to me. But I don't know. Luckily, someone who might know is here with us: Alexander Winchell. I invited him here to study the water composition, the same way I invited you, Jon, to study the...rocks." Jon smirked at Oliver's avoidance of mentioning the actual carvings, which were the only reason the rocks were of any interest. "We'll have an excellent dinner, and we'll all talk. Lobster, steak, and an octopus salad served in a clam shell. Have you all had octopus? No? You'll love it. Look, we'll figure this out, I promise." He offered what seemed to Jon a sincere smile. "Alright?"

There were reserved nods of approval from all in the hallway, although Jon could see Niamh was unimpressed.

They said their goodbyes, and people returned to their rooms and to the elevator. When Jon and Niamh were alone in their suite, Niamh grabbed his arm.

"It was Danny. He was right in front of me. I could smell him, Jon." Her face fell. "I know there aren't ghosts. The Lord would never allow it. But if it was an hallucination, then I don't care for hallucinations."

"I know, dear," Jon said. "And, remember, I did see the flies. I did. But Clem didn't. Which means they weren't real. And that's all that matters."

Niamh nodded gravely. "We should talk to the scientist or water expert or whatever he his, and if there's a rational explanation, or some sort of antidote tonic, I'll support you if you want us to stay. And in the meantime, I'll keep away from the baths. But Jon, if it happens again, I don't think I can stay here."

"I agree," said Jon. "There's a train back to Lansing every afternoon. We've missed today's, of course, but we can take tomorrow's if anything else happens."

Niamh smiled. "I suppose I should dress for dinner. Though, in truth, I'm not particularly excited about the octopus."

Jon's eyes followed her body as she entered the bathroom. He then sat beside the bed, took his journal off the end table, and began to write a brief description of what had just taken place, including the imaginary flies. It was his tenth entry of the trip so far, counting the six entries he had composed before their first day here. After he had finished, and since Niamh had not yet emerged from the other room, Jon went back and reviewed some of the sketches and rubbings he had made of the strange carvings. As he studied them, it sure didn't seem like the Indians were describing "harmless, mild hallucinations." These petroglyphs depicted a tangible threat. And Jon was beginning to feel, at the back of his neck, the first real rustling of fear.

nineteen

"Oh my God," Sam said as they stared at the water in the stairwell. "What if Al was down there?"

"What the hell could have happened," demanded Sarah. "How could five floors have flooded so quickly? This doesn't make any sense."

"It smells terrible," Janet observed. "Maybe a sewer line broke?" She was remembering a horrible moment from childhood, when their own sewer had backed up and flooded the basement almost a full foot and a half high, past the lowest step, so it looked like you were about to step down into a wading pool filled with sludge.

"A hundred years without use," Vaughn laughed. "Did anyone use a toilet since we've been here?"

Sam was irritated at Vaughn's insensitivity. "You want to make jokes when Al might have been down there?"

"Well hang on," Janet interjected. "Sarah's right. This type of flooding takes time. Even if Al had gone all the way down, he would have seen the water pour in. He would have climbed or swam up as fast as he could. So maybe it means he's on one of the higher levels."

Sarah was shaking her head. "No, something isn't right. It's just too much." She began to approach the water, kneeling down to the edge.

"Stay back, Sarah," Vaughn advised. "That shit is nasty."

Sarah winced as she inhaled the pungent odor. It smelled

worse than it had just moments earlier, like dog excrement combined with the mushroomy semen stench that had accosted her an hour ago. Every instinct in her body told her to get away from it, to run up the staircase to vomit. But she couldn't. Though her body was convinced, her mind told her something was wrong. And now that she was certain about the fake Kedzie, she no longer trusted anything she saw, especially if it was unusual.

Sarah slowly reached out her hand to touch the water, despite Sam and Vaughn's shouted protestations, but she snapped her arm back when she saw a creature move below the surface. It looked like a long, slender fish, but then it lifted its head out of the water and snapped its teeth.

"A piranha!" exclaimed Vaughn. "Sarah, get away from there!"

Sarah's fears subsided, and she laughed. "A piranha? Ten stories below the surface? *In Eaton fucking Rapids?*" Without thinking twice, Sarah turned and stepped down into the water.

"No!" Sam exclaimed. But in an instant they could see she was right. It had been an illusion. As soon as her foot broke the plane of the water, the liquid flickered and vanished, as if a bubble had popped.

Sarah turned to her friends defiantly. "The sooner you start to understand that we can't trust everything we see, the sooner we have a chance to get out of here."

"But how did you know," Sam asked, incredulous.

"Because," Sarah replied, irritated at her boyfriend's dimness on the matter. "It didn't make any sense. It *had* to be an illusion."

"What about Kedzie," Sam protested. "She may not have been real, but she wasn't an illusion. We touched her. She touched us back. You bandaged her wound. You can't have physical contact with a damned hallucination."

Sarah shook her head. "Look, I have no idea. Really, I don't have any answers at all. I just know that if there had been an actual water break, I'd be soaked to my knees right now. And I'm not. Which means maybe something doesn't want us to go down there. Which means that we should. So let's keep going."

"No, wait a minute," said Sam, holding his hands out. "We need a plan. What if Al's not down there? What, we just go floor to floor again like we did with Kedzie? What if the next hallucination convinces us to fall down a flight of stairs? Or worse, what if we do see Al again, and it's *not* Al, and we have no way of knowing because he was out of our sight? Then what the fuck do we do?"

Sarah recognized the tone in Sam's voice. He was starting to panic. She had heard this only twice before, both times when he had lost complete control of a situation and saw no way out. It was different than his momentary spasms of fear, like he had with the imagined mouse in the back room of the hotel lobby. Everyone had those. But panic was different. She loved Sam's strength in a crisis, and he had been great through this, but she knew his strength lasted only as long as Sam felt he could make decisions that could conceivably improve the situation. Once all appeared lost, or when no decent options were left, Sam crumpled, and became as helpless as a child. In those moments, he leaned on Sarah. Now was not the time to admit she didn't have all the answers. Like she had earlier with the gun, she would need to take charge.

"Alright," Sarah decided. "We're going to go floor by floor, peek our heads in each hallway, shout for Al, and if we find him, we ask where the hell he went, and take the journal and see what's in there. We ignore anything out of the ordinary and we stick together."

Sam nodded at Sarah. "And if the journal doesn't tell us how to get out, should we try the transit level again?"

"That's a dead end," said Vaughn, shaking his head. "The tunnel just *stopped*, remember?"

Sarah frowned at this, but said nothing.

Janet, however, seemed more shaken than she had earlier. She kept tilting her head to listen to imagined sounds, or felt spider webs across her face that weren't there. Even with the illusions of the elevator and the water, she had trouble accepting the idea that Kedzie hadn't been real. It seemed much more logical that Sarah had been mistaken about the tattoo, and that Kedzie had been killed and taken. Or what if Sarah hadn't been mistaken, and had instead been lying? Maybe the reason Sarah knew about her roasting marshmallows on her stove had been because she could read her mind. Maybe Sarah was the monster. And now she was leading them deeper into the bowels of the hotel. Into a trap.

"No," Janet squeaked. The others looked at her with surprise.

"No what?" demanded Sarah.

"We don't go down," Janet insisted. "We try to fix the elevator first and get out of here. Maybe get help. Let someone else track down Al."

Sam took a step toward his friend and agent. "Janet, we need to find him. Even if the journal doesn't tell us anything, Al's still the only one of us who would have any idea how to repair a century-old elevator. Sarah's plan makes sense. And we shouldn't split up."

They argued for a few moments, before Janet began to cry.

"Guys," she said, tears streaming down both cheeks. "I can't take this. I'm trying to be strong, I am. But I can't keep going."

"We're going to help," Sam assured her. "It's going to be alright."

Sam looked up at Vaughn, and the two friends shared a brief, sad smile. They had been through a lot together, and Sam wondered if Vaughn was having the same specific memory from several years prior. They had known each other casually at the time, through mutual friends, and hadn't yet hung out one-on-one, but somehow at a party they came up with the idea to have a double-date. Sam had been getting serious with a girl named Katherine, and Vaughn had hung out once with Katherine's new roommate Brooke, with whom there seemed to be a mutual connection.

A hot new club had opened in the city of Pontiac, an outer ring suburb of Detroit about ninety minutes from Lansing. Pontiac's nightlife district had flourished in the previous decade, and it seemed every former church and warehouse within three city blocks had a liquor license and a dance floor. One small block by itself contained a jazz and swing joint, a dueling piano bar, a country line-dancing bar, an industrial metal club, a gay disco, a douchey frat bar, and an R&B club with rap battles on Fridays. The new club, Venue A, was on the corner of this legendary block, in the former location of NozzleZ, a firefighter-themed hangout whose male bartenders went shirtless, serving sweet drinks such as the "Abs-Salute" and the "Massive Cock-tail." Venue A was trying to stand out in the city by having no defined theme at all, to the point that house DJs were instructed to deliberately choose music in contrast to the newest arrivals. If a large group of people sauntered over from the country bar, the music would morph into hip-hop. If twenty people poked their heads in from the R&B club, they were treated with back-to-back hits by Dave Matthews. Even the aesthetics of Venue A were painstakingly neutral, espousing no particular point-of-view at all. The club's proprietors, if their interview with The Oakland Press was to be believed, were trying to create an environment "foreign yet approachable," under the assumption that a "melting pot" could "bridge the disparate populations on the strip," becoming everyone's "starting bar" and "last call spot." At least for now, it seemed to be working; in its first two months, business was solid and crowds were common. As a double-date location for a white couple and a black couple with few mutual interests, Venue A was an obvious choice.

Neither Vaughn nor Sam had appreciated how long a ninety minute drive would feel among relative strangers. Sam had volunteered to drive, and so Katherine sat in the passenger seat, meaning Vaughn and Brooke had to sit in the back, which made Sam feel a touch uncomfortable for perceived racial concerns, and Vaughn feel uncomfortable for reasons of his physical height and leg length. Conversation between Sam and Katherine was necessarily stunted, as they could only talk about trivialities among company, and conversation between Vaughn and Brooke was equally artificial, as they felt the standard "getting to know you" chatter was unbalanced in the presence of an established couple. They had each imbibed in a beer beforehand to loosen up, but full sobriety had kicked in after thirty miles on the road, and the artifice of the double date proved too obvious to ignore. The four had no musical tastes in common, so even the CD and radio selections were awkward. By the time they arrived at the common parking lot, paying a toothless gentleman the rather outrageous sum of $10 to park in an unlit, unmonitored concrete slab which was a private lot during business hours, each couple couldn't wait to ditch the other pair and start their own quality time.

There wasn't a line at Venue A this evening, though a decent crowd greeted them with indifferent nods as they entered. It was just after 11:00 p.m., so Sam reasoned that they were too late for the groups starting their evening and far too early for those ending it, thereby stuck between the two time periods the bar was best known for. As a way of finding a private spot and getting to have some actual date time, it was perfect. Each couple found a two-person table along the same wall, not adjacent but not so far apart that anyone felt they were being rude, and the double date transitioned into two single dates.

A half hour later, a group of young Latino men walked in, and so in keeping with the club's theme of counter-programming, the DJ spun a Middle Eastern techno hip-hop fusion song which was unknown to everyone in attendance. For some reason, however, the sparsely-attended dance floor began to fill in, and Katherine grabbed Sam's hand to dance at the same time Vaughn grabbed Brooke's. The four swapped knowing smiles as they began to strut their stuff and grind their bodies to the bizarre beat, and by the end of the song, the whole dance floor was applauding and laughing. The DJ took the hint, and played another unknown track Sam guessed was in Korean, and the crowd ate it up. Sam and Vaughn exchanged an amused and curious look across the floor, as neither had ever witnessed a DJ increasing the number of dancers through obscure song selection, rather than relying on popular standbys.

As the drinks flowed, the two pairs mingled back into a foursome, albeit a closer and more giggle-prone foursome than they had been in the car. A passerby would have likely concluded the four had been friends for years, as their conversation had developed an intimate quality of asides and in-jokes.

At one point, Katherine and Brooke excused themselves to the restroom, and Sam and Vaughn were able to talk one-on-one. At first they commented on the beer they were drinking, and the short, tight skirt of a tattooed woman who passed before them, but then Sam looked around and said:

"Ya know, someday I'd love to own a place like this."

Vaughn's interest was piqued. "Really? Do you mean 'it would be cool to,' or 'I actually want to'?"

Sam took a long swig of beer. "I'm not sure," he said. "But I think maybe I actually want to. Though not this big...maybe more of a cool cocktail bar than a dance club."

"You'd still have dancing, though, right?"

Sam nodded. "Yeah, sure. I'd want it to be fun. Look at all these little crowds here." Sam gestured across from them to a standing cocktail table, where six people of varying ages and skin tones were laughing so hard they couldn't catch their collective breath. "I bet those guys and girls didn't even come in together, and now they're having the time of their lives."

Vaughn smiled. "Alcohol's pretty amazing, right?"

"Right," Sam laughed. "But it's also atmosphere, and music, and fun waiters, and all of that. It's why some places can seem dead even when packed, and others seem alive when they're half-empty."

"Spent a lot of time studying bar life, Sam? Getting a degree in clubbin'? This all research to you? Wanna cover my tab so you can write it off at tax time?"

"I'm just an observer," Sam laughed, shaking his head and downing the last of his beer. "I like observering."

"And drinkering," Vaughn chuckled.

"I know, I know, you think this is just drunk talk. But you shouldn't be surprised if you're walking downtown Lansing or somewhere someday, and see me hanging a neon sign on some beautiful old building, and getting all jealous of my name in lights."

"Yeah, well you just let me know if you need a DJ."

"You know someone?"

"I *am* someone," Vaughn said, with an exaggerated air of sophistication. "Well, or I will be. I got a couple Numark's tied into an old Behringer that's pretty decent. My cousin hooked me up. He does a few clubs in Ann Arbor and some private parties. Nice little supplemental income, ya know what I'm saying? And it's fun as hell."

"Well alright then," Sam agreed. "Let's do it." He clinked his empty glass against Vaughn's half-full one with a flourish.

"What was that about," asked Brooke, approaching the table with Katherine. "That better not have been the 'I'm getting laid tonight' toast."

"Nope," said Sam brightly. "Just business."

"Okay, good," teased Brooke.

"Wait," Vaughn interjected with a serious, pained expression. "You mean I'm *not* getting laid?"

No one had time to laugh before a gunshot exploded behind them. Sounds of breaking glass and screaming drowned out the music, and most of the hundred people in the club instinctively ducked down, crouching and looking around for the shooter.

Sam motioned to the others to follow his gaze. The person with a gun was a short, tattooed white guy in his early twenties, standing on the other side of the dance floor from where the four had crouched. The man had apparently fired his weapon high, on purpose, to scare the target of his rage, but now had aimed it at her, staring the woman down with an intensity approaching madness.

"Everyone here is a witness!" the man shrieked, and then a nervous look of discomfort flooded his face, as if he registered how unhinged his voice had sounded. He took a breath and repeated the phrase with more authority, gaining strength from the mass of eyes upon him.

The man turned to the DJ, who had also crouched down,

and ordered him to "shut that shit off." The DJ complied, and the thumping beats were replaced by a soft chorus of sobs and whimpers from the frightened crowd.

Then, in a flash, the man turned his gun toward the front door and fired another shot, blasting a large hole in the safety glass on the door itself, showering glass pellets onto the couple who had been trying to slip out unnoticed.

"The next fucking person who tries to leave is dead! *Am I being clear enough for you?*" The man sounded even more unhinged than before, screaming and spitting the words in a sort of broken-sobbed cackle, but he no longer seemed distressed by his own tone. "No one gets out of here until this diseased bitch has confessed to whoring around on me!"

The woman he was referring to, a pretty tattooed girl with short dyed-red hair and a tight black tank, fell to her knees, sobbing in a panic. Sam and Vaughn had noticed her earlier. "Jimmy!" she croaked between gasps. "Oh, Jesus, Jimmy. Jesus!"

Jimmy kicked her in the gut.

"Get up!" he barked. When she resisted, he made a motion threatening to pistol-whip her face. She stood, trembling, and seemed to be mouthing his name inaudibly, over and over, almost in prayer. "Will whoever has had their cock inside my girl please raise their hands, right now! Raise them high, so I can see them, and *don't fucking lie to me!*"

No one seemed to be raising their hand, and the few that still had their hands raised in surrender before the request lowered them safely to their sides.

"Oh really?" Jimmy laughed. He turned to a young dark-skinned man in a white dress shirt who, Sam remembered, had been dancing with the attractive woman earlier. "Not even *you?*" Without waiting for a response, Jimmy fired a round into the man's shoulder. The man was thrown back by the force of the bullet, his body flailing and crashing into a cocktail table, sending him, the table, and its drinks to the ground. People screamed, including the tattooed girl, but no one moved to help the fallen man, who was in an obvious amount of pain, making agonized, guttural cries as blood pooled beside his collapsed body. Jimmy raised the gun back into the air, waving it around indiscriminately as if shooing away a mosquito. "Who's next to testify? Or do I have to start shooting anyone who I caught looking at her tonight?"

Sam shot Vaughn a look of panic. He had looked at her. Hell, half the guys in here must have looked at her. But Vaughn was calm, and he placed a gentle hand on Brooke, then Katherine, and they turned back to him.

"We're in this together," he whispered. "Together, we're strong. The guy shot a hole through a glass door that everyone outside must have seen. Cops will be here in two seconds. We're in this together, and we'll get out together. We're strong, he's weak. A gun doesn't change that. Okay?"

Brooke and Katherine, who had been both been shivering as if they had been locked out in the snow, began to take deeper, slower breaths. They turned back to the crazy man on the other side of the dance floor, but did not look him in the eye when his gaze passed over them. With any luck, given the distance and the chorus of sobs and crying around them, Jimmy hadn't heard Vaughn's whispered pep talk. But Sam had, and it calmed him down as well. Vaughn's logic was sound. They would get through this.

And it did a lot to allay the feelings of helplessness to know they were a team.

"You!" shouted Jimmy, and Sam froze. The maniac seemed to be looking right at him. But then, mercifully, an awkward, overweight man crouching in front of Sam said "Me?" and Jimmy nodded with solemnity, motioning the man to approach the panicked young woman. Sam's heart was racing, but he had never been so relieved in his life. *Thank God,* Sam thought, and then felt a pang of guilt for feeling joy at someone else's misfortune.

The chosen man was nervous and sweating, but Sam thought he carried himself with a surprising amount of dignity given the situation. He didn't sob, and he didn't protest, but simply walked toward the psychotic man with the gun and awaited instructions.

"You noticed my girl?" demanded Jimmy.

"Sure," was the man's honest response. "She's beautiful."

The terrified woman couldn't hide a hint of a smile. Jimmy didn't notice.

"Ever seen her naked?" Jimmy pressed.

"No, of course not," the man stammered. "I've never even met her, not really."

"Not *really?*" said Jimmy, holding the gun to the man's head. "Explain that."

"Well," gulped the man, "I said I liked her hair."

"And what did she say in response?"

The man looked down in the direction of his shoes. "Well, I'm not sure that she heard me."

"She didn't respond to you at all?"

"No, sir," said the man, his voice growing weaker. He

looked up to see a pitying expression on the tattooed woman's face. She *had* heard his compliment, but she had looked at his face, his plump body, found him unworthy of a response, and had walked past him without a second thought.

Jimmy's anger seemed to subside a bit, observing this pathetic man. His eyes darted about the room, unsure what to do next. But then something seemed to snap inside him, and the rage flooded back into his face. He raised the gun to the fat man's head.

"But you *wanted* her to respond to you, didn't you? You thought about what it would be like to hear her thank you, maybe let you buy her a drink, where you could then impress her with your incredible personality, am I right? Cause that's all you have, isn't it, you fat piece of shit? I bet you have a great personality. You'd almost have to have a great personality if you wanted to get laid at all, am I right? *Answer me, damn it.*"

"I…suppose that's true," the man said miserably.

Jimmy's eyes sparkled in triumph. He was giddy now, so excited to speak that he stuttered.

"Then…then you *did* want to fuck her, right? You saw her body, in those little slutty clothes, and you thought, *if only she'd see I'm a really nice guy, she'll suck my little dick.* Right? *Am I right?*" Jimmy was trembling now, and the man couldn't keep his eyes off the barrel of the gun in front of his face. Beads of sweat covered both men's foreheads, and the room had grown as silent as a stage. "And you know what? You were right. If she had talked to you, she would have gone home with you. Or sucked you off in the parking lot. Or fucked you in our own bed like she did with this bloody motherfucker right here." He gestured to the bleeding man on the floor and spit in his direction. "So tell me, if you wanted to fuck her, and she would have fucked you, then what's the difference between you and this guy? So I think it's time to blow your brains out right now and get on to the next asshole."

The fat man's eyes went wide. He could see that Jimmy was serious. And he had nothing to say. His skin went white. He knew he was going to die.

In the theatre of his mind, Sam was entertaining a heroic bid to save the poor man. He would stand up, as heroes do, and say "leave that man alone, Jimmy!" Jimmy would be flummoxed, and the overweight man would walk off to the side, safe, and Sam would take his place, challenging him on behalf of the innocent others. He would say something like "put the gun down, my friend, and no one has to get hurt." Or, maybe, he would challenge him another way, saying "yeah, I fucked your girl—what are you going to do, kill me?" and then knock the pistol out of his hand and wrestle him to the ground, to cheers from the crowd. Sam was so convinced that he was about to act that he at first thought it was his own voice saying "come on, stop this shit."

But it wasn't Sam's voice. It was Vaughn's. Sam had only *thought*, while Vaughn had *acted*.

Vaughn stood up and stared the maniac down. Jimmy, who had been a fraction of a second from shooting the man in front of him, lowered his gun a bit, unsure whether to keep it pointed at his original target, or to turn the gun on this new man instead.

"Who the fuck are you?" squealed Jimmy, in a furious voice which Sam thought was starting to sound like Bobcat Goldthwait.

Before Vaughn could answer, Jimmy's head exploded into a wet, red shower of gore, as if explosives had been placed around his neck. The crowd reaction was dumbstruck silence followed by a wail of screaming unmatched by the heaviest of metal concerts. No one could figure out what had happened for several seconds, which felt like minutes, until Jimmy's headless body fell forward, his strings cut, revealing the Venue A staffer with a smoking shotgun behind the falling red snow left by Jimmy's brains.

Just then, as Vaughn had predicted, cops burst through the door of the establishment, weapons drawn, causing more chaos than comfort among the panicked patrons, until time returned to normal speed, and everyone was able to breathe. The bad guy had already been vanquished, and the people were safe.

Sam, Katherine, and Brooke stood up from their crouched position of safety behind the three-inch metal tube that held up the cocktail table. They cried, they smiled, they hugged, and they exchanged the meaningful glances of those bound forever by a life-altering event. Sam was so relieved, he wasn't even hurt by the girls' extra hugs and kisses for Vaughn, who had been their anchor to sanity during the last few minutes of hell.

Not a lot was said on the drive back to Lansing. While they spoke of the crisis cementing their friendship in the following days, Sam and Katherine broke up less than a month afterward, and Brooke and Vaughn never had a second date. Venue A shut its doors, at first temporarily, then for good.

After a short time apart, Sam and Vaughn began to hang out again. At first, they just talked about how messed up the experience had been, but soon talked of other things, and then, as good friends are apt to do, began talking about everything. They shared stories from childhood. They talked about girls. They even started talking again about someday owning a bar, since despite the shared trauma, their determination to create a place of fun and joy wasn't destroyed by the jealous bastard whose head had exploded in front of them. The only change to their plans was in its proposed location. "Maybe a smaller town club would be okay," Sam had said one day. "Small, but great. Somewhere...*safe.*"

In The Eaton, it seemed Vaughn was having the same memory, for after another shared smile with Sam, he took Janet's arm and said, as he had then, "We're in this together. Together we're strong." And as it had then, somehow, these simple words seemed to help. A quiet dignity was restored to Janet, and she raised her head a little higher, as if she were no longer ashamed of her moment of weakness. When you lived and worked alone, as Janet did, there was no one to lean on when times were hard. But in a group, you didn't have to be strong every moment. The weight of life could be spread around. She had almost forgotten, single so many years now, what such companionship was like.

"Here, I'll take your purse," Sarah offered. Janet handed it over with gratitude, another weight lifted. She was ready for the stairs now, and Sarah helped Janet steady herself against the makeshift pool cue crutch.

The search resumed.

At each floor, Sam opened the door to the hall, shouted Al's name, waited several seconds in silence, and joined the team for the next set of stairs. There was never an answer, and never anything out of the ordinary.

The stairs fanned out a bit into a short hallway at the lowest level, with the larger, more ornate door to the lobby positioned further down than the other floors, reflecting the first floor's unique floorplan. When they reached the door, Sam hesitated, concerned that if Al wasn't on this level, they had nowhere else to search.

"Gonna open it?" Janet asked dryly.

"Yeah, sorry," Sam said. He took a breath, turned the knob, and went through, followed by a limping Janet who was still somewhat leaning on Sarah. Sarah turned behind her to Vaughn, the last of them in the stairwell.

"Hey," she said to him as she passed through the doorway into the lobby. "Before we get too far, can you grab your DJ lights from outside the maintenance room a floor up?"

At first Vaughn said nothing, and Sam thought his friend might be nervous to run up there by himself. Before Sam could offer to accompany him, Sarah added: "We might need them down here, and you're the one that said there's nothing to be afraid of."

Vaughn nodded, and shot Sarah a small grin. "Alright, I'll be back in two seconds."

"Thanks man!" Sarah replied with a smile, continuing through the doorway as Vaughn sprinted up the stairs.

The moment Sam, Sarah, and Janet were safely into the lobby, however, Sarah pulled the keyring from Janet's purse, found the "Stairwell" key they had used hours earlier, and locked the door as fast as she could.

Sam was incredulous. "What the hell are you doing?"

Sarah spun around to her boyfriend, glaring at him. "Dammit, Sam, that's *not Vaughn*."

Through the door, they could hear him coming down the stairs, accompanied by the sound of clinking metal tripods.

"Sarah, give me the keys," Sam pleaded. "He'll be trapped."

"It's *not him*, Sam," she whispered, her eyes fierce and determined.

They heard Vaughn setting one of the lights down so he could open the stairwell door.

"How the hell do you know that," Sam whispered back.

They heard, then saw, the doorknob shake, unable to turn.

"*Because*," Sarah insisted, "Vaughn didn't come with us in the tunnel, remember? So how the hell would he know that the tunnel just stopped?"

twenty

Oliver's heart was throbbing in his lower abdomen. A third person, Clyde Bernero, had just stood up at the banquet and announced a supernatural sighting, and the murmurs from the crowd had developed a nervous, uneasy energy. He overheard snippets of conversations, and uncomfortable utterances of "haunted hotel," "too close to hell," and "we should leave right now." Some of the crowd seemed intrigued and fascinated, wanting to hear more stories from those who had seen or heard disturbances. But others seemed close to panic, their eyes flitting around the room, expecting a demon to burst through every wall seam.

As the mood continued to darken, Oliver caught the eye of Jonathan, who was listening intently to the current story, making frequent notes in his journal. *Christ,* Oliver sulked. *Does he have to record this too?* Oliver considered walking over to Jon's table and asking him to stop, but realized that would be perceived even worse than keeping quiet and pretending this was all normal and expected. His only chance at preventing a mass walkout would be an appearance of nonchalance and absolute, unwavering confidence.

When Clyde sat down, and before anyone else could begin, Oliver stood up.

"Gentlemen, ladies," he began. "There is a reasonable explanation for all of this, and I assure you no one is in any danger." Oliver walked to the front of the dining hall, smiling brightly, a spring in his step, as if giddy to at last reveal an exciting secret to the assembled. He would have just one shot at this.

The expectant crowd grew silent, and all eyes were on the young, handsome, wealthy investor.

"As some of the construction crew discovered early on," he lied, "there are indeed some special, almost magical properties of these magnetic mineral springs, especially when one is so close to their source. My friends, we have been documenting all occurrences of hallucinations, and are confident it's related to the adjustment period for new arrivals. Those of us who have been down here for days or weeks are completely immune to the effects, as you will likely be by tomorrow. There is nothing real about these apparitions. They are not harmful in any way. Just as some of our finest modern medicines which contain opium or morphine can cause temporary visions, so too do the medicinal properties of the mineral springs confer similar effects. And, just as the human body becomes accustomed to opium or morphine when used in a medical setting, allowing their healing effects to function as their side effects decrease, so too will you be free of the hallucinations after a short time, while the restorative and rejuvenative powers of the baths continue to work their wonders."

Oliver looked around, and saw an increase of nodding, approving heads among the skeptical stares. He continued.

"My friends, I would not remain down here if I thought there was any chance of danger, or any ghostly presences, or any long-term ill effects of the mineral baths. I myself saw a hallucination more than three weeks ago, and could have sworn my grammar school teacher was lecturing me about my mathematics." There were some smiles at this, and even a few chuckles. "Tis true! All two hundred pounds of her, staring me down as sternly as ever, a ruler in one plump, sausagey hand and my poorly graded homework paper in the other." A few people laughed. "But I didn't leave. I know better than to believe in ghosts or monsters, as I suspect *you* know better. And I know there can't be any lingering effects, as these are the same, safe mineral springs which have delighted Eaton Rapids visitors for more than fifty years. We're just closer to their source, and that's all. The powers are more concentrated. But, my dear guests, that is why this hotel is destined to be such a success, and why we are all so lucky to be here together."

There were some nods of approval now, and the murmuring returned with a brighter tone. But a few didn't seem to buy it.

"Excuse me," said a voice from the back. Oliver recognized him from the floor with the flies, and suspected what he was going to say. "There were several of us that saw the same thing: a door covered in thousands of black flies. Are you saying we all had the same hallucination?"

Oliver was prepared for this. Although the three people who had spoken of their visions so far had been alone at the time, the joint delusion was indeed harder to explain. Oliver was about to offer his theory on the matter, when he was preempted by a woman at one of the front tables.

"Folie à deux," announced a confident voice from the back. Heads turned to see Dr. Hernietta Carr rise from her seat and smile at the assembled guests. "It's a syndrome discovered recently by Dr. Charles Lasègue in Paris. We studied it in London." Dr. Carr was known to some of the guests, for most had never met a female doctor, much less a female psychiatrist. She had even studied under Dr. Elizabeth Blackwell, the first woman to receive such a degree in the United States. "It means," she continued, "quite literally, a shared psychosis. There have been numerous documented cases of multiple individuals sharing the same vision or hallucination."

The man was skeptical. "But how?"

"It comes from the power of suggestion," she continued, folding her hands in front of her body in the manner of a lecturer. "When multiple people are susceptible to visions at the same time, one person might see something, identify it out loud, and another is convinced that they, too, are witnessing the illusion. It would explain your flies, would it not?"

Oliver was relieved, though he tried to maintain a neutral expression. He had planned to propose a similar idea, that perhaps one person had the hallucination and planted it unintentionally in the minds of others, but it sounded much more believable coming from Dr. Carr, who had a medical-sounding term to describe the phenomenon. She couldn't have offered a better, more timely explanation if they had coordinated in advance.

"Thank you Dr. Carr," Oliver said, with clear gratitude. She bowed in response and returned to her seat. He made a mental note to have a bottle of French wine delivered to her suite that evening.

Oliver turned back to the questioning man, and tried to avoid looking triumphant.

"And as some of you know," he continued, denying the man a follow-up question, "we are also joined by Dr. Alexander Winchell, the famed professor from New York City, who is doing research on the mineral springs themselves, and who more than thirty years ago published the first proof of Eaton Rapids water's ability to impart magnetic properties onto non-magnetic metals." He gestured toward an ancient man of at least 80 years of age, who remained seated at his table but offered a kindly, labored wave and a smile. His wife beside him, at least 70 herself, didn't seem to notice the attention paid to her husband. "His research represented the definitive medical evidence that these springs could cure erysipelas, gravel, salt rheum, sciatica, neuralgia, dyspepsia, and nervous debility. So is it so hard to believe that such magical water might, too, have the power to impart an unwanted hallucination? My friends, I am indeed sorry if anyone has been frightened or inconvenienced by these tricks of the mind, but it seems a small price to pay for a longer, healthier life, wouldn't you agree?"

Oliver glanced at Jonathan, who was making more notes in his journal. He tried to read the man's expression when he looked up from his book, but was unable. Jonathan had the detached countenance of a scientific observer. Thankfully, he didn't look like he was going to speak, but his wife beside him was one of the few remaining skeptical faces. Oliver knew Niamh's vision had been dramatic and personal, and she would be less likely to dismiss her experience as a simple, temporary delusion.

"I have a proposition," Oliver announced with renewed confidence. "I overhead a few of you discussing the possibility of cutting your stay short." He raised his hands up in a playful, defensive gesture. "Now, of course you are always free to leave. You're my guests, not my prisoners, after all! But the last train out of Eaton Rapids has already left, and as you know, the station is closed. So there really wouldn't be anywhere for you to go tonight, except for the few of you who live in the village. Therefore, since you're stuck in this luxurious place until morning anyway, I say you enjoy a night of free wine and spirits on me, and music as long as you like. We have more than 100 records available for the ballroom gramophone, and since most of you are dressed so lovely already, I encourage you to dance and be merry with me. And if anyone still wants to leave tomorrow morning instead of Monday morning, my feelings will not be hurt." He flashed the group another genuine smile, and saw that now, finally, he seemed to have won them all over.

After dinner, Jonathan approached each of the people who had experienced a sighting and jotted down some basic information in his journal. He thanked each individual and assured them that Dr. Carr was likely correct, and not to worry. But as he reviewed his notes, and mapped the approximate times that each person reported an hallucination with a rough sketch of the hotel's vertical layout, he knew his suspicions had been correct. Before he could bring the information to Oliver's attention, Niamh entwined an arm in his, and asked Jon to stop working for a moment and to come dance with her. He smiled, closed the journal, and accompanied her to the ballroom floor.

The alcohol poured freely throughout the night, and only a handful of guests turned in early. Oliver noticed that even Jonathan and Niamh seemed to be enjoying themselves. Before long, the crowd thinned, and Jonathan took Oliver aside to announce they, too, were heading to bed. But he asked Oliver to be honest about his claim of hallucinations from weeks earlier. Oliver wasn't prepared for the question, and accidentally revealed the truth, that he hadn't had any hallucinations at all. When Jon's face hardened in response, Oliver protested that he was only trying to make people feel comfortable, and that his theory was supported by Dr. Carr.

"Be reasonable, Jonathan," he said. "There aren't ghosts. What else could it be than hallucinations triggered by the magnetic springs? It makes perfect sense, and now people aren't scared anymore."

"But you don't know that," Jon warned. "And I have to be honest with you, Oliver—what I saw didn't seem like a hallucination. It seemed as real as you are. I believe I could have touched those flies. And my wife believes her brother was in her room."

"Did you get a chance to talk to Dr. Winchell?" Oliver asked. "Surely, a man of his credentials might have greater persuasive powers than a mere building owner."

"Dr. Winchell is a century old," Jon scoffed. "I did look for him after your speech, but he left with his wife right after dinner, for a good fifteen hours of rest I imagine. But from what I understand, he can barely hear anyway."

"Well, what alternative explanation are you proposing,"

Oliver asked with manufactured innocence. He knew perfectly well what Jon was going to propose. He had been obsessing over those damned stone carvings, and had demanded details about when his team had moved the boulder blocking the empty cave.

"Oliver," he said, lowering his voice even though no one seemed in earshot. "As my dear wife reminded me earlier, there are many things I cannot explain from my travels across this great world. I have heard legends told by the peoples of six different continents, and while my scientific mind might demand proof, my gut requires no such evidence to be persuaded." Jon looked around to assure the conversation remained private, and then lowered his voice to a near-whisper. "Did you know that every civilization known to man has myths about demons who can change their physical appearance? Every one?"

A fleeting look of doom flashed across Oliver's face, but was soon masked by his usual, good-humored charm. "Jonathan," he said, licking his lips. "How much have you had to drink?"

Jon shot him an annoyed glance. "Not much at all, thank you," he said stiffly.

Oliver's face melted into an expression of benevolent pity. "My dear man, I assure you there is nothing to worry about. It's just—"

"If you tell me it's just a hallucination one more time," Jon shot back, "I will wring your damned neck, I don't care who you are." As soon as the words has escaped his lips, Jon realized that perhaps he had indeed imbibed more than he had estimated, and he held his hands up in an apologetic salute. "Sir, I am sorry."

Oliver was unphased. "Jon," he asked, with a conspiratorial raise of his right eyebrow, "do you believe in ghosts?"

Jon shook his head. "No, I do not."

"Then why in our Lord's name would you believe in demons?"

A memory from Jon's childhood, one he had tried to suppress most of his adult life, came rushing into his brain with such force he actually shuddered. He was a child of ten, living in the Michigan town of Kalamazoo, which had still been named Bronson back when his family had settled in the small village. Titus Bronson, the town's original founder, was Jon's great uncle, and although he had passed on years before Jon himself was born, his family related many an amusing tale of the eccentric old coot. Indeed, the town had been renamed in 1836 precisely because of Titus' wild actions, including the bizarre theft of a full-sized cherry tree from a neighbor's property. Jon could only imagine how low the opinion of the townsfolk must have been of his uncle to have replaced the sturdy-sounding town moniker "Bronson" for the rather ridiculous mouthful of "Kalamazoo." Titus' youngest sister, Jon's grandmother Edwina, defended her late brother the best she could against the town's persistent accusations that the man had been crazy, but as she descended into a similar manic dementia in her later years, her defensive claims convinced others that the entire family was out of their minds.

Edwina had lived alone for years, but there had been an incident involving Edwina and a neighbor which resulted in a judge declaring her incompetent. Jon wasn't told the details, but his father Charles had explained that his grandmother was "sick in the head" and would have to come live with them. Unfortunately, it meant that their already modest house had to make room for an extra bed, and Jon had to share his bedroom with Edwina until their father could complete a long-overdue addition. An only child, Jon had been proud of having his own room, as most of his friends shared a room with at least one sister or brother. Even at ten years of age, he had understood the benefits of privacy, and knew that his days of staying up late to read by candlelight, or exploring his own body under the blanket as he thought of his attractive blonde schoolteacher, had come to an end.

The first two nights had been uneventful. Edwina fell asleep quickly, and didn't snore or move around much, so Jon was unaffected by her. But the third night was different. He awoke to her choked screams of nonsense, writhing around in her bed as if in pain. Jon wasn't sure what to do. He debated waking her up, which he felt would be merciful, but was also terrified that she would begin screaming at him instead. His father had been awoken by the noise, and had come into the room to see what was wrong. He shook his mother awake, and she bit him on the arm, not knowing where she was or who the man shaking her had been. He slapped her across the face, and she came to, sobbing uncontrollably and apologizing for her behavior. Jon pretended to be asleep, but listened to all of it, as his dad spent a good half an hour calming her down and whispering to her until she slept again. But Jon couldn't fall back asleep.

His eyes stayed open in the dim moonlit room, hoping his grandmother wouldn't have another episode and bite him, too.

The next few weeks were worse. Jon learned to sleep lightly, to respond to and prepare for unexpected sounds and behavior through the night. Once he awoke to found his grandmother peering over him, frozen like a statue, only to cackle like a hyena when Jon asked if she was okay. Another night, he awoke to find her missing altogether, and left the room to look for her, only to discover she had never actually left, but had crawled underneath the bed to sleep in total darkness. On yet another night, she couldn't fall asleep at all, and recited her rosary aloud for hours and hours, her voice growing weaker and more panicked with every run, as if the fate of the world depended upon her successful iteration of a thousand Hail Marys.

Jon complained to his parents, begged them to find another room for grandma to sleep in, but although they were sympathetic, they insisted it was temporary, and to try and have more empathy for his grandmother's plight. "She's not well, is all," his mom would say. "She's still the same person who brought you treats on Sundays and bathed you when you were little. And she's your only living grandparent. We need to give back to her, after she's given so much to all of us." Jon would feel guilty at this, and chastise himself for complaining. After all, his own life was better than hers. What gave him the right to be so judgmental? Didn't he, too, hope to be old someday, cared for and surrounded by family he loved?

For several nights after that conversation, things seemed

better. Jon no longer felt sorry for himself, but felt sorry for Edwina. He went out of his way to help tuck her in at night, tell her how much he cared for her, and even read her poetry to help her fall asleep. She, too, appeared to have calmed down, her erratic behavior now seeming eccentric rather than scary. She would tell him "you're such a good boy," and "I'm so lucky to have this family." Which made it especially shocking when Jon awoke one night to feel his grandmother's frail, naked body pressed against his, under his covers, her breath against his neck, her hands under his pajamas.

He tried to scream, but no sound emerged from his throat. It felt like someone was strangling him. His heart began to race, and his face broke out in a sweat. Was this a dream? What was happening?

"Love me," Edwina whispered harshly into his face, her sour breath drowning him like viscous syrup. "Love me, love me now. Show it to me, oh Jesus. Oh Jesus."

He could feel her sharp nails pierce the delicate skin of his abdomen. He was sure he was bleeding. Again, Jon tried to cry out, for his father, and again no sound came.

"Oh Jesus," she repeated, her whisper evolving into a sort of croak, her body stiffening against his, her nails digging deeper.

Jon's voice returned to him. "Father! Father!" He was shouting now, repeating the word over and over like a man on fire screaming for help. He felt he said it a hundred times before his dad stormed through the door, accurately assessed the situation, and pulled his naked, clinging mother off the body of his terrified son. The shriveled, wrinkled pile of flesh on the floor began to shake and shudder, and even in the dim filtered light, Jon could see her wide, black eyes darting about, demanding answers. She had a wild, caged animal quality that seemed as awake and alert as Jon had ever seen her, and he was struck with the notion that this could not be his *true* grandmother, but instead was some demonic imposter. She did little to help disprove this fear when she bit her tongue so hard that it began to spray blood across the rug, adding yet another level of horror to a macabre performance.

Jon's father was sure she would come to after he shook her, for this must all be a terrible nightmare for her, but she didn't return to normality. Edwina tried to bite her son, but he was ready this time, and slapped her hard across the face, only to be greeted with a bloody smile and a dark, humorless chuckle.

"Go on," she teased in a tongue-injured lisp. "Hit me. Hit your mother again, you ungrateful child. Hit me in the face." She stared him down, blood trickling from her lips to her impossibly thin, wrinkled neck, coating her translucent onion-skin flesh in streaks of crimson. Her voice grew deeper then, as if all light had been extinguished from her soul. "I will kill your son. Sweet merciful Jesus, he will die slowly and horribly, praise God." And then, confronted with stunned silence, she filled the void with the loudest, more gleeful laughter Jon had ever heard.

Charles Wesley sent his son out of the room to get chains from the cellar. When Jon returned, Charles tied up his naked mother and methodically chained her to the iron bed posts. She didn't say a word in protest, but panted with exertion even though she had stopped all voluntary movement. Jon had to explain the situation to his mother, who held him tight and rocked him back and forth, promising everything would be okay. He spent the rest of the night in his parents' bed, too scared to go back to sleep, as his father stood guarding the monster who had once given him life.

At noon the next day, two priests arrived. Charles had sent Jon's mother into town for them at the crack of dawn, to explain the situation, and they had come prepared, with crucifixes, holy water, and a Bible Jon thought looked a thousand years old. Although forbidden to enter the room, Jon could hear the priests' Latin verses, his grandmother's screams, and his father's sobbing. Even when he left the house for air, the terrible sounds of exorcism followed him into the yard, and even into the nearby woods, where Jon collapsed by a tall tree and cried like an infant, until his exhausted body fell asleep on the mossy earth.

When he awoke a few hours later, all was quiet. He crept back to the house, one side of his face caked with dirt and both arms covered in bug bites, but still heard nothing even as he stood by the open front door. A fear crept across his body that his grandmother had killed his parents, and the priests, and had freed herself from her chains, and was now looking for him. But then he saw his mother, sitting still and silent on the uncomfortable divon, eyes wet but staring ahead, seeing nothing and somehow everything, uncertain what to say or do.

"Mother?"

She turned to him, and offered a small, hopeful smile.

"Hello, my son."

"Mother, what has happened?"

She said nothing at first, out of kindness rather than uncertainty. She didn't want her baby to grow up this fast.

"Come sit by me," she offered at last. He did.

The house was empty save the two of them. There was no sign of his father, or the priests, or Edwina.

"Jonathan," his mother said sweetly, placing a hand on his. "Do you know what a demon is?"

Jon nodded. He knew of the Devil, and demons, and Hell. He had learned such things from school and church.

"Well," his mother continued, looking down at where their hands touched, "a demon was possessing your grandmother. A vicious, cruel demon had taken over her body, and her mind, and voice. It wasn't her fault, you understand. The Devil is much stronger than a man or a woman. She was not a bad person, I promise you, child. It was not her fault."

Jon became vaguely aware that his mother was referring to Edwina in the past tense. "Did the priests get the demon out?" he asked.

His mom smiled. "Yes, I expect they did. But Jon, it cost her. To save her soul, they had to end her life. Do you understand?"

Jon nodded again. He did not understand, but saw the importance of understanding for his mother's sake.

"The world is full of demons, my love. Full of them. They creep in every shadow. They hide beneath the earth. In dark places, in caves, in holes in the ground, closer to hell, protected by blackness and dust and silence. They took hold of your grandmother's spirit, and they tried to suck its life away, tried to suck all that was good and Christian in her, until she was just a shell, an empty shell, which they filled with hate, and evil, and lust, and sin. It's important that you know it wasn't her, Jonathan. You must forgive her, if you hold any ill will against her for making you uncomfortable. She was not an unvirtuous woman. Her soul is with God now. But her body belongs to the earth, and your father, along with Father Mark and Father Thomas, have gone to put her where she belongs."

It was a hard lesson. Jonathan had loved his grandmother once, before he had grown fearful of her. He took comfort in the idea that the wrinkled, naked woman who crawled into his bed and touched his body with her sharp fingernails was not his grandmother, not really. Perhaps his grandmother had been an empty shell for some time, filled by the demon's dark energy before she had even moved in with them. She had not been herself. She had been possessed. And maybe now, with the demon expunged and her body empty of consciousness, she could find peace.

In The Eaton, Jon recovered from this memory, and looked at Oliver with a touch of embarrassment. "I do not know if I believe in demons," he said at last. "I have seen much in my life to suggest their presence, yet there have always been possible alternate explanations. And I agree there are multiple interpretations of the past day's events. But that doesn't mean we stop trying to find the right interpretation. Whether or not I believe in demons, I do believe in answers." He opened his journal. He had sketched a cross-section map of the hotel's floors, and made notes concerning the location and time of each known vision.

Oliver leaned in to see what Jon had written. "Answers," he repeated.

"Look here," Jon said, tapping his pen at each point of interest. "The first reported hallucination is on the second floor, around two o'clock. Then another, here, on the third floor, at half past two. Then another, here on the fourth floor, at a quarter past three, and then my wife's, at four o'clock right here, and the one I witnessed, also on our floor, at a quarter past that."

Oliver studied the sketch, but didn't seem to follow. "So?"

"So," said Jon, fighting to suppress a note of irritation, "the cause of the hallucinations was mobile. It traveled up the hotel in a simple pattern, floor by floor. If this were merely the effects of the mineral water, then people should have been affected at random. But instead, the visions were caused by something that *moved*."

"I see," said Oliver, stiffening. "So that's why you wanted to know if my hallucination story was true or false. Because I've been here for a long time, as has my construction crew. If it was the mineral water, we would have been affected. But we weren't. So, instead, you're trying to determine whether these anomalies are related to our moving of that cave boulder. Am I right?"

"That's right," Jon replied, his voice hushed. "Now, I can't claim to know much more than I can observe. I'm not saying there's a demon, or a ghost, or anything specific at all. I am only pointing out to you that the cause of the hallucinations seems to be able to move. And if it can move, then it stands to reason that it might also once have been trapped, and has now been let out."

twenty-one

"Come have a drink," Al shouted with joviality from the bar at the other end of the lobby. Janet screamed, and Sam jumped three inches into the air, but Sarah took the distraction as an opportunity to place the keys back into Janet's purse and postpone the argument over Vaughn. The look on Sam's face had been severe, and she half-believed her boyfriend was preparing to overpower her and let the not-Vaughn through. But although they could still hear pounding from the other side of the thick wooden door, the urgency of the situation had passed, and confronting Al was the most important task at hand.

"What the hell, Al," Sam snapped. He took a step toward the open doors to the bar, then stopped, remembering Vaughn. Sam shot a look to Sarah to see if she had relented, but she shot him a strong look back. He huffed, then called through the door "Vaughn, hang in there, I'll be just a second," before turning back and jogging toward Al's location.

Seeing the ferocity in Sam's gaze as he approached, Al raised both hands in surrender, as if expecting to be punched in the face.

"Easy there, kid," Al implored, his voice higher than normal and a bit slurred. "Lemme talk a second."

Sam stopped two feet before Al's barstool and crossed his arms in defiance. "What's going on, Al," he demanded.

"First Kedzie runs off, then Vaughn, and now you? What, is this just a game of hide and seek to everyone? Janet's right. We need to be working together to get out of here, not chasing each other around."

"Now wait a minute, champ," Al responded. "You know as well as I do that your bimbo friend was never even here, and I'm sorry to break this to you...but your girl's right, and that ain't Vaughn."

"And how do you know that," Sam demanded.

"Cause unlike you, you dumb cluck, I actually listened to the chick." Al picked up his drink again and took a quick gulp. "Think about it. You can't trust anyone who haven't had your eyes on this whole time, and I was there in the tunnel too."

"We haven't had our eyes on you either," Janet interrupted. "So why the hell should we listen to you?"

"You shouldn't listen to me," Al chuckled. "You should knock back a few and see for yourself."

"Getting wasted isn't going to help, Al," groused Sarah.

"Ohhh, excuse me," Al responded with the sarcastic flourish of a practiced drunkard. "Well how about you read a little bit of this journal and tell me why not." He motioned for the open book on the bar beside him. "Go on, girlie. Or let me spell it out for you. There's a creature down here with us. He can look like anything he wants to, any person from our memories, from our experienthces..." Al paused for a moment, recognizing his slurred speech, and continued again at a more manageable pace. "It can read our minds, find people, find memories, and recreate them. But it's not changing shape. It's only our perception of his shape. It's like a projection, like a hologram mask or some shit, I don't know. And if he's around, he can make you see *other* things, too, things that aren't there, pulled from your memories like a fuckin' plagiarist."

Sarah was listening to Al, but had also taken the book and was skimming the pages with trembling hands.

"That's what the writer of this journal said?" Sam was curt, but curious.

Al and Sarah looked at each other and nodded.

Sam was unconvinced. "And how could he be so sure?"

Al laughed. "Because the fuckamotha tracked it." He turned to Sarah. "Sweetie, show him the page with the...with the chart thing."

Sarah flipped back a few pages and held out the page to Sam and Janet. It did indeed show a cross-section of the hotel, complete with people's names and sighting times.

"There's another one a few pages further," Al advised. Sarah hadn't seen that one yet, but when she flipped ahead to it, her face froze in terror.

"Oh, shit," she whispered.

Sam looked over her shoulder to see another cross-section of the hotel, more hastily drawn than the first, that had many more times and a dozen people's names written down beside different floors. But this time, two names were crossed out, the word "missing" scrawled beside each.

While this sunk in, Sam became aware that he could hear Vaughn's knocking once more, dull from the distance across the lobby but with an increased urgency. He looked back toward the stairs door, but made no move toward it. He could not believe his friend was an illusion. But he could not really believe Kedzie had been either. He whirled back to Al, finger raised in accusation, but trembling too much to inspire authority.

"That doesn't explain why the hell you ran off," Sam said. "Or got wasted."

Sarah was back to reading the journal, and was about to come to Al's defense, but he beat her to it.

"Listen, son," Al said. "There's a way to see what's real, and what ain't, and this is it." He raised his nearly-empty glass. "This thing uses the complex machinations of the brain to fool itself into seeing, hearing, feeling, even smelling something in your memory. But it needs the fleshy little computer to be fully operational. Alcohol interferes with the illusion." Al turned to Janet. "I saw a split second of this with the elevator shaft, where it was both there, and…not there, at the same time. Like an old fluorescent light flicker. You understand?"

Janet nodded, and the memory sent new pain up her injured leg. She leaned heavily on her burgundy pool cue.

"And," Sarah added, without looking up from the journal, "drinking might interfere with the creature being able to read your memory with total accuracy. Did you read the part about the flies?"

Al nodded. "Right, for the same reason your own memory is slower and fuzzier when you're drunk, apparently this thing reads slower, fuzzier memories from you too." Then he glanced in his glass and added: "Slower, fuzzier, fluzzier." He laughed in the form of a hiccup. "That should be a word, fluzzier."

"Al," Sam protested, "even if I buy all of this, and even

if this guy did figure it out, if we get wasted we don't stand a chance against the thing. We need to be sharp, and fast, and you're neither right now. So what if you can see it coming if you can't move fast enough to get out of the way?"

"Hey, man," Al said, pouring more scotch into his glass. "I'd rather look my real killer in the eye than think I was being offed by my dear old Mom, know what I'm saying? My Grandpa…" But he didn't finish the thought, downing his shot instead.

Janet limped closer to Al. "I know what you're saying," she said. "And I agree. So pour me a double."

Sarah placed the unfinished journal down on the bar. She looked at her boyfriend with wet, pleading eyes. She wanted to get out of here, but her strength was wavering. The adrenaline that had given her swagger earlier had been replaced with a low, dull dread, almost hopelessness. Sam walked over to Sarah and embraced her, her head nuzzled in his shoulder as she quietly sobbed. She would get her confidence back, they both knew, and her steely determination and will to survive would return. But she just needed a moment, one moment of weakness, to be held and comforted and told everything would be okay. And he was there for her.

Al had uncorked another bottle of spirits and had poured three new glasses in addition to his own. Each of them downed the drinks like water, until half of the new fifth had been consumed. Sarah was particularly grateful for the drink, as the throbbing pain in her breast still occasionally threatened to overwhelm her. Janet held a hand to her mouth, ready to be sick, but held it in and belched instead, sweat dripping from her forehead as she hunched over, clutching the pool cue for support. Al skipped the last round, having been so far ahead of them to start, but Sam, who maintained his college-level tolerance, did a shot from the bottle as well.

The four looked at each other in silence. In this quiet, foreign space, away from the panic and running around, the reality of the situation was finally, fully sinking in. They were being pursued by a creature of incredible power, who could trick them, make them see things from their deepest memories, and who, they believed, massacred dozens of people before them without a trace. They, too, were likely to die here, forgotten by history, unless they could figure something out that had eluded the victims a century before. And, they had to be drunk. It seemed so hopeless it was almost funny, and Sam couldn't suppress a sick chuckle.

"Well, this sucks," Sam assessed. He had no idea what to do.

Sarah stiffened with authority. There were several issues demanding resolution. "First of all," she said, "we have to agree on Vaughn. Sam, do you believe me now that he's not there in the stairwell?"

Sam nodded, but then froze.

"It's silent," he observed after a beat.

Janet shot him a confused look. "What's silent?" But then she, too, understood. The dull sound of Vaughn's pounding on the door was gone. How long had it been quiet? No one could say for sure.

Sam looked around. His eyes darted behind Al to the pizza-box-sized door on the wall. "The dumbwaiter," he said, pointing.

Al spun in his seat and stared hard at the device. "No, I don't think so Sam," he said after a bit of drunken silence. "If they were right, it's not a shapeshifter, not quite. It has a large physical form. It can make us think it's something smaller, or project little things, but it can't itself be little. None of us could fit in that thing, so neither can it. Otherwise, it couldn't have been trapped behind that boulder hundreds of years ago, or trapped in that stairwell now. It's not a ghost, Sam."

"Just a monster," Sam added dryly. It occurred to Sam that, as a matter of fact, they couldn't even be sure it had been trapped in the stairwell. If it was as powerful as Jonathan's journal implied, it might have broken down the door, and was projecting an unbroken door into their collective minds. A sharp paranoia swept over him, and his eyes inventoried the room, looking for anything out of place, eventually staring at the far door, trying to see any hint of the "flicker" Al had described. But the door seemed as solid as ever, and nothing was attacking them.

Sam left the bar area and walked to the center of the lobby, mentally cataloging the hopeless options before them. There was a back office area that could be locked, but to what end? They would hide in there until someone rescued them? Even if the door held, they could be trapped for days before someone discovered the hidden hotel, and even then, there was no guarantee they would be found. The kitchen would contain knives and other implements of self-defense, and they still had a gun as well, but what were the odds that the demonic creature could be injured by such things, especially when it could disguise its form and make an impossible, ever-shifting target?

He felt Sarah's hand take his. All four of them now walked together in the beautiful lobby, Al clutching the half-drunk fifth of whiskey, Janet leaning on her impromptu cane, and Sam and Sarah leaning on each other, trying to find peace in the panic, comfort in the futility of it all.

"So if it can't get through the dumbwaiter," Sarah said, giving voice to the unspoken thought they all shared, "and it can't get through the stairwell door, its only other option is that elevator."

"The elevator's broken," Janet reminded them.

"Is it?" slurred Al.

They stared in silence, transfixed on the elevator gate before them, and the curved brass floor indicator above it, waiting for something to move. Through the holes in the gate, Sam kept imagining fingers, claws, and watery shadows, but they all disappeared when he blinked. Everything was dimming around the edges from the alcohol, and he couldn't trust his eyesight.

After several long moments, the brass indicator arrow did indeed begin its slow, silent arc to the left, from "8" to "7" to "6," causing Janet to burst into tears, and Al to curse under his breath.

Like it had as Kedzie, the creature was traveling down in an elevator car to greet them in the lobby. Only this time, they all knew what it was.

twenty-two

Jon had been awakened by an insistent knock at his hotel room door. He called out asking for a minute, stumbled into yesterday's clothes, and answered. Before him stood Clem, Oliver, and Oliver's assistant Matthew, who seemed agitated, and looked like he hadn't slept.

"What time is it," asked Jon, rubbing his eyes. It was impossible to have any natural sense of the time of day so deep underground.

"Almost 5:00, I think," said Clem.

"This couldn't wait until morning?"

"It *is* morning," Oliver interjected. "Morning enough, anyway. Get your journal."

Jon returned to his nightstand, retrieving the journal and pen. Niamh asked from the bed if anything was the matter, and Jon assured her everything was fine. He stepped out into the hallway as not to bother her further.

"I'm listening," Jon said.

Oliver placed a gentle hand on Jon's shoulder. "Let's go down to the lobby."

They took the stairway down, rather than the elevator, which Oliver said was "still off for the night." At the end of the flights, Jon's tired body was quite alert. He observed that Oliver had to unlock the door to the lobby, and asked him about it.

"The main level has to be locked after hours," Oliver

explained. "Wouldn't want someone coming down at night to drink all my whiskey. That's also one of the reasons the elevator shuts down from midnight to six."

"It's automatic?" asked Jonathan as they entered walked across the lobby, curious about the elevator's technology.

"No," Oliver admitted, "though that's something we're looking into. Right now, we have to hold the elevator gates open on one floor to prevent access from the others. That's not ideal in terms of ease-of-use or guest safety, but it's temporary. Most of the hotel's moving parts, as you see, are run by pneumatics, which in turn are run by the pressurized steam. You've noticed the copper tubing along many of the hallways?"

Jon nodded. "I assumed they weren't decorative."

"No, though we tried to make them a bit prettier on the upper floors, with a little more molding and so forth. But they're still there. We'd have built them into the walls, but frankly when the copper tubing is under that kind of pressure, the soldered and brazed joints need to have occasional monitoring and maintenance, like any standard steam boiler. Now, the elevator needed to be operational long before the steam and pneumatic system was functional, which is why it's not on pneumatics itself. But when the transit system is in place by next year, we might have it swapped out then. Those types of enhancements will be easier to accomplish starting next week, of course, when the hotel has publicly been announced and we can work with more than a skeleton crew down here."

"Is that why the transit is delayed, too?"

"Yes," Oliver agreed. "It would take years to complete

the ten-mile track if it was just the twelve-or-so of us, but we've gotten it in great shape so far for the starting stations and the general technology. We didn't have to tunnel as much out as you might expect, given the existing cave system we're taking advantage of. And we actually only need the tight pneumatic tunnel surrounding the first half a mile of each side, because once the car gets going, there's no friction and no wind resistance, so it can virtually coast to Charlotte and back once it gets up to speed."

They sat down at a table, and Jon took out his notebook.

"Alright," said Oliver, wishing he could continue to delay this conversation by discussing The Eaton's positive attributes. "Here's what happened since you left the party."

Oliver and Matthew began to detail a number of strange occurrences they know of that happened through the night, as reported by several guests. Oliver had taken notes himself, showing Jon that he remembered to record the exact times, as Jon had done. Matthew had been the one fielding complaints from the beginning, which was why the poor chap looked so exhausted, soon enlisting Oliver's help to talk to guests and contain the panic. Clem had joined them soon afterward, as one of the reported disturbances affected a neighbor in 402, whose screams had awoken several of the guests on that floor. Jon wrote down the narrative, making notes in the margins when someone remembered additional information, and eventually drawing another cross-section of the hotel and plugging in Oliver's recorded names and times.

"So, Jamie Biddle," Jon asked, "wife of Clive Biddle, is the one who woke you up screaming, is that right Clem?"

"Yes, she said there had been a knock on her door at night, and she heard the voice of her sister, so she answered."

"She answered the door herself? Not her husband?"

"Her husband didn't hear it," Clem explained. "He had had a bit too much to drink."

"But not Mrs. Biddle?"

"No, I don't believe she imbibes."

"And why did she scream?"

Clem frowned. "She said when she opened the door, it was indeed her sister…but at the age she had been when they were kids together, not her age today. And she had blood covering her little dress, which meant, to Mrs. Biddle, that it was the night her sister had found their mother dead from a hemorrhage. And this little girl, her sister, was laughing, saying that she wished Jamie had joined her to 'dance in mommy's blood.' Which, I might add, Mrs. Biddle says is not something her sister had ever said."

"But when she screamed," Matthew interjected, "and Mr. Biddle woke up, he ran to her, and couldn't see the girl his wife saw, except for maybe a flicker in the air—nothing like the real, physical presence Jamie saw and heard."

Jon took notes.

Oliver, Clem, and Matthew shared several other stories involving hotel guests. The first of the late night had involved Garrett and Margaret Freeman, "the negro couple working for me, Garrett on maintenance and Margaret in housekeeping," Oliver explained. They were one of three married couples who combined a construction worker or hotel staff husband with a housekeeper wife, which Oliver encouraged to maintain secrecy. They had stayed late in the ballroom, cleaning up after the party, and were taking the stairs together back to their room in 308, as the elevator had already been stopped for the night. On the stairwell, they turned a corner and both saw and heard a man in a white robe and hood, carrying a lit torch, telling them to turn back. It was a figure from Garrett's memories as a child in Tennessee, "some sort of white supremacist group that scared their family off their farm." They ran down to the lobby to get help, which is when they told Matthew, but when Matthew accompanied them back up the stairs, they found nothing.

"Do you know if Garrett and Margaret drank any alcohol last night?" asked Jon.

"I don't think so," Oliver answered. "They're Baptists."

"Hmm," said Jon, making another note.

Matthew had retrieved the guest manifest from the front desk, allowing Jon to know where each guest was staying, assuring his notes were accurate and everyone's names were recorded. As the additional stories were discussed and compared, Jon understood why Oliver seemed to be coming around to Jon's creature hypothesis. As Jon had observed the night before, whatever was causing the visions was moving through the hotel, not just affecting random people at random times. There wasn't a single case of two visions happening at the same time in two different places, and each disturbance was separated by the previous disturbance by one or two floors. Alcohol, too, seemed to play a role, as being intoxicated appeared to make the hallucinations invisible, or at least much less real. This also matched Jon's own experience with the flies, and why Clem seemed to be the only one who didn't clearly see the swarm.

"So, do you want me to grab a bottle for us?" asked Clem, hopefully.

Jon groaned. The thought of alcohol this early in the morning made his stomach churn, and his head was still buzzing from the evening before. But he nodded, and Clem sprinted off to the bar.

Oliver forced a smile, and Jon looked at him carefully. There was more that Oliver hadn't yet shared, but he was uncertain how to proceed. Throughout the night, Oliver and Matthew had used their intelligence and charm to convince each of the affected people that their experience was an isolated hallucination, caused by the reasons explained by Drs. Carr and Winchell, and there was no cause for alarm. But in the morning, the guests would talk to each other. They would compare notes. They would realize that the visions were increasing in frequency, and some might even figure out, as Jon had, that the cause of the disturbances was mobile, some sort of ghost or demon moving through the hotel. They would panic, and they would leave, and Oliver would be ruined. The fact that Oliver was now on board with Jon's hypothesis underscored the seriousness of the situation, but Jon could tell the man was still holding back.

"I must ask," Jon began, "if there's anything you're not yet telling me."

Oliver and Matthew looked at each other. While Oliver was more skilled in projecting confidence, the look of grave concern that flooded over his assistant told Jon that he was right to suspect something more. Oliver must have recognized the transparency of Matthew's fear, for he shot him an annoyed, chastising smirk before turning back to Jonathan.

"Yes, there is something," Oliver began, as Clem returned with two bottles of scotch and four lead-lined glasses. "There are at least two people missing."

Jon's eyes went wide. "Missing?"

"Two workers of mine, Tim Elshoff and Mark Hinkley, are not in their respective rooms and cannot be found."

"Where were they staying?"

"All the staff and construction workers are staying on the third floor for this opening," Oliver explained. "Part of their agreement to develop the hotel in secret included a stay in the hotel for the first two weekends, as long as they keep the rooms spotless, for tours. We know they're missing because we went through all the rooms after Garrett and Margaret insisted on looking for them with the torch."

"But you haven't gone through all the rooms," Jon frowned.

"No, just the third floor, because they work for me. And we didn't want to create any sort of panic."

"That means you don't know if others are missing."

"No, we don't," Oliver admitted. "But we have no reason to believe any more are gone."

Jon's eyebrows scrunched disapprovingly at Oliver's unjustified optimism.

"Maybe they got out," offered Clem, handing each of them a full glass of scotch.

"No, they couldn't have," argued Matthew. "The elevator's been locked down since midnight, and they both were still here then, helping with the linens."

"They could have taken the stairs," Jon reasoned.

Oliver shook his head. "No, the stairs don't go all the way out. They stop at the Mastersuite."

Jon was taken aback by this. "You mean to tell me there's just one way into and out of this place, and you don't even allow its operation at night? What if there's an emergency? My God, man, what if there's a fire?"

Oliver held his hands up. "Now wait a moment, I didn't say there *never* will be, there just isn't *now*. The stairwell will eventually break through to the surface, just outside the wall of the train depot, for emergencies, but we couldn't very well build that before the existence of the hotel was known. It's coming, within weeks, it really is. But right now…"

"Right now," Jon shot back, "you chose secrecy over safety, and the only way out is an elevator that you control."

"Well, technically, there's also the transit level…" Matthew began.

"But that doesn't go anywhere yet either," Jon interrupted. "So our choices are a staircase that doesn't reach the surface, a train tunnel that doesn't reach Charlotte, and an elevator that Oliver currently has blocked. And somehow, we need to get forty people out of here, and fast."

Oliver stiffened. "Well wait just a damned minute," he said, eyes cold. "I've worked very, very hard to make sure this weekend goes smoothly, and there are some very wealthy and well-connected people here. We can't just…"

Jon cut him off by showing the pencil rubbings of the petroglyphs contained in his notes.

"Do you see this?" he demanded. "This is the creature

that is terrorizing your hotel. The Indians knew the creature. These carvings describe exactly what we're now seeing. A thing they trapped. That *you* let out. A demon who can project a different appearance, anything it wants to, by raping the memories of its victims. Like the old shape-shifter legends, only it's not really a shape-shifter, is it, because it's hiding behind its illusions, not actually changing." Jon pushed the journal closer to Oliver's face. "It's *real*, and it looks like this clawed monster right here—and the only reason we're not seeing it for what it really is, is apparently because we haven't had enough damned whiskey. So don't tell me that 'we can't just' get out of here. Because I happen to think we are in very real danger here, and if we don't leave now, we might not get another chance."

Jon's words hung in the silence for a long time. He lowered his journal back to the table, grabbed the whiskey glass, and pounded back its contents. Drinking while hungover was not something he enjoyed, although he could tell from Clem's vacant expression that it was a regular occurrence in Clem's world. *God, what an asshole,* Jon thought, not for the first time. *Why do I work with this guy.* Although, he supposed, had Clem not been a drunk, he might not have figured out the alcohol connection in time. *Even a broken clock...*

"No one's gotten hurt," said Oliver meekly. "There's no reason to believe anyone's in danger." But there was a look of defeat on his face, like a child caught doing something awful and was now in deep trouble with a strict parent. Jon had empathy for the man, who had poured so much of his heart and soul into the place, only to have it become a house of horrors.

"We don't have to alarm anyone," Jon assured him. He glanced up at the clock hanging on the far wall. "Look, it's after 6:00 now. People will be waking up anyway. You and Matthew can walk around, knock on each door, apologize profusely for the inconvenience, but advise them to pack up their things."

"We can explain it as a steam leak in the mineral baths," Matthew suggested. "We can say that the reason for the hallucinations is due to the leak, and out of an abundance of caution, we're evacuating the hotel, just to save the guests the discomfort of having scary visions, even though they're harmless."

Jon nodded. "That's right. It matches up with Dr. Carr and Dr. Winchell's theories, so you're not a liar. But it also is compatible with the stories the guests are going to be hearing about from their neighbors. It avoids a panicked rush to the exit, but still gets people out before the creature turns violent." Jon did not add his concerns that the creature might have *already* turned violent, given the unsettling fact of the missing people from the third floor.

Oliver nodded gravely, then knocked back the final swig from his whiskey glass. "Alright, Jon. We'll do it your way. I don't want to see anyone get hurt."

"How do we restart the elevator?" Jon asked.

"It's just blocked on the Mastersuite floor," Oliver explained. "I stick one of the lobby chairs over the threshold. The car can't move if it's blocked." Jon glanced down at the guest manifest, which listed the Mastersuite as occupied by "Waldorf Astor." Oliver caught his confused gaze and laughed. "That's me," said Oliver. "I'm staying in the Mastersuite for our maiden voyage."

"You used a pseudonym in your own hotel?"

"For luck," he admitted. "Thought a famous name like Waldorf Astor would get us off to a good start."

"Alright," Jon responded with authority. "You wake up the staff, enlist their help, and start at the upper levels. Then you can start explaining to the guests in the suites what's going on. They're the high-society visitors so I'm sure they'd appreciate an explanation from you personally. Matthew and I can help with the lower levels. We'll tell everyone to stay calm, pack up, and we'll start taking people up and out within the hour. And we'll all get through this, including you, Oliver."

Oliver smiled, but his eyes were wet and glassy. He knew as well as Jon did that even if everyone got out safely, the reputation of the great and mysterious Oliver Stanton was very much on the line.

Clem got a shoulder bag from the back and began filling it with several bottles of alcohol, just in case. Oliver began the trek to the third floor, hoping the combination of whiskey and climbing stairs wouldn't expel the contents of his stomach. Matthew and Jon were behind him, Matthew stopping at the fourth floor, but Jon advanced to the eighth floor, figuring he owed his wife an explanation first.

As he had feared, Niamh had indeed been worried.

"Christ, Jonathan," she said after he opened the door. "Where have you been?"

"We have to leave here, now," Jon explained, motioning to their traveler trunk. "Pack everything up."

"It's the hallucinations, isn't it," she said.

"They aren't hallucinations, exactly," Jon began, then thought better of it. She didn't need to know the whole truth, at least not now.

Niamh scrunched her nose. "Have you been drinking?"

Jon ignored her question, tossed his journal onto the end table, then went into the washroom to splash water on his face. The alcohol was just starting to take effect, and he knew he would be tipsy soon, but it was important he look sober if he was to help with an orderly evacuation. He dried himself with a towel and took a deep breath before entering the bedroom again. Niamh hadn't moved, and was standing there in her nightrobe, eyeing him with fearful fascination.

"Jon," she started, but he cut her off.

"Niamh, my wife, it is okay. You were right to want to leave yesterday, and I'm sorry I didn't fight harder for that. But we're going to leave now. There's…" Jon stopped himself. He was going to try out the cover story, that there had been a leak in mineral water steam, and that it was causing hallucinations, but he couldn't bring himself to lie so directly. He would tell her the whole story later, once they were safe and free. For now, he smiled and kissed her. "Trust me," he said instead, and headed toward the door to the hallway, which he had left open in his distracted state. Realizing anyone walking by might have seen his wife in her nightclothes, he added "and get dressed, for God's sake!" before racing out.

Niamh poked her head out the door. "Where are you going?" she called.

"I need to help with the evacuation," Jon called back as

he reached the stairwell. "Everything will be fine, and I'll see you very soon, but I promised I'd help with the lower floors first, alright? Just, pack up as quick as you can." He didn't wait for a reply, and soon he had vanished through the door on his way down to help Matthew.

Niamh looked around, backed fully into their room, and pulled the door shut behind her.

All of this was wrong, she knew. They shouldn't be here. They should never have come. There was a coldness to the room that she hadn't noticed before, and a chill went through her body. She could hear something, too, and it took her a moment to realize what it must be. Jon hadn't shut the water off entirely, and there was a soft drip-drip-drip sound coming from the bathroom. She sighed and walked toward it, turning the corner into the bathroom's open door, freezing in her tracks.

The drip-drip sounds hadn't been from the sink, but from her brother's soaked body dripping water onto the tiled floor.

Niamh cried aloud, stepping back from Danny but never looking away, as the boy stared back, his accusatory eyes blazing at her with anger. He was bluer now than he had been during her first hallucination, and his skin was taut and bloated.

"Neeeevie," the boy taunted, though his voice stayed monotone. "I'm not thirsty anymore, Neeeevie."

"Get....get away!" Niamh stumbled backward into the main part of the room. He followed her, stepping slowly, leaving wet footprints behind him.

"Neeeeeeeeeevie," he said, adding a note of malice.

Niamh realized for the first time that he had a hand behind his back. "I have something for you, my sister. I know how much you like these." He produced a decaying bouquet of wildflowers, which seemed to blacken and wither before her eyes, shedding rotten black petals onto the carpet.

"Stay away," she sobbed. "I know you're not real."

"Oh, but I *am* real," Danny assured her, his hand crushing the flowers into an ashy paste. "You know I am real. And your husband, didn't he just say we weren't hallucinations? I heard him say that, Neeeevie."

Niamh was breathing in spurts and sobs now. She crawled backward away from him, hitting the far wall and then pushing her body hard against it, as if she could knock it down with sheer force and create an escape.

"I know you've been sad for years over my death," Danny said, his voice developing a raspy tone as if unable to breathe. "And I want you to know that you were right. It *was* your fault. God knows it was your fault. Every day you spend alive is an insult to our Lord." He leaned in closer, conspiratorially, and smiled. "And so we both know that the longer you stay on this earth, the more your skin will bubble and burn in the flames of eternal hell."

Against the wall, Niamh's body trembled and turned in on itself like a crushed ant. "Oh, Danny..." she choked. "Oh I'm so sorry, oh Christ I am."

"The longer you wait to join me in death," Danny continued without mercy, still creeping toward her thin, twisted body, dripping water from his blue skin and matted hair, "the more I will take everything you love. I'm the one who made sure you were childless. And I'm the one who will make sure your husband dies a slow, cruel death. I'll make sure his skin will burn in flames in this life like yours will burn in the next."

Niamh was covering her face with her hands now, shaking and sobbing, trying to drown out her brother's taunts, to convince herself that it was still an illusion, and that if she just closed her eyes it would go away. But she felt him getting even closer, could smell the wet hair and the scent of decaying flowers, and before she could cry out again, she felt two cold, wet hands seize her by the wrists, pushing her arms apart with incredible strength, uncovering her face, and putting his own face an inch from hers. When she opened her eyes, her entire vision was overtaken by that face, that blue, bloated, rotting face, water still dripping from his hair onto his taut skin, and her mouth locked open in a silent scream.

"Neeeeevie," he said, through loose teeth that seemed ready to fall out on their own, his breath humid and sour. His eyes locked into hers, daring her to look away. "Neeeeeeevie."

She squeaked a soft, strangled "what?" and he smiled at her, cocking his head and leaning in until his nose was almost touching her own.

As if sharing a secret, his voice dripping with hate but absolute authority, Danny whispered the last words Niamh Wesley would ever hear:

"*You know what you have to do.*"

And she did.

twenty-three

"Run!" cried Sarah in a half-scream, half-whisper, uncertain how much her voice might carry up the elevator shaft. The four hurried to the stair entrance and Sarah whipped out the keys from Janet's purse.

Sam had a disturbing thought. He placed his hand against the lock just as Sarah was about to thrust the key inside. Her face shot up at his. "Wait, Sarah," Sam urged, "what if this is a trick?"

Janet was keeping her eye on the brass arrow across the room. The blessedly slow-moving elevator was now at "4."

"What if it sent the elevator down empty," Sam continued, "so we'd open the door?"

Sarah hadn't considered this, and took a beat.

The arrow fell to "3."

"Guys…" urged Janet.

A thought came to Sarah. "No, Sam, this is right," she said. "It wouldn't send down the elevator because the elevator's the only way out."

The logic behind this clicked to Sam as well. From the creature's perspective, giving them the elevator was too risky. With the stairs, they could only get so far. He snatched his hand back from the lock and Sarah opened the door.

The arrow fell to "2" as they hurried into the stairwell, praying they closed the door behind them fast enough to avoid detection. Sarah locked it from the other side the instant it was closed, and they started up the staircase.

"Where are we going?" asked Al.

Sarah had an idea. "We just need to get to the next level," she said, panting as the alcohol made its way through her fast-pumping blood, slowing her progress. "Then we can race across the hall and call the elevator ourselves while the thing is trying to get into the stairwell."

Sure enough, they heard pounding on the locked door below them as they raced up the last few stairs, Sam and Sarah in the lead, followed by Al, and Janet in the rear, still limping in pain and dependent on her pool cue crutch.

"Come on," Al said, falling back a bit to help Janet by the arm.

Sam wasted no time, though the scotch gurgled in his stomach, begging him to slow down. He swung open the door to the second level and raced to the elevator call button, Sarah just yards behind him. The instant he pressed the button, he heard the elevator whir to life, and he stepped back.

Or had he heard the whir begin an instant *before* he pressed the button?

Sam looked back at Sarah. She must have had the same thought, because her eyes did not show relief, but were asking a question. His face revealed that he didn't know.

Al and Janet had entered the hallway and were walking toward the elevator, just as Sarah and Sam began to back away from it. If the car was occupied, they would have to return to the stairs. But would they have time to climb another flight to try again?

They could see the top of the elevator now.

Shit.

The second Vaughn's head was visible through the gate, Sarah and Sam bolted for the stairs in panic. Al followed behind, as did Janet, though the cane continued to slow her down.

"Guys!" called Vaughn's voice from the elevator car. "Wait up, guys! I'm hurt!"

Sam's heart was screaming to go back, to help his best friend. Even his mind tried to make excuses and rationalizations, urging him to return, insisting on a logical explanation that would make the pursuer the real Vaughn after all. Only his gut instinct, and his faith in Sarah's logic, propelled him forward.

They could hear the elevator gate opening just as Janet made it through the door.

"I'm hurt!" cried the voice of Vaughn. "I need help!"

Sarah seemed to sense that Sam had slowed, and grabbed his arm roughly.

"It's not him, Sam," she pleaded.

"I know," Sam assured her, gasping for breath.

Sam and Sarah had made it to the third floor, with Al close behind, but Janet was trembling so hard as she climbed that she lost her secure hold of the pool cue. It propelled itself out of her grasp and clattered down the half flight she had ascended, only to roll against the boot-clad feet of Larry Blair.

Janet looked back, and screamed.

Her husband was dressed in the same red flannel and ill-fitting faded jeans he had been wearing the night he had beaten her. His hair and stubble were the same, too, and that look on his face...Janet would never forget that crazed, hate-filled expression as long as she lived. Larry had been angry with her before, sure, and said the most hurtful things one could imagine, about her being fat, and worthless, and "not even a good lay." Once he had even spat in her face when she had performed an unsatisfactory blow job. But the night he had beaten her, *truly* beaten her, it was different. He had looked like a man possessed, hungry for violence, like a rabid animal, drool and all.

There was something else, Janet realized. The image of her ex-husband was flickering somehow, as if under a faulty fluorescent light. Behind the image of Larry, or perhaps, inside of it, was an oily blackness that seemed to ooze underneath the surface, never quite matching up with the illusion of skin and bone. Each time Janet blinked, she thought she could almost see the other creature, the *real* creature, but it was just for an instant, like seeing the echo of a bright light after closing one's eyes.

"Where are you going, *Janet?*" The voice was blood-curdling, dripping with hate, using the same words he had spat at her before he landed the first blow. In his right hand, Janet remembered, would be an empty beer bottle. He would beat her with that bottle until...until she...

What was in his hand?

She was frozen now on the stairs, jaw agape in terror, transfixed on Larry and his right hand. And Larry knew he had Janet's undivided attention, even as Al, realizing she was no longer behind him, had sprinted back down, turning the corner just in time to see the stranger holding something horrible in front of his body, just six feet from Janet's terrified face.

"Jesus," Al gasped.

As a fisherman might hold up a trout still dangling from the line that snared it, the right hand of Larry Blair dangled a dead, bloody, tiny child from a foot of grey umbilical cord.

"Looking for *this?*" he sneered.

Larry shook the cord, causing the body beneath it to convulse, making the doll-sized head appear to turn in mid-air, until its little black eyes snapped open, staring right at Janet.

Janet screamed again, and kept screaming, flashes of pain shooting through her belly as she remembered the beating, and the bloody miscarriage on her kitchen floor tile. "I'm sure it will come out in the wash," Larry would say heartlessly an hour afterward, when he found her crying in front of a heap of bloody clothes, as if she had been distressed over the laundry challenge and not the loss of her only potential child. It all flooded back to her now, and Janet kept screaming up until the second Al fired the shot that knocked her ex-husband back a half flight of stairs.

Sam and Sarah had heard the screaming from a flight above and had slowed. The gunshot, they knew, had been from Al. But had it been effective? They stared at each other, uncertain, not knowing if they should save themselves or try and help their fallen sister. And then all Sam could think about was the first time he had heard a gunshot in person, at Venue A, and could hear Vaughn's whispered voice ringing in his head. *Together, we're strong.*

He closed his eyes for half a second, gaining strength

from the darkness, and raced down to help.

Sam arrived just as Al fired a second shot, presumably as a warning, as the stairwell appeared empty. He raced down a few stairs past Al to help Janet to her feet. As Al stood straight and tall, feet wide in a shooter's stance on the half-landing, Sam half-dragged his panicked Realtor up the stairs as fast as he was able. Al stayed in the back, gun raised and taking the stairs backward, slowly, making sure not to lose focus, ready for anything that moved, human or otherwise.

Sarah was there to help with Janet when they reached the third floor. The couple each took an arm and carried the woman across the hall to the elevator. Sam pushed the call button, repeatedly, trembling with panic and nausea and believing the slow-moving elevator was even more glacial than he had remembered. But it came, empty this time, and he ripped the gate open and they piled inside, Al the last to enter the car, still with gun raised and eyes staring down the hall to the stairwell door.

Sam hit "12" and the car whirred to life, leaving behind the third floor. But within moments of the start of their ascent, they saw through the gate the stairwell door burst open, the figure of Larry Blair standing before them down the long hall, the same murderous rage on his face that Janet had witnessed moments ago. But instead of racing down the hall and toward the ascending car, the face of Larry merely smiled, turned around, and re-entered the stairwell.

"What the hell?" demanded Sarah.

"Oh God," said Sam. "He's going to try and cut us off on one of the other floors."

Sarah whirled to Al. "Can he do that? Can he stop the

elevator?"

"I…don't know," Al admitted.

They could see the fourth floor hallway now through the gate. No one was there. They continued upward.

"Janet, who…" began Sarah, but upon seeing the woman's ashen face, didn't pry further. It didn't matter who it was. It only mattered that it had been someone from Janet's past who had terrified her. Or, perhaps more accurately, it only mattered that it *hadn't* been someone. It hadn't been anyone. It had been an illusion, designed to terrify, to catch them off guard, and to make them victims.

But they weren't going to be victims, Sarah vowed to herself. Not today.

They could see the fifth floor now, and could see the baths through the double doors they had left open. This floor, too, was deserted.

The tension rose as they approached the sixth, then the seventh floor, both empty. Sam wanted desperately to gain confidence as they traveled higher, but couldn't shake the feeling that it was some sort of trap. The elevator was moving so slowly that the creature could ascend the stairs just as quickly, perhaps even faster, unless Al's shot had done more damage than it had appeared. Sam reasoned the last floor it could ambush them at would be the tenth floor, the transit level, for they knew the stair access door to the Mastersuite on the eleventh was blocked, and only the elevator reached the twelfth.

The eighth floor became visible through the gate. Still nothing.

Sarah reached for, and found, Sam's sweaty hand. She

felt sick, and dizzy, the combination of alcohol and adrenaline proving too much for her body to bear. Her right breast ached as well, and when she looked down, she saw that the action of dragging Janet had ruptured the bandage which was covering where her nipple and piercing had been. Blood was seeping out, not in spurts but a slow trickle, down to her waist and pooling atop her studded belt in a crimson stream.

Sarah applied pressure with her free hand, wincing but endeavoring to stay in control, as the ninth floor hallway came into view.

The hallway was not empty.

Sam cried out in sorrow as he saw Vaughn's broken body. As the slow ascent continued, Sam saw the smeared trail of blood which led from the outer gate of the elevator to where Vaughn now lay. Sam looked down at the floor of the car, and noticed for the first time that here, too, was evidence of dried blood. He closed his eyes in pain, realizing what must have happened.

"When he went up to get the gauze," Sarah said, reading his thoughts.

"And it was his body that was blocking the elevator door," Al added, in the hushed, respectful tone of a funeral attendant.

Sam cut them off with a raise of his hand. He didn't need it discussed.

Together, we're strong, thought Sam again.

And Vaughn had been alone.

The car reached the tenth floor, the last floor Sam figured the creature could ambush them. But it, too, was empty. For the first time, Sam allowed himself to feel hope. He squeezed Sarah's hand tighter.

The Mastersuite level, like the baths, opened into a small lobby with two waiting chairs and a set of wooden double doors. When they had passed it on the way down, they couldn't get a good look at it through the cage with Vaughn's battery-powered lights. But now, with the hotel lighting turned on, they could see clearly that one of the doors was badly damaged, a gaping, torn hole through the wood, and hanging from one of its iron hinges. Sam strained to look closer, but the room beyond the broken door was quite dark, and the single lobby light couldn't cast enough past the splintered door to make anything out.

"Can you see inside?" asked Sam of the others.

"No," said Sarah, and Al concurred, though Janet wasn't looking and didn't respond. She was silent, rocking her body softly, looking down at her abdomen in misery.

They passed the Mastersuite and slowly, impossibly slowly, arrived at the small lobby in which they had first found the elevator. The car purred to a halt, and nobody moved.

They couldn't see a thing.

The floor, assuming they had actually arrived, was pitch black. The dim illumination of the elevator car seemed to travel mere inches into the space outside. When they had entered this space before, they had Vaughn's DJ lights to guide their way. But now, there was only the dark.

Sam had a dim realization of what this meant. Either the large trap door that revealed this room had closed, or the trap door was still open, but it was too dark for any daylight to still seep in. He took his phone out of his pocket and turned it on. It was just after 7:00 p.m. Sam laughed aloud at this, not because it meant the sun had not yet set, or the corresponding implication that they could be trapped under a closed trap door, but the darkly comic realization that the entirety of their adventure so far had lasted a mere six hours.

"What's so funny," Sarah demanded.

"It's only 7:00," said Sam, and laughed again, the kind of laugh that could melt into a sob if he didn't stay in control.

"So what?" she countered. But then she understood.

They four stood in silence for a moment. Even with the frantic desire to leave The Eaton, none of them wanted to be the first to enter the dark unknown.

"Wait," said Sam. He fiddled with his phone until the LED light came on. Under normal circumstances, the flashlight app he used couldn't provide much illumination, but in the total blackness, it was quite effective. Sam could see through the gate that the waiting room was empty.

Al opened the elevator gate and the four stepped out, walking slowly to the staircase which seemed to ascend into a solid ceiling.

"Why do you think it's closed?" asked Sarah, since someone had to.

"It might be designed that way," Al ventured. "To come back on its own mechanism after a short time."

Sam frowned. Something felt wrong. On instinct, he turned back to the elevator.

"Janet," Sam called, "don't let the car leave, just in case."

Janet nodded, and limped back, placing her pool cue crutch

across the threshold, which she hoped was enough to stop the car from being called back from a lower level.

"What now?" asked Al.

"We push," said Sam.

The two men climbed a couple stairs and began to push upward on the heavy panel. It lifted on its hinges with ease at first, and to Sam's great relief, the dim light from the dusk-filled station filtered into their space. But after about eight inches, it stopped, and could go no farther.

Sarah gave Janet back her purse, so she could assist in the effort, but even with the three of them working together, the panel wouldn't lift more than eight inches from the opening.

"What's wrong?" called Janet from back near the elevator car. There was a tension in her voice, a tension they all felt. Could they really have escaped The Eaton only to be trapped a few feet underground?

"It's okay," Sam reassured them. "I can probably get a signal on my phone now." But the display still reported no reception. He asked Sarah to check her own phone.

Sarah's phone also showed no reception, but more worryingly, she realized that her earlier text to Kedzie informing her of their whereabouts was reported as "not delivered," having been attempted from this very room.

Just as Sarah was about to panic, she heard the muffled sound of a woman's laughter from somewhere in the train depot. A distinctive laugh they knew well.

It was Kedzie. The *real* Kedzie. She had come after work, just like she said she would.

"Oh, thank God," said Sarah, then cupped her hands to

shout through the opening. "Kedzie! We're in here! Come help us!"

But then they heard another voice, and another muffled laugh, this time a man's.

Sam and Sarah exchanged a glance. Had Kedzie brought someone else by? Well, that was good, wasn't it? The two could help them out.

"Kedzie!" Sam shouted. "Can you hear us?"

The voices didn't seem to notice.

"What's happening?" Janet called behind them.

Al stepped down and joined her near the elevator. "I don't know," he said. "I think their friends are here, but they're in the other part of the depot."

Sam and Sarah screamed louder, and it was impossible the two of them could hear Kedzie's laughter without Kedzie being able to hear their shouting. The couple exchanged a nervous glance, and strained to listen instead of scream.

They began to hear fragments of Kedzie's voice, although the male voice was still too low and muffled to make out. She was giggling, a bit flirtatiously, and they heard things like "…it's so cool…" and "…it's going to be amazing!" Perhaps she was bragging to her male companion about what she knew of the plans for the bar. But then Sam heard her say something that seemed to stop his heart cold, and he gasped, and lost his balance, having to catch himself on the stairs by his knees.

What Kedzie had said was "…*it's pretty sexy that you own all this.*"

He looked at Sarah. She, too, had gone white.

It was clear why Kedzie couldn't hear them. For the same reason they didn't see Vaughn's real body when the fake Vaughn was with them, Kedzie couldn't see or hear the raised platform in the presence of the creature, who had taken the image of Sam.

"Oh, Jesus," Sam whispered.

They had to do something. Sam and Sarah both forced themselves to peer through the eight-inch opening, trying to see what was going on, screaming Kedzie's name again and again, but it was no use. Then, to Sam's horror, Kedzie and the creature "dressed" as Sam entered their room, and Sam cried out as he saw his own face on the man walking Kedzie into the very space where they were trapped beneath the floor.

"*Sam,*" Kedzie protested with a playful giggle. "I'm flattered, but you mean you and Sarah didn't christen this place already?"

"No," the voice of Sam said earnestly. "You know how she is. She doesn't think this is a mature venture. She doesn't understand."

Kedzie laughed. "She's never been any fun."

"Not as much as you, anyway," the creature teased. Sam and Sarah watched as the Sam-creature playfully picked up Kedzie by the waist and placed her on the desk opposite the opening, the creature's back to them now, giving them a perfect view of Kedzie wrapping her ankles around the backs of its knees. Every few seconds, to Sam and Sarah, the illusion appeared to flicker, revealing a sort of inky black shape, but it was clear that to Kedzie, the Sam mask was a perfect fit.

"You're such a flirt," Kedzie admonished.

"Oh, it's not that," the Sam-creature said. "The thing is, Kedz, I've fantasized about owning this place a long time. You know I have. But you're the only one I've fantasized about inside it. Of having you, *taking you*, those strong legs of yours wrapped around my back, telling you how incredible you look, how amazing you are, and how you make me feel alive."

"*Sam*," she blushed. He was saying all the right things. She had been feeling so unsexy since the bad breakup, and the pregnancy, and he had always been so nice to her, and this place…well, it didn't look like much now, but she, too could see his vision for it. She could imagine his success, and how much fun it would be to be with him as he ran his nightclub, and how much carefree laughter they could have, like the endless party of her early twenties.

Sarah noticed Kedzie had raised her legs up to the backs of his thighs, pulling him closer. *What the hell is she doing?*

"Kedz," said the soft, husky voice of Samuel T. Spicer. "I can't stop thinking of you. I need you."

"Oh, Sam," Kedzie replied in a sort of sympathetic purr, "I want you too. But that night…that was a one-time thing. I can't do that to Sarah again."

Sarah made a sound like she had been stabbed in the chest. She grabbed Sam by the shoulder and forced her to look at him. Was it possible it isn't Kedzie after all? Could they both be an illusion? Was this just another trick? But the unspoken questions shooting like daggers from Sarah's eyes were received by a flustered expression of guilt from Sam, and Sarah had her answer. The bastard had cheated on her.

With her best friend. *Jesus, was it Sam's child, too?*

"What's going on?" called Al.

"Are they going to get us out?" added Janet.

But Sarah and Sam barely heard the questions, and offered no response. They stared at each other in agonizing silence, until they could take it no longer, then turned again to stare at Kedzie, who was in real danger.

"Kedzie!" shouted Sarah again, this time with a touch of anger, Sam noticed. But she still couldn't hear them, still did not seem to see the raised floor panel, and still had her legs wrapped around the creature. Only now the creature's jeans were becoming loose, and they dropped to its ankles.

"Oh, God, that feels good," whispered Kedzie. "But you really have to stop. We can't…ohhh Sam how do you know *exactly* how to touch me…"

Within moments, the creature was inside her.

Sarah looked away, but Sam's eyes were transfixed on the image of his own body thrusting into Kedzie just ten feet from their position. And as he watched, he could see the strange flickering, too, the patches of oily blackness that revealed true portions of the creature. But the creature's body wasn't matching up with Sam's. The human figure was upright, tall and narrow, while the creature underneath was bent and hunched to the left. Sam could see the hints of something like a shoulder where Sam's back would be, and some sort of black spike along the contours of his right thigh.

"Oh…hey, hey, Sam…not so rough…" Sam saw Kedzie struggle, and attempt to push the creature back, but with one of Sam's hands it pinned her down, by the throat, and increased its speed. The true form of the monster began to melt through the illusion, piece by piece, like wet paper revealing the surface underneath. Sam could see the creature's right arm now, and its right hand, a sort of slick, shiny claw with three long coppery nails sharpened to points. And he observed again how the creature was hunched, and understood where the other claw was.

"Sam...*Sam! What the fuck!*" Kedzie was shrieking now, wailing in desperation and pain and confusion as the thing began to push its claw further into her body, tearing her flesh from the inside. Sam saw her blood spurt and pool underneath the table as her panic increased, and it was clear that she, too, now saw the true form of the demon inside her. It had ceased pretending altogether, the last flickery hint of Sam's form vanishing like steam, leaving just the rich black form of a child's nightmare. Its thick skin was shiny, like patent leather, but pitted and imperfect too, with signs of age and abuse, deep grey scars along its back like welts from a whip. The legs were strong and muscular, tapering down toward the feet like overturned wine bottles, ending at feet which resembled the claws of the hands, but sturdier, as they didn't move an inch as Kedzie fought against its strength with all of her own.

Sam tried to scream, to cry out and beg the monster to stop its brutal assault, but could not manage a single croak of protest. Helplessly he watched the creature's back constrict and tremble as it used all its force to destroy Kedzie's body, tearing the muscles off her bones as Sam himself might have torn the meat from a rotisserie chicken. Kedzie's own screams were gone now, replaced with the gurgling sound of her torn throat, and the chunks of meat falling onto the wooden floor.

Sam was vaguely aware of Sarah's voice shouting at him from a few stairs below, but he couldn't respond. He couldn't even move. He was still watching the large alien silhouette standing there amidst the carnage, its back rising and falling in heaving breaths, clear sweat glistening on its shiny taut skin.

And then it turned, slowly at first but then reeling around to face Sam, staring him down defiantly with two dark inset slits for eyes, smiling a hideous, wrinkled, toothless grin, face and chest covered and dripping with Kedzie's blood.

Sam felt someone grab his shoulder. Sarah was still shouting at him, yanking and pulling him down the stairs toward the elevator. They heard a dragging sound above them, and Sam dully realized that the creature had moved a piece of furniture, which he guessed had been the object preventing the floor panel from opening. *Oh God,* Sam realized. *There's only one reason it would be moving the furniture.*

The floor panel sprung open on its hinges above them, flooding the space with light. The monstrous form of the creature took just moments to assess the situation, then came bounding down the stairs.

Al was standing off to the side of the elevator entrance, in a wide stance with his gun raised at the beast, but he couldn't fire. "It's beautiful," he whispered instead. The creature seemed aware of Al's hesitation, and slowed its pace, confident in its ability to stop the group before the elevator car could descend. It fixed its gaze on Al and his gun, and began approaching him with a leisurely strut, challenging Al to act, somehow knowing he wouldn't.

"Al!" Sam shouted. But Al didn't hear him. He was a statue.

"The Eaton," Al whispered in a sort of hypnotized reverence. The creature smiled at him in reply, and there was something so *alien* about the black, toothless grin that Sam thought a full set of sharp teeth would have been less terrifying.

"Shoot it!" yelled Janet, who was standing at the elevator threshold. When Al didn't respond, Janet panicked, reached into her purse and threw the only projectile she had access to—the plastic bottle of water she had refilled in the baths. She had intended to create a distraction, giving Al time to snap out of his frozen state, but the creature had seen the bottle coming, and raised its left claw to bat it away. But the sharpness of one of its coppery nails had caused the thin plastic to become pierced instead, and the liquid splashed over the creature's arm and chest like a burst water balloon. Its unexpected reaction was not that of annoyance, but of extreme pain, and it uttered the first sound they had heard from the thing since it has abandoned the Sam illusion—a tortured, inhaled shriek like that of a great bird. It stumbled backward, grabbing its wet arm with a free hand, then recovered and fell forward instead, on its knees.

For a moment, they were all too stunned to move, but Janet's actions had indeed succeeded in bringing Al back to reality. He dropped the gun to his side and rushed into the elevator, motioning the rest to follow. Sam and Sarah did, but Janet's gaze was fixed on the stairs. She had no intention of descending into that prison again. The creature was directly in her exit path, but she could run around it, she was sure, and be free. Without a word of explanation to the others, she sprinted right, forgetting her leg injury and her tight, restrictive skirt, and did indeed make it past the kneeling demon, if only for a moment.

"Janet, no!" cried Sam from the elevator car, moments too late. Janet's leg gave out before she reached the first stair, and she fell forward, arms flailing, just as the creature regained strength, spun around on its knees, and attacked. On impulse, Sam tried to run to help, but Al stopped him from leaving the car by sliding the gate closed just inches from his face. Stunned, Sam tried to protest, and reached for the gate handle himself, but Al had already pressed "5," locking the mechanism and whirring the motor to life. The car began its descent as they saw the creature break Janet's back.

twenty-four

The plan was simple. Oliver would gather the staff, they would climb to the upper levels, then walk down floor by floor, urging everyone to pack their things and walk up the stairwell to the Mastersuite. They wouldn't mention the creature hypothesis, to avoid a panic, but to convey urgency, they would strongly imply that it wasn't safe to remain until the source of a "steam leak" was found. Oliver reasoned this would fit in with the average guest's understanding of the problem, although Jon suspected the real reason might be a desire to save his professional reputation.

Since the elevator was halted on the eleventh floor, the creature couldn't use it, either, leaving the stairwell as the sole means of passage. There was a danger in this, they all knew, but also a sense of security—the creature couldn't ambush them from the elevator side. If the creature revealed itself, they would know for certain where it was, and then try and take action, such as locking it on a specific floor, or better yet, trapping it in an individual room. With Oliver and his staff starting at the top floors and moving down, and Jonathan, Clem and Matthew starting at the lower levels and moving up, the chance of a confrontation with the creature was high. Still, it seemed the most logical course of action that assured all had a chance of escape.

Oliver had knocked on all the doors of the third floor, and the staff and builders had wearily stumbled out of their rooms and into the hallway. He explained the situation and the plan, urging them all to pack quickly and be prepared to help the guests to the Mastersuite. There were several nods of approval, but also a few smirks. Oliver realized that he was slurring his words a touch, and had to explain why.

"It's alcohol," he said. "But I am not drinking for fun. We have discovered that the consumption of alcohol seems to interfere with the...hallucinations. It is easier to determine whether something is real or imaginary with alcohol clouding the brain, allowing the illusion to be less convincing when it appears." Oliver considered explaining the creature hypothesis as well, but decided against it. All they needed to know was that some things they were seeing were not real; the cause wasn't important and might foster panic.

Solomon Sabo, one of the construction staff who had been giving a skeptical glare, cleared his throat. "If that's true, shouldn't we also have a nip or two before we begin? You forbade us from drinking last night, you recall."

Oliver stiffened, reflexively defensive at his previous night's orders being challenged, but couldn't disagree with the man's point. They were the most sober people in the hotel, at a time when he needed as many accurate eyes and ears as possible.

"Alright," Oliver agreed. "Take five minutes to pack your things, anything absolutely necessary, and I'll run back down to the bar for some liquid courage. Is that acceptable?"

It was. The men and women scurried back into their bedrooms to gather their things, and Oliver ran back into the stairwell and sprinted down the stairs. He thought he might run into Clem on the way down, who he had last seen gathering alcohol. But Clem must have already made it to a higher level, as when Oliver entered the lobby, he was alone.

Oliver was about to jog to the bar, but stopped. It was so *quiet*.

"Hello?" he called to the room. A dull hint of his own voice echoed back.

A chill melted its way along Oliver's spine, causing his shoulders to shudder and a gasp to catch in his throat. He spun around in the silence, convinced someone was there, but saw nothing. He found himself intently aware of every dark place within the range of his vision, and imagined something horrible oozing out of each shadow—a black, cold liquid tar which would drown and consume him.

In the silence, the pounding of his heart could be heard and felt in his head, and he began to feel nauseous. He was certain he was going to vomit, and raced to the bathroom behind the bar. When he reached the porcelain, though, he realized it wasn't vomit, but an intense hot diarrhea that was consuming his innards, and he unfastened his pants and sat down within a second of being too late. The force of the expulsion made him cry aloud in surprise and agony, and his headache took a new direction, no longer pounding with his heartbeat but rather ratcheting up to a squeal deep beneath his eyes and extending to the base of his skull.

Oliver became aware of a voice in the room, a sort of panicked whisper, and was surprised to find it his own. He was speaking a prayer, some automatic verse from his childhood he scarcely recognized. Embarrassed, he stopped himself, and soon felt another forceful expulsion from below. He put his elbows on his thighs, and his head in his hands, and tried to breathe at a deliberate pace. *I have never tried to drink so much so quickly,* he thought. *That's all it is. I'll be fine in a minute.*

It took several minutes, but the headache began to lose its edge, and as his intestines were thoroughly expelled, Oliver cleaned himself and left the bathroom. The floor was as silent as it had been upon his arrival, and he no longer felt the need to call out. He had a job to do, and that was to procure alcohol for his staff, give them instructions on how to assist the guests' orderly departure, and then find some way of salvaging his dignity and good standing in the community.

His stomach gurgled with discomfort as he picked up two quarts of J & A Mitchell scotch whiskey. Oliver's vision was still blurred, and he knew his time in the bathroom had not affected his sobriety, so he decided he didn't need any more himself. But would two quarts be enough for the sober staff? He tried to do the math, though it threatened to bring back the headache. Fourteen people? Fifteen? Was that counting himself and Matthew? He couldn't remember.

A loud clanging sound from above startled Oliver, and he almost dropped one of the glass bottles. It was a familiar noise, just the inner mechanisms of the steam boiler which he had heard countless times, but Oliver had never realized how loud it sounded in absolute silence. Had it always been that loud? Surely he would have noticed before. Oliver supposed he always stayed in the Mastersuite, far away from the maintenance room on the second floor, but the volume of the metallic scraping and banging still distressed him. For the first time in The Eaton, Oliver didn't feel *safe*.

You can do something about that, whispered a voice in his head. Yes, Oliver realized, this was true. The back office held two revolvers and more than a hundred rounds of ammunition in the top drawer of the desk. He had never cared for such weapons as a younger man; his father had left him his Civil War Remington when he passed away, but Oliver had kept it in a display case and never fired it. In fact, he had never fired a weapon of any kind, until these two Colts were purchased a few years back, in response to a wealthy friend of the family's being robbed and murdered in her Detroit home. Oliver remembered thinking that if a sweet old widow could be murdered in *Detroit*, one of the safest major cities in the world, then he too had best be prepared to defend his home and investments wherever he lived.

He set down the whiskey and made his way to the back. He found the weapons in no time, chose one of the guns at random, and loaded it with ammunition. Oliver even grabbed a handful of additional cartridges and placed them in his vest pocket. Although on some level Oliver knew there was no guarantee simple bullets would be effective against a supposedly shape-shifting monster, he still wasn't convinced of Jon's full assessment of this danger anyway. At the very least, a gun could help him restore order in the event of a full-scale panic.

Oliver tucked the loaded revolver into his inside jacket pocket. He retrieved the two bottles of scotch and made his way back to the stairwell. Although his confidence had been bolstered, he made an involuntary sound of disgust as he looked at the stairs before him. The thought of climbing to the third level was hard enough; accompanying the group to the tenth level was almost too much to contemplate. But Oliver steeled himself and took each step at a deliberate pace, pausing at each half-landing to catch his breath, and remembering to prepare a nice, false smile of self-confidence before opening the third floor door.

To his surprise, the hallway was empty. He was expecting a group of people with suitcases and steamers, waiting impatiently, for he was later than he had promised. Were they all still in their rooms? He knocked on the first door to his right. No answer. He knocked on another. Still nothing. *What the hell?*

He began trying the doors. Most were locked. One was open, but was empty, the bed neatly made. Another door was open, this one with an unmade bed and a steamer trunk open on the floor, packed in haste, but no room occupant in sight. Something was wrong.

Oliver backed into the hallway, then sharply turned around, as if trying to catch someone hiding in the shadows. No one was there. And, he noticed, there were no shadows in the evenly lit space. The soft vignetting of his vision, which he presumed was due to the alcohol, were the only shadows in view. A dark paranoia was creeping over him, and again his stomach gurgled in a threatening manner.

The clanging sound of the steam boiler, this time from below his feet, caused a momentary sense of disorientation, and Oliver drew a sharp intake of breath. He put down the quarts of whiskey, reached into his jacket pocket, and retrieved the loaded revolver. Although he had loaded it mere minutes earlier, he checked the cylinder to assure all six chambers were filled. He closed it with a flick of his wrist, then pat his vest pocket to check for the additional cartridges. Everything was in order. Of course it was.

Finally, it dawned on Oliver what must have happened. He had told his staff they were going to meet on the transit level, hadn't he? Well, then, when he had been detained, his staff likely just assumed they were supposed to meet him up *there*. Sure, Oliver didn't remember telling them that was the plan, but since that *had* been the plan, Oliver *must* have mentioned it. It was the only thing that made sense.

Relief swept through his mind and calmed his nerves. He gingerly holstered the revolver, picked up the two bottles, and made his way toward the stairwell door.

As he made it to the fourth floor landing, he began to hear excited utterances above him, and a woman's scream. Alarmed, he quickened his pace to the eighth floor, where he saw the door was open, with a few people standing in the hallway.

A bit out of breath, Oliver approached the nearest man, Brett Miller. "What happened?"

"Well sir," said Brett grimly, "there's been a suicide."

Oliver's mouth dropped open. *A suicide?* He pushed past those on the landing and into a group crowding the first part of the hall. He recognized some of the guests as those from the fourth floor, and some from the sixth they were on, which meant Jon and Clem must have already succeeded in evacuating the fourth floor and were moving up as a group. But where was Jon?

And then he saw the poor man, on his knees in the

doorway to his room, weeping in front of his wife's dangling corpse.

"Oh, Christ," Oliver whispered.

He didn't know what to do. He felt ridiculous still holding a quart of whiskey in each hand, and put the bottles down on the floor, approaching Jon from behind. "Is it…" Oliver began, thinking to ask if it was real, and not one of the strange hallucinations, but he could tell from Jon's agony that it was. Or at least, Jon knew it was, and that was good enough for Oliver.

He became aware of the murmurs in the crowd. There were whispers about "this terrible place." And the tone was accusatory, too, and Oliver could feel words of anger and disgust boring into him from all sides. Although no one said it directly, the mood of the crowd was clear. They were blaming *him* for this tragedy. Not this place, not the magnetic mineral baths, but *him*.

Clem approached Oliver with a nasty expression. "What are you doing back down here so soon?"

Oliver blinked, confused. "Back…down?"

"We saw you going up with your guys. You can't be done with the top floors already."

Oliver was baffled. And then his face went white.

It must have been quite an obvious change in his expression, for Clem's face changed as well, from a look of annoyance to one of worry, almost sympathy. "What? What is it?"

Oliver didn't answer, not even when he saw Jon turn around to face him too, tears wet on his cheeks, sending the same confused, worried glance Oliver's way. He just backed away slowly, turned for the stairwell, then sprinted toward it, knocking Jasper Hayden off balance and stumbling into the wall.

"Hey!" shouted the toppled man.

But Oliver didn't hear him. He kept sprinting up the steps, even though it was making him physically ill, the alcohol sloshing through his insides and his brain, until he reached the transit level.

He opened the door in a panic, just in time to see the end of the slaughter.

The entire staff and building crew of The Eaton were there, most of them on the tracks, including Matthew, or what was left of him, his body ripped in two like a broken doll, still gasping and gurgling blood from the half which contained his face. Solomon was running down the tracks into the darkness, but something was chasing him, and then caught him, breaking his neck. One of the housekeepers, Sally Lorent, was screaming but frozen as the creature approached her, not even raising her hands to protect her face when the thing lunged, smothering her mouth and nose with a large black arm and seeming to crush her bones into powder against the curved brick wall.

Oliver was frozen, too, staring at the back of the black monster before him. He had still not seen its face. He needed to see its *face*.

As if reading Oliver's thoughts and wishing to oblige, the creature allowed Sally's destroyed body to crumple, and turned around.

Oh, sweet Jesus. Oh God.

Though an inky ape-like creature in all other respects,

the thing still wore the face of Oliver Stanton.

The staff never had a chance, thought Oliver in horror. *They were sober. They followed it willingly. They followed... me.*

The creature smiled with hate at Oliver, human blood trickling down from its stolen visage and onto its ample, heaving chest. In silence, it began to inch closer to Oliver, and the two stared at each other intently, Oliver with horror, the creature with glee.

A survival instinct kicked in, somewhere deep inside Oliver's psyche, and on impulse his right hand thrust itself into his jacket, retrieving the pistol and pointing it outward in a single motion. It surprised the creature, as Oliver saw the dark parody of his own face register shock, then alarm.

Still running on instinct, Oliver fired. The bullet hit the creature straight in the chest, and the mask of Oliver's face flickered darkly, replaced with sputters of what must have been the creature's own revolting countenance. He fired again, but this time the creature's reflexes had improved, and it whirled its body backward with impressive speed, dodging the lead. For an instant, Oliver thought he saw the creature's face smiling—a horrible, rotting, toothless smile—and then the thing faded out somewhat, still visible in low-opacity spurts of darkness but no longer distinct at all times. Oliver knew he was in grave danger, and his survival instincts kicked in again, his feet sprinting toward the stairwell door before he felt his mind give the order to.

He made it through the door, and ran as fast as he could up the stairs, knowing his only chance of survival was into the Mastersuite, where he could access the elevator, reach the surface, and never return. He could hear his name shouted by someone a couple flights down, but didn't respond. With the speed of a much younger and more sober man, Oliver made it to his door, thrust his key into the lock with minimal fumbling, opened it, thrust himself through, and closed and locked it from the other side. For now, at least for a moment, he was safe.

Christ, Oliver thought for the first time, *all those people… they're all trapped with that thing*. And then, from a darker place inside himself, *I'm ruined*.

But there was no time to think about either concern. He had to get out of here. And right now, it didn't matter that he was the only one who could.

Keeping a firm grip on his gun with his right hand, Oliver rummaged for his billfold with his left, stuffing it unartfully into his pants. There was a ledger here, too, that held information on his investments and his business transactions, including some of the quasi-legal tricks he had pulled in constructing this hotel. He grabbed it as well, tucking it first under his right armpit, then realizing that might affect his ability to aim, shifting it to his left armpit instead.

"Oliver!" shouted a voice from the stairwell door, followed by loud pounding. "Let us in!"

Oliver didn't recognize the voice, but could tell whoever it was wasn't alone. There was more pounding, and another man's voice shouting his name. It sounded like Terry Laurent, the obese banker who had been one of the first on Oliver's guest list.

Are they real? Is one of them the monster? Are they all the monster?

Oliver surveyed the space, seeing nothing additional of importance, and raced to the other side of the large room for the other exit door, the one that led to the small elevator lobby.

For a brief, terrifying moment, Oliver felt convinced that when he opened the door, the creature would be there, smiling at him, towering over him, ready to strike. But when the door swung free, all Oliver could see was the empty little lobby, the open gate, the elevator car's warm glow, and the chair which he had used to keep the elevator from running.

Far behind him at the other end of the Mastersuite, four men were using the force of their bodies, including Terry's ample form, to bash and weaken the door lock into the room. On the third rush, the door jamb cracked and gave way, Terry's body tumbling comically into the luxurious space beyond. Oliver turned to see Jonathan Wesley, Peter Barclay, and Cecil Bickenbach jumping around the fallen man toward the elevator room.

They're trying to stop me. They're not going to let me escape.

"Stand back!" Oliver shouted shakily, pointing the gun at the approaching men.

Jon, whose face was still twisted by grief, looked dumbstruck. "Oliver, what the hell are you doing?"

"I said stand back!"

Peter Barclay, who ran much of the nearby Horner Mill, was an athletic man who under normal circumstances could have overpowered Oliver and beaten him into a pulp. But when he tried to lunge toward Oliver through the open doorway, Oliver shot him dead, a hole ripping through his chest as if he'd caught a live grenade.

From a distance, down the stairwell, Oliver could hear a woman scream. What did that scream mean? Had someone discovered the bodies on the floor below? Or had the creature escaped and was on its way up to finish what it started?

Everyone here is going to die.

"I said...I said, stand back," Oliver croaked in desperation. Jon and Cecil remained still as Oliver backed into the elevator, gun still aimed on them from his right hand, as he closed the gate with his left. But the awkward arm movement caused the ledger tucked under his left shoulder to fall to the ground, and Oliver took just a quick second to scoop it back up before reaching to press the button marked "12," the button that would assure his successful evacuation.

Oliver realized in a horrible instant that he was too late. A floor below had called the elevator before his own button could be registered.

Oh God. Which floor?

But Oliver knew.

There was a bustle of commotion behind Jonathan—someone had undoubtedly heard the gunshot—but he could not look away. As others began flooding into the Mastersuite, Jon stared through the iron gate in awe as the great Oliver Stanton punched the 12 button, over and over, screaming in abject terror, not ascending into freedom as he had planned, but in his final moments of life, descending into hell.

Cecil shook Jon's shoulder. "Come on, man, I need

help!"

Jon blinked and pivoted around. A dozen people were now in the room, some with luggage, some in their coats, all sporting the terrified expressions of wounded children. They didn't know what to do.

"Get everyone in here," Jon heard himself shouting. "Go on, anyone on the staircase still, shout down to the lower levels. Everyone get up here as quick as possible."

A few men raced out of the Mastersuite and began barking directions down the stairwell. Soon the room was filled with a dozen men and women, with more on the way. Cecil and Jon helped with luggage and shepherding those who were paralyzed with fear.

Jon knew they didn't have much time, as only a minute or two would pass before the creature was finished with Oliver. But in a flash of dread, Jon remembered that it could masquerade as any of them, and so what would stop it from ascending the stairs with the rest of the guests? For all Jon knew, he had already assisted the creature inside this very room. His alcohol-filled insides curdled.

Jon dropped the bag he had been carrying and raced from person to person, sometimes grabbing their faces and staring intently, looking for any clue, any of the strange blackness shimmering beneath the surface which identified the intruder. But everyone seemed real. Panicked, he pushed past a lady entering the room and watched others coming up the final lap of stairs, his eyes locking on an elderly man. Something was wrong about him, Jon knew, and even before he saw the shimmery blackness which confirmed its true identity, Jon remembered seeing this man, the real version, already present and accounted for inside the Mastersuite.

"Stop!" Jon shouted. "Stop that man!"

The people around the old gentleman looked confused, and the creature itself gave an excellent performance as an offended innocent, but within moments it seemed to realize the futility of the charade and lashed out, grabbing the nearest person, Clyde Knapp, and hurling him down the stairs, knocking the man unconscious. The black flickers grew darker, and Jon watched its human-looking hands melt into black claws before his eyes. A young woman tried to race past the transforming mass, and never saw the claw coming as it sliced through her chest, tearing her clothes and flesh with equal ease. She continued to stumble upwards, blood spurting out behind her, and a man grabbed her and helped her up just as the creature reached for her too, to pull her down. But it slipped on the blood and missed, giving the man time to drag her bleeding body to the landing. The hideous, shifting thing tumbled backward, shrieking as it hit the lower landing, but Jon saw it right itself just as the woman's body was dragged across the Mastersuite threshold.

The last man in the landing, Jon stared with fury down at the creature for a second. Still wearing the face of a human but transforming into something far more grotesque, the thing pounced upward, two stairs at a time, and was mere feet from the door to the Mastersuite by the time Jon had sprinted through it and closed it shut. It pounded with its claws on the hard wood, certain it could break through, but on the other side, Jasper Hayden and Cecil had already succeeded in barricading the door with an armoire, and the door would not budge.

On the other side of the great room, several people were at the elevator, including Clem, pushing the "up" button frantically. The car wouldn't come. Clem tried to pry open the iron gate, though it wasn't clear to the others what his plan would be if he succeeded in exposing an empty shaft. Climb the elevator wires? But soon it was too late, as the creature had stopped pounding on the door to the stairwell, which meant it had traveled down a floor and might be coming up in the same elevator they were trying to call.

"Get away from there!" shouted Jon, pushing his way past a dozen guests and stumbling toward the small room that housed the elevator door. "It's going to be coming up in that! We need to barricade this door as well!"

"Then we'll all be trapped," countered Clem, though he knew Jon was right. If the creature did indeed travel up in the car, they were sitting ducks.

The elevator motor began to whir. Jon ran back behind the Mastersuite door and urged the other men to follow. The fear of what might be coming up in the car trumped the fear of being unable to escape, and they all rushed in. Like they had with the stairwell door, several men pushed furniture in front of this door, too, though nothing was as high and sturdy as the armoire had been on the other side. Within moments, as Jon had predicted, something was knocking on the other side of the wood.

Thump. Thump. Thump.

"Now what," Clem demanded.

Jasper, who Jon had met on the first night, pointed to

315

the two men standing on a dresser, attempting to remove the tin ceiling tile, one with his bare hands, and one with a crude tool that Jon guessed was a leg from a photographer's tripod. "You help us dig out of here," Jasper huffed. "We're right below the entrance lobby which goes in the depot. We just need to bust through the floorboards."

With what, Jon thought. It seemed terribly optimistic to believe they could tear their way through thick floorboards before the creature could bust through one of the blocked doors. But it was also the only plan. The creature controlled the only known exit, so they had to make their own.

Yet the futility of it all overwhelmed Jon, and the adrenaline which had kept him standing poured out of his body as if someone had pulled the plug on a drain, and he felt the full effects of the whiskey at last. His vision blurred, and his legs became weak. He tripped backward against the nearest wall and slid down it, feeling his insides quiver as his ass hit the floor.

The others ignored him, and Jon became nothing more than an observer, as he had been through so much of his life. "Isn't it nice to be a part of something new," Niamh had said on their first night here. "Rather than always researching the past." Jon thought of all the conflicts, disasters and lost civilizations he had devoted his life to studying, and chuckled aloud. He began to ponder if any of the historical figures he had written about had realized, when they themselves were dying, that someday, others would find their bodies, and judge their actions and inactions as Jon himself had done. After all, someday people would discover the victims of The Eaton as well. They would even discover him. The researcher would, at long last, become the subject.

twenty-five

Once the creature was out of view as the car descended, Sam whirled around on Al. "What the *fuck*, man?"

Al held up a defensive hand. "Now wait a minute, Sam," he argued, voice slurred with intoxication but attempting a commanding tone. "We both know there was no saving Janet after she tried to make it up those stairs. Our best chance of survival was to go back down."

"You didn't even *try* to save her," cried Sam. "You have a gun. You could have shot the thing."

"I would have," Al snapped. "But I was waiting. Then it was too late. We only have a few bullets left, and it didn't seem to hurt it much in the stairwell…"

"Damn it, Al," Sam said, his voice breaking with emotion. "That might have been our only chance to leave! Why the hell are we going back down? Why '5'?"

"You saw how it reacted to the water," said Al. "It became stunned, and weak. Think, too, of the place we think it was trapped."

Sam took a breath and considered Al's argument. The cave they had found, behind the boulder which seemed to have been moved, contained nothing but a trickle of an underground stream. Perhaps those who had once captured the creature had also realized this weakness, and tried to keep it in a weakened state.

"The fifth floor," Al continued, "is also a floor with two

locked doors. There's the lockable stairwell door, and the door to the small waiting area with the elevator. It gives us a defendable space, with a weapon—water—which we know can slow it down, and when it finds its way back inside, through whatever its second exit is that he used to get out, and starts breaking through the stair door, we hurt it as best we can, then leave in the elevator."

Sam did not respond for several moments. He was impressed with Al's ability to reason in a crisis, particularly in what appeared to be a rather tipsy state. "Okay, Al," he said at last, as the car passed the ninth floor. "I understand that if we slow it down, we could get out the elevator side and hope, if it's weak, that it can't beat us to the surface again. And I'm assuming you're saying we would lock the elevator somehow so the fucker can't use it." Sam shuddered as he thought of the last thing which had blocked the car from being able to move: his best friend's corpse. "But why can't we just find the other way out ourselves? It's gotta be through the Mastersuite, right? That's the only floor we haven't seen, and it's closest to the surface."

"I think so too," said Al. "But that's probably how the creature is trying to get back in right now. I don't want to go that way, do you?"

Sam shook his head. He turned to Sarah for her opinion, but she was still silent, looking at the floor of the elevator car. He had seen her like this before, when she was too angry to speak, or when she was close to vomiting and needed to concentrate on a fixed spot. Sam realized her current state of shock could be both, and empathized. The images of Kedzie's death, and Janet's, flashed in his mind each time he blinked, as if he had stared into the sun.

He was about to express support of Al's plan, when the elevator car experienced a violent jolt, shifting the three off balance and knocking Sarah's head against the back wall.

"What the…?" Sam regained his footing, and instinctively looked up, realizing that the creature must have forced open the gate and jumped down the elevator shaft, landing on top of their car. He looked over at Al in a panic, and Al had no answers, his own plan having been dependent on the damned thing taking the stairs. Sam wondered how powerful the creature's ability to read their thoughts really was, and if the mere act of strategizing about the fifth floor plan made such a plan doomed to failure. If that was the case, there was no chance for them at all, as anything they strategized would become known, and therefore fail.

There was another jolt, and the sound of metal scraping against metal, and Sarah snapped out of her hypnosis. "Where are we," she demanded.

Sam understood what she was asking. "Sixth floor's coming up," he said. "Do we try and make it to five?"

Nobody said a word, though they all were thinking the same thing. If the creature above them kept trying to disrupt the elevator, perhaps severing the cables, the entire car could plummet, killing them all. But if they stopped at the sixth floor, they might not be able to make it to the fifth floor before the thing could catch them.

"Keep going," Al said at last, his voice cracking. "We're almost there."

The car jerked again as they saw the sixth floor hallway pass slowly before them. What was it doing up there? Even though it had been imposing in its true form, Sam reasoned that it couldn't be any *heavier* now than it had been when assuming the role of Kedzie or Vaughn. It must be jumping with its full weight, perhaps grabbing the cables or interfering with the mechanism, either trying to actively disrupt their descent or trying to scare them into stopping early. If its intent was to scare, then maybe they were doing something right, and Al's plan was correct.

The fifth floor came into view. Sam opened the internal gate early and reached out to the external, yanking it backward before the car came to a complete stop. The three leapt from the car to the small waiting area, throwing open the left of the double doors to the baths with such force that it flipped around and slammed into the wall. Sam was grateful they hadn't locked it, but knew they had to lock it now. He called to Sarah for the keys, but she was racing toward the other side, the stairwell door.

"Sarah, wait!" called Sam, then stared back at the empty elevator car through the open door. It was lurching now, as if the creature was jumping up and down on its roof with as much force as it could muster.

"Stair door first!" she cried back in response, arriving at the opposite door and fumbling with the keys to lock it. Sam understood. If the creature was on the roof of the elevator car, it might choose to jump into the sixth floor hallway instead, run down a flight to the fifth floor stairwell entrance, and be upon them just as they had sealed their fate by sealing the other exit. But this plan was risky, too, as it seemed the car was inching downward with each thump of the creature's feet. Sam and Al stood inside the opulent room, staring through the one open double door at the shuddering elevator, waiting for Sarah's return to their side.

Then, something snapped. There was a cry of pain, or perhaps triumph, from the creature, and the car began to fall. Sam could see the creature falling too, still in its full, black unfiltered form, standing on the roof of the car just as they had believed, but thrusting its arms out toward them, as if trying to leap onto their floor. It couldn't get the right leverage, however, and its body fell out of view, giving Sam a momentary hope that perhaps it would fall to its death. But then he could see the claw, and then an arm, and then two arms, the creature forcing itself upward, pulling its body through the open gate and glaring at them in fury.

Sarah raced beside them, saw the creature's progress climbing out of the shaft, and helped the stunned Sam and Al close and lock the double doors securely before it could advance further. Within seconds, they knew the creature had completed its ascent, and had reached the entrance. It began pounding against the wood doors.

"The water," whispered Al as he counted the rounds in his revolver, and Sarah and Sam ran to the back shelves to search for cups or tubs they could use. Al stepped back from the locked double doors but stared them down like a sheriff at high noon. He adopted a shooter's stance, and raised the weapon toward the direction of the pounding. He considered shooting through the wood, then dismissed the notion, realizing the solid heavy construction of these doors might act as Kevlar to the creature, wasting Al's three remaining bullets and accomplishing nothing.

Sarah had found a small metal wash tub, and Sam a

ceramic mug, and the two filled their containers with water from the nearest mineral bath. Within moments, they were back at Al's side, as uncertain what to do with their weapons as Al was with his.

The pounding had grown louder, more forceful, and the first crack in the center of the left door appeared as a jagged yellow line before their eyes.

Sam motioned to Al and Sarah for their attention. "We should take the stairs," he mouthed in silence. "We can get out."

Al shook his head. "We don't know that for sure," he replied in the same silent whisper. "We should fight first."

Sarah had the same thought, but chose to act rather than join the muted debate. She had observed a gap of about an inch between the doors and the tile floor, and so heaved her tub to expel the water towards it. The water splashed on the floor and on the doors themselves, much of it bouncing back at them in a wave, but at least some found its way through the gap and into the small waiting area. There was a harsh cry from the creature, and the pounding stopped.

Sam stared at Sarah with a look of wonder and respect, before he too splashed the contents of his cup toward the gap, and they ran to the nearest bath for refills. When they returned to the doors, they instinctively waited, listening for any hint that the creature was still fighting. But the only noise coming from beyond the doors was the faint, hollow sound of water draining into the empty elevator shaft.

"Do you think it's dead?" asked Sam.

"No," said Sarah dryly. But a horrible thought occurred to her. What if the creature had jumped away from the water, climbed back into the elevator shaft, and hoisted itself up to the sixth floor, or lowered itself down to the fourth? It wouldn't be too difficult, and it would explain the silence.

Sarah backed away from the main doors, and sprinted to the door to the stairwell on the other side of the room. Here, too, she listened, but heard nothing. As a precaution, she poured some of the water under this door as well, but the only sound that followed was a gentle trickle of water down the empty stairs beyond.

From across the room, she telegraphed a "what now" message to Sam and Al, who responded with their own confused shrugs. The thing didn't seem to be anywhere. Cautiously, Sarah walked back to the main doors, refilling her metal tub with water on the way. The three stood in silence upon her return, listening, waiting, holding a collective breath.

Sam broke the tension. "We don't even know for sure if the water makes it weak," he said. "This is crazy." Then, again, with emphasis. "This is *fucking crazy!*" In a flash of anger, he hurled the full mug across the room. It shattered against the wall tile, exploding in a shower of wet shards, and Sam felt water on his cheeks. He first thought the drops had been from the splash, but was surprised to discover they were tears. He hadn't even realized he had been crying.

A dark, soft chuckle bubbled up from the other side of the large wooden doors. It was a man's chuckle, filled with age and anger, and Sam knew the creature had put on a new human face, one they couldn't yet see. The laugh didn't sound familiar to Sam, and he glanced at Sarah, who had a similar reaction. They turned to Al, who had lowered his gun and was stepping closer to the doors, transfixed on the muffled sound.

"Hello?" Al asked.

"Hello," the voice responded.

"What's so funny," Sarah deadpanned.

"Oh, I don't know," the voice replied weakly. "I suppose it's all quite amusing, on some level. You found a weakness that *I* never found, but others had, long ago." There was something peculiar in the way the voice emphasized the word "I," and Sarah got the feeling the "I" might be referring to the person it was pretending to be, not the creature itself.

"*You?*" she asked. "Who are you now?"

"Begging your pardon, madam, but you and I are not acquainted. I'm afraid I passed on long before you were born. Before any of you, in fact."

Sam and Sarah exchanged a confused glance. Al, however, seemed to be trembling with excitement. Although it was true he had never met its owner, he did know the voice. He remembered it well.

Al had first discovered the stack of old reel-to-reel recordings when he was ten. It was the summer, and his parents were both at their respective places of employment, leaving a very bored boy exploring the house. He found the reels nestled in an old wooden trunk hidden under blankets in a seldom-used closet, and all ten were unlabeled, still in their thin cardboard boxes. Al first assumed them to be blank, and wouldn't have given them much thought if they hadn't been so intriguingly hidden.

His mom had a reel-to-reel recorder which she used for

dictation and transcriptions in her capacity as a legal secretary, and he had seen her use it enough times to have an idea on its operation. He threaded the first reel, adjusted the volume, and sat on the rug with a bowl of crispy Better Made potato chips.

Over the next few hours, he listened to an old man ramble about visits to other countries, exploring ancient temples, and researching lost civilizations. But more than half of the reels were devoted to a single impossible tale of visions, murders, and some sort of monster, though the narrative rarely made linear, logical sense. It occurred to Al that during the telling of this story, the man was getting progressively drunk, and in fact at one point he even began detailing and extolling the virtues of specific types of alcohol which might keep monsters at bay. Near the end of the final reel, the speech was so soft and slurred that it could barely be understood, and Al had to strain to hear the conclusion of the story, and its haunting descriptions of "absolute darkness." As it finally unspooled to silence, Al sat still, fascinated and terrified. When he heard the back door open, his mom coming home from work, he jumped.

Hurriedly, Al had packed up the reels and hidden them under his bed. Over the next few weeks, Al listened to them again and again, when the house was empty, never telling a soul about their existence. One day, though, he had been careless, and left the equipment out when he ran to play outside with a neighborhood friend. When he returned home for dinner, his mom had explained he should not have listened to those "mad rantings," and to Al's horror, she had destroyed the recordings "to protect the good man's honor."

Tears streaming down his cheeks, Al had stormed down the hallway to his bedroom, and didn't speak to her for days. Though he eventually forgave his mother, he never forgot the strange, dark tale of the underground monster.

Al never thought he'd hear this distinctive voice again. He stepped closer to the double doors, close enough to touch them, his shoes sloshing on the mineral water still puddled from the splash back of the emptied tub.

"But even though I've never met you all," the voice continued, "you do have something of mine. And so you do know a good part of my story."

"The journal?" asked Sam.

"The journal," the voice confirmed. "Yet, you see, it's incomplete. I left it here. And so you don't know how the story ended."

But Al knew. He took a final step toward the door, and placed his free hand against the dark wood, against the long, thin crack, as if trying to feel the life behind it. Sam and Sarah said nothing, and made no move to stop him, as Al swallowed hard, and addressed the door with a rough whisper.

"Grandpa?"

twenty-six

Jonathan Wesley awoke in a fog. The smells of death, excrement, dried sweat and blood were overwhelming, and his eyes wouldn't focus for several minutes. Even before he could see, though, he knew where he was, and knew it hadn't been a dream. The creature who had massacred the men and woman around Jonathan had, for some reason, overlooked him. He searched his mind for his final memories of the horror, and realized he must have passed out. Perhaps the creature had assumed he was already dead.

He sat up, a bit too quickly, and an ache gnawed through the back of his skull.

The light in the room was mercifully dim, trickling in from the hallway and therefore obscuring the gore, but still Jonathan could sense that he was alone among the living. He tried to stand, but could not, at least not yet. His muscles were stiff and ached, and he realized he had no idea what time it was, or even what day. Based on the discomfort of his legs and back, he guessed he had been out for many hours, but being cut off from any light from the outside world made an accurate assessment impossible. Out of habit, he reached across his chest, looking for the small watch which resided in his left vest pocket, but remembered it was in his suite, likely sitting on the dresser near his journal. He was overcome with nausea at the thought of ever returning to that room, again seeing his beloved wife dangling from the ceiling, and vomited to his right. The bile pooled and oozed its way to the lifeless corpse of the woman beside him, and Jonathan took several minutes to sob into his hands.

After a quarter of an hour, he tried to stand again. His right leg had been punctured by some sort of shrapnel, but it had stopped bleeding, and was relatively numb. Once upright, he found he could walk, or at least limp, and so made his way toward the light coming from what was left of the Mastersuite's shattered front door. He tried his best to look past the broken bodies surrounding him, imaging them as long-mummified corpses, which allowed him to progress in the detached manner of the professional archaeologist he was. By the time he made it through the door and into the short hallway, however, he was trembling, and his breathing had developed the raspiness of a panicked child. He had to lean against the nearby wall for a long moment, closing his eyes and concentrating to get his heart rate under control.

Jon stared at the buttons for several long seconds. Then he stepped forward and, holding his breath, pressed "up."

To his shock and great relief, the motor whirred to life. He could hear the muffled sound of the elevator car through the gates, traveling toward him from a considerable distance, perhaps as far down as the lobby. As he waited, a great concern crept into his relief, as the elevator seemed so loud in the absolute silence of the hotel, it seemed clear that the creature would hear it, too, and put a stop to his escape. Maybe the creature would shut it down. Jon imagined hearing the elevator grind to a halt before it reached him, leaving him trapped on the floor forever. But the whirring continued, and the car kept inching closer, and Jon allowed hope to enter his heart. He was going to get out after all, perhaps the only one of the doomed guests to do so.

He saw the top of the car through the gates. Then he saw the man inside. His father.

Jon burst into tears. There was nowhere to go. There was nothing more to do. He had survived all this time, only to be destroyed by the creature just moments before his escape. And in the form of his father, no less, looking as healthy as he had right before his accidental death a decade ago.

Defeated, Jon backed into the nearby wall and allowed his quivering legs to fail, his body sliding into a seated position in front of the monster. The image of Charles Wesley stared back at him, a concerned expression on his face.

"Are you alright, my son?" The body of Charles Wesley knelt in front of Jonathan, and the face of Charles Wesley wrinkled its forehead.

"You're not my father," was Jon's choked reply.

"Of course I am, Jon," said the voice of Charles Wesley.

Jon shook his head, slowly and sadly, finding anger and indignation impossible. "You look like him," he said. "Right down to the grey stubble on the cheeks." When Jon was young, he thought it felt like sandpaper when his dad kissed his forehead goodnight, but he never complained because he loved his father so. "And you sound like him—the deep, kind voice. But whatever you are, you are not my father. My father is dead. And I suspect I will be joining him soon in heaven."

The Charles creature looked offended, even hurt, and

Jon was briefly overcome with sympathy for the illusion. Was it possible that the creature believed it was the person it pretended to be? But then Jon saw a hint of a smile pass across his father's face, a humorless, dark smile, and he knew it was all a game to the thing. It was *toying* with Jonathan, the way a cat will toy with a mouse before crushing him with its teeth. That's all it was. Maybe humans tasted better if they died afraid.

"Son," said the voice of Charles Wesley, "you've just had a bad fever, is all. You're seeing things. Maybe you've been consumed by bad dreams. Perhaps we should get your mother."

"Yeah, sure," was Jon's weary reply. "I wouldn't mind seeing her again. Go ahead, conjure her up, you bastard."

Again, a look of hurt flashed over his father's face. But an illusion of Jon's mother did not appear. The creature seemed to be debating something within himself, and the two stared at one another. After several long, silent moments, the creature spoke again, but although it still looked like his deceased father, the voice had developed an unusual timbre, a darkness underneath the words, and the false warmth was gone.

"This is mine," it said with unmasked bitterness, stretching out the vowels as if through clenched teeth.

Jon didn't know what the creature meant. What was his? This moment in time? The body of his father? The hotel?

"Tell me," Jon prodded, out of obligation rather than interest. "Explain it to me in a way I can understand."

"This is mine," it repeated in a harsh monotone, still lengthening each word for emphasis. "It has always been mine. These are my caves. You can decorate my caves, adorn my walls with wood and plaster and paint, but they are still mine. They will always be mine. And you will always be the invader." The face of his father smiled. "And I will always defeat you."

"We didn't know," said Jon, his voice hollow and hoarse. "You must understand that. You can read our minds, see our innermost thoughts. You didn't have to kill innocent people."

The creature chuckled. "Innocent! None of you is innocent. Clyde Knapp, the man in the room next to yours, had been stealing from his employer for more than six years, and fabricating evidence to frame a work companion if he was ever caught. Dr. Henrietta Carr cheated on her exams and even plagiarized her dissertation. Your associate Clem repeatedly fondled his younger cousin, then threatened to kill her if she told a soul."

"My wife was innocent," Jon countered meekly.

"I did not kill your wife," the creature reminded him. "But she was not innocent. She let her little brother die. She had fantasies of sexual intercourse with your neighbor William while you were away on your trips. She was jealous of her friend Elizabeth, whose husband was home every night, and who gave her three children. Such extreme jealousy that she resented you, even though she was the one who was barren."

"No one is innocent," said Jon. "It's the preponderance of good deeds that defines a man or woman, not the mistakes. We all make mistakes. Even you, creature."

The creature nodded with Jon's father's face, and forced

a smile. "I do not like you, my son," the voice again sounding like Jon's dad, but with the dark hint of hate underneath. "I do not like any of your kind. You are weak, twisted animals. You are liars and hypocrites. And so it is fitting for you to end your existences here in my caves. You deserve death in the dark, not life in the light."

Jon stiffened. "And you, creature? So noble in your torture and slaughter of other living entities?"

The creature smiled. "You are the invaders, not I."

"You were trapped behind a boulder," Jon reminded his enemy. "Others had imprisoned you, years before. Oliver rescued you. You repaid him by murder."

"He destroyed my home. He was worthy of death."

"Who among us is not?"

"Then why be surprised when it comes?"

"It comes to all of us in time," said Jon. "But those carvings were old, by our standards. I suspect our lives are short compared to yours. So why not let us live them? I can leave your cave. I can board it up. I can assure you aren't bothered. But if you kill me, too, others will find you. Maybe the United States Marines will find weapons to destroy you. They will come in large numbers to avenge the deaths of their fellow countrymen. And all your murder would have been for nothing. You would not have peace. We 'invaders' would win."

"If I were to let you leave, avoiding the judgment you deserve, what guarantee would I have that you would keep your word? And before you answer, remember that I know of times you have lied and not kept your word in the past, as you're thinking of one right now, when you told me, your own father, that you didn't steal the fruit when you were six years of age. And just now, your thoughts drift to the time last week when you told the newspaper delivery man that you hadn't received a paper, when you actually had received it and accidentally destroyed it with water before you had the chance to read it."

"None of us is innocent by God's standards, and I cannot claim to have led a completely truthful life. But surely you see that on large issues, I have been a man of my word. Do you see that, creature?"

The creature smiled a father's smile. "I do, my son."

"Then let me be," Jon concluded. "I will cover up for you. I will board up the entrance. I will try and plant stories in the local papers that might explain the absence of some of the more prominent residents that were killed here. I promise you, creature, it is in my best interests to do so, and also in the interests of my fellow men, who might be spared death by your hand, should they go looking for answers. I can make this go away, and you will not be bothered anymore."

His father's face smirked. "You, an archeologist, have this power?"

Jon almost laughed. "Don't you know what I can and cannot do? Can't you read my mind, my every thought?"

The creature shook his head. "No, it isn't like that. It's more that I can read your *past*. I can see your memories, particularly of people, especially when the memories are strong, and you've thought of them often, and recently. You invaders all live in the past, and it's constant. Everything you see and do reminds you of something else. You continually replay scenes in your head, even ugly memories that serve no purpose other than to upset, scare, and anger you. These memories ooze out of you. To me, they are a dirty, yellow liquid, and I can see and taste those memories, literally taste that sour fluid that drips from your pores, from your eyes and ears and mouth, and I can feel what you felt, see what you had once seen." The creature was overcome with disgust. "I cannot stand its taste, the dripping, eggy mucus, but I admit, without shame, that my lust for making you suffer means I can stomach as much of it as you have to give. And with each release of that thick pus, you give constant clues to me as to what you expect an individual in your past would do or say, and so I can comply, when I feed the ooze back to you. But, if you thought of a random number, I could not penetrate your thoughts to retrieve it, nor can I predict your future actions, except when they are similar to your actions in the past, and I can guess."

Jon said nothing. He had no response that seemed adequate.

"To me," the creature continued after a pause, "it seems a strange way to live your life, thinking always of yesterday, especially when it must just reveal, over and over, how disgusting you are, how disgusting your actions have been your entire time on this planet. And when you're not congratulating yourself for getting away with yet another disgusting act, you're wondering what you might have done differently in situations in which you could not have affected the outcome. No other animal does this but you."

Jon nodded gravely. "It's how we learn."

"And no doubt, you will replay this scene in your head

for years, if I allow you to live, dripping your putrid nectar of fear and regret and futility, spilling and oozing your memories onto the earth, where no one will see it, and no one will taste it without me. You, Jon, will convince yourself that you could have saved your wife. That you could have saved them all. That perhaps you could have killed me at this very moment, but were too pathetic, too weak to do so. These dark memories will drip out of your sick, decaying body every day of the rest of your life, poisoning the ground as it poisons your soul."

Jon was silent for a long moment, absorbing the truth of what the creature was telling him. The rest of his life, if he had one, was indeed bound to be miserable, and sad, and obsessed with the past. But wasn't that better than no future at all?

"Are you a demon," Jon said at last, more a statement of futility than a question.

"Like your grandmother?"

Jon's eyes widened. "Was she? Was she possessed?"

"I can't know anything more than you remember."

Jon nodded. "Then what are you?"

His father's image stared back at him, a foreign expression melting across his otherwise familiar face. "I don't know, exactly," the creature revealed in a fleeting moment of humility. "Would a demon know they were a demon? I'm just…here." The face hardened somewhat. "And here, is *mine*. Here, is *me*."

"You don't remember how you first came to be in this place? To…*be* this place?"

"I do not," his father's voice admitted. "I may have been

hunted. But I do not much care. Unlike you, I live in the present, not the past."

"Then how do you learn?"

"I do not need to learn. I need to live."

The two stared at each other for some time. The monster seemed capable of rational argument, yet was utterly alien, despite looking, and even smelling, like the man who had raised him. Could this really be some sort of undiscovered, intelligent life, as explainable by Darwin as man himself? Sure, perhaps an evolutionary advantage could be gained by absorbing people's memories and mastering mimicry—a chameleon of thought instead of form. But where could the giddy, indiscriminate evil come from? If it had indeed been hunted, had there been others? Was it the last of its kind, doomed to hate humanity without knowing why, using its powers to torture those it found unworthy of life? To what end? Jonathan couldn't wrap his head around it. This monster couldn't exist, yet there it was. Whether it knew itself as a demon or not, a demon it must surely be.

"Creature," Jon began, addressing an earlier question, "I cannot give any assurance that my plans will be successful, only that they represent your best chance for privacy. 'Tis true my motives are of self-preservation, and perhaps preservation of others, but I am not lying to you. I am not a man without means, and I will do what I can to prevent anyone else from falling into your judgment. Ultimately, it is your choice. You have the power to destroy me, and I do not have the reciprocal ability. I am weary, and we have talked enough. So please, if you are to kill me, then do so without haste. If you are to accept my proposal, to let me escape and try and stop others from pursuing you further, then stand aside and let me begin my work. I will speak no more on this, and await your decision."

Jon sensed a deep loathing from this face of his father, and knew that his own hatred for the beast could not approach the bitter, unhinged abhorrence the creature felt for humanity. Jonathan tried not to think of anything from the past, not even the recent past, for fear of offending the creature with vile emanations of memories that only the beast could see and taste. But he couldn't look at the monster, either, because it was impossible to stare in the face of one's father and not be flooded with imagery of the past. So, Jon turned his head and stared at the wall, attempting to concentrate on counting the shapes of the patterns etched in the wood, filling his mind with abstract math, hoping it wouldn't remind him of a damned thing.

At last the creature stood up, brushed off the illusion of his father's slacks, and walked back into the elevator. Jon remained seated, paralyzed by uncertainty, until he understood the creature intended Jon to join him in the car. He got to his feet, wincing again at the pain in his leg, limped over the threshold, closed the gate, and pressed the glowing "12" to exit.

The two arrived at the waiting chamber, and Jon left the elevator alone. The electric light from the elevator bathed the room in amber, but Jon did not feel safe just yet. The staircase before him ended at the floor of the depot, and he realized he still had no idea what time it was. He would have to listen at the underside of the floor to assure the depot was closed and free of people before he would attempt the mechanism that would free him. Jon heard a noise behind him, and turned to see his father's form closing the gate and pressing a button. As Jon watched the car descend, he saw the image of his father fully transform into the black, terrifying beast he had only glimpsed in drunken flickers before. And, to his astonishment, he found the creature to be beautiful.

Jonathan Wesley smiled in spite of his pain. He had communicated with an inhuman lifeform of great power, one who had slaughtered countless others and caused his own wife's suicide, but he had learned from it, and survived. And in surviving, he had a duty to protect others, to devote the remainder of his life to protecting the incredible secrets he now possessed. It may not have been a mission from God, but it was a mission nonetheless.

He waited for over an hour until he was sure no one was in the station, lifted the floor on its hinge, and entered the deserted depot office. He drank water, which he was desperate for, and found day-old bread in a trashcan, which he devoured with impunity. Then, calculating that he had but hours before a morning crew might arrive, he began to systematically board up the elevator shaft, disassemble the lights in the basement waiting room, and apply thick wood glue to the seam around the hidden entry panel, which Jon was sure would hold a hundred years. If Oliver had been careful, and it was true the secret had been maintained, then every person who knew of the hotel had died within it, and no one would be looking for a way in. And, if the creature were to be believed, as long as its home was safe, it would have no interest in a way out.

In the months that followed, Jon did his part to obscure and hide the true nature of the disappearances. His experience as an archeologist had required an ability to discern the authentic from the forgeries, but he found that also gave him a unique talent at crafting forgeries as well. Jon was able to write letters, create false travel documents, post official-looking notices in area papers, send convincing certificates to numerous jurisdictions, and develop a number of plausible, documented scenarios which could explain the deaths of those he knew from the hotel in an untraceable, pattern-free collection of freak accidents, spread over the course of a year as to not arouse suspicion. He got a job selling train tickets at the depot, on a forged recommendation letter of course, and on the rare occasion someone would mention something peculiar, he would do his best to send them off the scent. With Oliver missing and presumed dead (according to documents mailed to his estate, he had traveled far into Canada to hike the dangerous northern trails), the depot was sold to another wealthy magnate, who liked what he saw in Jon, promoting him to manager, where he stayed for the remainder of his career. He even got remarried, to a young, ambitious redhead he met at the station, and at the advanced age of 58, Jon fathered his first child, a daughter, who they named Anna.

"This is mine," the creature had said, referring to the space below the earth. But also, more cryptically, "here, is me." Jon could never grasp the meaning of this claim, and it haunted him, but not as much as the idea that his memories were physically oozing out of his body, a thought which disgusted him. As he got older, he began to drink more heavily, and became emotionally distant to his family, even abusive. In his twilight years, the same dementia which had claimed the life of his grandmother claimed Jon's sanity as well. After being told by doctors that his time was near, he began to record hours of nonsensical voice recordings up until the moment of his death, ranting both about a secret, evil hotel, and also a terrifying creature, which he referred to as *The Eaton.*

Years after her father's passing, Anna would fall in love with and marry a dashing young Detroit salesman named Milhouse Horner, and after several miscarriages and a decade of assuming she was barren, the Milhouses would have an unexpected child when Anna was nearly 40.

More than a century had passed since the creature had spared the life of Al's grandfather. Jon had promised the creature would be left alone. But the presence of these intruders proved that this clemency had been a mistake.

The Eaton would not make this mistake again.

twenty-seven

"Let me in," purred the voice of Jonathan Wesley from behind the wooden doors. "We'll talk about things. I can tell you about myself, about this place. We'll have a nice talk. We don't have to be enemies. You're my family. You're my grandson, Albert. A boy I never got to meet."

Al placed his right palm gently against his side of the door, as a visitor might attempt contact with a prisoner behind bulletproof glass. Sarah stepped forward, alarmed at Al's proximity to the danger. "Step back, Al. Come on."

Al ignored her, or perhaps didn't hear her at all. He was transfixed, as if hypnotized by the familiar baritone voice just inches from his hand. He even had a decent idea of what the creature must look like, based on old photos he had inherited when his mother had passed away.

"You've been looking for me, haven't you," said the voice.

"All my life," Al whispered.

"Then let me in. We can talk."

Sarah stepped closer once more, but Sam placed a hand on her arm and shook his head. "He's not going to let him in," he assured her. Al still had his right palm resting against the door, but was making no motion to reach for the knob or lock. He was simply standing in place, mesmerized by the voice but not seduced by its message.

Al stifled a laugh that might have been a sob. "You know

I can't."

"Why can't you," said the voice.

"Because," Al replied with genuine effort, "I saw what you did to Janet."

"She tried to escape," the creature reminded him.

"But so will we."

"Now, Albert," the voice replied in the soothing, yet condescending tone Jon sometimes had used on Clem. "You must know you're never leaving here. You *know* that, right?"

"My grandfather left."

"Did I? Oh, I wouldn't agree with that my child. See, you seem to think that just because Jonathan Wesley lived for years outside of this place, that means he isn't still here. But of course he's still here, because here I am. I retain his memories, from the innermost corners of his mind. That's more than I can say for his original, rotting body."

"He lived a life after you. He lived decades after you, memories you can't possibly know. You're incomplete."

"I know some of them," Jon's voice countered. "Because I recorded them, and you heard them, and retained them. Recordings, too, that no longer exist, as I understand. So again, I am all of me that is left."

Al said nothing to this. He let his hand fall from the wooden barrier before him, and turned to face his companions. Sympathy flooded Sarah's face when she saw him, as Al's cheeks were now drenched with tears.

"Are you okay?" she asked.

Sam shot Sarah an irritated scowl. "He's fine." He turned back to Al, and his face held a mix of heartbreak and fury. "You *knew* about this place? You knew about...*that?*"

"No, not…not really. I mean, I've always wondered if his stories were real. I've imagined it…like any kid digging in his backyard imagines buried treasure, you know? But you never truly *believe*…" Al looked and sounded like a confused child now, without a trace of the sarcastic, weary man Sam had gotten to know. But this didn't dissipate Sam's anger. Sam was still carrying a full container of water, and was tempted to throw it at the bastard.

"You didn't think to mention it when we pulled up the floorboards? When we were standing in a fucking underground hotel lobby? Or even when you found the damned journal?"

The reel-to-reel tapes had offered few specifics, and Al had spent his younger years searching Michigan's abandoned hotels, only later considering underground possibilities which might better match up with his grandfather's recorded ramblings of "the dark." It had been chance that he had met Sam a few months earlier, and learned of the kid's plans to purchase the old depot, offering to help on a very slim chance of discovery. But once it became clear that they had indeed revealed The Eaton, making his grandfather's legends true, Al couldn't wake himself from the dream.

"Sam…I'm sorry."

"Tell that to Kedzie's parents. Or Vaughn's."

"Would you have believed me?"

"That would have been my choice to make!"

Sarah raised her hands in a truce-calling gesture. "Guys, we don't have time for this."

"On the contrary," interrupted the voice behind the

door. "You have as much time as you like. You've destroyed the elevator. There's nowhere to go. And Albert," it said, lowering its voice to a conspiratorial level, "I'll even tell you a little secret."

Al, who had turned back toward the door and was still inches from it, leaned forward to hear.

"Unlike you three," the voice insisted, "I *am* getting out of here."

Before Al could process this, a single black talon pierced through the face of the wood and sliced deep into Al's chest.

From behind, it took Sam and Sarah a moment to realize what had happened. Al's body just seemed to jerk suddenly, spasming in place as if he had touched an electric fence. Then he fell back, the claw making a thick, watery sound as it was freed from Al's flesh, and the blood spurted up in a deep arc, hitting the door and even the ceiling.

Sarah rushed to his aid, but Sam hurled the water through the crack beneath the door, and they all heard the creature squeal, not in the voice of Al's grandfather but something more primal. Sam raced to refill his container and repeated the maneuver. When he turned back to the others, Sarah was helping Al press down on a bloody mess a few inches above his navel.

"It's bad," Sarah gasped. "Oh my God."

Al nodded. He was still alive, but understood he wouldn't be for long, and accepted this fate. Maybe it was just the alcohol, or being down a pint of blood, but it felt somehow predestined, as if he had always known if he ever found The Eaton, his life would be in its hands.

"Listen to me," Al commanded in a phlegmy whisper.

"You can't let it leave. You need to destroy this whole place."

Sarah and Sam exchanged a look of astonished panic. "And how the hell do you suggest we do that," Sam said.

"Steam pipes, everywhere," Al coughed. "The huge machine and boiler. Sarah, you're technical right? Cars?"

Sarah nodded.

"Stuff the vents, override everything, set every dial to 11. Then get out. I can keep him weak here. Just prop me up by the bath closest to the door and give me some buckets. I'll buy you as much time as I can."

"We're not leaving you," Sam said, a bit unconvincingly.

Al chuckled in response. "You were ready to kill me a minute ago."

They heard a moan, then a light tapping sound on the door from the other side. *What,* thought Sam, *does it think knocking politely will change our minds?*

Al winced with pain, then recovered. "Sam, you need to find the way out. It has to be the Mastersuite. I think that's where my grandfather was breaking out from, I'm not sure, but it makes the most sense."

Sam frowned. "We couldn't open that door. It's blocked."

"If that's where it got out to kill your friend, I think it unblocked it for you."

"Al…"

"Look, now you *are* wasting time. Get going. One of you take the gun."

"Absolutely not," insisted Sarah. "Al, if that thing makes it through, just unload as much as you can. Even if it doesn't kill the thing, we might hear it, and know we're out of time."

Al agreed. He was also thinking that, if the creature was not easily stopped, he would be glad for the chance to put a bullet in himself, too.

Sam stood up and poured more water under the crack in the door. Again, they heard groans of discomfort. Sam returned to Al and, with Sarah's help, dragged and propped Al up by the water supply closest to the doors. Sam filled two containers for him to start, and helped him load new cartridges into the revolver. Al motioned to the whiskey bottle nearby, and Sarah retrieved it. Sarah and Sam each took a swig of whiskey from the bottle and handed the remainder to Al.

"Now get out of here, both of you. I mean it."

Sam and Sarah steeled themselves, then sprinted for the stairwell door. Sarah flung it open, half-expecting to find some dark figure from her past smiling there, but it was empty. She began to run down the first flight, and caught Sam following her.

"No, Sam, you have to go up. Al's right, one of us has to find the way out and it might take muscle, okay? My part takes brains." Sam winced a bit at that, but Sarah didn't care.

"I'm not letting you go alone."

"Samuel, you will get your ass upstairs and find us an exit, or I'll kill you myself."

He stared at her. She meant it. He turned and sprinted, the shot of whiskey sloshing in his cramping stomach.

After two flights, Sam had to stop to catch his breath. He wanted to vomit, but didn't want to reduce the alleged effectiveness of the alcohol against the creature's powers should he encounter them again. A few deep breaths brought his world back into focus, and he set a deliberate rhythm for himself, climbing the remaining steps in a sort of structured agony. On the tenth floor landing, he noticed the DJ light which had been left behind, and briefly considered grabbing it to use as a cane, but didn't want to lose momentum. By the time he arrived at the eleventh floor, Sam's head was spinning, and he again was in danger of retching, but fought it back. Hands on his knees, Sam indulged in five full breaths before looking up at the door before him.

He had been expecting the door to have been forced open, reasoning, as Al had, that the creature must have used it as an exit when they were traveling up the slow elevator. But the door was just as they had left it hours earlier—unlocked, pushed open a small crack, apparently still blocked by a piece of furniture on the other side.

Still, he had come this far. It was the only logical exit. Sam closed his eyes for a moment, building up courage, and then threw his entire body into the door like a linebacker. The pain started sharp at his shoulder, then flooded over his chest and up to his head. He cried aloud but remained upright, checking to see if he had made any progress. The crack had indeed grown, but was still less than an inch of space, enough to see that the room behind the door was dark. If he did somehow break through, Sam would need a flashlight. He kicked himself for not grabbing the DJ light a floor below, and considered using his cell phone light instead, but decided he wanted to retain the phone's remaining battery.

After another deep breath, Sam sprinted down the stairs, grabbed the DJ light, and climbed up again. He had to carry the light in his left hand, as his right arm was still aching from the attempted bashing of the door. As he considered ramming the door again with his left shoulder, it occurred to him that the sturdy aluminum and steel tripod he held could be used as a makeshift crowbar, at least now that he had a small opening. Sam unscrewed the LED light from the top of the tripod, tightened the legs into a closed position, collapsed the tallest section into the middle section to give the tube more strength, and inserted it into the crack about four feet off the ground. He kept his left foot on the ground and pushed his right against the stuck door, pulling on the base of the tripod while simultaneously pushing the door with his foot. The maneuver worked for a few more inches, before the space became too large, causing the tripod to become loose, hurling Sam backwards against the stair landing.

"Shit," Sam said.

Encouraged, however, he got back to work, this time using the larger base of the closed tripod as a lever on the bottom of the doorframe, against the ground. This seemed to work better than his first attempt had, as heavy furniture was always easier to move from the bottom rather than the top, and soon the door had opened enough for his body to squeeze through. Sam moved the tripod out of the way, recovered the LED light, flicked it on, sucked in his gut, and pushed inside the Mastersuite for the first time.

He tried not to think about the dark cellar at Aunt

Eleanor's. He had steeled his nerves for the unexpected. But nothing prepared him for this.

The first thing the light hit was a broken skeleton, patches of mummified flesh visible under torn clothes. He flicked his light away, to another part of the room, but it only revealed another body. Then another. Then *another*. One skeleton seemed to have been cut in half somehow. Another corpse had fingers of both hands pressed deep into the skull's sockets, as if in the end he had clawed out his own eyes. It was too much. Sam couldn't hold it back this time, and dropped the light onto the carpet as he collapsed, vomiting and crying and choking back screams. The taste of the whiskey and the smell of the bile caused him to wretch again, until his body could give no more, and he gasped and dry heaved, kneeling and panting, the puddle of sickness oozing over his right fingers, but Sam without the strength to move his hand away.

Sam realized the LED light was still lit on the floor beside him, shining over and upward toward the center of the room. As his eyes adjusted, he began to make out a hole in the ceiling. Underneath the hole, someone had moved a heavy wooden desk, and two more bodies lay atop this desk, with pieces of another corpse strewn beside and around its base, mixed with what looked like wooden panels and plaster which had fallen. These dead people had been trying to escape, but the creature must have attacked them before they could.

We were right, Sam thought. *It's a way out.*

Sam wiped his hand off on his jeans, grabbed the light from the ground, and walked briskly to the center of the room, hopeful for the first time since Kedzie's death. He shone the beam into the hole, and his heart sank.

"No," Sam whispered. "Jesus, no."

The previous guests of The Eaton had indeed tried to escape through the ceiling. But it had been in vain. Above the ceiling plaster and wood supports lay solid, impenetrable rock.

To be sure, Sam pushed one of the bodies off the desk and climbed up himself, reaching to touch the stone. He clawed at it like an animal for a moment, then pounded it with the knuckles of his left hand, bloodying them in an instant. There was no use. It was the roof of a cave. And without incredible tools and a great deal of time, of which Sam had neither, there would be no exit through the Mastersuite.

It occurred to Sam that perhaps there was a way out after all. He hopped down from the desk, nearly slipping on what looked like a leathery femur, and raced to the other side of the suite, to the door to the elevator room. Faint light crept in from the cracks and missing chunks of the door, and Sam tried to concentrate on only these lit shapes to avoid being affected by the dozens of destroyed bodies around him. When he opened the damaged door and stepped into the light, his body shuddered with relief.

It took some effort, but Sam was able to force the exterior gate open, allowing him to look into and up the shaft. He held the gate with his left hand, allowing his body to lean over into the shaft, using his right hand to angle the handheld light. He thought there was a chance that he and Sarah could climb from the eleventh level to the twelfth. But

Sam soon realized that this was also a dead end. The shaft itself was smooth on all sides, and the entrance lobby was not just a couple feet away but at least eight feet up. If the elevator had still been in place, there may have been a way to climb the cable. But that cable had snapped, and was now likely coiled around the roof of the worthless elevator car a dozen stories below.

He returned to the small lobby, but his knees buckled at the thought of entering that room of horrors so soon. He fell onto one of the nearby visitor's chairs instead, catching his breath and trying to make sense of what he knew.

The creature had somehow gotten to the surface while they were riding the elevator. Which meant there had to be another way out. But if it wasn't through the highest floor, and the stairs didn't reach the surface, and the elevator was in use, then what was left?

Then, it hit him.

"Oh, fuck me," Sam said aloud, shocked by his own obliviousness. Of course there was another way out, because there had to have been another way *in*. The hotel hadn't existed when the Native Americans had trapped the creature behind the boulder. It was just a series of caves. There weren't staircases and elevators in the age of petroglyphs. The caves must have reached the surface, at least back then. And, Sam realized, they almost certainly must have reached the surface when the hotel was being built, too—how else would the place have been tunneled out, and building materials moved in, in secret, underneath an existing train station? It would have been impossible unless the construction workers could come in from the side, already underground. And the exit still must be around, because the creature must have used it an hour ago. The Eaton wasn't trapped down here, after all; even without a cave tunnel, it could have taken the elevator years ago. It was *choosing* to be here. Which means it could also choose to leave. And so could they.

The way out was through the Transit level. Sam was sure of it. He had to tell Sarah.

He stood up, powering through the dull aches that panged his right shoulder and bloody knuckles. He hurried through the ghastly display of skeletons and fossilized flesh. He squeezed back through the opening he had made with the stairwell door.

And as he raced down the first flight of stairs, Sam heard the unmistakable pop-pop-pop of Al's revolver.

twenty-eight

Sam froze on the stairwell, uncertain whether to continue down, or retreat. Al would only have fired at the creature if it had broken through the doors. Maybe The Eaton was dead. Or maybe Al was in trouble. Or, maybe Al was already dead, and now Sarah was in trouble. Or maybe the thing was coming for *him.*

Sam continued to descend the stairs, trying to make as little noise as he could and listening intently for any clues to what was happening below. He made it to the Transit level, and a part of him longed to escape this way, but he knew he couldn't abandon Sarah, and Al, too, if he was still alive. Sam kept descending, quickly and carefully, but only made it to the ninth floor when he heard the creature lumbering up the stairs to intercept him. He darted into the level, Gameroom and Apothecary, closing the door behind him. Sam observed that the door to the stairwell itself could be locked, as had been the case on the other common levels such as the Baths and Maintenance.

He found the correct key, locking the mechanism just seconds before the creature itself arrived at the landing. Sam stepped backward, seeing the doorknob shake.

"It's me, guys," came Al's voice from behind the door. "The thing is dead. We can get out now. Come on, open the door."

Though his mind was still affected by a haze of alcohol,

Sam recognized the significance of "it's me, guys." The reference of "guys" implied that the voice behind the door was not Al, as the real Al would have known that Sam and Sarah had separated and were on different floors. It was therefore also likely that the creature had not been able to extract that information from Al, which meant that Al had either been too drunk for the creature to read his mind, or Al had died before it could.

"Open up," Al's voice called again.

Sam had just seconds to consider his next move. There was a chance the creature was bluffing, and did not know Sam was behind the door. If Sam did not respond, it might give up and try another level, perhaps even finding Sarah. For the moment, Sarah was relatively safe, as long as the creature thought they were both on this level.

"Come on, Sarah," Sam said, in an audible voice but not conspicuously loud. "We'll hide in here!"

The bluff seemed to work, as the pounding on the door continued.

Sam's eyes darted between the Apothecary side and the Gameroom, trying not to notice Vaughn's body by the elevator door. The Apothecary would provide little protection with its glass windows, one of which was already broken. He couldn't imagine finding a drug that could harm the creature, and he knew there was nothing that could be used as a weapon, as Janet couldn't even find a simple crutch, having to resort to a pool cue. He ran into the Gameroom instead, also wondering if he could make use of a cue, but realized that if a gun provided little protection, a stick of wood was rather worthless. Sam briefly fantasized that he could cover the hallway in billiard balls, and the creature would slip and fall down the elevator shaft.

The hallway door was being hit with greater force now, as if the creature was ramming his entire body against it. It wouldn't be long.

Sam closed and locked the Gameroom door, providing a bit of extra protection, though he thought that it only made his coffin smaller. He wasn't going to get out of this. The Eaton was too strong, and too insistent on Sam's capture, to be stopped or outsmarted. But it could still be slowed.

There was a small bathroom in the corner of the Gameroom, and Sam wondered if the toilet and sink water might be mineral water as well. It was worth a shot, he knew. Buying Sarah more time had to be his fundamental objective. She still had a chance. The problem was, Sarah didn't yet know about Sam's deduction about the Transit level. He had to get her the message, or she, too, would race up to the Mastersuite, and be trapped.

The small dumbwaiter on the far wall caught his eye. Could he send Sarah the information that way? There was indeed a dumbwaiter door on the second floor, but it was in the laundry room, not the maintenance room, so even if Sam had sent a note, there's no way Sarah would know to look there. He cursed at his inability to call or text her, but as he knew well, there was barely any cell reception in the train station itself, let alone underneath it.

A crash in the hallway seemed to announce the collapse of the stairwell door. The Eaton was one door closer.

Sam considered barricading himself in the small bathroom, perhaps buying a few more minutes, but there was something so horrible about the thought of dying in a bathroom that he couldn't bring himself to accept the plan. He did, however, think he might be able to use the bathroom as a ploy for more time, if he could convince the creature that he was keeping Sarah safe behind the door. But, sacrificing his life for Sarah's only made sense if Sarah could make it out.

Like many couples, Sam and Sarah had a "special song." The song's chorus had been playing on a loop in Sam's head since he locked himself in this room, grief and longing churning inside him the more certain he became that he would never see her again. Sam realized that there might be a reason his subconscious was blasting this particular station. He took out his phone, checking to make sure the song was in his library. It was.

"Let me in, guys," called Al's voice from beyond the Gameroom door. "We have to get out of here!"

Sam suppressed a chuckle. Did the creature think Sam would be fooled by that ruse, after just breaking down the stairway door with inhuman strength?

He set the song to loop, keeping the phone volume low for now but preparing to raise it to maximum once placed in the dumbwaiter. To make sure that Sarah got his message, he had to improvise. She had to be able to read it the moment she touched the phone. Sam decided the fastest way would be to compose a text message, even though he knew it wouldn't get through, and then take a screenshot of the text message, which would create a photo he could set as his phone's background and lock screen. That way, the moment Sarah touched or picked up the phone, even without unlocking it, the message would be there.

The Al creature had given up on verbal entreaties and was beginning to pound the door with its fists.

Sam hurried to the dumbwaiter, set the looping song to maximum volume, double-checked that the message did indeed show when the phone was touched, and closed the inner and outer dumbwaiter doors. He was relieved to observe that the sound, while muffled, was still quite audible through the doors, and with luck would resonate from the laundry room into the hallway, in the silence of an empty hotel. He pressed the "2" button beside the box, and the message in a bottle began its descent. The music faded slowly, deeply away.

The creature's fists had begun to crack and splinter the center of the Gameroom door. Sam was almost out of time. He ran to the bathroom, found it could only be locked from the inside, and so closed it and looked around for a barricade. The nearby billiards table was the only suitable candidate, so he raced to the far side of the table and hefted it across the room. At a suitable distance from the bathroom door, he picked up one side with significant effort and tipped it ninety degrees. It came down with an enormous thud, several billiard balls bouncing out of pockets and rolling across the floor around him. He shoved it flush against the bathroom entrance, then turned around just in time to see a hole form in the far door, the blackness of The Eaton behind it. It no longer had any interest in pretending to be Al.

The creature bent down to peer at Sam through the splintered hole. Sam backed into the overturned pool table, then tried to look as protective as possible of the covered up space. The Eaton had to believe Sam was trying to protect Sarah, or none of this would matter. It smiled a toothless smile, then backed away from the opening. Sam was sure the creature was preparing to ram the door a final time. But then, inexplicably, it didn't.

Sam took a cautious step forward. He could no longer see or hear the thing at all. Had it figured out the truth about Sarah? Had it left him for the second floor? If so, what could she do? What could *Sam* do? Should he stay put, in case the creature came back? Should he run after it, and try and attack it before it reached Sarah? Or, should he abandon Sarah and escape out the tenth floor himself?

Sam was paralyzed with fear. He realized it was not fear of the creature, but in not knowing what to do, feeling helpless, powerless, with every option before him impossible. He had to act, yet could not.

A memory crept up on him, bleeding into his mind, demanding attention and respect. Sam shuddered, trying to shoo the image away. He hadn't thought about that day for a long time, as it was the only traumatic experience he had never shared with another person, not even Sarah. It was the only other time in his life he had felt this level of terrified indecision and helplessness. Even that awful night at Venue A with the gun-wielding nut job hadn't left him frozen with indecision, as the correct path had been obvious: stay down and shut up. But that day at Aunt Eleanor's was different.

"Oh God," Sam whispered. "Why am I thinking of this?"

And then he could hear it, at least he thought he could,

from a great distance. As it had been, it was still the weakest, most pathetic little kitten mew imaginable. But was it in his head, or in the hallway?

Sam listened, stepping closer to the broken door. He tried not to breathe, demanding total silence of himself, convinced the sound had been real, then equally convinced that it hadn't been.

Sam tried to make sense of the situation. He stared at the hole in the door. The Eaton was either waiting out there, or it wasn't. If it was still in the hallway, then it was toying with him, trying to smoke him out. It would surely kill Sam the moment he stepped outside the Gameroom. But why would it do that? The door had already been breached, and the thing could enter whenever it liked. Was there something special about the Gameroom itself? Some magical force that kept the thing at bay? Seemed unlikely. There wasn't even any mineral water. Perhaps it had indeed read Sam's mind, despite the alcohol, figured out Sarah's location, and ran to attack her first. But this, too, seemed unlikely, as The Eaton would know that left Sam with an escape route, and Sam didn't believe for a moment that the thing would allow one of them to reach the surface without a fight. Unless it was counting on Sam being unable to abandon Sarah, which meant chasing after the thing was precisely what it wanted.

"Shit," Sam hissed. Waiting was doing nothing. He had to do *something*.

He ran for the door, opened it, and raced into the hallway, intending to sprint down the stairs. But his path was blocked by an enormous fourteen-year-old boy.

Sam screamed. It was his cousin, Pete. And the kid stood

seven feet tall, his head inches from the hall ceiling.

Pete grinned.

Sam turned on his heels to run the other way, perhaps back into the Gameroom. But now he was facing his other cousin Matt, also seven feet tall, with the chipped front tooth and perpetual smirk Sam remembered, looking down on his younger cousin with amusement and contempt.

Sam shuffled in place a moment, uncertain what to do, his head and eyes darting back and forth at the two cousins. They looked just as they had twenty years ago, only larger. But no, they *weren't* larger than he remembered, not exactly. They were proportionally correct from the point of view of a short and scrawny ten-year-old. As Sam recalled, they were more than a head taller than him when he would visit Aunt Eleanor's, and so now here they were, more than a head taller still.

Then Pete hissed the words Sam had spent his adolescence praying to never hear again.

"*Here, kitty, kitty.*"

twenty-nine

It was Christmas Eve in Mio, and the first time Sammy Spicer and his family would visit Aunt Eleanor in the winter. It would also be their last. Sam's mom had an intense fear of driving in the snowy season, particularly if it involved the narrow, winding roads which peppered Oscoda County. As a child, she and her father had come within inches of driving off a steep cliff overlooking the Au Sable River, and that precipitation had been only a mild rain. In snow and ice, the risk of driving anywhere, especially *north*, seemed irresponsible. But Aunt Eleanor had been insistent, as it would be her and the boys' last Christmas in the old cabin, for they were moving to Oklahoma in the spring. "Come on," she had pleaded. "I'll even make an extra batch of fudge!" Even Sam, who hated his summers up there with Matt and Pete, took his aunt's side when The Fudge was mentioned.

Sam had turned ten years old during the fall, and Sam hoped the important milestone would make him more accepted by the older boys. Somehow, Matt, now thirteen, and Pete, fourteen, didn't seem so much more mature when they were all in double digits together. Sam had even grown at least an inch since the past summer, and he had hoped to have caught up a bit in height. Alas, the cousins both had apparent growth spurts of their own, and still seemed to tower over Sam as much as always.

Sam's parents, Paul and Lynn, had brought some sort of eggnog that Sam wasn't allowed to try, and the three grown-ups had suggested that "the kids" play outside before it got too dark. Sam thought this a terrible idea, for it was freezing outside, and he knew he would get pelted with hard, icy snowballs the moment they were alone. But, he did as he was told, taking his time to slide on his boots and coat and hat and mittens, and counting to five with his eyes closed, just to build the courage to leave the safety of the fire-warmed cabin, filled with safe non-violent adults.

"Come on, slowpoke," taunted Pete from outside. "What, didja wet yourself?"

This was not promising.

Sam attempted a cool, deliberate stride from the cabin to the center of the snowy yard where Pete and Matt were waiting. He wanted to convey a sense of nonchalance, that of an equal rather than a young kid. But the cousins seemed to recognize his reluctance had been out of fear. Matt and Pete looked at each other, and both laughed.

"Dude, we're not gonna hurt you," said Matt. "You're too old for that shit."

Sam must have flashed an involuntary look of skepticism, for Pete added "aw, he doesn't believe us Matty."

Matt pouted. "And we were going to show him our clubhouse and everything. Invite him to share in our secret place."

"Guess he's not ready for that," Pete said.

"Guess not," Matt agreed.

Sam couldn't tell if this was a trick, but was prepared for

the worst. As was often the case with these boys, there was no way to win. If he said he didn't care about the clubhouse, they'd use his rudeness as an excuse to get even. If he said he'd love to see it, they'd attack his naiveté, and either admit there wasn't a clubhouse, teasing him for falling for a lie, or confirm there was a clubhouse after all, but since he had insulted them, he was no longer invited.

"I'm ten," Sam offered, which seemed safe. It said nothing directly, but could be interpreted as either an argument of being old enough for whatever they wanted to show him, or an implication that he was too old to be deceived.

Matt looked at Pete. Pete shrugged. They turned back to Sam.

"Alright, we'll show you," said Matt. "This way."

They walked for several minutes, across the long yard and into a wooded area Sam knew well from the summers. It seemed so different now, with all the leaves gone and the trees looking like skeletons. Sam always thought of this area as a sort of dense and endless forest, but today, he could see where it opened into a clearing not far away. Panting now, the three trudged through the snow, a foot high in some spots, until they arrived at a rather impressive sheet of ice.

"Was this lake always here?" Sam didn't remember it.

"It's not a lake," Pete snorted. "It's a field. But it's low, so the water collects in it after a rain, and sometimes, it just freezes. It's totally solid. Like a skating rink."

"Pete loves to ice skate," Matt teased, flashing Sam a conspiratorial smile. "He's a regular Brian Boitano."

Sam smiled. He had no idea who Brian Boitano was, but

he liked that Matt seemed to be sharing a joke with Sam at Pete's expense. He couldn't remember a time that had ever happened.

"What?" Pete looked confused. "Who the fuck is that?"

"He's a figure skater," Matt explained. "You know, the spinning around and being gay."

"Fuck, there's nothing gay about skating," Pete said. "Steve Yzerman's a fucking badass. And, let me say you're the only one here who knew the name of an *actual* gay-ass figure skater, so fuck you, you gay fucking figure-skating cocksucker."

Pete had a way with words.

"Yeah, well you got eyes for Yzerman," Matt retorted. "Got a life size picture of the guy. In your bedroom. By your *bed*."

"I told you, he's a fucking badass."

"And so *dreamy*."

Pete looked like he was going to clobber Matt for that one, but he held back. He was the first one to make it onto the ice, and needed to concentrate. The snow had given the ice a decent amount of traction, but one false step could cause a lot of pain.

Sam was initially nervous to cross the ice, and so was glad Matt and Pete were ahead of him. He saw how they were able to traverse the slippery sheet at a deliberate speed, and Sam was able to follow. You couldn't run across it, but you could walk comfortably if you used your arms for balance.

Finally, Sam was able to make out their destination. On the other side of the icy clearing was an unmistakable boy-made structure. It was a sort of improvised teepee, with fallen tree branches tied together in a point with what looked like a hundred feet of tan rope. Abandoned sheets of wood were affixed somehow to the sides, and the floor was lined with brown blankets.

"Wow," Sam said. "That must have taken you forever."

"A couple days," Matt confirmed. "The first one we made was too small. We'd have to take turns in there. So we tore it down and built this one. It's ten feet tall at the point, and about eight feet by five feet along the bottom."

"Just the right size for getting down and dirty," Pete boasted. Then, his face reddened, and he clarified his comment. "I mean, me and a girl, of course, not Matt and me."

Sam was intrigued. "You have a girlfriend?"

"Nah," Pete admitted. "But when I do, that clubhouse is where I'm going to see her pussy."

Sam had no response to that.

"Oh shit, man," said Matt, peering into the tent. "You got pussy in there, alright."

"That fat barn cat again?" Pete seemed annoyed. "Why doesn't that mangy bitch find her own clubhouse?"

Matt was on his hands and knees now inside the structure. He was moving the blanket a bit, feeling around as if he had lost something.

"Hey Pete, I think that barn cat had kittens in here."

Sam smiled, fascinated. But Pete became furious.

"What? How do you know that?"

"Well," Matt said, "there's a lot of frozen blood and goo here, and two kittens. I think one's dead, but the other is…"

As if recognizing her cue, the tiny kitten mewed. The

sound was harsh, and a little pathetic, cut short as if ending in a cough.

Pete was unimpressed. "Give me the dead one," he said without emotion. Matt passed him what looked like a small stuffed animal. Pete gave it a perfunctory glance, scowled, and then hurled the thing into a cluster of nearby trees. The animal flew in a grand arc, twisting end over end, and Sam braced himself for the sickening thud. Mercifully, the fuzzy flying ball missed the tree trunks and plopped soundless into the snow. Pete looked unsatisfied. "Now the other," he barked.

Matt hesitated, locking eyes with Sam for a beat. He must have seen the terror in Sam's face, for he looked down, ashamed. They both knew Matt wasn't going to deny his older brother's request, and if anything, Matt would be angry with himself for sharing even a glimmer of doubt with his young punk cousin. Sam stared at Matt, desperate for their connection to be restored, but he could see Matt's thoughts evolving in his furrowed brow and darting eyes. *It's just a dumb kitten. No more than a rat, really. It would probably die out here in the cold in a few hours anyway. Who cares what Pete wants to do with it. It's not worth the fight.* After a moment, Matt nodded to himself, turned back to the rear of the tent, and called it.

"Here, kitty, kitty," he coaxed. "Come on, girl."

The kitten allowed herself to be picked up and held by Matt's hands. It mewed weakly, a shallow, high-pitched sound, more a mouse squeak than a meow. Matt brought it out to Pete, who had one hand held out to take the creature, and the other curled in a fist.

Pete snatched the kitten from his brother, then looked at it for several long seconds. For a moment, Sam thought the boy's cruel heart might have been softened by the adorable, big-eyed tabby staring back at him, and dared to hope that Pete would abandon his original plan and set the kitten down gently on the ice.

Instead, Pete laughed. "They say cats always land on their feet, right?" Then he raised his arm and spiked the kitten on the ice a few feet away. The little fur ball bounced, and in the upward arc she seemed to extend all four legs into a darkly comic jumping jack.

Matt, who had been Sam's only hope of saving the kitten's life, was now guffawing along with his brother. "Do it again," Matt urged. "She's got eight more lives left!"

Pete walked over to where the kitten was squirming on the snow-dusted ice before him. She seemed to have broken at least one of her legs, and was unable to stand on her own. "Here, kitty, kitty," he said, not with the same faux sweetness his brother had affected minutes earlier, but with a pungent malice in his tone that chilled Sam more than the snow. He grabbed the kitten and tossed her to Matt. Matt hadn't been expecting it, and so missed the catch, the kitten hitting the ice behind him instead. Again, the little creature bounced, but not as high this time, and again she was unable to stand, though this time she began dragging her body along the ice, away from the boys.

"I think she's trying to get away from you, butterfingers," Pete taunted.

Matt walked up to the kitten, chuckling at her futile attempt to flee. "Don't be scared," he assured the cat. "I'm not going to hurt you."

But he did hurt her.

Sam felt invisible and helpless. He lacked the courage to stop either cousin. He lacked the speed to whisk the kitten to safety. Pathetically, he even lacked the will. The backlash from interfering with his cousins would be unspeakable, and likely painful. He couldn't fight them. He couldn't even tattle on them, because they would back up each other's stories and say Sam had it wrong, or that he was jealous of something. And he sure as hell couldn't participate in the abuse. He could do nothing. Any move would be the wrong move. Any choice he could imagine seemed the worst possible choice.

Sam turned away when the animal was in flight once more. He heard the soft thud, and thought he might be sick.

Pete picked up the nearly-lifeless kitten by her feet. He smiled as he observed one of her back legs had broken with such savagery it had twisted upward, as if growing from her back. By deforming this creature, Pete was feeling powerful, and very much alive. Sure, he had pulled wings off of flies, and burned ants with a magnifying glass without a second thought. But this was so different. And delicious.

For the first time in several minutes, Pete seemed to notice Sam's eyes on him. Sam had tried to convey a hard expression of disapproval and horror, but his sadness must have softened the glare, and Pete interpreted Sam's look as disappointment of being left out.

"Aw, sorry, kid," Pete said. "You want a turn?"

He chucked the kitten at Sam. Sam panicked, desperate to catch the animal before it endured another harsh landing on the ice. Unlike Matt, Sam actually did catch her, though barely, one of her legs catching in his fingers and seeming to pop out of its socket in the recoil.

Sam brought the kitten close to his face, examining her. Her eyes were closed, her face covered in frozen blood. She was no longer mewing, but her twisted body was convulsing, random spasms shooting through her as if attached to a current.

"Throw it!" shouted Pete. "Don't be a pussy!"

Again, there was no way to win. No option before him would allow Sam to be victorious. He couldn't save the dying kitten. He couldn't earn his cousins' respect. He couldn't fight. He couldn't flee.

Sam closed his eyes, took a breath, and threw the kitten against the ice as hard as he could.

Even now, twenty years later, Sam would tell himself that it was the only way of stopping the kitten's suffering. He believed, or at least tried to believe, that he got no pleasure in his cousins' impressed cries of "ooh" and "damn" as the cat cracked open on the ground before them.

Sam had never seen his cousins after that final holiday. Pete had been killed in a car accident his senior year of high school, and although Matt went on to graduate, no one in the family seemed to have any idea where he had ended up. But here they were in a hotel hallway, towering over him once again, hateful mischief in their eyes, daring him to act, knowing as he did that any choice would be the wrong one.

"You're not real," Sam said, trying to sound tough. Yet if Al's grandfather had been right, Sam knew one of them must be more "real" than the other. Could he figure out which was truly The Eaton, and which was the projection? Would it make a difference if he could?

The Pete creature was down the hallway toward the exit to the stairwell. The Matt creature was on the other side, toward the elevator shaft and Vaughn's body. One of them should be nothing more than vapor, as the piranha had been, and he could run right through the illusion without harm. The other would be as solid as he was. If the projection was Pete, he reasoned, he might be able to make it to the stairwell door in time, perhaps run up the flight to the transit level and escape, or down to the baths level and the safety of the mineral water, and Al's gun. If the projection was Matt, running through him helped less, as jumping down the elevator shaft was certain death, and the pharmacy provided no protection at all.

Sam's stomach churned. He was still affected by the alcohol, but was it enough to help here? He tried concentrating on Pete, then Matt, then Pete again, looking for some clue, some imperfection, some sort of flickering that would give the game away.

Then, he saw it. Pete's face, for just an instant, became semi-transparent, shimmering into nothing and then reforming itself.

There was no time to think, and no time to second guess his instincts. Sam charged the Pete character, expecting to run right through him toward the stairwell door. But Pete was not made of mist. He was as solid as a wall, and Sam was knocked backward on the ground, dazed and aching.

The Pete creature smiled, bending down to show Sam the transparent flickering again, proving its intentionality.

"Fooled you," it said.

Sam glanced behind him, but the Matt apparition was gone. It was just the two of them now.

Before Sam could stumble to his feet, the Pete creature had him by the neck, lifting him into the air. His hands were impossibly large, and they too had begun to shudder and flicker in the light, only not into transparency, but into the black tar beneath. Even Pete's smiling mouth began to lose its large crooked white teeth to reveal the dark gummy smile of The Eaton.

Sam tried to speak, but could not. He clutched at the large hands, trying to pry the fingers from his neck.

The creature laughed, then threw Sam through the door into the Gameroom. Sam's body tumbled in the air and crashed with damaging force onto a wooden chair, which shattered and splintered with the force of his landing. He cried aloud in agony, then found the wind had been knocked out of him, and he couldn't catch his breath.

The distorted Pete figure strode into the room, its eyes fixed on Sam.

"Here, kitty," it said. "I'm not going to hurt you."

Sam tried to crawl away, his legs frantically trying to find friction in the carpet, but it was like trying to stand up on a sheet of ice. He got only a few inches before he was picked up again by the monster and thrown, with more force this time, onto the second billiards table, the one that wasn't blocking the door to the bathroom. Unlike the wooden chair, the pool table held, but the felt top provided no comfort to the hard blow. Sam heard, and then felt, his right arm shatter. He cried aloud, then again as he rolled and fell from the table onto the floor. The pool table separated Sam from his attacker, but the haven was temporary, as with minimal effort, the creature lifted and toppled the table out of the way, then turned to face his prey.

Sam's mind was on the kitten, which he now had become. And then, the mouse. And then Janet's unborn baby. And then Kedzie, and *her* unborn baby. And then another wave of fire surged through his body, and he could barely focus.

"Why?" Sam wailed, the pain unbearable. "Why make us relive these memories? Why are you so obsessed with our pasts? Why not just kill us, you sadistic fuck! What *reason* can you have for making us suffer like this?"

The Pete creature laughed. Then it lunged forward, right arm outstretched, grabbed Sam by the neck, and yanked his body straight up into the air, feet dangling, until the two were eye level.

"I don't *want* to see your memories," it spat. "I hate your rotting memories. I hate everything about you weak, selfish, evil creatures. I *know* you deserve to die. There is no question in my mind about that. The only enjoyment I get is when I get to show you *how* and *why* you're worthless. Because then I can feel vindicated, happy even, for doing shit like *this*."

The creature hurled Sam neck-first against the far wall, his back cracking the wood paneling with the impact. In an instant, Sam felt a wave of electricity flood through his entire body, as if every muscle was falling asleep at once, and he soon felt his arms and legs spasming in some sort of seizure. The sound of a snapping twig overwhelmed his senses, seeming to come from somewhere deep within him, and Sam's body slumped to the right, all feeling in his legs severed, his upper body overtaken by a sort of icy fire.

Sam saw and smelled, but did not feel, the urine and blood saturating the crotch of his jeans. He was momentarily fascinated by this, as if his body had already moved on, and he was just a spirit observing his mortal end. But soon, the towering shadow of the flickering Pete creature brought him back to reality.

Sam was not dead. He was paralyzed. And the creature knew it.

"You're all so weak," the creature hissed, a thick gurgling sound audible underneath the English. "Weak in mind, and spirit, and especially in body."

Sam coughed, and spat blood onto the front of his shirt. "Says the all-powerful being who can't get wet," he said.

The Pete monster smiled, gesturing toward the barricaded door to his left. "I'm going to tear your whore apart, piece by juicy piece, right in front of you, right here, and you can't even stand up and defend her honor. So I'd show a little more respect if I were you." Then it walked over to where the overturned pool table was covering the restroom door, pushed it aside, and forced its way in.

For a moment, Sam was panicked for Sarah. He had almost forgotten himself that Sarah was seven floors away. When he remembered, he tried to block it from his mind, to think of anything other than where Sarah was and what she was doing, to delay as long as possible The Eaton's ability to pluck that information from his brain.

It only took seconds for the creature to determine the

emptiness of the room, and to realize it had been deceived. It stormed out and towered over Sam's broken body, demanding answers.

"Where is she, Sam," the Pete creature hissed, but it hardly looked like Pete anymore. The blackness of The Eaton's natural form was bleeding through almost everywhere, and for the first time, Sam could see that Al had indeed shot the thing. There was thick, inky fluid seeping from at least two unnatural holes in the creature's chest and lower abdomen. Sam was certain they were bullet wounds, and couldn't suppress a smile. When The Eaton saw this, it became infuriated, and dropped to its knees, lunging yet again for Sam's throat. The Pete mask had melted away entirely now, and the creature's eyes—its *real* eyes, black and uncompromising—seemed to be boring deep into Sam's skull.

"Go to hell," Sam whispered, all his mental efforts devoted to blanking his mind, denying The Eaton any more knowledge for as long as he could.

"*Where is she,*" the thing demanded once more, a mere foot from Sam's face now, its mushroomy breath wafting over him, its right claw now wrapped tight around his neck. But Sam stayed resolute, finding a hidden courage he himself had been unaware of until just this moment. There was a strange sort of freedom in knowing he could no longer save himself, and that his only remaining mission in life was buying Sarah a few more minutes of time.

Go on, kill me, thought Sam. *Do it. Do it quickly, and then maybe she'll be safe.*

Something happened then, to the atmosphere in the

room, and to the walls and the floor of the room itself. All the energy and light appeared to flicker and drain away, replaced with an oozing darkness that seemed to come from everywhere all at once. Sam thought, deliriously, that the room must be on fire, but in a new world where flames were black rather than yellow and orange, and gave off an icy chill rather than heat. And through it all, the creature was staring at him, through him, into him, trying to force its way into Sam's deepest thoughts.

All at once, the room returned to normal. The creature let go of Sam's throat, and backed away from him. For an instant, Sam thought he registered fear on the face of the monster, but it was soon masked by a confident, toothless grin.

"Got her," it said. Then it stood up, turned, and bounded for the hallway.

thirty

It had taken genuine effort for Sarah to enter the maintenance room again, her sliced breast aching as if in warning, a Geiger counter for pain. Thankfully, the liquid courage she had consumed earlier had given her just the extra push needed to get done what needed to get done.

She had started by making a mental catalog of the various gauges and levers, determining which pipes served as steam release valves and safety overflows. One by one, she worked to disable and seal off as many pressure points as possible, endeavoring to create a sort of ticking time bomb of pressure and heat. Sarah had to double-check her readings several times, both because she was more than a little tipsy, and because she couldn't fathom why the hotel needed to generate such high levels of pressure. Although she had no direct experience with steam pressure or pneumatic systems, she knew that oil pressure gauges at her dad's shop tended to max out at around 100 psi, and tire pressure gauges were half that. These dials, however, were measuring pressure in the tens of thousands of pounds per square inch. Sarah guessed that perhaps such capacity was needed not so much for the hotel baths and general power, but for the planned pneumatic transit train to Charlotte. Attempting to rig such a high pressure system to explode was terrifying, as she was not confident in what she was attempting, paranoid that her lack of sobriety would lead to a serious miscalculation that could kill her before she had the chance to escape.

After several minutes of learning, working, and sabotaging, Sarah believed she heard gunshots in the distance. She froze, waiting for some sort of confirmation, but none came. Sensing she may be out of time, she redoubled her efforts, certain that she was getting closer. With some reluctance, she even restarted the energy generators, with their guillotine-like powers to destroy phones and nipple rings, which allowed her to shut down and reroute power as needed.

A few minutes later, Sarah realized she was humming "The Book of Love" by The Magnetic Fields. It had been Sam and Sarah's song, but she couldn't imagine why it was in her head at this moment. Sarah was focused on the task at hand, and even if she had been thinking of Sam, it would not have been positively. For an instant, she could have even sworn she heard the melody in the distance, over the whir of the energy generators, but dismissed this thought as impossible. She knew the tune couldn't be coming from her cell phone either, as she had propped the phone beside her feet in flashlight mode to aid in the reading of schematics printed on the back of an access panel.

How long have I been working on this, Sarah wondered. It must have been ten minutes. Had the gunshots meant the creature was dead? If so, Sam would have come to get her, wouldn't he? *Maybe he escaped out the Mastersuite already, the selfish bastard.* Or, she realized, the creature might have killed Al and ran up toward Sam, rather than down to her.

The song was playing louder in her head now. *The book of love is long and boring. No one can lift the damn thing…*

Sarah found herself thinking of her father as she finished the last few adjustments. The specific memory flooding her mind, perhaps because of the pain surrounding her absent nipple, was of her dad comforting her after what she only called "the Tony thing." She had called him first, even before calling the police, and he must have driven like a maniac to reach her for he arrived before they did. She sobbed and screamed into his chest like an injured toddler as they waited for the sirens, and he had whispered in her ear how proud he was of her, and how strong she was. He swore to her that some men were good, and decent, and she would find someone special. Thinking of Sam and Kedzie, Sarah wondered if her dad had been wrong. Maybe her dad had been the only decent man who ever lived.

Tony Generaux had picked up Sarah on the Saturday following the frat party at which they had met. He arrived on time, held open his car door for her as a gentleman would, and they had sushi and sake at a new place Sarah had mentioned she wanted to try. To Sarah, Tony seemed to have many qualities she was generally attracted to. He was smart and witty and liked to show off, but in a confident rather than cocky way. The only time he sounded a bit narcissistic was when he was describing his workout routine and the effect it had on his body, but Sarah admitted to herself that she, too, was thinking about his body, and what his abs would look like under the thin black dress shirt he was modeling for her. Pretty boys were not Sarah's type, yet she was somehow drawn to him. That is, until he started talking politics.

Tony had grown up in Grosse Pointe Shores with every

possible advantage in life, yet somehow believed he was a self-made man who didn't need any handouts, convinced things like welfare and affirmative action gave the poor and talentless an unfair advantage over *him*. Sarah must have stiffened at something he said, for he held up his hands and apologized.

"Sorry," he said. "Didn't mean to offend the liberal."

Sarah smirked. "How do you know I'm a liberal?"

"Aren't you?"

"Yes, I am, but I haven't told you that."

"Well," he stammered attractively, "I mean, I just assumed…"

Sarah glared at him, though she tried to do so in a playful way. She had not given up on Tony just yet, and knew perfectly well that her spiky hair, nose stud and clothing didn't scream "Republican." But she was trying to make a point to him that he shouldn't judge a book by her cover.

"Because of how I look," she said.

"Well, not just that. You also said you're going to be a journalist."

"There aren't conservative journalists?"

"There don't appear to be, no."

Sarah laughed. "Oh my goodness, Tony. Is your world so small as that?"

Tony smiled, and attempted to change the subject. "I'm sorry I judged you."

"*Judged* me? Interesting word choice there. I, for one, could have assumed by your perfect teeth and all-American good looks and expensive shirt that you were a Republican, but I gave you the benefit of the doubt and came out anyway."

"Ah, but is 'benefit of the doubt' any less offensive than being 'judged'?"

"Yes," explained Sarah. "Because by your own admission, you *knew* I was a liberal, a class you're prone to 'judge', but asked me out regardless. I *thought* you might be conservative, but didn't want to assume either way, when I said yes."

Tony dismissed this with a wave of his hand. "A distinction without a difference, as they say. But honestly, it doesn't matter to me. Besides, I *like* liberals."

Sarah smiled at this, and said "good." But there was something about the way he had said "I like liberals," with a raised manicured eyebrow and a slow, hungry smile, that made Sarah think his real meaning was "…because they're easy to get in bed." Although she was enjoying the evening, she vowed to make sure she did not sleep with this Grosse Pointer anytime soon.

They had shared two pots of sake during the meal, so when Tony had suggested a martini bar for their next stop, Sarah countered with a juice and coffee shop instead, where it wouldn't be so loud. Tony thought about this, and made a compromise suggestion.

"Well look, we're super close to my apartment, and I make a killer chocolate martini myself. Plus, you can meet my roommate who will convince you I'm not evil, and we can end the night at the coffee shop. Sound good?"

It did. Sarah was a sucker for a chocolate martini, and both the presence of a roommate and the future plan of the coffee shop made the offer seem safe.

When they arrived at the beautiful loft apartment, with its exposed brick, expensive modern kitchen, and window walls overlooking the city, Sarah was impressed. The place was decorated in a tasteful fashion, and was actually clean— a rarity among boys of any age, but extraordinary for those in their twenties. She wondered if he had a cleaning service. She was also aware they were alone.

"Huh, Nick must still be out," explained Tony, sensing her thoughts. "But that's okay, I'm sure he'll be back soon. Do you have a vodka preference?"

"Whatever you think works," she responded, not wanting to pick a brand that he did not have or looked down upon.

Sarah sat on a stool at the dark granite bar, and Tony began taking bottles down from shelves behind the counter. He made the drinks in a metal cocktail shaker, which eased Sarah's mind a bit, knowing they would each be drinking the same concoction. She did notice, however, that the martini was all alcohol—without the chocolate milk base she was used to. It didn't *taste* much stronger, but she knew it must be, and paced herself.

"What's in this?" she asked.

"It's a coffee-infused vodka mixed with Bailey's and a splash of Godiva liqueur," he boasted, as if he had recited this secret recipe a hundred times before. "Kind of like an Arby's Jamocha shake, right?"

"Better," Sarah conceded. "Good job."

They ended up talking and laughing quite a bit, and when Tony suggested just "one more drink," Sarah didn't object. This martini used Amaretto and a different type of

Irish Cream, and tasted something like the inside of a chocolate cherry cordial.

"I'm going to need that coffee soon," Sarah giggled. "Shall we take off?"

"You can take off whatever you like," Tony teased. He had been sitting across from her, but came around to her side of the bar, placing a hand high on Sarah's leg.

"Hey now," she smiled. "It's only a first date." But she didn't stop him when he leaned in to kiss her. It started nice, but felt aggressive for a first kiss, as if he was signaling with his tongue and teeth his ownership of her. In a sobering moment, she remembered the roommate who had still not arrived. She gently pushed him back.

"What about your roommate," she asked.

"He's in Detroit for the night," Tony said, then leaned in again to bite her left ear. It felt good, but Sarah was concerned about being lied to, and pushed him back again, with more force this time.

"You said he'd be right back," she reminded him.

"Don't worry, he won't be."

"I'm more worried that you lied to me." Sarah stiffened. "Come on, you promised me coffee." She managed to wiggle away from him, standing up.

"You sure?" he asked.

"You can't always get your way, Tony," Sarah said.

She walked over to where her jacket and purse were hanging on the wall. Tony followed her close, and before she reached her destination, she felt his arms around her waist, and his breath on the back of her neck.

"Tony," she said, annoyed. But he was holding her

tighter this time, and when she tried to break free, he spun her around and pushed her body against the wall, hands encircling her wrists.

"I think you should stay," he said.

"Look, I've had a good time, but you're really hurting your chance for a second date here."

Again, she tried to break free, still believing his holding her to be playful, but he tightened his grip, and moved her hands above her head in a single swift motion, forcing them tight against the wall. His lower body was crushing hard against her as well, keeping her upright, and she could feel his erection through his jeans as he grinded into her.

"Please stop," she insisted.

But Tony didn't acknowledge her wishes at all. They seemed to be of no particular concern to him. In a matter-of-fact tone that terrified her more than a slap or a scream, he had answered, simply, "no."

Sarah didn't know why this memory had come back to her in the maintenance room, but she tried to shake it away as she stepped back to examine her work. If everything was accounted for, the steam pressure would build up and, with a great deal of luck, would cause a massive steam and water explosion which might destroy The Eaton. *Both* of them. She dialed everything to maximum, as Al had suggested, and waited for something to happen.

Within seconds, a white plume of steam shot up from a four-inch pipe near the back of the room, and Sarah realized her oversight. She had remembered to close all the release valves, but there was an emergency steam release pipe that could not be closed mechanically. She would need to find something to stuff into the pipe. Glancing down at her own clothes, Sarah considered using her shirt or jeans, but then remembered the laundry room across the hall. There would be bed sheets perfect for the task, and she wouldn't have to escape in her underwear.

As she entered the hallway, she was shocked to discover the song, which she had assumed had been in her head, was actually playing in the laundry room. At first Sarah thought it must be another illusion, like the record player in one of the first rooms had likely been, and whirled her body around, looking for the monster. But she was alone.

The song ended, then started over from the beginning. It was on a loop. She tracked down the source of the song, the laundry room dumbwaiter, and opened the small door to reveal Sam's phone.

But I, I love it when you read to me. And you, you can read me anything…

Sarah picked up the phone and unlocked it. She expected to find the music app showing the cover of The Magnetic Fields' album, but instead it was on the messages screen. She dismissed the "low battery" pop up warning, and saw the text message. It was marked "Not Delivered" due to the lack of cell service, but was legible to her just the same.

No exit on 11. Exit is on 10. Follow tunnel. Will see you there. All my love. Hurry.

Sarah paused for a just a moment, absorbing the instructions. She wondered if it was possible for this to be just another trick of the creature, though she knew the phone itself wasn't an illusion. She also wondered, for an instant, if she'd be able to forgive Sam if they got out of this alive. Obeying the "hurry," she silenced the music, shoved the phone into her pocket, grabbed a white bed sheet, and raced back to the maintenance room.

She had to climb on the equipment itself to reach the pipe, careful not to step on any levers or dials. At first, she tried to shove the sheet into the pipe while steam still billowed from it, but it was too hot to get her fingers near. She cursed herself, climbed back down, disabled the steam, and tried again with the system off. With as much speed as she could manage, she rolled and shoved the bed sheet into the release pipe, as far down as she was able. At the end, she was pushing so hard with her fingers she thought they would break off.

She could force the fabric no further. Either the sheet would hold, allowing the system to overload, or the wadded sheet would shoot out like a spitball from a straw. She climbed down and, once again, activated the generator.

This time, the pressure did begin to build. The metal slicers on the wall were spinning into a high-pitched wail. Sarah could feel Sam's phone in her pocket vibrating with a sympathetic, magnetic reaction of its own. Soon, some of the ancient dials had needles in their respective red zones. Sarah felt as if she were staring at the controls of a submarine plummeting into depths that could not be safely maintained. Since she had no way of knowing how long the machine would take to overload, if indeed such a thing was even possible, she considered the noble option of going down with the ship, making adjustments as needed to assure the great metal contraption exploded with the sufficient force necessary to destroy the creature, even at the expense of her own life.

As she debated this in her mind, Sarah became aware of another presence in the room. She spun on her heels, turning toward the door.

Standing casually just a dozen feet from her, sporting a cocky smile, was Tony Generaux.

Of course it was.

She almost laughed.

thirty-one

"So how does this work, exactly," Sarah challenged the creature. "Are you standing there now because I was thinking of that bastard? Can you only pluck from my strongest, most recent memories? If I had been thinking of a different thought, some birthday party perhaps, would you be showing up as my Aunt Vivien, holding balloons?"

Tony continued to smile at her. "I don't know what you mean, Sarah. I knew you were feisty, and I like feisty. That's why I knew you'd come back someday for another round. You know you want me just as much as I want you."

Sarah's eyes darted around the room, cataloging everything that stood between them, looking for some sort of escape route, or something that could be used as a weapon. She thought she could perhaps force the creature in front of the magnetic slicers, but knew she would be too easily overpowered. She thought instead she could just keep stalling until the generator exploded, but knew The Eaton wasn't stupid, and would know what she had been trying to accomplish.

"I know you're not Tony," she said flatly. "So why pretend? Especially now, when I've seen your true form, which is a hell of a lot scarier than some asshole from my past. What does this accomplish?"

"You don't think I might enjoy drawing this out a bit?" Tony's smile melted into a grin. "You're the last one, after all."

Sarah's face blanched. That meant, if the thing were being honest, that Al and Sam were dead. But Sam had just sent her that cell phone note.

"You're lying," she said.

"Oh, sweet Sarah, if only you could access my memories the way I can rape yours."

The r-word stung her, especially from Tony's sneering mouth. She stiffened, but again tried to come up with some sort of plan, an action she could take to either kill the creature, escape, or both.

As if reading her mind, and perhaps it was, the Tony creature laughed aloud. "Oh, come now. You must know this is the end." It began walking toward Sarah, who was backed against the control panel as if held by unseen hands. Soon the creature was ten feet away, then eight, and she was trapped.

But then Sarah noticed something that gave her hope. It came to her that the creature had not quite rendered Tony's face as well as it had with Kedzie or Vaughn. There were subtle details missing from the real man, as if he had been smoothed out—airbrushed in real life. There was no visible stubble, for instance, even though she distinctly remembered stubble on both occasions she had been with Tony in person. Something about the eyebrows, too, which seemed a bit too manicured, and the skin a bit too free of blemishes or pores.

Sarah's mind searched for an answer. Was it because her memories of Tony weren't as vivid as others? That couldn't be it, since otherwise she would not be noticing the discrepancies now. Was the creature just being lazy, or perhaps injured, and not operating at full strength? Maybe, though this could be wishful thinking. Was the alcohol in Sarah's system affecting the thing's ability to fully read her past, therefore having to produce an approximation, rather than an exact copy? This thought gave Sarah just the slightest sense of empowerment, that the creature was imperfect, that it could make mistakes, and perhaps did not know her past as intimately as she once assumed.

Six feet from her now, Tony's smile hardened into a contemptuous smirk, and his blue eyes bored into Sarah with a newfound intensity. Although some of the details of Tony's face may have been missing, the creature had nailed the coldness of those eyes. She knew the line that was coming next, and braced for it.

"This is going to happen," it said.

In Tony's apartment, Sarah had spat at him when he had uttered this line, hoping his grip on her hands against the wall would loosen from the shock. But the bastard had merely smiled, and made no movement to dry her saliva from his cheek. Instead, he had pressed his erection harder against her, and tightened the grip on her wrists until she cried aloud in pain.

"Look," he said coolly, inches from her face, martini breath wafting over her in waves. "I don't want to hurt you. I just want to fuck you. I've wanted to fuck you all night. And I know you want it, too, or you wouldn't be here in my apartment, in that tight t-shirt and that fuck-me red lipstick, waiting for me to make a move. Well, this is my move."

He leaned into her side then, grazing his lips on her neck,

below her left ear, running his teeth against her earlobe, gentle but threatening. Sarah had started to cry, and her body trembled against his.

"Please," she whispered, hating the weakness she heard in her voice.

"It's okay to want it," he whispered back. "Or, don't. It's your call. As I said, this is going to happen, whether you want it or not. The choice of whether or not we're going to fuck has already been made, by me. *Your* choice is whether you want to have a great night, too, or whether you want to allow yourself to become a victim. It's whether you want to walk out of here feeling empowered and sexy, or feeling ashamed, like used-up garbage. What's it going to be?"

Tony started to kiss her neck again, slobbering, like a dog at a water dish. He used one foot to kick her left leg a few inches from her right, so he could grind into her more directly. Sarah felt something painful then, pressing against her right buttock which was being pushed into the wall. It took her only a moment to remember what was in her back pocket.

He was back on her left earlobe, biting harder this time, trying to create a sort of rhythm between the action on her ear and the rubbing of his clothed erection against her crotch. She knew what must be done, and let a soft, convincingly pleasurable moan escape her lips. He moaned back, pleased with himself, but did not yet reduce his grip on her wrists. She moaned a bit louder, and let one of her ankles rub against his own, signaling desire for the first time. Against her ear, she could feel Tony's lips curl into a smile. He loosened the grip on her wrists, tentatively, then fully, as his hands dropped to his belt, working to free his erection as soon as possible. Sarah's hands dropped to her own jeans, but while her left hand went to her front button, in case he was watching, her right hand reached into her back pocket and retrieved the small, iron weapon.

Tony was looking down, unlatching his belt, and so never saw it coming. The Kubotan hit hard against his left temple, making an audible crack, and he staggered away from her, tripping backwards over a pretentious glass coffee table which exploded under his weight. Tony's body shook violently, as if in some sort of seizure, before his eyes rolled back into his head and he slipped into unconsciousness.

Sarah, who was still clutching the iron Kubotan for dear life, walked over to his body, terrified that she may have killed the man. But it was clear he was breathing, even snoring a bit, so she relaxed. She opened her right palm for the first time then, staring down at the weapon in wonder. She had picked the thinnest, most delicate Kubotan the shop had, yet perhaps because it was iron, it had held firm. The weapon felt indestructible and powerful in her trembling hand, a thing of magic which had branded its ribs and contours into the soft flesh of her lower palm and fingers.

Putting the Kubotan back in her pocket, she walked shakily over to the coatrack where her purse was hanging, retrieved her phone, called her father first, and then the police. By the time officers had arrived, Tony had regained a sort of fuzzy consciousness; when they asked him if he had told Sarah that he was going to fuck her whether she liked it or not, he sealed his fate by responding not only that he *had*, but "so the fuck what?" The officers, one of whom was female, were not amused, and Tony went to the hospital in handcuffs. Sarah had been worried the police would confiscate her Kubotan as evidence, but they had let her keep it, perhaps due to her father's commanding presence and his demands that they be allowed to leave.

No charges were filed against Sarah for using the weapon, but she did press charges against her attacker. It took more than a year for the case to go to trial, as Tony's wealthy parents were able to delay hearings repeatedly through carefully crafted motions. Sarah's attorney had warned her that attempted rapists rarely got much jail time, especially when the rape had not even begun—Tony was still clothed when he was arrested, after all, and had no prior convictions on his record. Sarah had argued with vehemence that a woman shouldn't have to let a rapist inside her just to increase his jail time, but her attorney just shrugged and agreed that it "sucked."

Once the case had gained some publicity, however, three other woman had come forward to share their own stories, all three claiming full unwanted penetration, and one of whom had, through choked sobs, recounted her subsequent abortion on the stand. The judge railed against Tony from the bench, branding him a "sexual predator" in front of his parents and grandparents, and sentenced him to four years at Woodland Center Correctional Facility.

A few days after the sentencing, Sarah asked her friend Brad, a blacksmith she had met at the Michigan Renaissance Festival, if it was possible to turn part of the iron Kubotan into an intimate piece of jewelry. Brad explained that raw iron wouldn't be recommended for a piercing, but was able to modify a surgical steel nipple bar to accommodate the end pieces of the Kubotan, giving the illusion of a shortened Kubotan entering her right nipple and coming out the other side. It gave her strength whenever she admired it in the mirror, or looked down and saw its outline through thin fabric when she wasn't wearing a bra. She had lived her life less afraid from that point on. But even though a few hours earlier the body piercing had been ripped away from her flesh by the powerful magnets of the hotel's generator, likely aided by The Eaton itself, she knew the internal strength hadn't left her.

The Tony creature was less than four feet from her now, inching ever closer, still smirking, a hungry stare on its borrowed eyes. For the first time, Sarah smirked back.

"I think you're getting a little rusty if you thought the face of Tony Generaux would terrify me," she said, her right hand casually moving across the control panel behind her back.

The Tony creature cocked its head. "And why's that?"

He moved another step toward her, close enough to reach out to her now, to attack and strike and strangle, but Sarah showed no fear. Her right hand had found its mark, and the creature had stopped just where she wanted it to.

"Because last time," she said crisply over the whirring motors, "*I kicked his ass.*"

She pounded her fist on the pressure release valve, and from a pipe about four feet from the ground, a jet of hot steam exploded into Tony's left side. It seemed to cut right through its body, and its human facade melted away in less than a second, replaced with its hulking, monstrous true form. It seemed to fly as much as fall, thrown against the room by the force of the blast, and uttered such a piercing, primal scream as it landed that it drowned out the sounds of the generator altogether. The steam had acted like acid against its flesh, and at the point of impact, Sarah could see the oily hide had become charred straight through. A moldy stink filled the space as a viscous grey-green fluid poured out of the hole and onto the tiled floor.

The creature made new sounds of pain, then fury. It turned its head to Sarah with hate in its eyes, and gave a gurgling growl so utterly alien that she gasped. It may have been wounded, but it was still strong, and she had to get out of there *now*.

The pipe was still releasing a torrent of steam, although with less force than before. Sarah ducked under it as she ran to the door and into the hallway, racing for the stairwell without looking back. She knew the creature was hurt, but doubted it was a mortal injury. After all, she wasn't sure the thing was mortal at all. If it had any power left, it would pursue her.

Releasing the steam pressure had injured the creature, but had also made her attempt at sabotaging the generator a failure. It would not now explode; it would simply peter out. As she raced up the stairs, she again noticed the water pipes which lined the stairwell, remembering The Eaton's over-the-top illusion that one of the pipes had burst, filling the lower levels with piranha. As she sprinted, she kept her eyes out for valves she could spin, thinking that flooding the stairs with the toxic water would aid in her escape. She found one, and tried to turn it, but it required a special tool to move that she did not have and could not get. So she raced onward, stopping to catch her breath at the fifth level, the baths level, where she got an idea. If Al's gun had any remaining ammunition, she might be able to shoot holes in the water pipes, creating additional obstacles for her pursuer.

She flew through the stairwell door into the baths, and screamed.

Al was there alright, his body slumped against the wall with a gun in his lap, but his face had been torn away, leaving a mess of blood and gore that seemed to have gushed out of his head like a chocolate fountain. The combination of panic, the stair running, her alcohol buzz, and this horrific site, made the remaining whiskey in her stomach expel itself violently from her throat and onto the floor several feet in front of her. She wretched again, and cried aloud in agony, but would not permit herself any more time to recover. She ran over, grabbed the bloody gun from Al's lap, and checked the cylinder. Two rounds remained.

Racing back to the stairwell, she considered leaving the two bullets in the chambers for personal protection, but reasoned that bullets hadn't stopped the creature before, and likely wouldn't again. She took aim at the pipes, and fired both rounds. The first shot went wild, missing the pipes altogether, but the second hit, and rich Eaton Rapids mineral water began to spurt from the hole as if from a faucet. It flowed down the stairs, not as torrential as Sarah would have liked, but hopefully enough to further slow the wounded creature in its pursuit. Having no further need for the weapon, she tossed it aside and continued her ascent, faster than before, as though the purge from her stomach had given her strength.

All she had to do was make it to the transit level. If The Eaton was telling the truth, and Sam was dead, she would be alone. If it was lying, Sam might be there as well. If there was no exit after all…well, she just wouldn't think about that. The pneumatic train car was supposed to reach Charlotte, wasn't it? Perhaps the tunnel already did.

She had two floors to go when the lights began to flicker. Perhaps she had done more damage to the generator than she thought. The thought of being plunged into total darkness was terrifying, as she reasoned her pursuer had hung out in the darkness for a hundred years, and likely had night vision which she lacked. Still, she plunged ahead, passing the Gameroom level, stopping to catch her breath as her hand was on the doorknob of the tenth floor, which if Sam's text message was correct, would be her chance to escape. One deep breath later, and she threw open the door.

"Sam?" she called. There was no response. She tried again, a little louder. Silence. *Maybe he already got out,* she thought, and jumped down onto the track. She was able to activate the work lights they had used to explore the tunnel earlier, but as the overhead lights flickered again, the work lights flickered too. Whatever she had done in the maintenance room was affecting the electrical system, or perhaps the creature was still alive and trying to sabotage the lighting itself, to improve its odds. She again began to panic at the thought of total darkness, especially after realizing her phone was still propped by an access panel in the maintenance room.

She then remembered Sam's phone in her pocket. Even with the low battery, there would be enough for the flashlight app, at least for a few minutes. She called "Sam" a third and final time, and when again no answer came, she hurried down the tunnel.

Sam had not heard her calling, for his broken body remained slumped against the wall of the Gameroom a floor below. He had heard, or at least thought he heard, Sarah's footsteps race up the stairwell to reach the floor above. Sam had considered crying out when he heard her ascent, but his mouth was dry, and he didn't see the point in her stopping for him anyway. One look down at his once-white undershirt, now crimson and caked with blood, confirmed he hadn't a prayer. Any attempt to save his life would not only be futile, but risk Sarah's chance for escape. Better she should live than both of them die.

Not that, he thought morosely, she'd still care enough to want to save him anyway. She had been the love of his life, and he had still fucked her best friend. *She's better off without me*, he knew.

In those final moments, Sam had time to think of many things. He thought of his parents, and how his death would affect them. He thought of Vaughn, and that night at Venue A, where Vaughn had taught him what real courage was. He thought of poor Janet, who deserved not only a better death, but a better life. He thought of Al, and how he had made such horrible mistakes in judgment, but tried to redeem himself in the end by buying them time to escape.

But mostly, he just thought of Sarah.

His left arm had gone numb, like his legs, but his right arm and hand still had feeling and motion. With great effort, Sam managed to reach into his pocket and retrieve the engagement ring. It was in a small clear pouch, for Sam hadn't wanted the ring box to make a conspicuous shape against the pocket of his jeans. With his thumb and index finger, he was able to open the pouch, tilt it to let the ring fall into his lap, and pick the ring up, bringing it close enough to admire with his one remaining good eye. Even in the dim light of the Gameroom, he knew it was perfect, and that Sarah would have loved it. The diamond sparkled for him, an item of beauty amongst the destruction of his lower body and the disarray of the room. He turned it over and over in his fingers, smiling at what might have been. It was the last thing Sam Spicer ever saw.

thirty-two

The lights flickered one final time before going out for good. The blackness was fast and absolute, causing Sarah to stop in her tracks. She waited motionless for several moments, hoping for the lights to return. Her remaining senses were heightened, and she became aware of peculiar smells, of rocks and musty earth, and of the sound of escaping steam, which sounded like air being released from far-off balloons.

Sarah retrieved Sam's phone from her pocket and activated the flashlight. The light was quite strong in the total darkness, at least when illuminating the tracks beneath her feet, but visibility fell off quickly when she pointed it onward. The tunnel had been constructed with dark bricks which reflected little light, though she could still make out where the curved brickwork ended and the raw tunnel rock began again. Cautious and quick, Sarah made her way to where the tracks abruptly ceased, and where large piles of bricks and abandoned construction tools told the story of halted progress.

Once again, Sarah found herself in front of the large boulder, and the cave which had long ago held the creature. She let her light fall over the strange petroglyphs, remembering how she had deduced the nature of the monster hours earlier, and cursed the builders of the hotel for their stupidity in unleashing the thing. Turning back, Sarah's light fell upon deep scratches etched into the boulder, scratches she hadn't noticed before, but were presumably from the trapped creature trying to escape many years ago. Yet she still didn't see any obvious exit.

Had Sam been here, and found the way out? If so, why hadn't he left a better clue behind? Sarah considered the possibility that the exit Sam referred to wasn't at this end of the tunnel at all, but back by the train car and the ticket booth. She hated the idea of backtracking to the station, as it decreased the distance between her and the creature, but the desire to escape was building into a frenzy inside her, and she had to know for sure.

With a deep breath for strength, Sarah began racing down the tracks, phone held in front of her like a shield, casting as much light as it could. The blackness outside the beam of light was unrelenting, and seemed to be absorbing more and more of the beam as she ran. The smells and steam sounds were increasing as she got closer to the entrance, and her mind was still prepared for a dark monster to jump out from the shadows at any moment. It was a "beep," though, that caused her to falter, dropping the phone in front of her on the tracks. The flashlight app deactivated itself, but the phone still emitted a soft screen glow, allowing her to see the warning message which had replaced the beam. The battery was now down to 5%.

As she leaned to pick the phone up, though, it became clear that something was wrong. The steam sounds had coalesced into a sort of mechanical whir, and the air began to feel somehow lighter than before, as if she had been transported to a high altitude. A feeling of dread washed over her then, and she fumbled with the phone to reactivate the flashlight. Pointing it forward, she at first saw nothing, as the beam fell off into the darkness fifty yards or so from her position. Then Sarah sensed, before she saw, a sort of wall moving toward her, pushing the air in front of itself, and she turned back toward the cave and ran. The pneumatic train car, invisible in the dark and nearly silent in its operation, was picking up speed, and would crush her against the tight fit of the curved brick walls if she didn't make it back to the construction area in time.

Unable to hold the light steady in front of her, she gripped it with her right fist as she ran blindly along the tracks, trying to avoid disorientation as the strobe of the light confused her eyes. She was afraid she would run full-speed and head-first into bricks, or a cave wall, but couldn't slow down or she could be overtaken. Sarah's speed was incredible, as if the air was being pushed behind her, giving her a wind at her back, which in a way was literally true. At the last moment, from the corner of an eye, she saw she had reached the opening. She dove to her left to hit the clearing, just as the whispering train car reached the end of the track, jumped it, and crashed with a loud, explosive force against the wall of rock at its terminus.

On the ground, Sarah cried out and covered her head, expecting debris to topple down upon her, but nothing came. There had been a shower of light-emitting sparks when the car had hit, but now it was black, and she was blind. Sarah had again dropped the cell phone when she fell, and fumbled for it in terror, certain it was lost forever to the blackness, but it had only fallen face down this time, and was located by the faintest of glow from the rock it had landed upon. The screen was cracked, but still functional, though reporting just 3% of battery. Still, she had to risk the flashlight app again, to see what had happened, and to see what her options had dwindled to.

Sarah got to her knees and turned around, shining the beam on the train car which had almost crushed her. It was in bad shape to be sure, and its front was a mass of twisted wood and metal. The wreck had also blocked her from returning down the track to the station. The entry doors were on the other side, the platform side, and so were inaccessible, but she thought perhaps there would be a rear door to the train car, so if she climbed through one of the broken windows on this side, she might be able to exit from the back.

There were three visible windows, and the glass had shattered on all three of them, but they were small for train car windows, just a foot or so high and less than two feet wide each. Sarah figured this made sense, as there wouldn't be much of a view in an underground tunnel, and the windows were likely there to add aesthetic familiarity rather than function. She thought she could squeeze through one, but before she attempted this, she had to know what had caused the car to chase her down. If it had been a fluke of pneumatics, brought about by her attempted sabotage of the generator, she was likely still alone. If, however, the car had been controlled by the creature, she would be trapped.

As if in answer, a dark shadow passed by one of the windows inside the car. Sarah hoped it might be a trick of the light, and squinted harder to confirm this, but then heard a soft crunching sound, and knew for sure The Eaton was in the car.

She wanted to turn the light away, but could not. This would surely be her death, and she wanted to look it in the eye. Within seconds, as if knowing what was expected of it, the creature turned to look out one of the prison-like windows and stared Sarah down. There was another crunching sound from the car—what *was* that?—and then a sort of injured growl, but it kept his gaze on her, saying nothing, making no movement to attack.

What's it waiting for, Sarah thought. *Turn into something skinny, slide out the window and finish me.* Only then did she remember that it could not. As she had seen, The Eaton couldn't *change* its shape. It could only *project* a different body in the mind of a witness. The wretched thing could no more squeeze through one of those skinny windows than could a black bear. It was trapped. Like her.

But then it grinned again, that hideous, toothless smile, and disappeared from view. What returned was a leathery, human skull. It seemed to look out from the window, turning its head, hanging there a moment, as if in a macabre puppet show. Sarah watched in horror as its puppeteer flung it from the window, right at her, missing her head by inches and hitting a cave wall. She turned her light toward it on the ground, only to see a second skull and spinal column be thrown and crash beside it. *The train car was full of skeletons,* she realized. And then, more distressingly, *it knows my light's going to go out. It wants to surround me with horror. Even if it can't reach me, it wants me to starve and die in the darkness, covered in the rotted corpses of its long-dead enemies. Oh, Christ. This is it.*

Sarah glanced at the phone display once more. 2%. What was that, ten minutes? Maybe five? She arced the beam from side to side, desperate for something she may have overlooked. Could she climb over the train car to reach the tunnel again? No, because part of the train car was still wedged in the tunnel, and it was too tight a fit. Had the train done enough damage to the rocks blocking the other side? Not that she could see. Could she move the boulder which had once sealed The Eaton's prison? No, because if The Eaton with its superior strength had clawed at it and tried to budge it for centuries, it was no match for her.

As another pile of bones was thrown from the train car, Sarah walked over to inspect the claw marks on the boulder again. She really *hadn't* noticed them the first time. None of them had. So what if they hadn't been there for centuries? What if they were new?

Then, she gasped, figuring it out, and directed her beam upward, trying to ignore the strange rattling and crunching sounds from behind her. Sure enough, there was room on *top* of the seven foot boulder, opening into a cavernous space beyond. The creature had climbed *over* the boulder when it had escaped to kill Kedzie. Which means it must lead to an exit. It probably always did. The hotel builders used the natural cave tunnels to bring in supplies, and had blocked this tunnel inadvertently when moving the boulder to one side; it was the only place the large rock could have been pushed to. But could she climb over the boulder herself?

She turned around, looking for a step-stool-sized rock to boost herself up on, and screamed. One of the leathery skeletons had assembled itself from its pieces on the ground and was standing upright, hands casually on its hip bones, looking right at her. It took a rattling step toward her, and Sarah jumped back, preparing to defend herself, before remembering that this could not be The Eaton. This had to be a projection, like the piranha-filled water, and so could not touch or harm her. The creature was still trapped—she could see it. It was trying to scare her, perhaps stop her. But she would not be distracted.

Sarah found a suitable rock, disabled the flashlight to preserve battery life, and with nothing but the dim ambient light from the smartphone's small display, rolled the small but heavy rock a few feet into position. When the creature realized what she was doing, it began to thrash around inside the car, trying to break the wood paneling by the windows to create a larger opening for itself. Sarah pretended not to notice, as she knew the task would be impossible when the light died, and she may only have minutes, maybe even seconds, to climb over the barrier. Another skull crashed against the rock beside her, thrown by The Eaton, and a bone fragment pierced her cheek, causing her to bleed. The bones were not illusions. But as long as the creature's aim was poor, she believed she could make it.

She had to put the phone in her pocket to make the attempt, blocking all light. She needed to push hard from her feet, grab onto the top of the boulder with both hands, and by some miracle find the strength to pull her body straight up over jagged rock in complete darkness. Her first attempt was a failure.

"Sarah, please," said a soft voice from behind her in the dark. It sounded like Sam. "Please stop. I'm hurt. Wait for me." But she knew damned well it wasn't Sam, and the rage she felt at hearing the creature mimic Sam's voice was enough to make her second attempt successful.

Atop the boulder, still in the darkness, she flung her feet to what she assumed was the other side, the freedom side, and dropped down. It felt, sounded, and smelled the same as the side she had come from, and she was momentarily convinced that she had gone nowhere. But after retrieving the phone from her pocket, and activating the flashlight app for the last time, she could see she had made it. The cave opened up here, and Sarah could more clearly see where the cave network must continue on. She could smell, and faintly hear, the underground streams which might have carved some of this out many eons ago. And, Sarah almost cried when she turned to her left and saw the dirty stone path, leading blessedly upward, wheelbarrow tracks etched into the rock floor as proof of the hotel crew's long-forgotten use, a path which the creature must have used just hours earlier. A way out.

"Sarah!" cried Sam's voice, sounding more distant now. "Where are you? Don't leave me! *For God's sake, Sarah!*"

Sarah glanced at the phone's screen. 1% now. It would shut itself off at any moment.

Still breathless from climbing over the boulder, her entire body aching, she raced with the best of her ability up the embankment, again holding the phone out before her like a shield and trying to avoid anything that might trip her up. The path turned twice and seemed to double back on itself, but always maintained a slight upward angle that promised she was approaching the surface.

Sarah had nearly made it to the end of the path when the smartphone died, turning into a useless rectangle in her hand. She stopped in the blackness, terrified only for a moment, then got down on her hands and knees and crawled the rest of the way, feeling around with her fingers for clues of the cave floor's shape. A spider web brushed against her face and tangled in her hair, but she stayed silent. At any moment, she was certain a claw would grab her ankle, yanking and dragging her down back into the pit. She began to hallucinate, her mind creating specks of red and yellow light across what would be her field of vision, but she knew they weren't real, as they didn't move when she turned her head. Just as she was certain the road went on forever, she crawled directly into a rock wall at the end of the path.

Sarah tried to stand, but hit her head on something hard. Crouching back down, she cautiously explored the surface above her with her fingers, and determined it was some sort of wooden structure, perhaps something of a cellar door, parallel to the ground and about three feet above it. She tried to budge it with her hands, but she had no leverage. Finally, she turned to lay on the ground, and pushed upward on the door with her feet. That did it, and the door began to hinge upward in the blackness, showering Sarah's eyes and mouth with dirt. With one forceful shove, the invisible door opened far enough on its hinge that it locked into position, and Sarah was able to stand, climbing out of the horizontal opening and onto another cave floor. This time, however, she was able to detect a hint of ambient light, and knew she had made it to a cave near the surface.

Everything inside Sarah demanded that she run toward

the light at once, and she almost did, but became convinced that the creature might still be pursuing her. In a darkness that remained close to absolute, she fumbled to close the hidden cellar door as it had been. She felt around for some sort of latch, and found none. There were, however, quite a few small boulders and what she believed to be heavy concrete blocks. Methodically, she moved every rock she could atop the square wooden door, and over a dozen of the heavy blocks as well, until her energy gave out with a desperate, tortured gasp, and she knew she could do no more. If the creature was strong enough to get through that, then she wouldn't stand a chance anyway.

Shuddering with pain and exhaustion, Sarah found her way through the cave to the light. It was a cool, dark night in Eaton Rapids, but the glow of distant sodium streetlamps had found their way to her. She stepped over a heavy chain and a sign reading "DANGER—KEEP OUT," and was shocked to find herself under a bridge near the old Horner Mill, more than a half mile from the depot she had entered. The cave had become a tunnel, and had led her to an old water wheel which, perhaps a century ago, had helped power the grist mill whose smokestack still stood, iconic and proud, overlooking the once-famous Saratoga of the West. When she at last laid eyes on this familiar sight, and all the freedom that it implied, she burst into sobs.

epilogue

Sarah Davidson had walked just a couple hundred yards along M-99 before a passing patrol car picked her up. Covered in an unsettling mix of fresh and dried blood, she was driven to the Eaton Rapids Medical Center and admitted immediately. Night shift nurses stripped her of Sam's tattered shirt, bathed her, replaced her makeshift breast bandage with something sterile, and dressed her in a fresh medical gown.

At just before 2:00 a.m., Detective Lt. Peter Letterby arrived to take Sarah's statement from her hospital bed. Sarah reported that her purse and identification could be found in the lobby of the old Eaton Rapids Depot, and in the next room, they would find "pieces" of her best friend Kedzie Duffield. She was unwilling or unable to go into much detail, and the on-call physician kicked out the detective after several minutes, insisting that his patient get some rest. As the detective was leaving, Sarah called out that he should prevent responding officers from exploring the secret hotel beneath the depot, as the monster within would "know their nightmares."

The attending physician stopped the detective in the hallway, and opined that Sarah was in a state of shock. She had not only suffered severe trauma, but also seemed to have a high blood alcohol level. "I'm not saying she's lying," the doctor explained, "but it seems clear that she is quite confused. She may be having a sort of psychotic break." Lt. Letterby nodded, and made a note of this in his pad, but still felt obligated to call for an immediate investigation.

Within the hour, two officers had arrived at the old depot, found both Sarah's identification and Kedzie's barbaric murder as described, and called in the remainder of Eaton Rapids' on-duty night staff for assistance. Several officers braved the exposed stairs down to the elevator room, finding Janet's broken body as well, but as the only elevator car had been destroyed, they had no way of discovering the hotel itself. That would have to wait for the next day, perhaps even the next week, for a team of excavators and specialists. "You couldn't pay *me* to go down there," remarked an uneasy officer to another.

At 4:30 a.m., Lt. Letterby returned to the medical center, with the intent on prying more answers out of the patient. This time, he was refused admittance altogether, and the physician put a handwritten "Do Not Disturb" sign on the door to Sarah's private room. Sadly, Sarah was indeed disturbed, and often, by the physician himself, and the nurses, the orderlies, and even a lost patient who had wandered from his bed and entered her room by mistake. Each time a face appeared by her bedside, whether it was new or familiar, Sarah's heart rate shot up, and she broke into a cold sweat, certain that *this* time, the person would be a fake, and their skin would melt from their body, revealing the oily, toothless grin of The Eaton. "This is going to happen," it would say, and it would have her. It was only a matter of time.

Yet the creature didn't come, at least not this night, and

soon Sarah could see the first hint of daylight streaming into her room. She had been up for twenty-four hours, and she could feel her body giving in to the inevitable. For the first time it what felt like weeks, Sarah allowed herself, cautiously, to fall asleep.

*

Ten miles to the west, the early morning sun signaled the start of prep time at Jessica's, the coffee and bake shop which now occupied the former Michigan Central Depot in Charlotte. Several restaurants and ice cream parlors had operated out of the old depot since its decommissioning, including a small but well-reviewed Italian restaurant which had closed over financial troubles just two years prior. The new owner, Zeke Cartwright, had named the coffee shop after his daughter, who had gone missing ten years ago at the age of twenty-two. She had fallen into a bad crowd, and Zeke never knew if she had been killed, or overdosed somewhere, or just fell off the grid for a time, with the chance of someday returning to him. He felt by naming the old depot "Jessica's" he was sending a karmic message to the universe, and to her directly, wherever she may be, that her destination still awaited, and that returning home would always be within her reach.

As sometimes happened in the mornings, the circuit breaker flipped the kitchen panel off when the ovens and the old espresso machine were heating at the same time. Zeke knew one day he'd have to get an electrician to place that machine on its own circuit. But as it only happened in those early hours, never when customers were present, the minor nuisance had become part of the morning routine.

This time, when Zeke walked into the back room, he heard a knocking from the wall behind some ancient shelves beside the breaker. His first thought was some sort of plumbing problem, and he looked up and down the wall to assess which pipes and junctions might conceivably run back there. Finding no obvious candidates, he moved some boxes off of the shelf and listened closer to the brick. The knocking seemed deliberate, a repeating pattern of three knocks followed by a pause, in the manner of a persistent salesman knocking at a front door. The sound was coming from somewhere beyond the wall.

"Hello?" Zeke called into the bricks. The knocking grew louder, and expanded to groups of five knocks instead of three. Whoever was pounding had heard and acknowledged his call.

Zeke took a step back and examined the old shelving unit. He had always thought of it as built into the wall, but saw now that it was detached. He reasoned it had likely never had been moved, at least since this had still been a depot, as it had unbroken lines of dust and grime in common with the wall and floor. It was therefore impossible for someone to actually be behind it, but Zeke felt an overwhelming urge to investigate anyway. He moved the heaviest boxes off the shelves, then heaved and pulled the entire wooden structure at an angle into the room, allowing several feet of clearance for him to examine the bare surface.

At first, this newly-exposed section of brick seemed just as impenetrable as the rest of the room. But as he peered closer, he could see that the sides of the shelving unit had covered up a conspicuous seam in the brickwork, forming a six-by-six-foot square. Zeke tried pushing on the sides and corners of this square, expecting something to give and push forward into a secret area, but when he hit a specific brick, the door shifted and hinged back toward him instead, opening into the storeroom, dragging against the stone floor. He helped the door open a full ninety degrees, and it locked in its new position with an audible click.

Through the doorway, Zeke was shocked to discover not just a small hidden closet, which itself would have been a miraculous find, but a full wooden staircase descending at least a dozen steps.

"Jesus," Zeke whispered.

The pounding came again, louder than before. It was clear now that the sound was coming from behind a second door somewhere at the bottom of these stairs.

Zeke fumbled for a flashlight from one of the storeroom shelves, switched it on, and descended into the opening. When he reached the bottom step, he was in an empty cellar of perhaps one hundred square feet. It had higher ceilings than he would have expected from a cellar, and the room itself seemed to serve no purpose besides highlighting the large, wide wooden door before him. He approached this door, examined its composition, and removed its large iron latch. Zeke took a breath, believing himself prepared for anything, and opened the door.

He had not been prepared to see Jessica.

She stared at him, unblinking even with the harsh flashlight beam on her face.

"Daddy?"

She looked not a day older than he had remembered, even wearing the white cotton dress he had last seen her in all those years ago. But it was undoubtedly his daughter. He knew every inch of her face, and every detail was perfect. Was it an angel? A dream? He leapt forward and embraced her, tears splashing against his cheeks, his whole body trembling against hers. She held him, too, her arms wrapping around his back. She felt as solid as he remembered…perhaps even more so.

Zeke had his eyes closed for several seconds, but eventually allowed them to open, and while still embracing his daughter, he used the flashlight in his right hand to pan the cavernous space behind her. There was some sort of unfinished rail track here, with a large platform to the left of it, upon which was what looked like visitor seating and even, it seemed, a sort of unfinished ticket booth.

Had Charlotte once had a subway?

It didn't matter.

He stepped back from the embrace, looking with love and bewilderment at his long-lost little girl. Seeing her father's tears, she placed her left hand against his cheek. He was vaguely aware of the sharpness of her fingernails.

"It's a miracle," Zeke cried. "*How is this possible?*"

Jessica gave her father a sympathetic smile.

"Oh, you sad little man," she said. "It's not." And in an instant, the talon was through his neck.

author's note

The first seven chapters of The Eaton, along with the plot outline and character summaries, were completed in 2009. Alas, I could never seem to find the time to work further on the novel, and it was shelved for a rainy day. In late 2014, I willed myself to revisit the story, and finished the first full draft in Google Docs on an iPad with a Logitech Keyboard Folio, just a few paragraphs at a time, whenever a free moment could be found.

Although a lot of research went into The Eaton, particularly for the chapters taking place in the past, all characters appearing in this work are fictitious. Any resemblance to real persons, living or dead, is purely coincidental.

In addition, I am at least 99% certain there isn't actually a hotel underneath the abandoned train depot in which this story takes place, though admittedly, the only time I visited the real-life depot was to take the photograph for the cover, and it *was* pretty spooky.

John K. Addis is an award-winning designer and marketing professional in Lansing, Michigan. When not advertising the products and causes of his clients, Addis enjoys expressing himself creatively in as many ways as possible. In the past two decades, Addis has composed a variety of works for small music ensembles, drawn a daily comic strip for The State News (*Studentangle*), written & directed a microbudget feature-length film (*The Bells of Beaumont Tower*), and has seen his photography displayed at local galleries. He is presently the CEO & Creative Director of AE: Adventures in New Media, continues to perform keys and vocals in a Williamston-based cover band (The Black Barn Band) and has recently started writing his second novel, *The Paper*. Addis lives in Lansing's historic Westside Neighborhood with his brilliant wife Leah, creative daughter Sophia, and adorable toddler Julian.